ARARAT

ARARAT

CHRISTOPHER GOLDEN

 ST. MARTIN'S GRIFFIN ☙ NEW YORK

ARARAT. Copyright © 2017 by Christopher Golden. All rights reserved. Printed in the United States of America. For information, address St. Martin's Press, 175 Fifth Avenue, New York, N.Y. 10010.

www.stmartins.com

The Library of Congress has cataloged the hardcover edition as follows:

Names: Golden, Christopher, author.
Title: Ararat / Christopher Golden.
Description: First edition. | New York : St. Martin's Press, 2017.
Identifiers: LCCN 2016049035 | ISBN 9781250117052 (hardcover) |
    ISBN 9781250117069 (ebook)
Subjects: LCSH: Noah's ark—Fiction. | BISAC: FICTION / Horror. |
    GSAFD: Adventure fiction. | Horror fiction.
Classification: LCC PS3557.O35927 A89 2017 | DDC 813/.54—dc23
LC record available at https://lccn.loc.gov/2016049035

ISBN 978-1-250-18134-3 (trade paperback)

Our books may be purchased in bulk for promotional, educational, or business use. Please contact your local bookseller or the Macmillan Corporate and Premium Sales Department at 1-800-221-7945, extension 5442, or by email at MacmillanSpecialMarkets@macmillan.com.

First St. Martin's Griffin Edition: August 2018

10 9 8 7 6 5 4 3 2 1

This is not the first book I've dedicated to my wife,
Connie Golden, and it won't be the last.
"What do you want, the moon? Just say the word."

Acknowledgments

Thanks, as always, to the people who create the environment that allows me to do my work, including my agent, Howard Morhaim, my manager, Peter Donaldson, and my very excellent editor, Michael Homler, and to Lauren Jablonski and the whole team at St. Martin's Press. Gratitude forever to Connie and the formidable young people we are proud to call our children. Special thanks as well to Dana Cameron, Eric Simonson (of International Mountain Guides), and Leila Vardizeh, for their knowledge, kindness, and expertise.

All my favorite people are broken.

—Over the Rhine

ARARAT

ONE

Just past eight o'clock on the last morning of November, the mountain began to shake.

Feyiz froze, breath catching in his throat as he put his hands out to steady himself, waiting for the tremor to end. Instead it worsened. His clients shouted at him in German, a language he did not speak. One of the men panicked and began to scream at the others as if the devil himself were burrowing up through the heart of the mountain to reach them. They stood on the summit, vivid blue sky rolling out forever before them, the frigid air crisp and pure. An idyllic morning on Mount Ararat, if the world had not begun to tear itself apart.

"Down!" Feyiz shouted. "Get down!"

He dropped his trekking poles and sank to his knees on the icy snowpack. Grabbing the pick that hung at his hip, he sank it into the ice and wondered if the six men and three women in this group could even hear him over the throaty roar of the rumbling mountain.

The Germans mimicked his actions.

On his knees, holding on and hoping that the snowpack did not give way, Feyiz tried not to count the seconds. The Germans shouted at one another. One woman wore a wide grin, her eyes alight with a manic glee as she reveled in the terror of the moment.

A man grabbed his arm. Thin face, prominent cheekbones, eyes like the sky. "How long will it last?" he demanded in his thick accent.

As if this sort of thing happened all the time. As if a mountain guide could live to be thirty-two years old on a mountain that shook itself apart with predictable regularity. Feyiz only stared at him, then pressed his eyes closed and prayed, not only for his wife and their four sons down in the village of Hakob, but for anyone waiting in Camp Two. Here at the summit, all was snow and ice, but the terrain at Camp Two was nothing but piles of massive volcanic rock, and he did not want to think what might happen if a slide began.

"Twenty seconds!" one woman shouted in English, staring at Feyiz. "How much longer?"

He held his breath as the mountain bucked beneath him, the roar filling the sky. Eyes open now, he stared at the peak of Little Ararat in the distance. His heart thumped inside his chest as if it were suffering a quake of its own.

The ice popped and a massive fissure opened, the sound like a cannon.

One of the Germans began to pray loudly, as if his god needed him to shout to hear him over the thunder of the quake.

It stopped as suddenly as it had begun. Feyiz glanced around at his clients, the roar of the mountain still echoing across the sky, and shot to his feet. He forced himself to steady his breathing—he could not afford to hyperventilate up here in the thin air of the summit—and bent to retrieve his trekking poles.

"Come. We must descend now."

"No!" one client barked—the man who'd been praying. "What

if there are aftershocks? Or . . . there may be a quake worse than this one. Another on the way!"

Feyiz stared at him, watched his breath mist in the morning air. These men and women were not friends but workmates, all executives for the same technology firm in Munich. They knew one another but did not love one another. All save one were inexperienced climbers, dressed for the weather and equipped with quiet determination, but their lives had not prepared them for this moment.

"Listen carefully," Feyiz said, his lips brushing against the little bits of ice that had collected on the fringe of his mustache. "My wife and children are down the mountain. My cousins and their families are carrying packs and guiding horses even now, bringing climbers . . . bringing tourists . . . to this place. I must see to their safety. So how long will you wait here? If there are aftershocks, they may come in hours or even days. Will you climb down after nightfall? I am going now."

He turned, the crampons attached to his boots scraping ice and digging in as he began to trek back along the path they'd used on their ascension.

"Stop!" the praying man barked. "You have been paid to guide us! You must—"

Feyiz turned to glare at him. "Must what? Put your welfare above my family's? If you need a guide to get down, come along."

As he worked his way off the summit, he thought of the many hours ahead—hours in which his family would be just as worried about him as he was about them. Behind him, he heard Deirdre, whom he thought the most senior of the executives, snapping at the praying man. When Feyiz glanced back, he saw that they were following.

He had marched only another dozen steps when he heard the mountain begin to roar again.

"I told you!" the praying man shouted.

But Feyiz did not drop this time. Ararat did not shake beneath his feet, not the way it had bucked before. This time the sky trembled with the noise and he felt the tremor, but the sound had heft and direction. He turned toward the southeast ridge, and he knew the roar he heard was thousands of tons of ice and volcanic strata giving way.

Avalanche.

This late in the year, no one would be climbing the southeast face, but his village was at the base of the mountain's eastern edge, toward the sunrise. As he listened to the booming clamor of the ice and rock, he picked up speed, his clients forgotten. They would have to keep up or make their own way.

The mountain killed people. It always had.

Feyiz prayed that the mountain had not killed *his* people.

TWO

A light rain fell on the streets of London and nobody seemed to notice. Some of the people passing by on the King's Road had opened their umbrellas, but most just did up an additional button on their coats, unfussed about a bit of drizzle. Adam Holzer shoved his big hands deep into the pockets of his gray, woolen coat. Born and raised on Long Island in New York, Adam had spent plenty of gloomy November days cursing himself for not paying more attention to the weather forecast. Apparently, moving to London hadn't changed that about him any more than he expected the not-too-distant arrival of his thirtieth birthday would.

Thirty, he thought. *Shit.*

He'd climbed mountains all over the world—scaled Mount McKinley with his father at the age of seventeen—and now he would catch his death on the curb in front of his prospective venue because his fiancée was late again and he hadn't had the good sense to bring an umbrella.

He tugged his phone from his pocket and glanced at the time: 1:37 p.m. They'd been meant to meet at one o'clock. Granted, he'd made the appointment with the manager of the Bluebird for one thirty, anticipating that Meryam would be delayed as she always seemed to be of late, but soon he would have to go inside without her.

No texts from Meryam, either. He started to tap out another to her, saw the previous two he had sent, and changed his mind. She had either seen them and chosen to ignore them or she hadn't, and one more wasn't going to magically speed her arrival.

Adam glanced over at the front of the Bluebird, a low-slung white building completely out of place among the lovely brick and stone row houses around it. Most of them had shops on the first floor—he stared at the facade of the apothecary across the street. On a rainy day such places sold shitty umbrellas for five quid apiece.

But the manager of the Bluebird would be waiting. He tried to remember her name—Emily something—he'd written it down on a scrap of paper he kept in his wallet. The Bluebird had a wonderful reputation as a wedding venue, plenty of room inside for both the ceremony and reception. The pictures he had seen online showed a lot of silver and white and mirrored surfaces, happy people making toasts with fluted champagne glasses, and pretty little girls cascading flowers along a makeshift aisle. String quartets smiled in the pictures and the brides and grooms seemed very happy.

Perfectly lovely.

At this point, Adam would have gotten married at the statue of Admiral Nelson in Trafalgar Square with pigeon shit instead of rose petals, if only Meryam would agree to a venue. She wanted to be married in London, and he understood that. It was her hometown, after all. But a bit more guidance than just *London* would not have gone amiss.

Stuffing his phone back into his pocket, he started along the frontage fence, peering through the wrought iron, hoping Emily-something wouldn't be waiting for him at the door. A droplet of rain slid down inside his shirt and along his spine and he shivered, surrendering his mood to the gray of the day.

"Adam!"

He turned to see Meryam hustling toward him, her bright red umbrella bold as Lady Godiva out there in the mournful gray of that overcast day. The damp weather had turned her short brown hair into an unruly mop of curls and she wore a grin he knew all too well. It screamed a brand of mischievous glee that he found alternately terrifying and intoxicating.

"I started to think you weren't coming," he said.

Meryam tilted her head and the umbrella with it. "I wouldn't just leave you standing here, love."

"You mean like you did last Monday at Battersea Arts Centre?"

She swept up to him, sharing the cover of her red umbrella, and slid her right arm around him, yanking him in close for a kiss. Adam accepted the kiss, exhaling some of his annoyance, but he refused to let himself smile at her.

"I've apologized for that a dozen times," Meryam said. "You know what I'm like when I'm writing. I sit in Wilton's and lose all track of time."

The rain began to fall harder, fat drops whapping off the umbrella overhead. Its protection created an intimate space between them, as if the whole world had been shut out. The effect made it harder for him to maintain his gravitas, and after all, she was only ten minutes late.

Forty, he reminded himself. *As far as she knows, she's forty minutes late. You told her one o'clock.*

He had nearly forgiven her for last Monday, but only nearly. They were working on their third book together and taking it in turns, as they always did. Meryam certainly made a habit of losing herself in the work, so Adam could well imagine how easily she might have been sitting in the pub, drinking tea and tapping away on her laptop. Except it hadn't been the first time. He had proposed to her in Scotland at the beginning of May on the peak of Ben Nevis, which they'd climbed just to have a picnic. At first Meryam had seemed almost giddy with excitement, but ever since they had begun the actual planning of the wedding, that had changed. She'd been indecisive on everything from flowers to invitations to the venue and had been late for nearly every appointment.

Now she held him firmly against her. The umbrella swayed backward and a curtain of rain slid off the edge and splashed them.

"Stop it," she said.

"Stop what?"

"You *know.*"

Adam kissed her forehead. They were equal in height—five foot ten—and sometimes she returned the gesture. Not today.

"Let's go inside," he said. "The manager will be waiting—"

"If she hasn't given up on us entirely," Meryam finished for him.

"Yes." Adam stared at her. "Look, I'm glad you're in such a splendid mood, but I haven't eaten anything but an apple today, so I'd like to get this over with. And we both know you don't have any patience for the whole process, so let's just move inside, out of the rain, and then you can reject this place like you have all the others and I'll go on looking while you try to figure out how to tell me you don't want to marry me after all."

Her grin faltered. Sadness flooded her eyes and she pushed him away, out into the rain, out of the intimate shelter of her red umbrella.

"That's not fair," she said quietly, words almost lost as a truck rumbled past. "And it's not true."

He exhaled, then shoved his hands into his jacket pockets again. "What am I supposed to think?"

"That I love you, and I've been distracted with this book and with organizing our adventures for next year, and I know you're going to say there's only one adventure that you're interested in right now, but one of us has to focus on how we make a living and right now that's me."

Adam felt his shoulders sag as he mentally surrendered. He couldn't argue the point. She might not have been paying enough attention to wedding planning, but he hadn't been focused enough on the long months they would spend in South America, rambling around the Andes and climbing Aconcagua, the highest mountain outside of Asia. Their explorations would form the basis of their fourth book.

"I'm standing in the rain," he said, finally allowing himself to smile, if a bit halfheartedly. "Can we go inside?"

Meryam's mischievous grin returned. "Afraid not, love. Appointment's canceled. In fact, all other appointments are canceled for the forseeable future."

"You just said—"

"I love you and I want you to be my husband, but could you shut up a moment?"

Adam pressed his lips together, asking the question with only his eyebrows.

Meryam nodded in satisfaction. "Excellent. Here's the thing. Cancel it all, because we're flying to Turkey tomorrow. I got a call from Feyiz. You remember him?"

Of course he did. The man had become a friend during their time on Mount Ararat, and he was the best guide they had ever worked with. Feyiz and Meryam had shared an instant rapport that might have made Adam jealous except for one vital fact.

"We're invited to *Feyiz's* wedding?" he said. "He's already married."

Meryam grabbed the lapel of his coat and pulled him toward her, back under the umbrella's protection, and he felt her hot breath on his cheek and saw the thrill in her eyes.

"Don't be daft. You saw the news about the earthquake a few days back. And the avalanche."

"Terrible," Adam said.

"It is that, but it's wonderful, too. The Turkish authorities won't let anyone up there, afraid of aftershocks and the like, but Feyiz and one of his cousins went up anyway. The guides need to know what damage has been done, scout the terrain, all of that."

Adam gave a skeptical sigh. "And I suppose they found Noah's ark."

Meryam gave that curious head tilt again. "They spotted a cavern up on the southeast face that wasn't there before. Big one. Geologically, it shouldn't exist."

He took his hands out of his pockets and matched her head tilt with his own, studying her eyes. Had it been anyone but Feyiz, he would have insisted on more information. Hell, *con*firmation.

"It's probably nothing," he said in a tone that wasn't convincing even to his own ears. "And you know damn well the elevation is too great for any flood to have risen that high."

"*But.*"

He nodded slowly. "But what if it's something and we could be the first ones there? Feyiz loves us. Especially you. He could get all the gear we'd need, be point man for the team we'd need for this."

"I've already asked him. It's happening now."

Adam's grin matched Meryam's. "This is crazy. You said yourself the Turks aren't letting anyone up there. The Kurdish guides can scout around, sure, but we're foreigners. Even on an ordinary day, we'd have to go through the licensing process before we could climb."

Meryam held him close again, touched noses. "Let's just get there. Feyiz knows who to pay off. When they lift the ban, I want to be the first ones up the mountain."

"Aftershocks . . ."

"Oh, please, Mr. Holzer. I've seen you do the stupidest, most dangerous things—most of which could have killed you—and you're worried about aftershocks? This is the stuff we live for, and let's not forget how badly you want that television show you're always going on about. I want to see what's inside that cave, and I want to get there first. You try to tell me that you don't want the same and I will know that you are lying through your bloody teeth."

Adam laughed and shook his head at the insanity of it all.

Then he took her hand and together they hurried along the sidewalk, red umbrella bobbing overhead. But Adam didn't care about the rain anymore. By the time they reached Turkey it would be the first of December, and a little bit of chilly drizzle would be nothing compared to what awaited them on Mount Ararat.

THREE

In the summer, a newborn teacup monkey could climb Ararat. Or at least that was what Meryam had told Adam when they'd planned their first ascent three years earlier. In the warm weather the mountain presented no more challenge than a long, arduous hike until about forty-eight hundred meters, when the glacier began. Even then, a reasonably fit person needed only crampons strapped to her boots and an ice ax to make the climb, depending on the route.

In winter, however, the climb became complicated. The snow and wind whipped across the face of the mountain, the cold cutting through heavy clothing, sinking into your bones. In the dark or in the midst of a storm, temperatures could plummet to thirty below zero. Even so, neither of them had any interest in climbing Ararat in the summertime. The whole point of the climb had been to have a few thrilling chapters for their second book, *Adam and Eve at the Top of the World*. The series chronicled their exploits as a couple, the things they dared together that most people wouldn't dare alone, never mind have a mate to attempt with them. Which meant that climbing Mount Ararat in the summer would be boring as hell to their readers.

They weren't idiots, though. They'd made the climb in late October, not in February. Avalanches were not uncommon on Ararat in the winter months, and they only needed to make the climb seem slightly more challenging than the teacup-monkey version.

Of course they'd picked the mountain in the first place because of the ark.

Not that Meryam believed in the ark. She thought Adam might, but he had never outright admitted it to her. The story of the great flood had too much historical prevalence in disparate ancient cultures to be pure invention, but the biblical story could not possibly be true. To jump-start the human race—never mind all life on Earth—with only whatever animals you could fit on a single boat . . . the idea that anyone could accept that concept made her want to bang her head against a wall.

So she thought the idea of *the* ark was hilarious.

But *an* ark? A guy who might have been named something like Noah, who'd built a huge, crude ship and loaded up his family and whatever animals he'd owned—donkeys and sheep, that sort of thing—she could wrap her brain around that. She had studied enough folklore, history, and theology to know most of the ancient stories were either crafted to teach a lesson or passed down through generations because they had a kernel of truth in them that scared the shit out of people. The lesson of the biblical tale of Noah's ark was a simple one, a refrain that echoed throughout the Old Testament: *behave, or God will fuck you up.*

Adam, for instance. She could see in his eyes that a part of him still believed the things he'd been taught growing up, the things he'd memorized before his bar mitzvah. His mother had died when he was young and his father had worked too many hours, leaving him to be raised by his grandmother Evie, whose grim mysticism had left him scarred by faith. The old woman had insisted that *her* father had been possessed by a dybbuk toward the end of his life. Adam claimed not to have believed her, but she still remembered the first time he had told her the story and the shadow that had fallen across his eyes. Adam didn't want to believe, but she knew he did.

For her part, Meryam didn't believe in dybbuks or spirits or angels, but then she didn't believe in much. She had been raised a Muslim and long ago decided that the main difference between their religions was the name of the god they were all afraid would punish them if they broke the rules the faith set out for them. Meryam still obeyed some of those fundamental rules out of reflex and caution, but it wasn't God whom she feared would punish her for breaking them. Allah wouldn't spit on her in the street, imprison her, gang rape, or murder her.

Only men would do that.

Men like Hakan Ceven.

"How long before the government gives us authorization to climb?" she asked him.

Hakan sat directly across the table from her, spine rigid against the back of his wooden chair. He turned to his left, addressing his response to Adam.

"It could be hours or it could be weeks." His voice rasped like stone on stone, thick with the accent of the region, but he spoke better English than she'd expected.

Meryam glanced at Feyiz, the fourth person at their table. Like his uncle, who had become the new head of the family in the wake of deaths the clan had incurred in the avalanche, Feyiz would not meet her gaze. But Meryam knew Feyiz avoided her eyes out of embarrassment rather than disdain. Kurds were not typically as antagonistic toward women as many other followers of Islam in the Middle East, but judging by Hakan's behavior, he was an exception.

"Is there anything we can do to speed this process?" Meryam asked.

Hakan stiffened further, chin raised and nostrils flared. His thick, graying beard could not hide the scowl on his lips. He let his gaze linger on Adam's, trying harder to get the message across.

"My cousin is there now, speaking to a friend in the minister's office. If bribes will help, we will offer them and simply add the cost to your bill. Until then—"

"Hakan," Adam interrupted, not hiding his irritation.

Feyiz gave a brisk shake of his head.

"—all we can do is wait with the rest of them," Hakan finished.

Meryam gritted her teeth and glanced around the massive, rustic dining room. Three other climbing teams were already assembled there but more would be on the way. Feyiz had spoken to the other guides and learned that all of them were larger parties, most awaiting reinforcements, and all three were financed or led by Arkologists—the people who believed the biblical version of the story of Noah's ark and had dedicated their lives to finding its resting place. Two of the groups had small documentary crews with them and the third had a crew on the way. Meryam had her fiancé.

"I'm sorry," Adam said, lowering his voice to be sure only the four of them—the little circle of distrust at their table—could hear. "But this is not going to work if you insist upon—"

Meryam tapped her fingers lightly on the table, drawing the attention of the three men. Anxiety spilled out of Feyiz's every pore. Adam clamped his mouth shut in frustration. Hakan kept his gaze averted.

"Firstly," she said quietly, "don't speak for me, Adam. Don't be the knight who takes up sword and shield to defend his love. That's not who we are and you know that."

Later, he might argue that the circumstances demanded he intervene, but that was for when they were alone together, not a conversation he would venture to have in front of others.

"Secondly . . . Hakan, you can go on pretending I'm invisible, that the voice you hear comes from the Jew I'm going to marry, whom I guess you like only a little more than you like me. I imagine the concept of our marriage is an abomination in the eyes of a creature as ignorant and full of hatred as you are—"

Hakan snapped his head around to glare at her. His upper lip twitched and she could see the fury burning inside him that she would dare speak to him that way. He huffed several shaking breaths and then slowly turned to stare anew at Adam. A razor-thin smile parted his lips.

Meryam leaned over the table. "You're torn, I know. Lash out at me and you have to accept that I exist and that I am giving the orders here."

To Adam—always to Adam—Hakan replied, "And if I just quit? I could lead one of the Arkology groups. I could forbid my family and the other guides from helping you."

Night had brought a cold breeze and it slid along the floor like rising water. Laughter erupted at a corner table where a German climbing party was opening more bottles of wine. The crisp, dry air pulled all of the moisture from visitors' mouths, but there was always more wine to quench their thirst. Always more stories of the mountain, more dark-eyed guides with weather-lined faces, more prayers to a god who seemed so much closer here in the shadow of the mountains, and so much more callous in his disregard of those prayers.

"You could do any of those things," Meryam agreed.

Tired, she rubbed her eyes and cracked her neck. It had been a rush to get here, to gather supplies and ensconce themselves in this hotel carved out of a rocky hillside, each of its rooms practically a luxury cave. A fairy chimney, according to the Swiss hotel chain that had built it. Seen from the outside, in the dark, the golden lamplight illuminating the caves of its rooms in the face of the rocky hill, the place did have a bit of magic in it.

Hakan slid his chair back and stood. Meryam had let the argument hang in the air, a cloud of discontent that only grew heavier, and Hakan had chosen to flee. The forty-year-old guide had un-expectedly inherited his family's business without wanting the role or being suited for the compromises that naturally came along with it.

"You're making a mistake," Adam told him.

"If I am, this mistake is not the first of the evening," Hakan replied.

"You have your own ambitions," Adam said. "All due respect, Hakan, you're a mountain guide and your family—for all of their honored traditions—lives a life one step away from being nomads."

Hakan's fists clenched. "As it has always been."

"You're proud of the traditions," Adam said. "And you should be. But that doesn't mean you want to do this till you die, or that you want your sons to do it, or your daughters to marry men who may die in the next avalanche. You already supply the horses—or your cousins do—so why not own the hotels? Why not own the shops?"

"This isn't the life you want, Uncle," Feyiz said.

Hakan spoke to him in Kurmanji. Meryam understood the single word he said. *Silence.*

"We're paying you a great deal of money," Adam went on, his tone all business. Reasonable, where Meryam knew she would have been incapable of reason. "And you know damn well that once the climbing ban is lifted, we'll be the first ones up that mountain. It's just us. I've got my own camera and we're not wait-ing for anyone. The producer I'm working with is already talking to officials here who've checked our credentials and agreed that if we get there first and there's something to find—and we follow all established rules for an archaeological site in this country—the dig is ours."

Hakan rolled his eyes. "Without a monitor from the govern-ment? Never."

"If we find anything, they'll send someone."

The guide stroked his thick beard, lip still curled in distaste. "Without a guide, good luck to you."

This time he did look at Meryam, as if only now, putting the last nail in the coffin of her plans, would he acknowledge her.

"They have a guide," Feyiz said quietly.

Hakan shot him a withering glare. "You wouldn't dare."

Now it was Hakan's turn to be ignored. Feyiz refused to look at him.

Adam pushed Hakan's chair out a bit farther, a suggestion that he should return to his seat.

"We're going to climb," Adam said. "If there's nothing there, we'll have wasted a lot of time and money. But if there's anything worth finding, it'll be our dig and our documentary film. We'll need a project foreman who knows the mountain intimately and who doesn't mind being on camera, part of the film. Our backers will be funding the whole thing. If this is the ark, the interest level will be so high that money will rain from the sky."

Hakan held onto the back of the chair, the muscles in his shoulders relaxing, but he did not sit down. The wrinkle in his brow had turned from one of vexation to one of contemplation.

"There are many 'ifs,'" Hakan said.

Meryam exhaled. "You don't have to look at me when I speak to you. If your religious beliefs mean you must condemn me—and my relationship with Adam—in your heart, that's between you and God. But we *are* doing this, and it will be much easier for us and much more rewarding for you if we have the cooperation of the Ceven family."

Hakan glanced at her, locked eyes for a three count, then slipped back into his chair. He turned to his nephew, spoke in a low voice and in the language of their birth.

"Do you believe in the ark?" Hakan asked.

Adam frowned—he didn't know the language—but Meryam

gave the tiniest shake of her head to indicate he should say nothing.

"If it's there, I'll believe in it," Feyiz replied.

"The cave seems too small to hold it," Hakan said.

Feyiz shrugged, but Meryam leaned over and spoke to the younger man, as if his uncle were not there. She could pretend as well as anyone, could play this game if it would ease their way.

"These others," she said in Turkish, with a slight nod toward the nearest table of Arkologists, "they're looking for a legend. Any measurements ever written down are symbolic. If the ark existed, nobody knows how big it really was. If it's up there on the mountain, we can measure it ourselves. We'll *remake* the legend."

Feyiz smiled. He had been in from the start—committed deeply enough to defy his uncle and anger the rest of his family. He had lost three relatives in the avalanche, but all of his children still lived. Feyiz wanted to keep it that way and knew that finding the ark could change his life.

"Are we in business or not?" Adam asked.

"Uncle?" Feyiz said.

Hakan hesitated and Meryam knew he would not agree. The climb would have to go on without him, which would make it much harder to get horses, to replenish their supplies, and to have the support they needed up on the mountain if they really did find something that warranted archaeological attention.

The German Arkologists erupted with another volley of laughter. One of them reared back and nearly spilled from his chair before righting himself, knocking his wineglass to the floor in the process. The glass shattered, spilling deep red liquid onto the wooden floor.

Hakan scowled in their direction, and then Meryam saw his brows knit, his eyes narrow. Meryam turned to find a young boy weaving through the dining room.

"Zeki," Feyiz muttered.

Meryam took Adam's hand, a flutter of excitement in her chest. She recognized the boy as Feyiz's eldest son. Slim and handsome, not yet twelve years old, Zeki would grow up to break women's hearts. Tonight his furtive speed suggested that he might have a very different future from his forebears.

The boy arrived beside his father, but when he produced a folded slip of paper, Feyiz indicated that he should hand it instead to Hakan.

Zeki obeyed. Hakan surveyed the room. Meryam knew others would be watching them, wondering about the presence of the boy, but there was nothing they could do about that now.

"Well?" Adam prodded.

Hakan opened the paper, scanned it quickly, and then grunted. He looked up, straight at Meryam for once. "We must go."

"Now?" Feyiz asked. "It's an hour past dark."

Meryam grinned. "Which gives us all night to reach Camp One . . . an excellent head start."

As they rose from the table, Meryam paused to drain the last red bliss from her wine in victory. She and Adam were going to be first to the cave.

First to lay eyes on whatever waited there.

Feyiz drove the van, their gear piled in the back, and they wended through the sleepy streets of Dogubeyazit. Adam grinned most of the way, suffused with a giddy exuberance he had rarely felt since childhood. Under starlight, they drove along badly paved roads to a tiny village called Eli, where the pavement came to an end and they arrived at a parking lot at the base of the mountain.

Here in Turkey he felt relatively safe, and yet the presence of the Iranian border only kilometers away made the sky in that direction seem laden with menace. On one hand it seemed silly to feel as if the whole nation held a personal animosity toward him, like a cloud of malice waiting for a shift in wind direction so that it could swallow him whole. On the other hand, if he crossed the border and was caught, he would be instantly arrested and imprisoned. Stupid to think about—he had no intention of entering Iran—but such were the things that lingered in his mind.

The trek toward Camp One was a hike rather than a climb. They spilled from the van, checked their gear one last time, and then slipped on their packs. Adam pulled on a wool hat, tugged down the earflaps, and shivered as his body began to adjust to the cold night air. *This is foolish*, he thought, glancing up at the mountain as the wind whipped around them. Then Meryam turned toward him and he saw the ecstatic glint in her eyes and the grin she wore, and he remembered that foolish was their stock in trade. The whole point of their books and their online videos was to help ordinary people overcome their fear of taking risks.

He retrieved his camera from the back of the van, sighted on Meryam, and began to record. "So, what are we going to call this one? *Adam and Eve Find the Ark*?"

"Let's actually find the ark before we start claiming we've done so," Meryam said with the smile that always broke his heart. That wasn't a smile he could ever refuse, and it was as good an opening line as he could have wished for.

She adjusted the pack on her shoulders and turned toward the mountain. Feyiz and Hakan had already started up the path, neither waiting for them nor offering to help. Feyiz knew they didn't need his help. Hakan simply didn't give a shit.

They trudged a half mile or so before Adam bothered with the camera again. The terrain looked ghostly in the starlight and he wanted to wait until they were far enough from the parking lot that none of the lights from the village or the road would interfere with the atmosphere he wanted to create. Normally they would have had horses, maybe a mule or two, but there were only four of them and their goal was to reach the cave first, establish their claim. They couldn't spare anyone to wait behind with the animals as they made their way from Camp Two over to the part of the southeast face that had calved off. There would be no safe way to reach the new cave, but the least dangerous option would be to cut across to a place above the opening and descend to it rather than try to climb all the loose rock and earth below it. Starting another avalanche might kill them all. Adam and Meryam were making careers out of calculated risks, but neither of them wanted to die from being stupid.

"Feyiz," he said, catching up to the guide and rolling the camera again, "we've done this with you before, but for viewers who aren't familiar, can you give us some details on what's ahead?"

The younger guide glanced warily at his uncle, who had stiffened. Hakan's lips pressed together in a tight line of disapproval, but he sneered quietly and picked up his pace, getting out in front of them. He wanted to find the ark as much as anyone, but had zero interest in documenting their efforts.

"We left the van in the village of Eli, which sits at about two thousand meters," Feyiz began. "The hike to Camp One is nine kilometers and should take less than four hours total. The terrain is not difficult for climbers who are physically fit—"

Meryam stepped into the frame, glancing back at the camera as she kept hiking. "Right now, Adam is wishing he hadn't eaten that massive portion of kunefe after dinner."

He groaned. "So true."

The trek continued in the same fashion, with Adam acting as cameraman and interviewer, Meryam as on-camera host and narrator, and Feyiz filling in the details. In quiet moments, when the on-camera banter lulled with the lateness of the hour, he glanced up at the mountain and felt a whisper of dread slide up his spine.

Each time it dissipated before reaching his brain, the way dreams turned to mist and vanished in the first moments of wakefulness.

He shifted the weight of his pack and kept moving, watching his step. The next time he glanced up at the mountain he thought he could make out the gouge on its face where the avalanche had occurred, a fresh scar that had changed the shape of Ararat.

Meryam appeared at his side before he could even notice that she had dropped back to be with him.

"You okay?" she asked quietly, though in the dark silence of the mountain even a whisper could be heard. Feyiz and Hakan kept moving, ignoring them.

Adam nodded. "Sleepy, I guess."

"There won't be much sleep the next few days."

"If we're lucky, the next few months."

Meryam smiled, eyes alight. "From your lips to God's ears."

"God?" Adam asked, eyebrow raised.

"Whoever's listening," she corrected.

Adam took her hand. Holding his camera in his right and clasping her fingers with his left, he felt the balance of his life. These two elements were all he needed. Inspired and more awake, he released her and clicked the camera to record.

"What makes you so confident?" he asked Meryam. His boots crunched down on rough stone and brittle ice. "There are at least two competent teams of Arkologists in Dogubeyazit. They'll be on our heels."

Meryam shoved a mass of curls away from her eyes and frowned at him. At the camera.

"We've got a head start and we're traveling light," she said, more for the camera's benefit than for his. "If there are mysteries waiting up there, we're going to be the ones to solve them."

She grinned. Adam tapped the camera to stop the recording and returned her smile, but it felt like a mask. An uneasiness had settled into him like nothing he had ever experienced. It made his skin prickle and he thought of the scrutiny of hidden eyes. With every step, he felt as if he walked beneath the gaze of unknown enemies.

"You need sleep," Meryam said, concern etched on her face.

"Just a few hours when we get to Camp One," Adam replied. "Then we keep climbing."

Whatever had crept under his skin would burn off with the sunrise.

He was sure of it.

FOUR

Adam rushed up from sleep, fleeing a dozen ugly dreams. He felt the grip on his shoulder and had his right hand clamped on a human throat before he'd even opened his eyes. Shaking off the caul of slumber, he focused on the face above him and discovered that he was choking Feyiz.

"Shit," he hissed, releasing the guide. "Sorry, man. Really sorry. You caught me in the middle of a nightmare."

They'd made good time to Camp One, but without any sleep at all, they had all agreed that they needed at least a few hours of shut-eye before they continued their climb. Now Adam's head felt full of cotton and his eyes ached from tiredness. Sometimes a little sleep was worse than none at all.

Feyiz wheezed and massaged his throat. "Damn it, Adam . . ."

"Really. I'm sorry. It's like I was still dreaming for a second there."

For a moment it looked like Feyiz might be pissed, start a fuss about Adam's violent awakening, but a change came over his face. Whatever reason he had for coming into the tent and waking Adam took precedence.

"Olivieri's team is passing us by," Feyiz said. He cleared his throat. "Meryam sent me to wake you."

Shaking off the last mists of a nightmare—in which long, withered arms had reached out from behind the pendulum of a grandfather clock—Adam slid from his sleeping bag and dragged on his boots. The cold mountain air whipped through the open tent flap and he shuddered as he grabbed his jacket. Scraping at his bristly beard, he thought of his first trip to Alaska. It was cold here, but compared to that journey, the predawn morning on Ararat felt nearly tropical.

"Bad dreams," Adam said with a shrug.

Feyiz nodded. "We all have them."

True enough, but the unease left behind by his nightmare lingered. Adam pushed through the flaps and exited the tent. An inch of snow had fallen on the grassy pasture that made up Camp One and a few stray flakes eddied in the air overhead. The rock formations that jutted from the pasture made this a perfect spot for the camp, allowing tents to be erected behind natural windbreaks. For most of the year, it would be quite comfortable up here, but now winter had begun to knock on the door and the weather would be unpredictable on the best days.

Meryam and Hakan stood about twenty feet away, sipping coffee from thermoses. They had set up a camp stove and used water from the small stream that ran beside the camp—higher up they'd have to melt snow for water. Right now, the camp stove seemed an indulgence they could not afford, not when another group of climbers was passing right by the camp instead of stopping to rest. He counted a dozen heads, half of the group on horseback and the others leading mules laden with equipment. The third rider was a burly man with a prematurely gray beard and goggles on his forehead that Adam knew had the same prescription as his eyeglasses. Armando Olivieri was the kind of man who came prepared, and once Adam had learned about those goggles they served as a constant reminder of the professor's determination.

Olivieri spotted him by the tent and waved as the parade went by. Worried and irritated, Adam strode toward Meryam and Hakan. The two of them had ignored each other on the hike up to Camp One the night before and they didn't seem exactly chummy now, but for the moment it was clear they were on the same side.

"What the hell does Olivieri think he's doing?" Adam asked.

Meryam glanced at him. "Moving on to Camp Two, I assume."

Adam laughed softly. After the trudge to Camp One, it would have been smart for the professor's team to stop and rest, but he could see skipping that step, considering they were in competition. The next step would be to ascend to four thousand meters or higher—about the same elevation as Camp Two—and then come back down to allow for acclimatization, avoiding the risk of altitude sickness. A night's sleep would follow before the typical climber would rise in the small hours of the morning and make the much steeper trek to Camp Two, stopping there for another night before the last part of the ascent. If they'd been climbing to the peak, that would be another six hours up and then a much more rapid descent, but of course they weren't heading for the peak.

"You really think they're going to try straight for Camp Two and stay there?" Adam asked. "No acclimatization?"

Hakan grunted. "What choice do they have?"

Meryam turned toward them. "If Olivieri wants a crack at the cave, he has to beat us there."

"Shit," Adam rasped. He turned to shout for Feyiz but saw that the man had already moved the gear out of the tents and started breaking them down. At least he seemed to understand the need for speed.

"We'll overtake him," Meryam said. "Fifteen minutes and we go. Pack up, have a wee, and get your camera ready. Another day, another adventure."

"You can't pretend you expected them to catch up this quickly. We only slept four hours and here they are—"

"With no sleep," Meryam added. "And without Feyiz and Hakan for guides. Twelve people, most of them not used to climbing. Odds are some of them will get mountain sickness if they attempt it. Neither of us has ever been prone to it. If we need to skip acclimatization, I think we'll be okay, but Olivieri's got two tweedy Arkologists and a sixty-year-old rabbinical scholar on his team. They're going to need to acclimatize. They just are."

Adam nodded, telling himself it all made sense, but something niggled at the back of his mind. "What *about* those guides? Who the hell are they?"

He turned toward Hakan, who took a long drink of his steaming coffee, then poured the rest out on the fire and began kicking dirt and freshly fallen snow over it.

For the first time, Meryam seemed unsure of herself. Adam loved her for her confidence, but she didn't always think things through. He turned to see Feyiz zipping up a backpack.

"I thought your family had cornered the market up here."

Feyiz frowned and studied his uncle. "Uncle Hakan and his cousin Baris are not in agreement on who ought to be giving the orders. The family is split on this subject. A final decision has not yet been made."

Meryam swore, spinning on Hakan. "You let us think no worthy guide was going to help the Arkologists up the mountain, that you had them all under control!"

Hakan went and nudged Feyiz aside, knelt, and began to unzip and repack the backpack, a silent assertion of control. He knew better, he was telling them all. Feyiz might be a passable guide, but he was in charge.

"The silent treatment again," Adam said. "Perfect." The mountain wind whipped around him and he shivered, thrusting his hands into his coat pockets. "So Baris is helping Olivieri. And if they reach the cave first—"

"It is not only your professor friend who will find victory there," Hakan said. "The family will think my cousin more capable and he will become the chief guide. The argument will be settled by achievement. Baris will not worry about altitude sickness. If several become ill, he will have one of his men descend with them."

Meryam handed Adam her coffee thermos. "This is the only thing that's hot. There's some bread and honey. Eat fast."

Adam didn't want to bother eating anything, but he knew he would need some food in his belly. He turned toward Feyiz, who had begun to break down the second tent.

"Wait," Hakan said, digging a plastic bottle out of the inside pocket of his coat. He twisted off the cap and began to tap pills out into the palm of his glove. "Take these first. Two different pills, take one each."

Meryam didn't hesitate, plucking the medications from Hakan's hand.

Adam examined the pills, brows knitted. "I assume one of these is Diamox. What's the other?"

"Procardia," Hakan said. "For blood pressure. It should prevent . . ." He turned to Feyiz and said something in the language they shared.

"Edema," Feyiz translated.

"These medicines are no guarantee," Hakan continued, "but take them and drink a lot of water, and with luck we will not have to carry you off the mountain."

Adam selected pills for himself, studying Hakan's face. "This cousin you didn't tell us about? He'll have given his group the same medicines, I assume?"

Hakan closed the pill bottle, slid it back into his jacket, and stomped on the last embers of the fire. Meryam approached Adam and cupped his scruffy, bearded cheek in her hand. When he turned to her, she dry-swallowed the pills and grinned.

"Let's go, my love," she said. "We're in a bit of a hurry now."

"Olivieri's got horses and mules," Adam replied quietly, clutching his own pills.

"And you've got me. Get ready and then start filming."

"You have a plan?"

Meryam laughed. "The only possible plan. They'll want to use their animals as long as possible. They're going to Camp Two and then straight across to the southeast face, above the cave, just as we'd planned to do."

Adam thought about the broken rock and earth that the avalanche would have spread down the mountainside beneath the entrance to the cave. He thought of the inch or more of snow that had fallen on top of it during the night.

"So we stay just west of the rockfall. Straight up, but not in the avalanche zone," he said. "Not completely suicidal, but still dangerous as hell."

As the burning rim of the sun crested the eastern horizon, her eyes sparkled. "Exciting, isn't it?"

The next time Meryam saw Olivieri more than nine hours had passed. She had her pick buried in the icy rock in front of her and the claws of her crampons digging for toeholds. Her stomach twisted and bile burned up the back of her throat but she forced herself not to vomit with the pain inside her skull. Acute altitude sickness could be fought. She'd already taken more medication and she had both prayed to and cursed her own god and everyone else's. She told herself that she would be all right, and maybe that was true. As long as her lungs didn't fill with fluid and her brain didn't swell—the results of pulmonary or cerebral edema—the other symptoms would subside eventually.

If she did develop edema and didn't descend immediately, it would be quite a different ending to her story. She would die.

Breathing deeply in the thin air, Meryam dug the toe of her boot into the ice and hauled herself upward, ripped her pick out and smashed it back into the mountain overhead. Skipping acclimatization had been a stupid, stupid plan. Setting off on their own, even with guides who knew the secrets of the mountain better than the curves of their wives' flesh, had been idiotic.

The horizon had turned a deep indigo on one end of the sky, the sun gliding into hiding on the other. A hand touched her back and she glanced to her right, surprised to see that Adam had overtaken her. The wind whipped at his face, making him squint.

"Didn't you hear me calling you?"

"The wind," Meryam said, resting against the mountain. "What's the problem?"

"Feyiz is right. We should have stopped at that shelf we passed half an hour ago. I think we should go back to it."

Grip tightening on the handle of her pick, she stared at him. Queasy, head pounding, she had to play the words over in her head to make sure she'd heard them correctly.

"Hakan said we could make it! He said we were almost there!"

Adam's expression hardened with frustration. "That was an hour ago and where are we now? Do you see the damn cave? Even if we get there, you know as well as I do that there's no ark inside. It makes for great footage, but it's impossible for a flood to have reached this height—"

"Who's this talking now?" Meryam said. "Not my Adam. I'm the atheist in this relationship, remember? What's impossible when God's in the mix?"

Her parents and brother refused to speak to her or even acknowledge that she still shared the same planet with them. The alienation had both broken her heart and emboldened her to fulfill her dreams, but still it was so lonely. The last time she had been with them, on a hot July day in London six years before, she had seen sadness and longing in her mother's eyes but only hatred and disgust from her father and her brother. If her mother had the courage to flout her husband's wishes, Meryam thought they might speak again one day. But she doubted that time would ever come. Declaring herself an atheist had been as bad as spitting in her father's face and she had known that before she had ever spoken the words. She had done it anyway, determined not to hide her true self. Not ever.

Now here she was, desperate to claim whatever lay in that cave. Part of her wanted to find it empty, to throw that emptiness in the faces of the self-righteous bastards in every faith she had ever encountered. But another part of her wanted very badly to find something . . . anything to believe in. Anything that might ignite a spark of faith in her and lead her, if not home, then at least to a place where she and her family could speak again.

"Can we have this conversation later?" Adam said. "We need to do something. We can't make it to the cave before sunset and it's too dangerous to—"

She set her knees against the thin layer of snow and let go of the pick, just the crampons on her boots holding her in place. "Come on! It's not like it's a vertical face. I'll get banged to hell if I fall, but I'm not going to plummet to my doom."

He fixed her with a cold glare. "Stop it."

Meryam sighed and grabbed hold of the pick. Yes, they ought to have brought pitons and rope, and if they'd brought them they would have been using them here. And, yes, if she did fall at the wrong point and couldn't slow her tumbling descent, there was always the chance that she'd smash into a rock or fall into a crevasse, but the terrain to the east was so much steeper. A sheer, jagged face, even under the snow. As long as they kept climbing straight up—

"No," Adam said, reading her face. "We're already close to the rockfall. You don't know how close. Not even Hakan knows. We're going back down to that shelf and camping there for the night."

Meryam grabbed hold of the pick again, feeling herself deflate. "If we stop, I'm not sure how long it'll be before I can carry on."

Adam rested against the mountain beside her. "You should've spoken up."

Hakan shouted at them from below. Meryam felt her hackles rise, ready to snap at him for his impatience. Then she caught the tone in his words, and put the syllables together to form a name. *Olivieri.*

She glanced below her and saw Hakan pointing up and to the west, then she lifted her gaze and squinted into the burning golden light of the setting sun. Higher on the mountain, still at least eight hundred meters below the peak, a line of black silhouettes made their way across a snow-clad ridge.

"Shit."

"Meryam—" Adam began.

She whipped her head around to stare at him, heat rushing to her face, unable to explain her urgency, the necessity, her obsession with making this discovery herself. Rough and handsome in his scruffy way, it was the warmth and intelligence in his eyes that always got to her—that had supported her through so many journeys—but there were things she could not say to him. Not now.

At the moment she had only one word for this man she loved. "Climb!"

"What—"

"Adam, just climb!" she snapped. Hauling back her pick, she planted it in the rock and ice above her head and hauled herself up. She kicked her left boot at the mountain, caught the teeth of her crampon into a toehold, and scrambled upward.

As she moved out of his sightline, she heard Adam swear, as he finally registered what she and Hakan had reacted to. Meryam glanced over again and saw the line of half a dozen silhouettes moving along the ridge to the west, nothing but dark cutouts against the golden gleam of the dying sun, shapes moving through the hour of long shadows.

There were no more words. Adam climbed, his grunts of exertion after nine long hours a perfect, synchronous match for her own. They had stopped to rest multiple times and debated stopping for the night, but the combination of Meryam's fierce desire and Hakan's determination to beat his cousin had made them press on. More than once she had thought they were being ridiculous, that Olivieri's team would have camped and rested or fallen ill. There were only six or seven out of the original twelve members of that group remaining, which meant that some of them had stopped or gotten sick and had to descend, but between Olivieri and Feyiz's uncle Baris, they'd forced the rest to keep going.

Left hand digging into snow for a solid hold, she kept climbing. Pick, boot, hand, boot, using her knees to brace herself. The sun had been warm, but as it slid over the distant, jagged edge of the world the temperature dropped precipitously and the wind buffeted them, screaming as it whipped across the face of the mountain. Meryam scrabbled upward, an awkward, clawed spider. Feyiz and Hakan began snapping at each other, but she couldn't focus on climbing and translating at the same time, so she ignored them.

"Meryam," Adam said, "talk to me. You all right?"

She ignored him. Loved him, but could not draw the breath it would take to reply. The cold radiating up from the mountain had gotten inside her, aching in her bones. Her face and nose stung now that the wind had cranked up. Pick, boot, hand, boot. Heart slamming inside her chest, lips so dry she felt them crack, Meryam lifted the pick again but wavered. A sharp pain spiked through her head and she blinked, vision blurring at the corners of her eyes. For half a heartbeat she lost herself, forgot where she was, and then the sick twist of nausea clutched at her again and she felt hot bile rushing up the back of her throat.

No.

Refusing, spittle on her lips, she choked it back down and forced her guts to be still. Her head pounded as if huge fists smashed against her skull. She breathed deeply and steadily, waiting for the pain to abate. Dread prickled at the back of her neck, a feeling of vulnerability, as if all the cruel malice in the world had abruptly been directed toward her. That dread turned to a thousand tiny, icy points and spilled down her back, sliding over and through her before it was gone.

"What the hell was that?" she whispered to herself, barely aware she'd spoken. Frigid, salty little tears sprang to her eyes and she blinked them away.

Sound rushed in before she had a chance to even recognize that the world had gone silent. For a moment she had just blanked out, the same way the electricity in their flat went dark for just a blink during a bad storm. The lights flickered and the clocks all reset, flashing twelve. Heart thrumming, blood rushing to her face, Meryam sucked in a ragged breath and began to sag backward.

Adam called her name. He planted a hand on her back and in doing so, lost his own footing. Kicking out, jamming the toes of his boots into the rock and snow, he started to slide and the mountain slid with him. Loose rock tumbled and Meryam screamed his name, started to reach for him before another hand grabbed her from the left—Feyiz, keeping her from doing something stupid.

"Don't move!" he snapped.

A curtain of snow began to slide off to their right, stone and earth and white shifting and tumbling down. Hakan called out a prayer but none of them moved, just listened to the whispered rumble of the mountain's displeasure. Adam had gone silent but kept moving, grasping, stabbing his pick into the shifting rock. They'd come right up beside the location of the avalanche but the snow had hidden the rockfall, and Adam had climbed right onto it.

He's dead, Meryam thought, and the sickness in her gut turned to a hollow, icy pit. Pure emptiness. Her heart went numb. She held her breath.

With a sound like a chorus of voices shushing her, the cascade slowed and then stopped altogether. Adam perched at the edge of it, pick embedded in a tumble of loose rock, rigid as he waited to see if it would start again.

Meryam took a few short breaths, her heart thumping. She felt her pulse throbbing at her temples but the pain in her skull had calmed to a dull ache. She wetted her lips.

"Move!" she called to him, then flinched at the loudness of her voice, afraid even the sound might cause the slide to begin again. "Carefully, but move now!"

Hakan began to descend, the mountain still solid beneath him. They had been climbing right alongside the rockfall until Adam had moved over beside her, but Meryam knew there would be all kinds of fissures in the rock and earth so close to the avalanche zone. They had to be wary.

Adam shifted his left hand. Rocks skittered downward but he moved his left foot. A fifteen-foot segment of the rockfall shifted again, just slightly. Meryam let the mountain take her weight, cradle her as she breathed and prayed to any god that might listen. It wouldn't be fair. Just not fair.

Feyiz spoke softly to her, small encouragements and reassurances that all amounted to "He'll be all right." But neither of them knew that.

Ropes, she thought. *Pitons. A larger team, proper safety precautions. Oh, my God, I've killed him.*

Adam tugged his pick out of the rocks and it all started to give way beneath him. He didn't swear or cry out to God. Instead he shouted for Meryam, in that instant more anguished at being parted from her than at what might happen to him next.

"Roll!" Hakan roared at him.

The mountain flowed downward but Adam heard, and instead of fighting for a hold he rolled left. Even as he rode the shifting stone and snow, he made himself tumble to the side. All it took was half a dozen feet and he sprawled onto solid, unmoving mountain face. Hakan scrambled down to meet him as he managed to get a new hold, dig in his pick and the crampon claws at the toes of his boots.

"Adam," she whispered to herself, a different sort of prayer.

Forty feet below the place where she and Feyiz perched, Hakan reached Adam and talked to him quietly, checking his body for broken bones and his pupils for dilation, in case he'd suffered a head injury. To the west, the sun had started to slide out of sight, the upper corona turning vivid colors that spread along the horizon line. They had only minutes before even this golden light vanished and then all that would be left was the glow of the stars and the crescent moon. The incline was not difficult for climbing—the rockslide might have killed Adam, but otherwise this part of the face required only stamina, caution, and a modicum of skill. They had been climbing easily enough . . . but sleeping out here would be impossible.

In the dying light she could see the blood on Adam's face, a cut or scrape on his forehead that trickled dark red streaks across his cheek and into his beard. He'd been knocked around, but when he glanced up and met her eyes, she knew he was all right. Still with her. Still on this journey.

"We've got to climb," she said, turning to Feyiz.

From the moment when her body had seemed to give up on her, when that terrible feeling of malice had pressed down on her, until right now, she had taken strength from the guide's presence, but only as she saw the concern in his eyes did she realize that Feyiz was more than just a guide or an ally. He was a friend. She had a history of not recognizing friendships when they really took form, when they became true and solid like Pinocchio becoming a real boy. That flaw had cost her in the past, but she felt it now.

"Come on, Feyiz," she said. "We've got to—"

Hakan shouted for them to look up. Meryam cringed, put her shoulder against the mountain and ducked her head, afraid something had been dislodged above them. When nothing fell she blinked and craned her neck to gaze up toward the peak, but a jagged ridge blocked her view. A wave of relief swept over her—a shelf, perhaps seventy meters up. It would take time, but . . .

She blinked.

Feyiz had begun a prayer of thanks. In her peripheral vision, in that last golden gleam of daylight, she saw his smile. Only then did she understand, and broke out into a smile of her own.

The cave.

Meryam plucked her pick from the mountain's face and lunged upward, digging in. Pick, boot, hand, boot. Quicker than she'd been at the start, all pain in her head forgotten. She glanced over at the silhouettes of Olivieri's team, just inky black marks against the darkening mountain, and knew she was going to beat him.

Feyiz followed her. Forty feet below, injured or not, Adam had begun to climb again, with Hakan looking after him.

Remnants of queasiness lingered in her gut, but Meryam kept moving and breathing deeply. There would be more meds when they reached the shelf. But only a tiny part of her brain remained aware of her discomfort. The rest of her thoughts were dedicated to climbing toward the mystery that had brought them here. She tried not to fantasize, dared not to hope, but even if they found nothing but a gaping wound in the side of the mountain, at least she had reached it first.

Her back muscles burned. Her arms felt weak, as if she had been deceiving her body for the past few hours by continuing to climb, somehow persuading flesh and bone that she had not asked them to endure far more than she had any right to expect they could. Now she needed just a little more. Weariness set in, carved its blades deep. Knowing they were so close to finding rest made every handhold harder to find, made her body heavier with every inch she dragged herself up the mountain.

Below, Hakan and Adam spoke to each other. The words floated up to her but she did not bother listening to discover if their conversation was speculation or an evaluation of Adam's injuries.

"Meryam," Feyiz said, moving up beside her when she began to slow. "Do you need me to—"

She shot him a withering look. "Do *not* help me."

The hard edge in her voice went too far. She knew it, but she saw the shifting shadows across Feyiz's face and the moonlit gleam of his eyes, and she knew he understood. She hadn't come this far to accept help from anyone. This had been her quest from the start—not even hers and Adam's, but hers—and she wouldn't accept a hand up from anyone unless she started falling. Maybe not even then.

Moonlight, she thought. For the first time she noticed that while they'd been climbing, in just the past few minutes, the sun had gone down. The glow of it still haunted the western horizon but it had vanished off the edge of the world.

In the darkness, she reached up her empty hand and caught nothing but air. A glance upward, and she saw the edge of the shelf. The lowest corner of the new cavern that had appeared in Ararat's face.

She grinned, warmth flooding her chest, buried the point of the pick into the flat edge of the stone shelf, and dragged herself up and into the cave.

Lying on her back, watching the stars come out, Meryam began to laugh.

Then she turned onto her hands and knees and threw up.

Adam wanted to drop his pack onto the floor of the cave and collapse. The muscles in his calves and shoulders burned and his knees were stiff in what he imagined was a prelude of what it would feel like when his youthful tendency to overdo things brought his joints to arthritic ruin. He wanted water and a bite to eat and to take a moment to revel in the knowledge that they had beaten Olivieri's team to this cave, even if they found nothing at all.

Then Meryam started to retch.

"Meer?" he said, rushing to her side even as Feyiz and Hakan clicked on flashlights and began to scan the cave's deep shadows.

In the crescent of moonlight that touched the first dozen feet of the cave's interior, Meryam lifted a hand to wave him away. "I'm all right."

"Bullshit." He took her hand, felt her pulse, asked her if she could breathe all right.

"Not while I'm—"

Another thin stream of vomit interrupted her. Meryam stayed on her hands and knees, trying to catch her breath. Adam put a hand on her back and tried to soothe her.

"You're okay," he said with more certainty than he felt. "You'll be all right. If we need to get you down—"

"No."

"—we've already secured the entrance. We're here. Olivieri's team may show up on our doorstep at sunrise, but they can't claim the dig for themselves—not with the deal you made with the government. If there is a dig, I mean."

"I'm not . . . not going down."

"You can acclimate," Adam went on. "Take Feyiz with you. Rest here a few hours and then—"

Meryam whispered something he didn't catch. Adam leaned in, asked her to repeat herself, and she twisted round to stare at him. Her eyes caught the moonlight but instead of silver they glinted a coppery red for just a moment. A trick of the light, and the night.

Taking a deep breath, she reached a hand to him. "Help me up."

Adam went cold, felt the hairs on the back of his neck bristle. "You know what can happen with altitude sickness. Come on, don't mess around with this."

"I'm . . ." she began, before her body seized up as if she might be sick again. Breathing through her nose, teeth bared, she managed to fight it off.

Adam knelt beside her. He reached for her wrist again, worried about her rapid heartbeat.

"It's not altitude sickness," she said, jerking her hand back. "Stop."

"What is it, then?" He'd been feeling unwell himself—a clammy, almost feverish film on his skin and a thumping in his head. "No matter how many pills Hakan dishes out, you can't climb as long and as high as we did today and not have it wreak havoc on your body. I'm all twisted up inside myself."

"It's not altitude sickness," she said again. Firmly, hanging her head and taking even breaths.

"Then what?"

Meryam glanced up at him, her gaze pale and sad. "Fine, all right? Maybe it is. But I'm not climbing down. I didn't come this far to go back without at least—"

Feyiz called to them. Adam studied Meryam's face, searching for the thing he felt certain she must be hiding. It might have been that she felt worse than she wanted to let on, or it might have been connected to the wall she had been building up between them. Adam had been hiding from that bit of truth for a while, but now he felt it more keenly than ever.

"Meryam . . ." he began.

Feyiz shouted, and this time they both heard the urgency in his voice.

"Coming!" Adam called back. He unzipped Meryam's pack and dug out her light, handing it over before retrieving his own.

She took his arm and rose, unsteady as she clicked on her light. The floor canted slightly, slanting downward. Only when they turned together and stepped deeper into the cave—out of that corona of moonlight—did they hear the soft, muttered prayers that came from off to the left. Adam waved his flashlight beam in that direction and saw Hakan. Meryam's torch beam moved slowly across the floor of the cave and then froze as it illuminated a pattern that might once have been an animal. Shapes like bones lay under a layer of powder that seemed partly snow and partly a chalky dust. A ribbon of thin, leathery skin or fabric flapped in the breeze.

Meryam reached out and took Adam's hand.

Feyiz continued to call for them, but now neither of them seemed able to reply. Adam noticed Hakan moving toward the back of the cave off to their left but the man's presence hardly mattered. The only things that did were the next breath, the next step, and the way Meryam's torch beam and his own continued to sweep across the nearest parts of the cave. The mouth of it—this vast wound in the side of the mountain—must have been at least a hundred feet wide, and the flashlight beams were not powerful enough to disperse all of that darkness. But as Adam and Meryam moved deeper, hand in hand, their torchlight kept revealing more of what waited for them in the darkness.

A dusty array of buckled timber beams jutted slightly from the floor of the cave. No, they *were* the floor of the cave.

Adam felt as if he were far beneath the ocean, weighted down and wading in slow motion through the deepest, darkest waters. The beam of his torch picked out the half-collapsed remains of a creaking apparatus that might once have been stairs. Dust motes swam in the shafts of light that he and Meryam played across the beams, like plankton floating past undersea. Then the wind howled at the mouth of the cave and the timbers creaked again and the illusion of the ocean bottom vanished. His mouth and skin felt dry and his head throbbed and he stared.

Meryam released his hand and took a step forward, and the tilted cave floor groaned underfoot. Flinching, she looked down and Adam followed her gaze to see that her boot had pressed down upon another timber.

"Holy crap," Adam whispered, frozen.

He swept his torchlight to the right, revealing thick, rough-hewn wooden columns, partly blackened by thick smears of pitch. Short walls that might have been the walls of animal pens blocked parts of his view, but there were other withered, desiccated piles of bones, large and small. Most of the mummified remains belonged to animals, but his torchlight danced across two shapes that might once have been human. He shone his light upward and saw the lattice of beams that still held a second floor, perhaps a third.

Not floors, he thought. *Decks. God help me, they're decks.* The animal bones alone told the story but none of them thus far had been willing to say it aloud. Tremors of giddy joy shook his body.

Meryam took several more shuffling steps, dry timber sighing at the shifting of her weight. "It's real."

"Or it's the greatest hoax ever," Adam said. But no, it felt too real. Too quiet and ancient and looming, as if the ark itself had some impossible presence and awareness, like it knew they had come. Like it had been waiting. It even *smelled* real, though he couldn't have described what that meant to him.

"This way!" Hakan called, reminding Adam that Feyiz had been beckoning to them and they'd ignored him.

Adam peered into the darkness of the deeper cave and saw the flicker of Feyiz's flashlight beam. They'd have to learn what he wanted, but with Hakan so much closer—sixty feet away, investigating the western wall of the cave—Adam started in his direction first. Meryam blew air out between her lips, one hand on her belly.

"You all right?" he asked.

"Not important."

With torch beams lighting their tilted path, they walked carefully over to Hakan. Adam felt the soft, dry, ancient wood beneath his feet and slid back into the strange, waking dream that had enveloped him the moment he had seen the collapsed timbers and the animal bones. Now the combined light from their three torches seemed to generate enough illumination that a patch of darkness shimmered into haunting golden life. Meryam came to a halt twenty feet from Hakan, but Adam managed several steps farther before he understood what had brought her up short.

So close to the cave wall, Hakan's flashlight beam exposed a broad circle to detailed examination. The timbers were like long bones, almost as if they had climbed into the belly of an enormous whale, nothing but its skeleton remaining. Jonah, four thousand years on. The seams had all been treated with bitumen pitch to seal water out.

"I'm not an archaeologist—" Hakan began.

"Neither are we," Adam interrupted. "Probably a mistake not getting that degree, right?"

Hakan turned, forgetting himself for a moment as he included Meryam in his gaze. "This is not a cave at all. The whole cave *is* the ark. Buried all this time."

Adam could find no words.

"Smashing," Meryam said, a grin spreading across her features.

Then she punched Adam in the shoulder. "What are you doing, love? Get the bloody camera rolling!"

Adam swore. Exhausted and in awe, he'd completely forgotten. Laughing in amazement at the days and weeks—hell, the months—ahead of them, he dug out the camera and started filming, beginning on those beams sunken into the wall.

"It's extraordinary," he said.

Something shifted in the darkness to their right, farther into the cave. Adam whipped the camera around, its light revealing an unsmiling Feyiz. He had gone pale and looked like he might be ill.

"You think that's something?" Feyiz began, shielding his eyes from the glare of the light, staring into the camera. "Come and have a look at this."

Meryam started to ask if he was all right, but Feyiz turned his back on them. The beam of his torch led the way along a long passage, past a row of large stalls. Adam caught it all on film as he followed Meryam and Feyiz, with Hakan taking up the rear. The wind that howled outside did not seem to reach this far inside the cave—*inside the ark*, he reminded himself. Outside the temperature had fallen dramatically, but here in the recesses of the ark the air began to feel close and stagnant and strangely warm. Adam's stomach gave a queasy rumble but he kept the camera steady as they followed the slanting passage all the way to what appeared to be the rearmost section of the ark, what had once been its outer wall.

"Here," Meryam said, pointing to a mummified corpse propped against an upright beam. Its teeth were bared in something never intended to be a grin, mouth lipless, eyes nothing but powdery holes in a face more like papyrus than flesh.

"Naamah," Adam said quietly. The wife of Noah. The name had popped into his memory and then to his lips. Odds were whoever built this ship had not been called Noah, nor his wife Naamah, but the names didn't really matter.

"This is impossible," Meryam muttered, glancing around as if entranced. "No flood could rise this high. And even if . . . if somehow this is real . . . it couldn't be this well preserved."

"You're standing in it," Adam reminded her.

He couldn't argue her points—they were simple truth. And yet here they were. This ship was not evidence the biblical story had been a precise record, but it did prove the flood had taken place and that there had been a Noah—whatever his name might have been. No, the names didn't matter. Noah would be fine enough, and so they might as well call this one Naamah.

"What's this?" Meryam said.

Adam panned the camera away from the corpse, found Meryam, and let the lens follow her focus to a place on the floor where her flashlight had picked out a scattering of gleaming black stones.

"Volcanic?" he asked.

Hakan moved into the video frame, frowning as he knelt to pick up one of the stones. "Ararat is a volcano, yes . . . but no eruptions for almost two hundred years."

Meryam kept searching with her torch. "This thing has been here a lot longer than two hundred years."

"It's not volcanic rock," Feyiz said from the shadows ahead.

Meryam lifted her torch and shone it in his direction. Adam followed with the camera, spotted Feyiz's flashlight on the floor, shining its light into a pile of dust and black stone. He had set the torch down, but now the camera's own light joined with Meryam's and Hakan's to zero in on Feyiz. The bright lights and strange shadows made the bearded young guide appear almost two-dimensional, as if he'd been transformed from a man into a portrait painted on the air in front of them.

"It's hardened pitch," Feyiz went on.

On the floor in front of him lay an enormous object that Adam at first took to be some kind of obelisk made of that same gleaming black pitch, perhaps some sort of altar. But then Feyiz broke off a piece of the pitch and Adam took a step nearer, zooming the camera in for a close-up.

"What is it?" Hakan said. "A crate?"

Adam slipped over behind Feyiz. Now that it had been illuminated, he could see that the entire black casing on the far side of the obelisk had been broken away, revealing a different texture beneath. A large, rectangular wooden box, timber heavy and blackened. Its lid had been sealed with that same bitumen, but Feyiz had begun to run his fingers over the seam and Adam zoomed in to see that the seal had been shattered, broken bits of pitch all over the floor.

Zoomed in, the camera picked up strange markings carved in the black surface, both on the outside of the box and on the shattered seal.

"It's some kind of sarcophagus," Meryam said.

"It's Egyptian?" Adam asked.

She gave him a sharp look. "How should I know?"

"Sarcophagi are Egyptian."

"We've established there are no archaeologists among us," Meryam said. "I'm only saying I think it's some sort of coffin."

"A tomb," Hakan said quietly.

"So, not Egyptian, then?" Adam teased, the joy of discovery buzzing inside him. He could feel that everything had changed for them. The future would begin with this moment.

But Meryam had stopped smiling. Her features paled and fresh beads of sweat appeared on her forehead. Her pallor went an ugly yellow.

Still crouched by the tomb, Feyiz muttered something in his own language and then slumped onto his side in a sprawl, unmoving. Hakan shouted his nephew's name and shoved past Meryam. Adam reached for her too late. Meryam twisted to one side, dropped to her knees, and retched again. A moment later she clasped her hands to both sides of her head and began to scream in pain, crying out that her skull had split open.

The camera saw it all.

Outside the ark, the cold wind went on howling. A cloud passed across the moon and, atop Mount Ararat, all lay in darkness.

THREE WEEKS LATER

FIVE

Ben Walker turned up the collar on his coat and zipped it all the way, nestling his mouth and nose down inside its warmth. The military helicopter tilted leftward as the pilot banked toward the mountain. Thousands of feet of gray daylight separated the chopper from the ground, but it wasn't the height that troubled Walker, it was the wind. Commercial helicopters were not even allowed to fly this close to the mountain. The only way to get on top of Ararat without climbing it was to hitch a ride with the Turkish military.

An updraft buffeted the chopper and then they hit a moment of dead air—so thin at this elevation that when the wind died, the rotors whined and it felt like they were falling. The rotors thumped so loudly that the sound felt like a physical assault. Walker gritted his teeth and looked out the window as they came in view of the shadowy scar on the face of the mountain. His son, Charlie, a nine-year-old daredevil, always talked about his desire to ride in a helicopter one day. Walker thought he ought to take the boy up eventually, but when he did it would be in less perilous conditions.

Don't be an idiot, he thought. *Amanda would never go for it.*

His ex-wife, Amanda. Charlie's mother. The longer they'd been together, the more frequently Walker had been away, and the situations in which he'd found himself had only grown more dangerous and more frightening. His scars unsettled Amanda, but not as much as his unwillingness to talk about how he'd acquired them. She'd told him his secrecy meant that he did not trust her, and though he'd denied it, Walker knew it was the truth. Amanda had a beautiful smile and a carefree laugh that made her eyes gleam with genuine joy. She tried to see the best in people, which made her the worst sort of person with whom to share things that must be kept secret. Keeping secrets would have eaten away at her. Just knowing the world contained some of the horrors Walker had encountered would have tainted her, and he refused to be responsible for that.

Charlie couldn't have asked for a better mother. Amanda would raise him to greet the world with openness and optimism. So when she'd told him that his sullenness and privacy was poisoning their marriage, Walker had agreed. The stunned look in Amanda's eyes—the painful epiphany as she realized he would not change for her—still haunted him. But she had found a path away from him, started to build a life without him, surrounding herself with friends. Last time he'd seen Charlie, his son had told him that Amanda had started dating an artist named George, who would draw the boy cartoons full of ghosts and wizards and funny animals. It hurt him to hear the fondness in his son's voice, but it made him happy as well.

An elbow nudged him and he glanced to his left, realizing belatedly that Kim Seong had been speaking to him. With his collar up and the thrum of the helicopter, he'd missed the words.

"Sorry, what's that?" He leaned toward her.

"I said 'if this is weather they feel safe to fly in, I'm very happy you didn't persuade them to come up when it was snowing!'"

"So am I."

He smiled as he spoke, but he had not yet decided what to make of Ms. Kim. The Korean woman made a strange and possibly unwelcome addition to this excursion. Meryam Karga and Adam Holzer had reportedly promised the Turkish government excellent coverage in the documentary and book they were working on as well as a share of earnings from those ventures, but Walker thought the adventurers must have made other promises as well, having to do with media coverage, tourism, and their willingness to accept any rules the Turks wanted to lay down.

When Karga and Holzer were pulling their initial team together they brought in people from various nations and disciplines, and the Turks only insisted on having a pair of government underlings on site. But the moment the United States had asked to send a representative from their National Science Foundation—Walker himself—the Turkish government had decided they needed an independent observer and had appealed to the United Nations to provide one. Kim Seong was that observer. An expert on global policy, trained in international negotiation, Kim seemed a strange choice for the job, but from the moment they had met in Istanbul she had struck Walker as professional, intelligent, and most importantly, intrigued by whatever the adventurers had actually found on Ararat.

Still, he didn't like the idea of a babysitter, no matter how well he might get along with her.

Walker strained at his seat belt so he could glance over his shoulder. Father Cornelius Hughes had gone as pale as the snowy crest of the mountain but gave a quick nod to indicate his general well-being. The aging priest had a deeply lined face and an air of wisdom that seemed to come from another era entirely. He was an expert on ancient civilizations and languages, but despite the priest's academic background, Walker had been pleasantly surprised to learn that Father Cornelius had an open mind regarding the biblical story of the flood.

Not much of a team, but if Walker had tried to bring a security officer, it might have led to the revelation that the National Science Foundation was nothing more than a decades-long facade, a placeholder name for use when the U.S. Department of Defense didn't want anyone to know that DARPA was on the scene. Even the priest didn't know who he worked for, and Walker sure as hell wasn't going to tell Ms. Kim. The UN rarely approved of DARPA sniffing around without authorization, and they'd have informed the Turks, who'd have withdrawn permission for Walker to be on site.

The mission would have been scrubbed and Walker's superiors would not like that at all. The Defense Advanced Research Projects Agency had a fancy name but a relatively simple job— look into emerging science and unexplained phenomena and make absolutely certain that if it was possible someone could make a weapon out of it, the United States would be first to do so. Walker had never really liked working for DARPA—he didn't appreciate weaponized science—but he had a lifelong fascination with mysteries both natural and unnatural, a thirst for explanation that would not be quenched. And when those things turned out to be potentially dangerous, he did prefer they be in his own government's hands.

Not that he trusted his superiors. It was simply a case of better-the-devil-you-know.

"Mr. Walker!" the pilot called. "Time to move!"

Walker turned to see the snow-covered mountain beside him, the dark mouth of the cave just below. The left side of the cave measured about forty feet in height, but it slashed down across the snowy face at a jagged, seventy-five-degree angle, down to a height of only ten or twelve feet on the right side. The copilot unstrapped himself and slipped back to join them, bent over slightly. He began unraveling a length of thick cord that Walker quickly realized was a harness.

Kim Seong had radiated a pleasant serenity until now, but she took hold of Walker's arm and gripped tightly. "I am not going first."

He steeled himself. "I wouldn't ask it. My team, my risk."

"I'm sure it's perfectly safe," Kim quickly added.

Walker removed his safety belt and let the copilot help him into the harness.

The copilot slid open the door on the chopper's left side and beckoned to him. The other man would control the winch that lowered Walker toward the mountainside, but nobody could step out that door for him.

He tugged on the harness, let a bit of the cord play out, then turned his back on empty space before pushing off into freefall. He used his right foot, not trusting the left just then. The helicopter danced above him in a sudden terrible gusting updraft and he swung side to side in a dizzying arc before the harness cable began to play out and he found himself descending toward the mountainside.

The cave mouth beckoned below, off to his right, and he tracked it with his eyes as he began to spin on the end of the cord.

The wind gusted again, a blast so cold that spikes of pain shot through his skull and so hard that for several seconds he swung out like a pendulum frozen at one end of its arc. The chopper tilted along with him and then dropped twenty feet in the space between heartbeats. Walker cursed even as the wind died down and he began to descend normally once more. The cold sank into his bones, cutting through his clothes.

He closed his eyes tightly, teeth bared, and then it seemed a different sort of wind swept over and through him. A sickly sensation made him shudder from something other than cold. He felt as if he'd been dipped in filth that soaked deeper into his skin by the moment. His flesh crawled with revulsion and he opened his eyes, staring about him in desperation as he spun in the harness.

Below, people had come out of the cave and were waving to the helicopter pilot to swing him closer. Two figures had crept down to a spot twenty feet below the cave opening, where a kind of platform had been set up, posts sunk into the face of the mountain.

Fear swam up inside him, worming its way into his belly, roiling there like acid and bile. He felt himself go slack. For so long he had believed himself next to fearless, but this fear bit as deeply into him as the mountain chill.

For long seconds, he went blank. *What the hell is going on?*

Then a hand grasped his ankle and he snapped his head around, on the verge of a scream until he saw the face of the man who'd grabbed him. A face he'd seen in documentaries and on the back covers of books he'd skimmed on the plane from Washington, D.C., to Istanbul.

"Holzer," Walker said.

The adventurer hauled him in, unbuckling the harness as soon as Walker's feet hit the snow-covered mountain.

"Just 'Adam' is fine," the man said, giving the harness a tug. Immediately it began to sail upward, the winch retracting the cord so that the next member of the team could descend. "You must be Dr. Walker."

"Just 'Walker' is fine." The echo was meant to be funny, but he felt dizzy and some of that sickly feeling, the malignance that had swept over him, remained, and he worried that his introduction had come off as sneering. "It's good to meet you."

Holzer—Adam—thrust out a hand. "Welcome to Mount Ararat."

"Don't you mean Noah's ark?"

Adam's features clouded. "Why don't we let you decide that for yourself?"

"Listen, I don't want to get off on the wrong foot," Walker said. "I know you didn't want me here."

"The U.S. government wanted you here and the company financing the project was willing to oblige," Adam replied. "Which means you're welcome as long as you're useful or at least not in the way."

"Message received," Walker said.

Adam took him by the arm and guided him to another man, whose thick beard and weathered attire suggested plenty of experience with the mountain.

"Hakan is our project foreman," Adam said, raising his voice a bit louder to be sure he would be heard over the thump of the chopper's rotors. "He'll help you to the cave."

Walker glanced up to see Kim already standing at the open door on the side of the helicopter, the copilot barely visible as he coached her—apparently reminding her of the brief training they'd received on this procedure the day before.

"Don't worry," Adam said. "I'll make sure they get down safely." His smile faded again. "Trust me when I say this is not the scariest thing you'll encounter today."

Walker started to ask what he meant, but by then Hakan had already taken charge of him and he had to start climbing. Ropes had been secured above, somewhere inside the cave, and Hakan put Walker in front of him, showed him how to use the ropes as guidelines. Without the crampons on his boots, and the rope to steady himself on the unstable ground, Walker felt sure he would have fallen. On one particularly troublesome assignment, he'd incurred serious injuries to his back and leg, and with the cold and the climb, the old wounds were singing.

He glanced up at the helicopter, saw Kim Seong being lowered down. Once the chopper returned to its base, there would be no way off the mountain except to climb down. To his surprise, this thought left him deeply unsettled. With every step upward he felt an urge to retreat so powerful that he was barely paying attention when he reached the cave. He found himself kneeling on the cliff edge in front of several members of the dig team.

Walker recognized Meryam Karga from her books and documentaries, just as he had with her fiancé. The tension around her eyes and the hunch of her shoulders gave her an almost predatory aura, as if her default position was one of coiled, serpentine readiness. The others he saw seemed tense as well, and Walker wondered if the Ark Project had hit a snag.

"Come along, Dr. Walker," Meryam said, hugging herself against the wind. "We'll get you a cup of coffee while we await your people, and then you can have a look at what you want to see."

He glanced around, peering at the work lights and the ancient timbers and the people working all through the cave.

"Noah's ark," Walker said as he climbed to his feet.

"We think so," Meryam replied. "But you didn't come to see the ark."

A strange calm settled into him. The pain in his leg receded.

No, he thought. *True enough.* He didn't give a shit whether or not the timbers he was looking at had really once made up the structure of a boat—Noah's or otherwise.

His interest lay in what they'd found inside the ark.

The ark—if that was really the word for it—had been buried within Mount Ararat like a tumor nested in a human body, just waiting to be discovered. Walker would have said locating Noah's ark on Ararat was impossible after all the time and money people had spent searching for it over the years, but now he stood inside it.

They'd had a short introductory tour to the basic structure of the ark. Lights had been strung throughout but they seemed only to offer small pools of illumination. There were generators supplying power to small space heaters in some of the stalls that lined the three decks and the lights offered some warmth, but there were no fires allowed. With timber this old, the members of what was now being called the Karga-Holzer Ark Project—KHAP—had to be damn careful not to burn the whole thing to cinders. It was damned cold, and even deep inside the warren of stalls and walkways, the mountain chill spread with every gust of wind.

A quick visual inspection had confirmed what he'd seen from the chopper. The leftmost, or western, end of the cave showed that the avalanche had exposed the entirety of that side of the ark, from top to bottom. On the right, however, the rock and soil that had been in place for thousands of years still partly covered the ark, leaving some of the outer wall timbers still in place. On that side—the east—the opening angled down to a gap of perhaps ten feet. It would make that side of the ark's interior much darker, but Walker knew it would be a little warmer and less drafty on that side as well.

After the introductions, Meryam and Adam guided Kim Seong and Father Cornelius up to level three. Walker hung back on the first, stopping to watch a team of archaeologists at work around a dusty collection of human bones hung with gray remnants of both skin and clothing—human hide and animal hide were indistinguishable from each other. He noticed one of the bodies had a thick leather cord around its neck, a sharp chunk of black rock hung from it like some kind of charm. Studying the other cadaver, he thought there might be another necklace on that one.

"Two bodies?" he asked, because there seemed to be more limbs than there ought to be.

One of the archaeologists lifted her head, blinking in surprise, so entrenched in her toil that she had not realized their work was being observed.

"Three. Two adults, one child," she said in a British accent.

Walker winced at the mention of a child, then admonished himself. These remains were thousands of years old. In ancient days, children had lost their lives for any number of reasons. If a flood in any way similar to the one described in the Bible had actually taken place, countless children would have perished. Reacting to the news of this one child made him feel like a rookie, new to the kind of tragedy the world had always offered.

The flood, he thought, mentally tracking backward, surprised that he'd accepted the concept so readily. *Could this be real?*

He'd encountered monsters before, things that would make an ordinary person scream just from learning they existed, but all of them had turned out to have a solid, scientific explanation. Unnatural, perhaps, but not supernatural. Yet the very presence of this ship, buried in the side of a mountain, implied that there was truth at the core of one of the most widely known myths of world religions. Walker had made some hard choices where his family and his life were concerned and, in doing so, he'd lost faith in himself. Now, he was here, looking for something to believe in.

Christ, he thought. *All you need now is a bottle of beer and a sad country song on the jukebox.* He forced himself to focus on the archaeologists as they worked to preserve the ancient remains.

They were four thousand meters above sea level. All kinds of theories had been put forward regarding real events that might have inspired the original tales of the great flood. Some of those theories came from crackpots and others from respected researchers, but Walker had not seen a single nonreligious theory that would explain the ark landing at this elevation.

Yet here it had landed.

The ark lay at an angle, tilted toward the mountain. At some point it had come to rest on a mountain ridge and centuries of landslides had covered it, filled the ridge, packed rock and dirt around the ship. Meryam had said that her team believed there might be a crevasse beneath the ark, so they should all be treading carefully.

"Sorry, who are you, exactly?" the archaeologist asked.

When he introduced himself, she frowned, maybe wondering why the United States would send someone from the National Science Foundation—someone whose inability to identify aged human remains marked him as clearly *not* an archaeologist. *Or maybe she's wondering why nobody told her the project was getting new blood.*

"A pleasure to meet you, Dr. Walker," she said. "I'm Helen Marshall. Marginally in charge of the archaeological team. They dragged me out of Oxford for this. This is Polly Bennett, my right hand among the group of graduate students I shanghaied for this project."

Tall and muscular, Polly had a spray of birds in flight tattooed on the back of her neck, and she'd shaved the left side of her head and dyed the other side of shoulder-length hair a vivid green. Walker thought she didn't look the part of the archaeology grad student, but then he admonished himself for it. This job wasn't about how you looked.

Polly barely glanced up from the seriousness of her efforts, but she did offer a slight salute of greeting.

Professor Marshall cocked an eyebrow. "I'd shake, but . . ."

She held up both dusty, gloved hands and gave a small shrug.

"Understood. And I'm sorry to interrupt your work."

"Not at all. I'm glad you're taking an interest. It's not every day you see something impossible."

Walker nodded. "Agreed. Though why do I have the feeling you're not just talking about the elevation?"

Professor Marshall opened her arms to take in their surroundings. "This thing is at least five thousand years old, by my best guess. That's about the same time the Egyptians figured out how to lash planks together to build a hull, though this might be even older. But this ship—"

"The ark."

"If you like. The ark is far larger and more elaborate than

anything else built in that era. The Khufu ship was entombed at the foot of the Great Pyramid of Giza about five hundred years later, and that had similar length, but that was nothing more than a barge."

Walker studied her. "You're saying it shouldn't exist at all."

"Don't mistake me. I'm thrilled it's here. It's like a dream—the kind of thing I never imagined I would ever get to be a part of—but when I say it's like a dream, that's in more ways than one. It feels so surreal. If you want your mind boggled even more by just how impossible this seems, talk to Professor Olivieri."

He didn't ask who that might be, assuming he'd meet Professor Olivieri soon enough. The ark wasn't that big.

"So," Walker said, "you think the Bible story is true? God sent the flood to—"

Professor Marshall shot him a sharp look. "Don't bring God into it, Dr. Walker. We're here to examine and report, not to explain. We'll leave that part to others."

As she returned to her work, Walker stared at the wall just beyond where her team was working. He'd spotted long furrows clawed into the timbers around what appeared to be a door.

"Are those . . ."

She glanced up. "Sorry?"

Walker pointed at the scratches on the door—a door that had been tilted toward the mountain, pressed there, trapping people inside. "Is that what it appears to be?"

She gave a troubled, thoughtful nod, like an oncologist confirming the worst. "We believe so."

"But why? There were other people aboard. They must've had food stores—"

Professor Marshall smiled thinly, glare from the work lights turning her deathly pale. Only her eyes were dark, skin crinkling at the edges.

"There were food stores remaining when the last of the passengers died, not to mention animals they could've eaten," she said. "There were other ways they could have gotten out if they wanted to risk the climb down the mountain. They had to know this door was blocked but still they died trying to open it."

"So what's your theory?" Walker asked.

Her smile faded. The others had continued working, one of them taking photographs while the other busied himself preparing the bones for removal.

"We don't have one yet," she said, and turned away.

Sensing her frustration, Walker did not press her further.

"You all right?" a voice asked from behind him.

Walker turned to see Adam Holzer approaching, bearing two cups of coffee, one of which he held out for Walker.

"I am now." He tugged off one glove and stuffed it into his pocket. "I take it the ark didn't have its own Starbucks."

Adam raised his cup in a toast. "Oh, the coffee's terrible. But it's hot and full of caffeine."

"In other words, just what the doctor ordered."

Walker took a swig and tried not to scowl. Turkish coffee could be strong, but whatever the KHAP crew was drinking tasted more like rust.

Smiling, Adam glanced back at the archaeologists. "Your team is settled in. Ms. Kim declined the coffee—maybe the smartest of us all—but Father Cornelius is warming up. Why don't we get the formal introductions out of the way and then we'll show you the burial casing?"

A chill passed through Walker that the shitty coffee could not dispel.

He followed Adam deeper into the heart of the ark and then up stairs that had been sturdily reinforced and in some cases replaced by the Ark Project staff. On level three, they made their way through a doorway with a wide crack in the lintel timber, and Walker tried not to think about the roof collapsing on top of them and trapping them inside. He pictured the furrows he'd seen down on level one—scratches made by the fingernails of people desperate to escape—and didn't like that cracked lintel at all.

Voices could be heard farther ahead and Walker felt a little better when he recognized one as belonging to Kim Seong. She had a way of behaving like a queen in a room full of jesters, an arrogance that could be grating, but somehow she still managed to seem amiable enough.

At the end of the passage, they came into an open space at the rear of the ark's topmost deck. Something dry and withered lay on the floor in one roped-off corner, but it had no bones. Walker thought it must have been a sleeping mat five thousand years ago, though how a bunch of hay had not turned entirely to dust he didn't know. At the back of the chamber, the wall shared the wide timber struts that he'd seen on the lower floors, the ribs of the ark. The top of a ladder jutted up from a hole in the floor—not original, but something constructed by the Ark Project.

Meryam stood waiting for them with a cluster of people that included Kim and Father Cornelius.

"Hello again, Mr. Walker. Or is it doctor?" she said.

"Just 'Walker' is fine."

She gestured toward the others gathered there, rattling off introductions. The Karga-Holzer team included the site foreman, Hakan, and his nephew Feyiz. A ghostly pale, blond woman with a camera on her shoulder turned out to be Calliope Shaw, the filmmaker Adam had allied with to create a documentary about the project. Meryam introduced the professor Olivieri whom Helen Marshall had mentioned, a fiftyish biblical scholar with a thick beard and powerful girth. From a distance, he'd have looked like a future mall Santa, but up close it was clear Armando Olivieri might be fat, but he was solid.

"We welcome you all," Meryam said.

Olivieri wrinkled his brow.

"The professor doesn't seem very happy to see us," Walker replied.

Olivieri's frown deepened. "I assure you, Mr. Walker, my displeasure has nothing to do with you."

"But you don't think we should be here."

"I don't think any of us should be here," Olivieri corrected. "The ark has always been a fascination for me, one of the focal points of my research throughout my career. Finding it, knowing it is real . . . that moment was perhaps the greatest of my life. Now I think the best thing to do would be to plant explosives on the mountain face and bury this cave for another few thousand years."

Father Cornelius stiffened and his eyes grew stormy. "If this is what it appears to be, it's the greatest connection to biblical history we have ever found. And you want to bury it? Destroy it? What kind of biblical scholar are you?"

Olivieri sniffed in disgust. "The kind who understands that some things are better left buried. Don't pretend you don't feel it," the man said, scanning their faces. "It's so close in here that you can barely breathe, and I promise you it's not just from the elevation—"

"Armando," Meryam said, so quietly the word was almost lost with the howling of the wind that screamed through the seams between timbers.

Olivieri flapped a hand at her. "Enough, I know. Fine. Go about your business, but I'll have no part of it. If I didn't think someone had to keep watch over this entire, dreadful affair, I'd have left long ago."

Meryam looked as if she might lose her temper, but Adam took a step toward the ladder, breaking the moment.

"No point putting it off any further, then, is there?" he said as he grabbed hold of the handrail and stepped onto the uppermost rungs. "Come along, Walker. We thought your arrival might defuse some of the tension that's been developing up here in recent days, but apparently we were wrong."

"Defusing tension has never been one of my fortes," Walker said, glancing at Olivieri. "But stranger things have happened."

Disgusted by their levity, Olivieri marched back the way they'd come. The other members of the Karga-Holzer Ark Project muttered things to Meryam and returned to their own duties. Even Calliope retreated after handing her camera over to Adam.

"Where are they all going?" Walker asked when only Meryam remained of the KHAP staff.

"Limited space," Meryam said. "And they've all seen what's down there already. None of them wants to see it again."

An involuntary shudder went through him. Meryam could have been going for dramatic effect, but her fiancé had just descended the ladder with the camera, so there seemed little point in trying to spook the new arrivals. Kim glared at Meryam as she started down the ladder. If she'd been a cat she would have had her back arched, fur up.

Walker drank the last of his awful coffee, folded the paper cup and tucked it into his jacket pocket, and turned to Kim and Father Cornelius.

"You feel anything?"

Kim exhaled, relaxing. "A bit claustrophobic, yes, but if you mean do I feel anything *unnatural*, then the answer is 'no.' I'm not psychic."

"Do you believe in psychics?" Father Cornelius asked curiously.

"Of course not."

"Well, I'm no psychic, either," Walker said. "But don't be so quick to dismiss the unnatural. There are all kinds of things in the world that we don't understand."

Kim nodded sagely. "Yes, and there are always those who would like nothing better than to make a fortune thanks to the ignorance of others."

Walker knew she was right, but as he went to the ladder, took the handrail, and started down, he couldn't get the deep crease in Olivieri's brow out of his mind. There were millions of religious fanatics in the world, but Olivieri was a biblical scholar. Walker had encountered the arrogance of the faithful many times, but what he'd seen from Olivieri just now hadn't been judgment or disapproval.

That had been fear.

SIX

As Walker descended the ladder, he encountered a stale odor that made him wrinkle his nose. Something like rust. When he passed through the second level and down to the first, the now-familiar twist of nausea returned to his gut but he breathed evenly and told himself the power of suggestion had gotten into his subconscious. If so, it had deep roots there.

"What is that smell?" he heard Kim ask, below him.

Meryam admitted they didn't know, without bothering to offer a theory. In the wordless seconds that followed, Walker marveled at that. People like Adam and Meryam never seemed to be at a loss for theories. As unwelcome as he and his team might be, Walker decided KHAP needed them. New eyes, new ideas.

The ladder ended in what could only be one of the rear corners of the ark. A plastic tent had been erected, opaque sheets that blocked out a space that seemed to be a fifteen-foot square. Lights flickered and the plastic sheeting flapped in the draft that whistled through the timbers and along the several passages that seemed to end here. A generator hummed, but most of the lights it powered were inside the plastic sheeting. ·

"Weather conditions on the mountain are deteriorating quickly," Adam said. He made a slow sweep of the faces around him with his camera as he spoke. "The deeper into the winter we get, the more dangerous it's going to be to move people and materials up and down. The temperature gets unpredictable. There's a storm on the way, but up here the wind can make it much worse. We'd like to get this all packed up and preserved before that storm arrives in full."

"We get it," Walker said. "No worries."

Adam glanced worriedly at Meryam. Hesitant.

Father Hughes sighed audibly. "If you don't mind, Mr. Holzer, we didn't come all this way to stare at plastic."

Meryam turned to the camera. "For the record, Adam and I know Dr. Walker and Father Cornelius Hughes by reputation, but we've never met them before."

Walker smiled at her. "What, you're worried people will think we're all part of some kind of conspiracy?"

"I'm not worried at all," Meryam said. "I am absolutely certain of it. There are people who still think the film of astronauts walking on the moon was staged."

Kim gave a soft laugh. "It's not like we're on the moon."

Meryam pulled back the plastic curtain. "It's a little bit like that, actually."

Walker stepped toward the open curtain. He heard Father Cornelius speak his name but he shook his head, as if the priest's voice were a fly buzzing at his ear. That low hum seemed to build up inside his skull, a vibration in his bones. He almost asked the others if they felt it, too—almost asked Meryam and Adam if it might be the whole mountain trembling, precursor to a quake—but then he felt fine beads of sweat pop out on his skin and a terrible prickling sensation, like the legs of a hundred insects alighting on him.

"What the hell?" he muttered, pausing just outside the plastic sheeting.

"Yeah," Meryam agreed. "We know."

She had turned pale, a jaundiced yellow cast to her skin.

Father Cornelius took Walker by the elbow. The priest had a sheen of sweat on his own forehead but his grip was strong.

"We mustn't hesitate," Father Cornelius said.

Walker agreed. They had come a long way to see the one discovery that the Karga-Holzer team had done their best to keep under wraps. KHAP was a Turkish, American, and British coventure, with backing from museums and the financiers of the documentary. But so far the handful of people in various governments who had seen the report and the short bit of video KHAP had sent about the "sarcophagus" agreed on only one thing—nobody was to discuss it. Not until they had some answers.

Superstitious bullshit, Ben thought. But it was a superstitious world.

"Walker," Kim said, "perhaps you should . . ."

He had one hand on the plastic sheeting. The prickling on his skin had begun to subside, though the knot of nausea remained, along with that buzzing in his skull. Walker glanced at Kim.

"You coming?" he asked, thinking it strange that she hung so far back, still practically still on the bottom rung of the ladder. The UN had sent her to observe.

Kim nodded.

"Then come on," he said, and pushed through the opening in the plastic. Father Cornelius followed, though Walker didn't need his aid now. Meryam came in after them and the light of Adam's camera gleamed behind her, adding to the antiseptic, industrial yellow glare of the work lights. Walker felt that vibrating in his teeth and realized what it must be—the generators.

Just a rattle from the generators. That made him feel better. Comfortable.

He started to exhale as he studied the ancient wooden box that lay near the wall ahead of him. Broken pieces of bitumen pitch lay on the ground around it like thick shards of black glass, and he remembered the glossy charms on leather cords around the necks of the cadavers Professor Marshall had been working on. They'd been shards of bitumen. Walker stared at the hardened bitumen shell around the coffin, then studied the symbols engraved into the visible wood, at the way they seemed to shift and flow in the sickly yellow light. The insect legs crawled all over his skin again, mostly at the back of his neck, and he wiped a hand across his mouth.

Forcing himself forward, he looked down into the box.

The corpse seemed like a pitiful thing, a bit of fakery created for a low-budget horror film. His mind wanted to interpret it that way, to perceive the wrongness of the thing as absurd instead of monstrous. But as his mind began to take it in, he knew the remains were anything but fake. He'd seen monsters before. Inhuman didn't mean impossible, didn't mean evil. Walker had to remind himself of that.

The fingers were inhumanly long, curved into hooks by the millennia it had spent dead in that box. The skin stretched tight over its chest had a purplish-gray hue. It had withered, and there were spots in which the flesh had caved in. Bone showed through in various places on its skull and one cheek had crumbled to dust. The eyes had sunken to dried berries in its head.

The horns were pale, dusty white, like ivory elephant tusks dulled by age. Six or seven inches in length, the two points jutted from indentations just above its eyes. One had a broken tip, jagged as splintered stone, and both bore a gentle outward curve. The cadaver's skull was misshapen, bulging outward at the top and too pointed in the jaw. In life, it would have been a very odd-looking man. Ugly, even.

If it had been a man.

Farther back in the plastic tent, Kim made a small noise in her throat. She'd begun to breathe in short gasps, on the verge of some kind of panic attack.

"Kim, do you want to step back out?" he asked, trying to disguise his disappointment. He'd expected more professionalism from her.

She said something in Korean, then seemed to remember none of them spoke her language. "Does anyone hear that?" she said in English.

Walker tamped down his own nerves, forced himself to ignore the prickling of his skin. He glanced again at the horns on the corpse in the box, then at the long, thin, jagged teeth, yellowed by time but stained a dark brown in places. Whatever it was, they weren't going to be able to fully identify it until they got it off the mountain.

"What do you think?" Adam asked.

Walker sighed. The plastic sheeting rippled with a gust of wind that traveled all the way through the ruin of the ark. Despite the breeze, the air felt thick and close, suffocating. "What I think is that you never should've opened it outside of a controlled environment."

Meryam stiffened. "As far as we were concerned, this *was* a controlled environment. The other remains on the ark had been exposed for days before we arrived and they are in the condition they're in. We had no reason to expect—"

Father Cornelius pushed past Walker and strode up to the box. Bitumen crunched under the priest's boots as he got his first good look at the cadaver. For a moment he appeared to hold his breath, then he faltered. He slipped a hand into his jacket pocket and came out with a full rosary twined around his fingers, kissed it, and began to whisper a prayer that came as naturally to the man as breathing.

Walker sighed. "Father, come on. I asked you along on this jaunt because I expect more from you than that. You're a scholar, not some prehistoric shaman."

The priest held up a finger to hush him, muttering the last few lines of the Hail Mary. Then he shot Walker a grim stare. "Better safe than sorry. Which is the reason I'm glad they opened the box up here on the mountain."

"You think this thing's going to rise from the dead and go on a rampage?" Walker asked. He glanced again at the horns, the dry, leathery skin at their bases, where they jutted from the cadaver's forehead. "You really think you're looking at a . . ."

He left the last word unspoken. Sweat dried on his skin, beginning to itch. They both knew the word Walker had avoided.

"You think that's impossible?" Father Cornelius said. "I certainly do not. But even assuming this is just some deformity, there are other concerns. The body is better preserved than the other remains. It could be rife with diseases we're not ready to treat. A coffin, yes, but it could be a Pandora's box." He glanced at Adam. "Don't mistake me, it was borderline idiocy to open the box here, no matter how excited you or your documentary producers might be about the moment of discovery. But better to do it wrong here than wrong somewhere more civilized."

When Meryam spoke next, it was to the camera. If she needed to defend her actions, Walker knew, it was to her audience and not her present company.

"Initially we had planned to wait for Dr. Walker's team from the National Science Foundation before we opened the tomb. We photographed all of the symbols engraved on the exterior, removed and preserved the bitumen casing in pieces as large as possible. In doing so, some of the pitch used to seal the lid to the coffin broke away, and . . ."

Meryam smiled shyly, working the camera, knowing the audience would be on her side because she had given them what they wanted.

"Curiosity got the better of us," she confessed, finally turning that shy smile toward Walker and Father Cornelius. "We sealed off the area and only select members of our staff have been inside the tenting. Yes, we removed the lid and took samples of the wood, but no one has touched the body itself. We took what precautions were available to us. Can you honestly say you wouldn't have opened it yourself, Dr. Walker? With some of the seal breaking away?"

What could he say on camera? Of course he would have opened it, but he had years of experience in the field. Saying so would make him look like an arrogant, condescending prick. He didn't care about alienating the eventual viewers of this documentary, but he couldn't afford to alienate Meryam and Adam. Not if he wanted their cooperation.

"We all get carried away sometimes," he said to the camera. "Even without something like Noah's ark coming into the conversation."

The entire gathering seemed to hold its breath.

"You're saying you do believe this is Noah's ark?" Adam asked from behind the camera.

Shit. "Nothing of the kind. Noah's ark makes a good fable and the inspiration for some fun children's toys. Whoever built this ship, he wasn't called Noah."

Father Cornelius turned toward Adam. "Now turn your camera off, boy, and let's get down to business."

"This *is* my business," Adam replied coolly, focused on the priest's face for a response.

"Walker," Kim said, her voice a soft rasp.

He turned toward her, but she wasn't looking at him. Her gaze had locked on the coffin, on whatever part of the cadaver she could see from fifteen feet away. Her whole body trembled, but what troubled him the most was the look of gutting despair on her face. Not fear or panic, but grief. Sorrow so deep it pained him to look at her.

"What is it?" he asked, taking a step toward her.

"No!" she snapped, throwing her hands up, still not looking his way.

Father Cornelius began speaking to her in quiet tones, the kind of soul comfort that he'd been trained throughout his adult life to offer those in pain. Kim squirmed where she stood, twisting as if trying to escape an unwelcome embrace, though no one had touched her.

"What the hell is this?" Meryam whispered.

Adam said nothing, but he caught it all on film. Walker wanted to slap the camera out of his hands.

"Come on," Walker said, moving toward her. "Let's get you out of here. I understand this is a lot to take in. I promise, it isn't what it looks like. But there's no reason you need to be in here while we're—"

He reached for her arm, wondering how the UN had chosen a representative who would fall apart like this. Kim began to shake her head, mumbling refusals as she backed away, pushing into the plastic sheeting behind her.

"Walker, wait," Father Cornelius said.

The buzzing hit him again, the vibration inside his skull. His guts churned and suddenly he'd had enough of this circus. He reached out and grabbed Kim by her wrists, trying to pull her away from the plastic sheet.

A scream tore from her throat and she ripped free of him. She staggered backward, endless despair in those eyes, and then she bolted, dragging the plastic around her, pulling one corner of the makeshift tent down. The others began shouting as Walker put his hands out, batting the plastic away. He shrugged off the suffocating layer just in time to see Kim running into darkness.

"Crazy bitch," Meryam muttered, trying to prop up the fallen corner of the tent.

Walker swore, racing into darkness as he snapped a flashlight off his belt and clicked it on. Around a corner, he passed the same sort of storage or animal stalls he'd seen elsewhere. Kim lunged through the beam of his torch, banged into a wall, and then whipped past a heavy blanket that must have been hung up by the KHAP team.

Pushing through, Walker found himself in a long, rising passage along the western wall. He raced along, finding himself fighting a frigid headwind. Voices cried out up ahead. He bent forward, scaling the incline of the ark's broken deck, and moved around support beams that had been put in place only recently.

"Kim!" Walker shouted, knowing it was useless and feeling foolish. Despite whatever had driven her to run, his voice would not be the thing that soothed her.

He clicked off his flashlight. There were plenty of work lights ahead. The chase Kim had led them on had brought him back to the place he'd been standing not long ago, where Helen Marshall and a few others were working to uncover and preserve the remains of three of the ark's passengers. The British archaeologist knelt on the ground as if to protect the bones of the long dead, but the others had backed away.

They were all watching Kim.

She had gone to the door—the door pinned against the mountain, the door that could provide no exit—and was scratching at it, digging her fingernails into the ancient wood just as these dead people had done thousands of years before. She kept whispering to herself, the same words over and over. Though Walker didn't speak Korean, he knew the word for "please." That was one of them.

He had an inkling of what those other words might be, but only when he had approached Kim and carefully laid a hand on her shoulder, only when he had knelt beside her and gathered her against him for a moment, only when she had reached out with her left hand and continued digging into the wood and finally whispered those words to him in English, could he finally be certain.

"Please," she whispered, gazing at him with that bottomless sorrow.

"Please let me out."

SEVEN

Meryam climbed the reinforced stairs that led up to the ark's third level. As much as she had fancied herself a knowledgeable woman prior to this discovery, she had learned a great deal in the three weeks since she and Adam had made the climb, and she was still learning. The timbers were an array of different woods, from oak to pine to juniper that would have had to be imported if the ark had been built anywhere in this region.

What most fascinated her about the ship's construction was that it had been stitched or lashed together with woven cords, the seams filled with reeds and grass and then painted over with a hardening resin and patched with bitumen. They'd snatched Helen Marshall away from teaching classes at Oxford and Meryam milked her for information every couple of days. Same with Wynyfred Douglas, the American who was essentially second-in-command to Helen, the two of them overseeing the motley crew of graduate students from three countries.

The trio—Meryam, Helen, and Wyn—would gather and discuss any new findings on camera, with Meryam seeming much better informed than she was thanks to having been prepped in advance. She had never seen herself as a TV presenter, but in some ways, that was what she had become.

As exhausted as she felt, the thrill of their discovery had not abated. Word had already gotten out, and there was no question that the world understood the importance of this project. People were fighting about it across the globe, debating, arguing, and in more than one case actually coming to blows over the truth of the ancient ship that formed the cave around them.

The word *impossible* seemed popular. Even if one accepted that the entire region had once endured a flood event that lasted long enough and was pervasive enough to sweep across hundreds of miles, or even thousands, there was one fact that only the very religious seemed ready to embrace. Unless someone had picked up an ocean and temporarily relocated it, no flood could have brought waters so high that the ark would have been lifted four thousand meters up the mountainside.

Unless God had put it there. Of course, she didn't believe in any god.

Keep telling yourself that.

There were other theories—something about an ancient tribe dragging the ark up the mountain, or building it up there. History held stories of ships moved across land for purposes of war, but to move a ship this size up the side of Mount Ararat seemed—if not impossible—at least impractical. But Meryam had one advantage over the people with theories about the ark, including those who claimed the whole thing had to be a hoax. She had been living and working inside of it for three weeks. However it had gotten up onto the mountain, there was no doubting the reality of it when you walked its canted floor and breathed in the scent of its aged timbers.

The how and why were the entire point of this project. Perhaps the who would even be addressed at some point. But the what . . . of that, there could be no doubt. A ship. Buried in the side of a mountain four thousand meters up.

Despite her weariness, and even with the fear and uncertainty the morning had brought, the questions that buzzed around her brain made her smile as she worked her way up the reinforced steps.

Many of the KHAP staff had been bunking on level one, in a kind of camp they had set up, making their sleeping quarters in the stalls, with additional shelter they had shored up with plastic sheeting, heavy blankets, and hastily constructed new walls. She had a feeling that when the first real winter storm arrived—which would be soon—the level-one campers would relocate to the second or third floor, but for the moment they preferred to be near an exit, just in case the mountain decided to start shaking itself apart again.

Level two included additional staff quarters, storage, the infirmary, and the workroom, which was off-limits while the artifacts and remains and samples were being catalogued. That left stalls on level three for Ben Walker and his team. Meryam held onto the walls and picked her steps carefully as she moved down the slanted floor until she reached the two stalls where they had erected their tents.

She passed the stall that would be Kim Seong's quarters and poked her head inside the next one. The large tent filled about half of the space Walker would be sharing with Father Cornelius.

Meryam rapped on the wall. "Knock knock."

After a rustle, Walker poked his head out of the tent. She couldn't tell whether or not he was glad to see her. Considering that she and Adam had resisted the U.S. government's request to send him in the first place, she wondered why she cared. Walker and Father Cornelius both exuded an air of confidence and competence, so perhaps that was it. As Wyn Douglas would have said, they seemed as if they had "seen some shit."

Just your way of saying you like them because they're not afraid.

She thought that was more accurate. Ever since the box had been opened and the first whispers about the cadaver had traveled among the staff, the fear had been building. People didn't feel well or they had bad dreams and too many of them had succumbed to the temptation to ascribe those things to the presence of the malformed thing inside that ancient coffin. There had been a lot of what she called turbulence over the past week or so, and it was getting worse. Religion was making it worse. Faith, or more precisely, the warring of different faiths, and those who were faithless.

The man himself stood outside one of the stalls. When she approached, the two Americans dropped their conversation and stood a bit straighter.

"How's Kim?" Walker asked.

Meryam rested against the wall for a moment. "Dr. Dwyer is calling it a panic attack."

Walker had a pleasant face, but his expression just then was anything but pleasant.

"You were *there*. She had a total breakdown, complete with delusions or hallucinations. The only thing I've ever seen that remotely resembled what happened down there was a psychotic episode from a kid in my high school math class, but he had full-blown schizophrenia."

Meryam bristled. "I'd have thought this would be good news. Doctor says claustrophobia and general anxiety caused a panic attack. I suspected some altitude sickness, but your team already went through the acclimatization process."

Walker hesitated, unconvinced. "So she's all right?"

"It's all relative, isn't it? If she were home, she'd be all right. But up here, we can't be responsible for someone prone to panic attacks. She could hurt herself, damage the faunal remains, or even hurt someone else."

"You have no reason to think—" Walker began.

"I'm recommending to the Turkish monitors that she be evacuated and the UN send a replacement."

"You can't do that."

Meryam straightened up. "It's my project, Dr. Walker. You're a guest here."

"All I'm asking is that you put off any decision until morning," Walker said. "If Kim hasn't had another episode and seems healthy enough, let her stay. I'd really rather not go through the difficulties involved in bringing another UN observer up here."

Meryam cocked an eyebrow. "That's the issue you have with me wanting her gone?"

"You thought it was team loyalty?" he replied. "I'm here to do a job. Kim seems competent enough, but I hardly know her. The cadaver down in that coffin is intriguing and more than a little disturbing. I don't want to have to sit on my hands while the UN finds a replacement. And you said yourself there's a storm in the forecast and you want to get the cadaver packed for transport before it hits."

A shout rang out, echoing around inside the ark. Meryam froze, on edge until she heard a shouted reply, followed by a bark of laughter. She exhaled, and saw Walker do the same. He'd only been in the ark for hours and already felt the tension of the place. It wasn't just the mountain or the creaking of the timber as the weather shifted.

"You all right?" Walker asked. "You jumped a little."

Meryam smiled. "There's not been much laughter these past weeks. Just surprised me a bit. There's a weight to this work that Adam and I haven't encountered on other projects."

Walker's expression softened. "That's an understatement. No matter what you discover up here, no matter what conclusions are drawn, you're going to make a lot of people very angry."

"Better to pretend we were never here? Blow it up like Professor Olivieri wants?"

"I wouldn't go that far."

"Glad to hear it," Meryam said. "Because, honestly, it doesn't much matter what the UN says or does. Their approval is a condition for you being here, not for our project to continue. So while you're welcome to participate, my intention is to remove the cadaver from the box this afternoon so Patil can do a full examination and take samples before the body is prepped for transport."

"So we've got hours. This isn't just about a storm. What's your hurry?"

Meryam leaned against the wall and thrust her hands into her pockets. The chill she felt inside her and the unpleasant queasiness in her stomach were not new. They had been there all along and had been getting worse.

"You saw it, Dr. Walker—"

"Just—"

"*Doctor* Walker. You saw it. I waited for your team as a courtesy to your government. Now I just want that thing out of here."

He seemed about to argue with her, but apparently thought better of it, perhaps remembering that he and his team were guests, after all. This was the Karga-Holzer Ark Project, not something his National Science Foundation had put together.

"Who's this Patil? Have I met her?" Walker asked.

"Him," she corrected. "Dev Patil is our paleopathologist, recruited from Cambridge University by Professor Marshall—"

"You're not going to whip out their diplomas, are you? I have a few degrees of my own."

Meryam shook her head. "I'm not here to measure your manhood or to check your credentials. I've done the latter already or I'd have put my foot down about you even being here."

Walker nodded slowly. "It's your show. But I'd like to ask one favor. Hold off moving the cadaver long enough for Father Cornelius to study the writings engraved in the casing. Both what you've broken away and what's still there, as well as what's inscribed on the lid. Enough of it's already been destroyed. I know you've got photographs, but he'd prefer to look at the remainder *in situ*."

A suspicion rose in her, almost amusing . . . except that she wasn't amused.

"Please don't tell me you're worried Kim's episode was the result of proximity to the box," she said. "I've got enough superstition brewing in some of my own crew—Turks, Kurds, Americans—without you giving them the idea you believe in ancient curses."

Walker sniffed. "I'm more concerned about ancient diseases than ancient curses."

Meryam studied his face, searching his eyes.

She wasn't certain she believed him.

Adam stood with Calliope at the edge of the cave, looking out over the mountain range. The beauty and silence were breathtaking. It was as if the rest of the world had vanished and all that remained of civilization were the people gathered in the ruins of the ark. He wore his knit cap pulled down tight over his ears and the hood of his jacket snugged down over it. The wind slid in along his neck and slithered down his back, always finding a way in, snaking through flesh and right down to bone.

"God, it's stunning," Calliope said, camera in hand.

With her focused only on the view through the camera, he felt free to observe her. Of all the members of the dig, including the team that had arrived with Ben Walker, Calliope alone seemed at ease. Even the cold did not seem to trouble her as much. Her hair fell about her face, framing her even as she framed a shot of the wintry gray horizon with her camera. In his work, and as a young American male in London, he met plenty of attractive women, but pretty as she was, it was the easiness about her that made Calliope beautiful.

He loved Meryam. Intended to marry Meryam. Nothing would change that. But being around Calliope lightened his heart, and he needed that right now.

"You're awfully quiet," she said without taking her eye from the camera.

"Just admiring the view." *Shit*. He'd meant it innocently enough and hoped she didn't take it the wrong way.

"A bit scary, though."

"What is?"

Finally she stopped filming and lowered the camera to glance at him. "Being up here. Storm on the way. Left to our own devices if anything goes wrong."

"You don't seem scared."

Calliope grinned. "I have hidden depths."

She went back to filming, focusing on the roiling clouds in the distance. The real storm wasn't meant to blast in for a while yet, but the sky already seemed ominous enough, pregnant with the uncaring threat of nature's power.

"She'll be all right, you know," Calliope said.

"Sorry?"

Perhaps very purposefully now, she kept filming. "Meryam. There's a lot of pressure on her. I know the project is jointly yours and hers, the books and our film, all of that. But we all know she holds the reins. If something goes wrong, she's going to feel the weight of it the most. Blame herself."

Adam could barely breathe. Either Calliope had keen intuition or he and Meryam were just about the most transparent people who'd ever lived.

"True enough," he agreed. "So what makes you think she'll be all right?"

A smile, and she lowered the camera again, looking at him in that way women had of letting a man know with a single glance that his idiocy was almost adorable, but only almost.

"You're a good guy, Adam. If Meryam falls apart, you'll put her back together again." Calliope took a deep breath. The wind had scoured her cheeks to a bright red. "She'll be all right because she's got you to look after her if anything goes wrong."

I hope you're right, he was about to say. Opened his mouth and got the first word out before he heard footsteps scuffing across the rock behind him and someone called his name. He turned to see Feyiz approaching with the younger of the two Turkish government monitors, Mr. Zeybekci.

"What now?" Adam whispered to himself, sure Calliope's camera would have caught it but not caring.

Zeybekci smoothed his jacket in a way that made him seem even younger, like a high school student about to give a presentation in front of the class. The holstered gun on his hip seemed more like a toy, but Adam knew it was very real. He and Meryam had initially balked at the idea of Zeybekci and his older counterpart being armed, but the government had insisted. If they'd been under any illusions that Zeybekci and Mr. Avci were ordinary government functionaries, the guns—and the pretense that there was nothing strange about these men carrying them—would have erased those illusions. They were monitors, certainly, but though they might report back to the government, they were doubtless Turkish army officers.

Nobody talked about it. Mostly, everyone just pretended the guns weren't there, and Adam understood why. The whole team understood that they were there on the sufferance of the Turks, and they weren't in a position to object to the conditions the government exposed.

"Mr. Holzer," the monitor began, "there are certain concerns among the project participants that I feel I must bring to your attention."

He'd gone to some kind of private school in Istanbul with British instructors. His elocution and the accent of his English made it clear. But unlike his older counterpart, Mr. Avci, Zeybekci didn't come off as disdainful. He seemed honestly engaged in doing his job.

"Go on," Adam said, eyeing Feyiz, wondering what he was doing here. The guides were all Kurdish, and the Kurds did not traditionally pal around with Turkish government functionaries.

"I know you're well aware that there has been certain rumbling among the workers since word began to spread regarding the contents of the particular box—"

"Such delicate phrasing," Adam said. "Call it a coffin if you want. Everyone knows there's a corpse in it."

Zeybekci swallowed. "There are many corpses in the cave, Mr. Holzer. Many bones. You know this one is different, and that its presence makes your staff anxious. You've dismissed their unease as superstition for some time, but you'll find it hard to dismiss if they abandon the project."

"Abandon? They'll walk off the job because of a five-thousand-year-old cadaver?"

"They might," Feyiz confirmed.

Adam met Zeybekci's gaze. In his mind, an image flickered to life, dredged up from his childhood memories—the tall pendulum clock that had stood in the parlor in his grandmother's house throughout his childhood. Even now, a trickle of remembered fear made him shiver.

He understood superstition and the power to terrify that could be imbued within an object. At twenty-nine years old, he could still remember the way he had held his breath when his grandmother told the story of the dybbuk that had possessed her father, and the little ritual her mother had performed when the old man had breathed his last, meant to capture the evil spirit and trap it inside that clock.

If we let the dybbuk escape with my father's spirit, his grandmother had said, *his soul will never have peace.*

Adam had seen in her eyes that she had believed it entirely, that the belief had consumed her, and it was that—her faith and fear—that had convinced him as a little boy. Seven years old, that winter.

His grandmother had taught him how to wind the clock. Where to find the key, how often it had to be done. If the clock ever stopped, she'd told him . . . the dybbuk would be free.

And he'd fucking believed her.

It still pissed him off, that he'd fallen for such bullshit. Her fear had infected him, and he refused to allow that to happen again, no matter how many people in the Ark Project had the same sorts of absurd beliefs. He believed in God, wanted to believe in an afterlife, but even if he went along with the idea that the thing in the box was not human, it was dead. Really most sincerely dead, in the parlance of Munchkinland. Did it make him uneasy? Hell, yes. But he wouldn't be frightened of a dead thing, human or otherwise.

"I understand their concerns," he said, "but let me play—" He stopped himself before uttering the phrase *devil's advocate*. It seemed a bad idea. "The cadaver is so old that until we get a proper study of it, there's no way to know what caused its deformities. I don't for a second believe it's some kind of monster or demon, but for those whose religious or spiritual beliefs suggest otherwise, do they not understand that it's *dead*? That it's been buried in the side of the mountain for—"

"Mr. Holzer, you're not listening," Zeybekci said. Normally impossible to ruffle, he was letting his frustration show.

"Adam," Feyiz began.

"Don't tell me *you* believe this shit."

Feyiz tugged at his beard. "I've been doing my best to keep everyone calm. My uncle's not helping because he half believes it's a demon himself. Remember, he's actually seen it. Most of the dig hasn't. We're not just talking about Turks or Kurds, either. Don't make the mistake of thinking we're a bunch of ignorant savages jumping at shadows—"

"God, Feyiz, when have I ever given you the idea I was the sort of person who'd make assumptions like that?" Adam asked.

"I know that's not you. But I know enough about Western culture to know there's some of that hard-wired into all of you. Some of the Americans and British are just as nervous. My point is that I had it mostly under control, but now the whole dig is talking about the woman from the UN taking one look at the cadaver and turning into a lunatic."

"She's fine now," Calliope added from behind the camera.

Adam glanced at her in surprise. She never talked while she was filming. Her piping up like that made him realize just how serious this must really be.

"*Now*," Zeybekci echoed. "But many saw her suffering some kind of breakdown, and you can only imagine what that has done to their fears."

Feyiz thrust his hands into his pockets. "You and Meryam have to talk to them. Better yet, you've got to get it out of here as soon as possible."

"That *is* our intention," Adam said.

Something danced at the edge of his vision and he realized it had begun to snow. Lightly, gently swirling, but snow nevertheless. A precursor to the storm to come.

Zeybekci shrugged himself deeper inside his coat and glanced longingly back inside the cave, wanting the relative shelter of the ark. The walls inside. The blankets and portable heaters.

"My government will provide whatever cooperation is necessary to facilitate this," Zeybekci said. "We would prefer to avoid being made to look foolish."

Adam couldn't believe what he was hearing. "So you share these fears?"

"Not at all. But if the Karga-Holzer Ark Project becomes an embarrassment, it will affect all parties involved."

"Look, let me talk to Meryam—"

He saw Calliope shift the camera again, and turned to see his fiancée approaching.

"Talk to Meryam about what?"

Shit. This was not a conversation he wanted to have in front of other people, particularly as on edge as Meryam had been today. She looked tired, deep circles under her eyes. The snow fell around her, quietly beautiful, and Adam had to fight the urge to beg her to abandon the project and fly home with him.

"Our friends here," he said, "have come to demand that the cadaver be removed from the ark immediately."

"Not immediately," Feyiz corrected. "It's too late today—"

"We're working on it," Meryam interrupted. "Believe me, I'd like that thing out of here just as much as you would."

"It isn't—"

"As *any* of you would," she corrected herself. "But here's what bothers me. Adam is my partner, but I'm project manager. I can't escape the idea that you came to him so you could avoid a confrontation with me."

Adam narrowed his eyes, flushing with irritation. It shouldn't have bothered him—this was the very same conclusion he'd drawn—but the way she spoke it was as if she shared their impression that he was some kind of lackey. He was nobody's lackey. He breathed deeply. *She knows that,* he told himself. *It's not what she means.* And yet his teeth were on edge.

"I'm sorry," Feyiz said. "We meant no disrespect. It's just that you've seemed so exhausted, that we didn't want to trouble you with this until we'd had a chance to—"

"Of course I'm exhausted!" Meryam snapped, and Adam thought he saw her mouth tremble a bit. Was there a quaver of emotion in her voice? "We're all bloody exhausted!"

She shook her head, stared at the snowflakes eddying over the abyss as the daylight waned.

"Don't you think I want the damn thing gone? You have my promise that the cadaver will be moved off the mountain the moment it's possible to do so safely, but unfortunately that means after this storm. Thank you for bringing your concerns to our attention."

Zeybekci seemed about to argue, but Feyiz tapped his arm and a moment later they were walking back into the ark. Meryam glanced at the camera, and then apparently decided she did not care if Calliope caught her words on film.

"I'll speak to everyone during dinner and address their fears," she said. "After that, if anyone wants to climb down the mountain before that storm hits, let them go. I'd rather lose half the staff than deal with a bunch of children who think the bloody bogeyman's coming to get them."

EIGHT

Walker and Father Cornelius had one rough-hewn stall to themselves, with Kim in the next one over. They had blankets and heavy sleeping bags, but the stalls had no doors. As cold as it was during the day it would be far colder at night, but now that he'd seen some of the other sleeping quarters he felt a little warmer. Some of the KHAP team had created false walls by hanging sheets of plastic from the roof and nail-gunning them to the floor timbers. The plastic snapped taut with every gust of wind, rustling quietly when it eased, but it did nothing to keep out the chill.

Only the infirmary had more substance. There were walls of preformed, insulated plastic that Ben figured must have been airlifted to the cave and then locked together. The little mobile procedure room came complete with floor and ceiling, and plenty of ventilation. It looked like a children's playset zapped with some kind of growth ray, but Walker felt envious. There were several cots in the room, and he was sure Dr. Dwyer slept in one of them.

"This is cozy," he said as he entered.

Dr. Dwyer glanced up from his laptop and surveyed his new arrivals. Walker had entered first, but Father Cornelius was right behind him. "How's she doing?"

"Well, I don't think there's any need for last rites," the doctor said, smiling at the presence of the priest.

Father Cornelius gave a soft laugh. "I might need them myself if I stay up here very long."

Kim lay on her side on the cot farthest from the entrance. She faced them, and though her eyes tracked their arrival, she made no other sign that she had noticed.

"Is she all right?" the priest asked.

Dr. Dwyer closed his laptop and stood, clasping his hands behind his back in the manner of doctors and lecturers from the birth of time. "Seong is awake and alert and certainly able to speak for herself."

Walker understood the doctor's deference to his patient, but Dwyer hadn't been there when Kim had gone racing through the ark, screaming and muttering gibberish. If they were all a bit wary now, that was to be understood.

He went over and sat on the middle cot, facing her. "How do you feel?"

"Tired," the woman said, tucking back a lock of hair that had fallen across her face. "Embarrassed."

Father Cornelius kept his distance, standing with the doctor.

"You gave us all a pretty good scare," Walker said.

Kim's face went cold. Hard. Somehow it made her beautiful. Walker tried to ignore the observation when it floated into his mind, particularly because he had known such women before. There was fear and pain beneath that cold veneer, and he had plenty of his own. He thought of his ex-wife, Amanda, of the pain he'd tried to spare her and the different stripe of it he'd inflicted upon her instead.

"I'm fine now," Kim said. "That's all I can tell you. I've had panic attacks—anxiety attacks, I suppose—in the past, but never anything like that."

She spoke in a kind of monotone that made Walker wonder if Dr. Dwyer had put her on some kind of medication. He studied Kim's eyes, saw the super-dilated pupils, and realized that had to be it. No wonder she felt fine.

"They're going to be serving dinner soon," he said. "Are you up to it?"

Kim's upper lip twitched. He'd seen her do it before—a sign of irritation, though whether or not she was aware of it, he couldn't be sure.

"I said I feel fine. And I'm starving."

Walker glanced back at Father Cornelius and then the doctor. "Doc?"

Dwyer nodded. "Miss Kim is free to go."

"Good." Walker leaned toward her, gripping the edges of the cot beneath him. He studied Kim's eyes again. "This is not a place where it is safe to lose control of yourself. If you feel another attack coming on—if your heart so much as skips an extra beat— you tell me."

For a moment she just lay there staring at him. Then she sat up straight, blew in her hands to warm them, and stood so that— tiny as she was—she loomed over him.

"I'm not a child, Walker. And I'll remind you that I do not answer to you."

Walker stood as well, shrinking the space between the cots so now it contained only the two of them. He stared down at her, analyzing, evaluating, trying to follow the threads forward to find the worst-case scenarios that might spin out of this moment. They were too close, barely any light between them. Kim exhaled a warm breath and Walker breathed it in, an unwelcome intimacy that made him blink and turn away, suddenly too aware of her presence and her strength. She'd gotten under his skin, but he tried not to focus too much on why.

"I know you're not a child," he said as he walked away. "But if you snap and go off, raving and running around in here, you might run right off the ledge." He paused, turning to meet her gaze. "I don't want to have to explain to the UN why you fell off the mountain."

He thought he saw the flicker of a smile on her lips. Then Kim nodded.

"Understood."

Father Cornelius smiled softly. "Shall we go down to dinner, then?"

Kim took a wobbly step and caught herself. Whatever Dr. Dwyer had given her, it worked very well.

"Come on," he said, watching to make sure she didn't fall. "Maybe we'll get lucky and it'll be taco night."

This time Kim definitely smiled. She had a sense of humor underneath that hard veneer. Then again, it might have been the drugs.

Walker stepped out of the infirmary and felt a sudden surge of nausea that made him stop and hold the doorframe. He took a deep breath as his skin prickled and a sickly sweat beaded on his skin. *No, no. Not this again.* He'd thought it was the elevation or the helicopter ride, but now he wondered if he'd come down with some kind of virus. He couldn't afford to be sick.

"You all right?" Father Cornelius asked.

Another deep breath and Walker dropped his hand, forcing a smile. "Just a long day, I guess."

The chill wind snaked back through the ancient timbers and slithered around the manmade efforts to keep it out. To his left, plastic sheeting flapped in the wind, torn loose from the nails that had pinned it down.

Something moved at the corner of his eye, but when he turned to look he saw nothing but shadows.

"Can I have everyone's attention, please?"

The rumble of conversation continued for a few seconds, dishes and silverware clinking, and Meryam thought she might have to speak up again, louder this time. But then forks and cups began to lower and the staff shifted one or two at a time to face her.

There were half a dozen lightweight plastic tables, stackable things that were only brought out at mealtime. The chairs were just as lightweight, just as stackable, but there weren't enough of them. The crew took turns standing. From Meryam's perspective they ought to have been happy to have tables and chairs at all. Happy they weren't, scooping cold canned beans with their fingers.

Be kind, she told herself. But she wasn't in a charitable mood. She felt a buzz of aggravation at the back of her skull like a small headache that she couldn't seem to shake.

"I understand some of you are nervous about continuing your work on the Ark Project," Meryam began. She scanned the space ahead of her—the archaeologists and students, the workers, the guides, the doctor, the Turkish monitors and the paleopathologist, Olivieri, and Adam. Walker's little trio sat farthest away from her, near Helen Marshall, who Meryam knew wanted to keep in view of the roped-off area she'd been working in that day to make sure no one stumbled into it.

"Some of you are religious people. Some of you have superstitions that stem from those religions or from childhood," she went on. Anger flickered across several faces. Off to her right, Hakan uncrossed his arms with a sneer she had seen before. "I am not questioning your spirituality or suggesting that your faith is in any way illegitimate. There are Jews among us, as well as Christians and Muslims and atheists. I'm not here to tell you what to believe. What I will tell you is this—you have nothing to fear."

An American—an NYU student named Errick Noonan—sat up straighter in his seat. "How can you promise that?"

Meryam relaxed. It was the question she had hoped for. They would listen much more closely to her answer to a challenge than if she'd made a simple statement.

"You're all intelligent people. Many of you are experts in your fields of study, or on your way to becoming that. Others have an intimate knowledge of this mountain, of this region. We're living inside an ancient ship—an ark. There's a lot we don't know. Who built it? How did it get up here? *Why* was it built? These are the questions and the onus is on all of you to find the answers."

"Those aren't the questions on my mind tonight," Errick said.

"Must we bother with this idiocy?" called an older Turkish student, a master's candidate called Kemal. "Some of us are tired of the constant chatter. You want something to fear? Worry about the storm that's coming, or whether your foolishness will get you dismissed from a once-in-a-lifetime project."

Errick stood up quickly, plastic chair falling over backward. "Are you kidding me?" he demanded, jabbing a finger in the air, pointing at Kemal. "You can't tell me this isn't getting under your skin. Any of you."

"Sit down, Errick," Wyn Douglas said. "Meryam was—"

"I know what Meryam is trying to do. But I heard Dr. Patil talking about the cadaver you're all so protective of." He whipped around, gesturing at several other students, most of them Americans who were on Wyn's crew with him. "This thing's got horns. It's not human. Dr. Patil said himself that it looked like a demon—"

Dev Patil held up a hand. "Now, hang on a minute. I never said it *was* a demon, only that it had horns like a demon."

Errick threw up his hands. "There you go!" He spun to face Meryam again, voices rising around him, some in support and some calling for him to return to his seat. "Doc Patil knows more about this than anyone and he won't even use a human pronoun to describe that thing. Why? 'Cause it isn't human."

"Oh, for fuck's sake," someone shouted.

Helen Marshall called for Errick to sit and listen.

Kemal got up from his chair. "The only demons around here are the little terrors running around inside the heads of anyone who believes there is something to fear! There is no devil! There is no evil! There is—"

"I never thought so, either," Errick said. "But now we've got a goddamn demon about eighty yards from where you're standing, man."

"There is no—"

"No?" Errick echoed. "You keep saying 'no?'"

He twisted around, scanning for someone, and when he spotted Kim Seong he marched in her direction.

Walker stood abruptly. "Back the fuck off, kid."

Errick hesitated, and voices rose up to fill the pause, arguing.

"Hey!" Meryam shouted. "That is bloody well enough!"

The last few words made her throat raw, the quivering rage in her so startling—to her and her staff—that all eyes turned toward her again. At last.

"Errick," she said, quietly now, but her voice carried in the sudden silence. "Sit down. Don't make me say it again."

Meryam waited, calming herself as the student returned to his table, righted his chair, and sat heavily. Walker, Kemal, and several others who had leaped to their feet also returned to their chairs. Those who had already been standing seemed to wish they had somewhere to sit, if only to avoid Meryam screaming herself hoarse.

"I'm going to be honest with you," she said, and saw them all stiffen. Most of the time, people who had to announce their impending honesty were about to lie to you. But the words that followed surprised her with the way they made her heart thump and the way her cheeks flushed as she spoke them.

The truth felt raw, even as it came out of her mouth.

"I don't believe in devils or angels," she said. "Maybe there's some kind of great, wise being out there in the cosmos—I think there probably is, but mostly 'cause I think it's arrogant for us to think we're the smartest things the universe has to offer. But demons and ghosts, the voice of God, heaven and hell? Not a doubt in my mind that it's all shit. Here's my confession, though, and you need to understand this. I want it to be true. If the ark is real, if God told some bloke called Noah to build this old tub 'cause he was about to flood the damn world, that means there is a heaven. It means death isn't the end and we carry on afterward, and maybe I get to see my gran again someday. She never put much stock in God but was kinder to me than anyone else has ever been."

Several people glanced at Adam, wondering how he felt about this statement, given that she'd agreed to marry him. Meryam didn't care how he felt about it just then.

"Here is what I *do* know. The body we found is deformed. We haven't established its sex, so 'it' is a perfectly acceptable pronoun. As soon as the storm is over, we are going to transport it to Istanbul. Until that time, if it makes you nervous or your superstition is so great that you are actually afraid, I suggest you focus on your work and stay away from the tented area at the back of level one. Now, if that's all—"

Hakan clapped his hands once, loudly, the sound echoing.

Every head turned. Meryam wanted to murder him. He'd clapped to interrupt, to get attention, but he'd done it like a dog calling his master to heel, and he was the project foreman. He had been rude to her all along, dismissive, critical of her gender, but never this openly.

"You have something to say, Hakan?"

He sneered. "You say 'superstition' the way people say 'dog shit.'"

"I don't think—"

"It doesn't matter what you think," Hakan went on.

Feyiz swore and began moving across the cave, as if to separate Meryam from his uncle. Hakan saw the younger guide coming and dismissed him with a scowl. Feyiz was not a factor to him.

"Maybe you are right," Hakan said. "Maybe there is nothing to fear. But if there is, you are putting every one of us in danger by not giving us a choice if we want to stay or go."

The talking started again, the worrying, the doubt.

Son of a bitch, Meryam thought. His resentment at having to answer to a woman had been simmering for weeks, and now it had surfaced.

"You want to go?" she said, glaring at Hakan. "Then fucking go!"

Feyiz reached his uncle then, tried to grab his arms, to move him away. Hakan shoved him. Feyiz reeled, arms pinwheeling, and crashed into one of the plastic tables, cracking it in half.

All fell silent again. Meryam had said all she intended to say.

She glanced around, wondering why Adam hadn't intervened. She didn't need her man to stand up for her, to speak for her, but she wouldn't have minded some backup.

Then she spotted him, standing far off to her left, near the outside of the cave with his camera in his hands, filming the whole thing. Off to her right and at the back, just beyond Hakan, she saw Calliope, also getting the whole ugly business on camera. The disloyalty and the violence, the disdain for her gender and her leadership, the ignorance and fear. If they used this in the documentary, it would make her look like a fool with a bad temper and even worse leadership skills.

What the hell are you thinking? She stared at Adam.

Only his camera stared back.

Hours after dark, Kim moved quietly through the frigid space of the ark's topmost level. Her jacket and thick garments provided as much warmth as she could have hoped for, but still she felt colder than she had ever imagined possible. She walked quietly, as though only she and the ark itself were still awake, and she did not want to disturb the others who had taken up temporary residence within. Though she knew very well there were others awake, working late or standing guard or, like herself, unable to drift off after the events of the day, exhaustion notwithstanding.

Madness notwithstanding.

Her teeth chattered a bit and she sipped at the plastic mug of tea she had been given in the kitchen area. The cook, a Kurdish man whom she gathered was related to the site manager, Hakan, had taken pity on her. Too late for coffee, he'd managed to tell her in English, but he could heat water for tea. Kim had been—still was—so grateful. The tea had an earthy flavor and rich, herbal aromas, but it warmed her a little, and tonight *a little* would be enough.

Despite the lighting and the generators, there were long stretches of profound darkness on her way back to what they were calling their quarters. She didn't like those shadows, the way they seemed to grow deeper as she approached and closed in behind her when she passed. They made her think of the tented enclosure on the bottom level, of the black sarcophagus down there and the withered husk that lay inside it. She didn't want to think about the cadaver, or the way her mind had just slipped away and her heart had started its raucous tantrum in her chest. Liquid pools of black and red had coalesced at the edges of her eyes—of her mind—and then she'd felt as if she were drowning in shadows, and those shadows were full of slithering things that were reaching out for her, and if they managed to touch her . . .

The screams had come then. And she'd run.

What am I doing here? she wondered, not for the first time.

The wind slid along the floor, turning once in a lazy circle that swept up a skittering of grit and carried it away. Kim passed the stall Walker and Father Cornelius shared, and spotted Walker standing just outside their tent, knocking a couple of pills back with a chug from a reusable water bottle. When he noticed her, he shot her a guilty glance, as if she'd caught him doing something he feared she'd frown upon.

"Headache?" she asked.

"Long day," he replied, which wasn't an answer. His expression implied a certain gratitude for the out she'd provided. To Kim, it was as good as an admission that the pills he had just taken were not for a headache at all.

She wondered, of course, but she felt reluctant to inquire further. If Walker seemed to be distracted from his work by a reliance on some prescription medication or another, then it would become her business. If that never happened, she would not bring it up again.

Yet he seemed on edge, now, even a bit twitchy, and having seen what could not now be unseen, she could not help feeling a flicker of doubt about him. She had been assigned only to observe—what Walker did by way of research was not her concern. Still, she wondered.

And she wondered about herself, too.

She had to.

"You all right?" he asked, when the silence between them had become awkward.

"Couldn't sleep," she said, raising her travel cup. "The cook made me some special Kurdish tea."

Walker cocked his head, smiling almost in spite of himself, as if the hour had grown too late and the night too cold for him to remember the tension between them.

"You know tea has caffeine, right? If you're having trouble sleeping—"

"It soothes me," Kim said. "And I wanted something warm."

"That much I definitely understand."

They stood there a few seconds more, until it grew awkward again, and then she smiled and said good night.

"Sleep well," Walker said, but he showed no interest in returning to his tent.

Kim slipped back into hers and sat on her backpack, sipping her tea and listening to the wind moving through the ancient structure. It sounded as if the ark had fallen asleep and was breathing, in and out, a whispering of enormous lungs. Inhale. Exhale.

Inhale. Exhale.

She sipped her tea.

In her mind, she saw the cadaver's face again, heard the echo of her own lunatic screams, and she knew she would not be getting any sleep at all tonight.

She had never felt so far from home.

Arjen had drawn second watch tonight, standing sentry from two a.m. until dawn broke over the ridge of the earth. At twenty years of age, Arjen still loved his sleep, and so every time his turn in the guard duty rotation came around, he would spend those dark, frigid hours full of resentment toward his uncle Hakan. Life on the mountain had changed so much in the time since the landslide and Arjen's fondest wish was that it all go back to the way it had been before. But as he stood just a few feet from the windswept edge of the cave, with the treacherous snow-laden rockfall stretching out below him and the blanket of blustery night all around, he knew the past would remain the past. When he had been living that life—up hours before dawn, helping foreigners trek to Ararat's peak, making camp and breaking camp, teaching most of them what ought to have been rudimentary climbing skills—Arjen had wished for a different life.

Now he cursed that wish.

There had been funerals after the landslide. Cousins, mostly. In the aftermath, Uncle Hakan and *his* cousin, Baris, had vied for control over the business. Their extended family had been guiding tourists on the mountain for generations and now a new generation had to take the reins. Being a part of the team that discovered the ark—and being able to hire many of his family members as workers on the project—had solidified Hakan's position as head of the family, and the business. Arjen needed to stay in his good graces, but with every day that had passed his own resentment grew. He knew himself well enough to realize this was due in part to his natural laziness, but his indolence did not prevent him from forming an opinion of his uncle Hakan. The man had always been arrogant and cruel, even brutal at times, and this recent elevation had only exacerbated those traits. Fortunately, Arjen had Feyiz. Their mothers were sisters and Arjen had admired his older cousin growing up. Feyiz indulged him. Tolerated his laziness. Defended him to Hakan, as long as Arjen put in some effort.

Now something had changed. From the first day Arjen had been hired onto the Karga-Holzer Ark Project, Hakan and Feyiz had butted heads over Hakan's treatment of the workers and the constant, muttered insinuations about Meryam and Adam. His disdain had seeped into the attitudes of some of the others. Arjen had seen it in them, and been entirely unsurprised. His uncle had set the tone for the other members of the family who worked under him. They would provide whatever manual labor the project required, including bringing supplies to and from the ark, but they could not respect their employers. Not if Hakan had anything to say about it.

Only Feyiz and Arjen felt differently. But even Arjen had begun to view Meryam and Adam differently after tonight. Meryam seemed frayed at the edges, on the verge of unraveling, and the tension among the workers and students and professors hung thick and heavy in the cave. The box had done that. The horned, dead thing. How could they not have anticipated the damage the whispers would do, the fear that would infect the entire project? Arjen had not had much schooling and had never been more than twenty miles from his home, but he knew that much. Meryam should have seen it coming.

Tonight, at last, she had tried to reason with them all, and he knew that some had listened. But the fear remained, and Uncle Hakan had not helped. The look in Feyiz's eyes then had been worrisome. Arjen just wanted to stay out of it. Tonight, for the first time, he had not minded at all when his uncle had told him he would have the second watch. The more he thought about it, Arjen wondered if Hakan would let him do second watch every night, just take that shift as his main job. He could sleep most of the day, and most of his waking hours would pass while the rest of the crew were sleeping.

It's peaceful, he thought, staring out at the light, swirling snow and the indigo depths of night. In these small hours, it seemed like dawn would never come. He almost liked the thought of that, the idea that the rest of them would sleep forever. The tension had finally eased from his neck and shoulders and he could think of the meal his mother would cook for him the next time he came down off the mountain, and the way his second cousin Navbahar smiled at him when she thought nobody else might be looking. *Like music*, he had said once, the words whispered to the mountain wind, never to be shared. He'd chided himself for such fanciful thoughts, that bit of poetry, but her smile really did make him think of music. Or make him feel the way music made him feel.

Arjen sighed and turned away from the ledge. The sentries were supposed to walk the outer edge of the cave, not because Hakan really thought some journalist or religious fanatic or terrorist might sneak up the mountain in the middle of the night—although there had certainly been terrorist threats. No, the sentries were mostly there to reassure Meryam, Adam, and the archaeologists that nothing would happen to their artifacts, samples, and dusty bones while they were sleeping. Arjen supposed it was possible that a member of the team might attempt sabotage out of religious fervor or fear or because someone paid them to do it, or might take unauthorized photos or video and sell them. But in the ten nights he had stood second watch, he had heard nothing more than the mutterings and cries of people suffering nightmares and the grunts and moans of those who'd found warmth and comfort in each other's arms. Nobody got up and walked around in the night unless they were sick or shaking off bad dreams. Sometimes they would smoke cigarettes, breaking Meryam's rules, but Arjen didn't see the harm there at the edge of the cave, where the ashes weren't going to ignite the old timbers. The butts would be flicked over the edge, into the snow.

The wind kicked up, howling around him, so strong that it bumped him back a step. Arjen blinked in surprise, his heart racing, and moved a few feet farther away from the edge. With the wind so strong, only a fool would take chances. He shivered and reached up to readjust the cowl he wore around the lower half of his face. The years had made him used to the brutal cold the winter wind could bring to Ararat and he knew how to endure it, what precautions to take. But nothing could keep the icy air from penetrating down to his bones when he had to stay out in it, unsheltered, for so long.

Coffee would help. Something warm around which he could warm his hands. Something to heat him, down inside. Yes, a cup of coffee. Or Navbahar. The thought of her made him smile, though not without a certain guilt.

A cigarette, then. Now that he'd thought of the nights he'd caught Dr. Dwyer or Mr. Avci out here smoking, he craved the warm, curling smoke in his lungs. Surely just a few puffs on a freezing cold night would not give him cancer.

Another gust of wind and he frowned, then smiled under his cowl. Had he caught the scent of cigarette smoke on the air, or was his craving so strong that he had imagined it? Arjen glanced up, wondering if someone on level two might be smoking, despite Meryam's explicit warnings.

Then he heard a small cry in the dark, off to his left. The wind rushed at him as if to drive him away, but Arjen stood rigid, listening as he peered along the outer edge of the cave. Was that another human sound, some kind of grunt? And a scuffle in the inch of newly fallen snow, a thump against the stone beneath it?

Arjen felt his throat go dry. He wanted to shout, but stopped himself. This was the point of being on sentry duty, after all. Someone had been out there smoking and stumbled, that was all. He'd smelled the smoke, craved a cigarette.

He started in that direction, striving against the wind that tried to push him back. The icy chill buffeted him, but he straightened up, unwilling to be cowed by it. His thoughts were often full of silent griping, but in his heart he felt strong. His family had given him that strength. His heritage. If Arjen could not withstand the cold winds that scoured the face of Mount Ararat, he might as well never have been born.

The snow picked up, obscuring his vision, and he tugged his goggles down so that he could see better.

There.

Thirty feet farther along the ledge, a shape lay heaped on the snowy ledge. The cave loomed to one side, mostly shadows while everyone slept, and ahead the night and the storm breathed darkness. He caught another whiff of cigarette smoke and wondered if the cigarette had fallen into the snow.

The heap on the ground began to groan.

Arjen swore. Wary of the wind and the ledge, he knelt and dragged the heap toward him, away from the perilous edge. Even in the dark, the black spill of blood on the snow stood out in stark relief. He turned the heap over and tried to make out the face below him, tilted the man's head toward what little illumination came from the interior of the cave. He had not bothered to get to know the students working the Ark Project. If not for the argument at dinner, Arjen would never have recognized Kemal, but he knew him now.

"Hey," he said quietly. "Are you all right?"

A stupid question. He knew the answer, but he couldn't understand what had happened here. Had Kemal tripped and struck his head, or had he had some kind of seizure? Was he ill? The archaeology student lolled his head to one side and moaned in pain and confusion. His lips moved but formed no words, and his eyes searched the gusting snow and the darkness, unfocused but full of a primal dread that filled Arjen with an icy chill no storm ever could.

He stared at the black spill of blood on the snow and forgot to breathe. What if Kemal hadn't fallen at all?

Arjen drew back from him, knees whispering against the snow. As he glanced over his shoulder there was a lull in the wind, and he heard the hitching breath of the shadow even before he saw it rushing at him. A glint of light from the cave shone upon the curve of the ice ax and it whistled as it sliced the wind and lodged just below his heart, struck so hard it pierced every layer of his clothing, tore flesh and muscle, and punched between ribs.

He tried to scream as he stared down at the tool jutting from his chest, but instead drew in a gasp of frigid air. Pain flooded through him and he managed a high, keening wail that merged with the howl of the wind, torn from his lips and lost in the night sky.

His knees began to give out, but the shadow grabbed hold of him. He felt a flicker of hope that it had been some kind of misunderstanding, that he had stepped into a fight that was not his own, that he would see Navbahar again and would cast aside any guilt about her being his second cousin and profess his love to her. That smile. It lived in his heart.

Those hands danced him backward and over the edge, and then he felt himself falling. The wind whipped past him and he hit the snow and the loose rockfall, bounced, and kept falling. Sorrow swallowed him whole, and then his head struck a rocky outcropping as he fell, and Navbahar would never know his love.

Kemal tumbled from the ledge a moment later, cast farther out from the cave, hurtling faster, striking harder, tumbling over and over as his bones snapped and his limbs twisted grotesquely.

In time both dead men came to rest more than a thousand meters below the cave.

The snow kept falling, lightly but steadily. By morning, it would have obscured any trace of Arjen and Kemal.

And the real storm had not yet arrived.

NINE

Adam wakes from a nightmare in the guest room at his grandmother's house. He can hear a ticking from the baseboard heating and the occasional pop from the hardwood floor. He doesn't remember the nightmare, but his heart is still drumming hard and so he lies awake for a while, listening to the heat and the house and breathing in the powdery sweet sachet smells of his grandmother's house. He stays with Gramma Evie every couple of weeks and he loves being here, but he doesn't like being awake at night. Not when Gramma Evie's sleeping. And he especially does not like to get out of bed when the house is so quiet. But now he has to pee and though he tries to forget—thinking that if he doesn't focus on it, the feeling might go away—it's too late. If he doesn't get up, he'll wet the bed.

Sighing, he pulls back the covers and slips his legs out from under the covers. His toes are reluctant to touch the braided rug but he forces himself to get up, and then—once committed—he moves quickly, practically scurrying out of the room and down the short hallway. He passes Gramma Evie's room. She should be snoring in there. He can see her in bed, lying on her side like always, but without her usual snoring she looks almost . . .

No. He won't think that.

The noises of the house seem to hush now, as he arrives at the bathroom door. He reaches inside, fingers searching for the light switch, and he can hear his heart beating.

No. That's not his heart.

Adam glances to the left. At the end of the little hallway, just at the edge of the living room, is the grandfather clock. He blinks, because something isn't right.

It isn't right at all.

The clock is facing him, turned so that he can see the face of it from the hall. It should be facing into the living room and this doesn't make sense at all. Gramma Evie wouldn't have turned it like that. Heck, she couldn't have turned it like that, not without help from him. She calls him her big, strapping boy, and this is why he knows she has not turned the clock by herself.

But still it is facing him.

Ticktock goes the pendulum. Slowly, though. Tick. Tock. Tick. Tock. *Back and forth like a hypnotist's pocket watch in one of the cop shows Gramma Evie lets him watch.*

Heart thumping but strangely calm now, like the hypnotist has done his job, Adam lets his hand fall to his side and then he is moving down the hallway toward the living room, toward the clock that should not be facing him. Gramma Evie leaves a light on, a three-way bulb on its dimmest setting, an antique lamp with a frosted glass dome covered in hand-painted roses. The roses turn the light a reddish hue, so the living room has a hellish little glow.

The heat has stopped popping in the baseboards. The floors have ceased creaking underfoot. All he can hear is the pendulum in the grandfather clock. Tick. Tock. Tick. Tock. *His heart has slowed to match that slow cadence.*

His feet are cold on the long, braided rug in the hall, the one Gramma Evie made herself.

Ticktock. *The pendulum draws him on.*

Draws him with its rhythm. Draws him with the mystery of how it came to be turned toward the hall instead of into the room. Draws him with the memory of the story Gramma Evie has told so often. The story of the dybbuk inside the clock, the evil spirit that had possessed her father and had been driven out and trapped inside the clock. The warning that if the clock ever stopped, the dybbuk would escape and poison the soul of whomever it entered next.

An awful story, Adam's father said. An old wives' tale, meant to frighten small children. He'd been furious with his mother for telling it to Adam. Gramma Evie has never told it again, nor has she ever admitted it is anything but the truth.

His bare feet slide along the floor. Now the bed calls to him. Cloaked in silence, suffocated in it, he takes another step toward the clock. And another. He tells himself to run, to hide under the covers, at the same time that his father's voice echoes in his mind. An old wives' tale, that's what it is.

The red glow from the rose-painted lamp glints off the pendulum as it swings. Tick. Tock. Tick. Tock. Tick.

The next tock never comes.

The pendulum has stopped.

Adam's heart stops along with it. His breath freezes in his lungs. A scream rises within him, but never makes it to his lips. He stares with a horror that makes him tremble, stares at the darkness behind the stilled pendulum, waiting. A second or two or five. Seconds mean nothing with the clock stopped.

Something shifts there, behind the pendulum.

Hands appear. Long, thin fingers, withered things with mere wisps of flesh-covered bones. Eyes glitter in the darkness at the back of the clock case, the eyes of the dark figure standing in the rain in his dream, and he knows what it is. That it's here for him. Those skeletal fingers reach out past the pendulum, grip the sides of the case, and its face emerges from the darkness, nudging the pendulum aside.

It has horns.

Adam has seen it before. Impossible, but he knows that he has. He knows this evil. Knows it well.

He screams. . . .

He woke. The scream in his nightmare turned out to be silent. He sat up, casting aside the thick flap of his sleep sack, and whipped around the inside of his tent, searching for the grandfather clock. Fully expecting it to be there with him—there in the stall, in the ark, in the tent—facing him with the pendulum frozen.

For a moment all he could hear was the hammering of his heart. The sachet smell of his grandmother's house remained in his nose, but then the frigid air snapped him more fully awake and stole that dream away. A low snoring made him twist around, thinking he might see Gramma Evie there with him, but it was only Meryam. She lay on her side, a bit of drool at the corner of her mouth, snoring quietly. Her brows were knitted, her sleep troubled, having her own bad dreams.

"Holy shit," Adam whispered.

The timbers creaked as cold air moved in and out of the ark. The terrified sliver of paranoia left behind after any nightmare tried to convince him to get up, to check outside the tent, look out in the passage to make sure nothing lurked there that might wish him ill, but he wasn't about to do that.

Neither, however, would he attempt to fall back to sleep. Morning couldn't be very far off, and Adam decided he'd had enough dreams for one night. Enough nightmares for a lifetime.

Morning had arrived, but only barely. The sky hung low and dark, the clouds enveloping the mountain itself, and the snow swept lightly across the ledge and accumulated inside the cave, covering the timbers of the ark. This wasn't the storm they were expecting, just a taste of what was to come. At first light—what light there was—the crew had managed to erect new plastic sheeting to keep the snow from blowing in and covering up the areas where the archaeology team were focusing their work.

Feyiz didn't care about the snow. He stood three feet from the ledge and stared at Meryam. A pale calm had settled into her, though her face ought to have been pinked by the brutal wind.

"He wouldn't do this," Feyiz said. "Arjen wouldn't just leave."

Meryam glanced around as if to be sure she wasn't overheard. Feyiz thought she must be looking for cameras, but Adam and Calliope were up in the back of the cave with Father Cornelius and Walker. There were no cameras here.

"I'm telling you—" he went on.

"I heard you," she said curtly. Feyiz flinched. He understood the stress she had been under, but she had been harsh these past few weeks. He wished for a way to soothe her.

"Meryam—"

"Kemal wouldn't have just taken off, either," she said, meeting his eyes, and for the first time he saw her fear and vulnerability. "He's solid. A thinker. I'm not saying he wouldn't have left, but at the beginning of a storm . . ."

Feyiz wiped snow from his eyes. "Arjen could have gotten him down safely."

"Without saying good-bye?" Meryam asked.

The question hung there between them. People shouted inside the ark. A piece of plastic sheeting had torn away and the team were doing their best to protect the dig. Feyiz knew that he and Meryam should both be helping, but the mystery that had confronted them this morning had stopped them both in their tracks. He feared for Arjen and for Kemal, though he didn't know the student more than the occasional hello.

"Shit," Meryam said, shaking her head. At a loss for rational words, Feyiz knew, because he felt the same way.

She glanced past him and he turned to see what had gotten her attention. Hakan strode toward them through the blasting, snowy wind. Several of the workers followed him at a distance, but they paused twenty feet from Feyiz and Meryam. The younger Turkish monitor, Zeybekci, stood with them and several members of the archaeological team, watching Hakan approach.

When first he spoke, the wind stole his voice.

"What now?" Meryam called.

Hakan stepped nearer to them—nearer the edge. Feyiz felt the urge to move away, but he also felt the morbid, magnetic lure of the fall that awaited if he stepped too close. That was always the case with danger, he'd found. His heart felt drawn to it, even as his mind made him back away.

"They left on their own!" Hakan said.

Feyiz glanced at the people gathered a short distance away, sheltered by the walls of the cave. Could they hear from there, over the wind? He didn't think so.

"How can you know that?" Meryam demanded. "Did someone see them go?"

Hakan shook his head. "No witnesses. But I checked their sleeping quarters myself. They cleared out their things. Everything personal is gone." He turned to Feyiz. "I know you and Arjen are close. He is my family, just as you are, but he has always been lazy and cowardly. I have no trouble believing he would slip off in the dark—"

"He would not," Feyiz said.

"—rather than face me," Hakan finished.

Feyiz hesitated. His nostrils flared, the cold air freezing them inside as he dragged in a breath. Was it really so hard to imagine that Arjen would have snuck away rather than having to tell Hakan, man to man, that he was leaving?

Perhaps not.

But he still did not believe it.

Meryam and Hakan kept talking—both of them still tense and wary after the confrontation last night—but Feyiz had stopped listening. Spiders of anxiety crawled up his back and along his arms and neck, and he shuddered as he stared over the ledge, down into the yawning gorge. It would be some time before they could confirm whether Kemal and Arjen had reached the bottom safely—likely until the coming storm had passed and the chance of getting a mobile phone signal increased. Until then, he would pretend to himself that they had abandoned the project overnight, slipped out of the cave, and begun the climb down Ararat in the dark. In the snow and the wind.

For the moment, Feyiz would allow himself to believe that. Even force himself to believe it. The alternative—that they'd been victims of some unknown violence, some hidden malice—was too disturbing to consider for very long. But as he turned to study Meryam and his uncle again, he knew he would be keeping a closer eye on them. A closer eye on everyone in the cave.

For their safety, and for his own.

Father Cornelius sat on a plastic chair at a table that had been set up just a few yards from the tented area around the cadaver and its casket. A space heater helped take the edge off the cold, but still his bones ached. At his age, arthritis had become a constant companion, sometimes so familiar that it seemed it would never abate. With the icy wind drafting around, the ache seemed deeper than ever before. But he had work to do, so he offered his pain up to God and continued to study the broken chunks of the casket's bitumen encasement.

Bright lights had been set up around the table. The lid of the coffin—what the KHAP team liked to call "the box"—stood leaning against the tilted wall. Father Cornelius removed his glasses, rubbed at his eyes, and then put them back on before resuming his focus on the large fragments of bitumen. Professor Marshall—

Helen—had helped him lay them out as if putting together the pieces of a puzzle. She had photographs, she said, of the unbroken encasement, but he wanted to see the actual bitumen, to run his fingers over the smooth, glassy black surface, to feel the slashes and curves of ancient language that had been carved there.

"What've you got?" a voice said.

Father Cornelius blinked as if waking from a dream. He glanced up to see Walker standing at the end of the table as if he'd just manifested there, but from the expectant look on his face, he had the idea Walker might have been standing there awhile.

"You all right, Father?"

The priest nodded, but he did not feel all right. Despite the cold that had settled into his bones, he felt a prickling warmth on his face and the back of his neck. His skin felt clammy, almost feverish, and he wondered if he had contracted some kind of virus.

Walker moved around the table, crouching beside him. "Father?"

"I'm sorry. It is just a bit overwhelming. You understand." He took off his glasses and used them to gesture toward the wooden lid where it leaned against the wall. "You see the inscriptions there?"

"I see them," Walker replied, but he wore an odd expression. Unsettled, worried.

"There are elements reminiscent of Nashite, the language of the Hittites. But some of the symbols are variations on the Akkadian language. There is a third element, one with which I am unfamiliar, and I feel it would be the key to my unlocking the morphological, syntactic, and phonological bridges that make this its own fourth, original language. It's even possible that this— what's written there on the lid, and engraved here in these fragments of the bitumen encasement—is not a variation but the parent language from which the other three eventually sprang."

Father Cornelius rubbed his thinly gloved hands together for warmth, fingers aching with arthritis. He shifted one of the large fragments on the table, trying to match it up more closely with its neighbor.

"Maybe it's time he stepped away," another voice said. "Took a little rest?"

Irritated, Father Cornelius turned. He flinched, startled to find so many other people gathered around him. Helen stood there with Wyn Douglas and one of their Turkish students. A few feet away, Calliope held her camera, filming the exchange. How long had she been there? How long had any of them been there?

"Don't talk about me like I'm not here," he said, unsure which of them had spoken.

"Father," Helen began, her eyes so kind.

"I'm not a child you can send off for a nap," he said, heat flushing his cheeks and rushing down his chest and along his arms. "What I am, young lady, is your best hope at deciphering these writings. And I will tell you this much . . ." He turned to stare into Calliope's camera. "Based on what little I've been able to translate thus far, I can say without a doubt that this ship is the biblical ark, built by a man whose name could be translated as 'Noah.'"

Feeling a sheen of sweat on his brow, he wiped his sleeve across his forehead. His throat felt dry, but as he glanced from Walker to Helen, he was all too aware of the eye of the camera upon him.

"Father," Walker said, laying a hand on his arm, a deep frown etched on his forehead. "I didn't think you supported a literal translation—"

"I didn't!" Father Cornelius said, yanking his arm away. A bit of bile snaked up the back of his throat and he choked it down, wiped at his forehead again. "You recruited me for this trip, Dr. Walker. You know my credentials. I'm not saying we're to take the story of the flood verbatim, but—"

"Father," Wyn interrupted, crouching on his other side, so that she and Walker flanked his chair. "You need to go and lie down.

I'm worried that the elevation is affecting your brain. You seem unwell."

He sneered, pushing back from the table. "Don't be ridiculous. I've just begun the process of translating a language no one in the world has ever documented. Could I do that if I . . . if I . . ."

Father Cornelius stood shakily, to prove to himself as much as to the others that he was fine. The serpent of nausea coiled in his belly and slid once more up his throat, but he fought it back down. All right, he wasn't feeling well, but that was no reason for them all to be staring at him as if he had gone insane. There were references to the building of the ark, to a warning from God about the flood, to a gathering of animals. There were other bits, phrases here and there, something about a terrible darkness that he thought might refer to the storm that brought the flood. Given time he could work out a rough translation, he was sure.

"Cornelius," Walker said softly, rising to stand beside him. "Everything you've just told us . . . it's the third time you've explained it all."

First he scoffed, even scowled. Then he saw the worry in Walker's eyes, turned and saw the wary curiosity in Wyn's expression.

"That's absurd."

But didn't he sense it as well, the déjà vu echo of words that seemed too familiar? Father Cornelius shook his head and walked around the table, staring at the upright coffin lid. He ran his hands over the symbols there, the language so similar to others and yet unique, like some intimate coded message from the ancient world.

A dreadful suspicion began to form. No, not a suspicion. A certainty, though he could not express it to the others. Not yet. Memories of past research cascaded through his mind and Father Cornelius backed away from the lid, turned and stared at the plastic tenting around the box, and the terrible remains of its occupant.

His right hand shook as he unzipped his jacket and snaked his thinly gloved fingers inside his shirt, drawing out the crucifix that hung on a chain around his neck. He closed his eyes for a long moment and then walked toward the tent. Calliope took a step toward him, her visible eye narrowing as her camera followed his every step.

"Father?" Helen said.

The Turkish student, a young archaeologist with the scruff of a beard, asked her something in a burst of his own language before switching to stunted English. "What is he doing?"

From the corner of his eye, Father Cornelius saw Walker and Wyn hesitate, but as he drew back the curtain, they started after him. He let the plastic flap fall down behind him, knowing he had only seconds alone inside the tent. Alone with the horned cadaver, the misshapen thing that someone had taken the time to hammer into a wooden box and then to encase that box in hardened bitumen. It would take time for him to translate all of what had been written, but he could not hide from the ominous things he had already interpreted.

He kissed the crucifix, held it toward the horned thing in the box. Black shadows stared out from the empty sockets of its eyes.

The plastic curtain rippled behind him as others entered.

"The Lord is my salvation, whom should I fear?" he prayed. "I will not fear evil because you are with me, my Lord, my God, my powerful savior, my strength, Lord of Peace, Father of all ages."

The Turkish student shouted something. Father Cornelius barely heard the words, did not try to translate them. Helen started to argue with him, but the young man thrust her aside and rushed at him. Father Cornelius lifted the crucifix and kissed it again just before the student slapped his hand down. Marshaling a strange serenity that rose within him, he turned to face the angry young man and saw in his eyes more fear than fury.

Walker grabbed the student, twisted his arms behind his back, and marched him out of the tent.

"Damn it, let him go!" Helen barked, following after them. "He's just angry about the blessing. We're not supposed to establish any religious claims regarding the remains."

Outside the blur of the plastic sheeting, five figures moved back and forth. Strangely numb, his mind at ease, Father Cornelius heard the student demand to speak to Mr. Avci, the senior of the two monitors sent by the Turkish government.

"Fine, go!" Helen said. "Tell Avci I want to see him as soon as you're done talking to him."

The student stormed off.

"Is *everyone* a lunatic now?" Walker asked. "People are losing their minds up here."

"Your team included," Helen muttered. "And you've only been here twenty-four hours."

Father Cornelius pulled back the plastic curtain. "I'm sorry if I caused that. But prayers are a way of purifying the space around us and it had to be done. Whatever you want to call this dead thing, from what I've gathered so far it was something truly wicked. Natural or supernatural doesn't matter, really."

"It matters to me," Calliope said from behind the camera.

"Whatever you do, Professor Marshall—Dr. Walker—do not let Meryam move that body before the translation is completed."

Walker, Wyn, and Helen stared at him.

Then Helen sighed. "Go and talk to Avci, Dr. Walker. If he's unreasonable, Zeybekci may be helpful. The last thing we need is more turmoil on this project."

Father Cornelius clutched his crucifix. "Would you like me to come along?"

Walker glanced at Wyn, who shook her head.

"I think that's a bad idea," she said.

Walker turned and hurried off in the direction the student had gone.

"All right, Father," Wyn said. "Let's get you to your quarters.

Maybe you're just overtired, but I want Dr. Dwyer to take a look at you."

Father Cornelius didn't argue. He dropped the plastic curtain back into place, endured the kind, concerned gazes of the three women around him, and let Wyn lead him away. But even as he left his work behind, he could feel the horned thing watching him go, could feel the pressure of its regard, the malevolence of the dark shadows that stirred in the empty orbits of its eyes. He had never believed in tangible, physical demons. Though he had trouble confessing it aloud, that had changed.

A malignant aura surrounded the cadaver, poisoned the air around it and the people who breathed that air. Father Cornelius knew the truth of it, felt it in the trembling of his hands and the sweat upon his brow.

Thank God it's dead, he thought. *Nothing but the memory of evil now.*

Thank God.

TEN

Walker ran a hand through his hair, using a thumb to massage his temple. He'd had a low-level headache since waking up, and nothing that had happened so far this morning had done anything to make it go away. The current of hostility running under the surface of almost every interaction in the cave could have been ascribed to any number of origins. Most of these people had been crammed together inside the ark for weeks, unable to get truly warm or comfortable enough for a deep, restorative sleep. The Kurdish guides and workers shot one another suspicious glares, some kind of fracture within their own group. The project foreman, Hakan, seemed to hate pretty much everyone on general principle. And that whole stew of animosity existed even before they brought religion into the mix.

"This cannot happen," Mr. Avci said, lecturing Walker like some 1950s private school headmaster. He had little rectangular glasses and a thick gray caterpillar of a mustache. The gun at his hip should have looked ridiculous on this man, but instead it seemed very much a part of his wardrobe. A part of him.

Walker knew many such men. In truth, he was such a man. His

own pistol sat snugly in a holster clipped at the inside of his waistband, at the small of his back, hidden by his sweater and jacket. He'd rarely been without it since arriving on Ararat, but he wasn't going to show it off, mainly because there would be questions and objections, and it might jeopardize his presence at the ark. As far as anyone knew, he was here for the National Science Foundation. If the Turks knew he worked for DARPA, they would pack him off home immediately.

"Should I assume that you forgot to instruct the priest that he was included on your team as a linguist and historian and not for his spiritual affinities?" Avci went on. "That you neglected to pass along our explicit instructions that no prayers or rituals were to be performed outside of private quarters, and that any claims asserting the primacy of one religion's doctrine over any others' would be unwelcome?"

Walker had his arms crossed, leaning back in the same chair Father Cornelius had been using to examine the broken pieces of the bitumen encasement. He glanced at the coffin lid, which still stood against the wall. Meryam had led them all down here, into the cold recesses at the back of the ark, because no one else was supposed to come here. It would be quiet, and they could shout at one another in peace.

"Something spooked him, that's all I can say." Walker uncrossed his arms, throwing up his hands. "Did I pass along those conditions, give him those cautions? You know I did. But come on, Avci . . . right now people all around the world are fighting over the idea that this might actually be Noah's ark. Did you believe you could get this project completed without the staff doing the same?"

Avci raised his chin and stared down his nose. "Several of the Turkish archaeology students have voiced their objections. They find the presence of Father Cornelius troubling. It suggests to them that their work serves a Christian purpose as opposed to a purely archaeological one. They've asked that the priest be sent away."

A harsh laugh erupted from Meryam, but she cut it off abruptly.

"Come on," she said. "Where the hell is he supposed to go?"

The monitor's nostrils flared as if he'd just caught wind of raw sewage. "He could go wherever your two missing workers vanished to last night, I suppose. Though I don't guess he's in any condition to make his way down the mountain." Avci turned to Walker. "Remind Father Cornelius that he is here on an indulgence from my government. If he cannot manage to restrict himself to nonreligious inquiries, then you and he will both be leaving when the storm has passed."

Avci turned on his heel and marched away, clicking on a flashlight to push back the shadows that pooled in the distances between the work lights strung along the wall.

"He's a very angry man," Walker said when he was gone.

Zeybekci snorted laughter and then quickly composed himself, shooting Walker an admonishing glance. "If you tell anyone I laughed at that, I'll deny it."

"Understood."

Meryam smiled. "It does make us love you a little bit, though."

Zeybekci rolled his eyes, then turned and walked to the plastic tenting around the coffin. He reached out, but his fingers hesitated, and he lowered his hand without parting the curtain.

"No matter what brand of god we believe in, I think we'd all like very much to believe that thing in there is not what it appears to be."

Seconds ticked past as all three of them stared at the thick plastic sheeting and the dark shadows within the tent.

"I disagree," Walker said at length, crossing his arms again and leaning back in the chair.

Zeybekci frowned. "I'm sorry?"

Meryam cocked her head. "You're saying you want that thing to turn out to be an actual demon?"

Walker smiled. "So do you. You said so yourself. I've been an agnostic most of my life, but I'd be lying if I said it held no allure, the idea that something could confirm the existence of God."

The trio went quiet again. His headache had dulled a bit, but he wanted fresher air, a blast of the storm. He intended to follow it with a couple of shots of whatever liquor he could lay his hands on, but even without the cold air and the booze, he couldn't deny he felt a little better.

With all that had been going on, it was easy to lose focus. DARPA wanted to know what the thing in the coffin could be, if it might be something other than human. They wanted blood and tissue samples and a translation of the writing on the box. If it was inhuman in some way—monstrous, or somehow altered—they wanted him to determine if there was any way its monstrousness could be weaponized and used against them, or used *by* them against the enemies of the United States.

So far, Walker didn't know what the hell he would write in a report on the ark and the horned thing in that box. He hoped Father Cornelius could keep his shit together long enough to translate it all.

He started to walk away.

Meryam called him back. "If this storm gets as bad as it's been predicted, there's no telling what's going to happen in here. Supports could come down, never mind the sheeting and tents. We could have plenty of snow blowing in. The worst of it is supposed to hit by tomorrow afternoon. By then, I want our friend wrapped carefully so he can be properly preserved for transport when the storm's over."

Walker nodded. "Which gives us until, say, noon tomorrow before you pull him out of the box?"

"Eleven a.m. Not a moment later. And I'm assigning Professor

Olivieri to work with the priest. Father Cornelius isn't going to transcribe a line without Olivieri looking over his shoulder."

Walker snapped off a casual salute. "Absolutely."

She studied him a moment, as if unsure whether he was agreeing with her or mocking her. Apparently satisfied, she nodded. "Go and fetch them, then."

Walker knelt on the floor, studying the engravings in the coffin lid even as the glare from his work light made him squint. The wood bore a series of streaks, a pattern stained into the surface of the lid. They had drawn his attention the first time he had seen them, but now he had the time to take a closer look.

"I don't know why you've made this leap," Olivieri said behind him.

Walker did not turn. Olivieri hadn't been talking to him. The professor had been seated next to Father Cornelius—or hovering over the priest—for the past two hours, muttering his doubts and quietly haranguing the other man in a constant, irritating stream of words. But Father Cornelius kept to his word. Well aware of the dustup his earlier mental lapses and his fearful prayer over the cadaver had caused, he had vowed to cooperate with Olivieri as long as the man did not interfere with his work. Walker was there to make certain they played nicely together.

So far, that meant they hadn't killed each other.

But there had been something other than gentle patience in Father Cornelius's eyes when he'd given Walker his promise. His upper left eyelid had developed a tic and his gaze darted nervously about, as if he worried that something hostile might emerge from the periphery at any moment. Walker had asked him about it. *Just keep me on track*, Father Cornelius had said. *If I start to repeat myself again, or do anything else strange, bring it to my attention immediately.*

Walker had promised. And now he listened as he worked, wary of any shift in the priest's behavior. The promise had come easily, but not without igniting a fresh spark of real fear in him, for it was clear that Father Cornelius did not trust his own mind. His own self. What could any of them trust if they could not trust themselves?

"What is this, now?" Olivieri asked dismissively. "You cannot simply invent syntax in a language you have never encountered before. I agree that this grouping is quite likely to mean 'days of rain,' and this to mean 'darkness,' but logic suggests this symbol translates to something like 'eternity' or 'infinity'—"

"Hittite language provides variable syntax," Father Cornelius said patiently, "and they are cousins. Surely you see that. The translation is not 'many endless days of rain.' Why add 'many' to modify something 'endless' or 'infinite?' The author is telling us that the skies delivered many days of rain, and these were summoned to wash away an infinite darkness."

Olivieri swore loudly and pushed back in his chair. "And again I say, you cannot invent syntax! Your interpretation is nothing but guesswork! You read the message you want to find here!"

"It isn't invention, Professor Olivieri," the priest said quietly, almost sadly. His voice wavered. "It's intuition. In our line of work, it's sometimes all we have. Scribble down your own translations and I'll do the same with mine. Other eyes will examine them both in time, and they will decide which of us is right."

Olivieri gave a huff. "I was brought into this project for my expertise. You were brought here as a courtesy. My notes will be the official opinion of the Ark Project."

"How nice for you," the priest said with a twitch of his upper lip. "Can we get back to work, please? We waste time bickering."

Olivieri fumed, clearly trying to find a legitimate way to continue the mostly one-sided argument. When he could not invent one, at least at the moment, he shook his head and began furiously scribbling notes on a pad, half turned away from the priest as though he thought Father Cornelius might copy his answers on a middle school math test.

Walker smiled to himself, despite the ache in his skull. Father Cornelius seemed entirely himself, now. Troubled, yes, but not in the midst of any kind of mental crisis.

He focused again on his work, and his smile faded. The cold seeped up through the angled floor beneath him, emanating from the timbers as if the mountain were itself the icy heart of winter.

Flexing his fingers inside his thin gloves, Walker picked up the small scalpel he'd been using and reached into his kit for a tiny, plastic, sample container. Careful not to damage the engraving on the lid, he dug into the wood where one of those streaks seemed darkest. He carved a sliver, then another in the same spot, surprised at how deep into the wood the stain had spread.

Setting the scalpel down, he capped the container and held it up, staring at those two slivers. They'd come from the outside of the lid, not the inside, so they weren't stains from the bodily fluids of the cadaver.

He suspected they *were* bloodstains, but if that proved true, it meant the blood splashed across the lid had come from someone who'd helped close it, or cover it in thick bitumen paste. Walker knew it was a mystery he could never possibly unravel, but it troubled him almost as much as the way Kim had gone briefly off the rails yesterday, or the way Father Cornelius had suffered some kind of cognitive slippage this morning. It suggested that violence had been erupting around the horned thing's remains from the moment it had been sealed into that box.

DARPA would love it. But they would want to know why and how.

"What are you doing *now*?" Olivieri sighed behind him. "You can't use four different languages as the basis for a translation."

Walker turned in time to see the hard glare in Father Cornelius's eyes, and the way the priest's lips trembled before he finally allowed himself to speak.

"No, professor. *You* can't. And that is the real problem here, isn't it? Oh, certainly you understand bits and pieces of what I'm unraveling, but can we both just admit that you're out of your depth?"

Walker winced.

Olivieri stood, knocking over his chair. "You arrogant bastard. I have spent decades lecturing on the finest details of ancient language. My studies of biblical history are the basis for hundreds of university classes in more than twenty countries. How can you—"

Father Cornelius set his pen down onto his open notebook and stared up at Olivieri, not bothering to stand. "Your greatest skill is in rearranging information others have provided so that you can better communicate it to those less informed and less accomplished than yourself."

Walker hung his head, expecting Olivieri to explode in fury. When only silence ensued, he cocked one eye open and saw the professor fuming, dumbfounded, shaking his head slowly as he took one step backward.

Olivieri turned and strode away so quickly that he seemed to draw a gust of air into his wake. Walker watched him storm off and then turned to Father Cornelius.

The priest brushed at the air as if to wave him away. "I know what you're going to say."

"You were supposed to play nice."

Father Cornelius's face darkened, brows knitting so tightly they made him look like a bird of prey. "You're not the one to instruct me on the subject of playing nice. Kim is here to do her job, just like you, but you've treated her like an intruder since we all met."

"Can I help it if I don't like having a babysitter?"

The priest's glare darkened further, a hawk intent upon his prey. "She's only a babysitter if you insist on behaving like a baby. She's a professional, here to observe on behalf of the rest of the world.

Don't begrudge her that. In your words, play nice. One would have thought that surviving the ruin of your marriage would have taught you something about how to treat other people."

Walker's mouth dropped open. "What?"

"I'm talking about Amanda."

"Jesus Christ, I know my own ex-wife's name," Walker said, shaking his head, feeling as if he'd just taken a hard blow. "Who the hell do you think you are?"

Father Cornelius still did not rise. "I'm your colleague and I suspect the closest thing you have to a friend within four thousand miles of here. You're so lost in your own head that you can never see the needs of those around you. Change your approach to Kim, and when you get home, make peace with your former wife. Set an example for your son."

Walker drew a hitching breath that turned into a soft laugh of disbelief. The words cut him, but the mention of his boy, Charlie, stabbed deep, twisted the knife. He knew that Father Cornelius hadn't been himself today, that something had been troubling them all . . . haunting them. But the dull ache in his skull flared into a bright, suffocating pain and he felt anger uncoil inside him like a viper defending its nest. Twisting and uncontrollable.

"Hey, Father?" he said, jaw tight, fist clenched.

"Listen, Ben—"

"Go fuck yourself."

Shaking, Walker turned and left him there, not caring what Meryam would say about broken promises or about the priest having unfettered access to the cadaver and the box and encasement. What harm could the old man do? Better that he be left to his work, tonight. Better that he spend his time with a corpse.

He sure as hell wasn't fit to be in the company of the living.

ELEVEN

Walker missed music. He stood outside his tent in the stall and wondered how he could feel so exposed and so claustrophobic at the same time. Earbuds would have given him privacy, let him listen to the playlist of '80s alt rock that always calmed him, but he didn't want to block out other sounds. The only sound was the wind blowing through the ark's upper passages, like the tide rolling in, but he didn't trust the quiet. Didn't trust the night. Not with people on such a ragged edge, not with two people vanishing last night. Yes, they'd probably abandoned the project, but what if they hadn't?

The mountain felt heavy above him, as if it wanted nothing more than to close the cave down like a monstrous mouth, and swallow them whole. He couldn't shake off that bit of claustrophobia because it was all too rational. Not that Ararat might be some sentient rock monster, but there had been a small earthquake and a landslide here just a couple of months ago. Another one could trap them here, kill them all.

Softly, he laughed at himself. *So cheerful.*

He stuffed his hand into his pocket and plucked out a small

white plastic prescription bottle. His throat felt dry and his head muzzy. A spot on his left temple throbbed with the weird neuropathy that had troubled him for years. The pain in his spine and across his abdomen reminded him that he desperately needed to make time to stretch. He wetted his lips with his tongue and opened the pill bottle, tapped out a couple of dusty gray tablets, and recapped it.

As he tossed the pills back and dry-swallowed them, he caught motion in his peripheral vision. Kim froze when he turned toward her. Had she just started to emerge from her own stall and seen him, or had she been watching for a while and decided to withdraw when she saw him take his meds?

"Trouble sleeping?" he asked.

"I'd been wanting to ask you the same question."

Walker felt the mountain close in even tighter. A flush went through him, an almost feverish moment of warmth that forced the chill of the cave to abate. Kim still looked tired and pale, but her eyes were focused and alert, nothing like the woman who had briefly shattered yesterday. How could she seem so confident now when she might run off, screaming and spouting gibberish at any moment?

"That really the question you want to ask?" he replied.

Her lips thinned into a dark smile. "I'm not feeling my best, Walker. My diplomacy is malfunctioning at the moment. You accepted the presence of a UN observer because you had no choice. I accepted the assignment because someone had to do it and it seemed like an opportunity to impress my superiors. Something happened to me yesterday that I don't understand and it's broken down my ability to be polite."

"You were polite before yesterday?"

Kim's expression flickered with anger, but then the mask broke and she gave a tired laugh. "All right. Perhaps I confuse courtesy and politeness."

Walker did not laugh. He clutched the prescription bottle in his hand, then tossed it to her. She caught it with one hand. "Go on, Kim. Do your job. Ask the question you wanted to ask."

She studied the label. "Zohydro?"

"Painkiller. Banned in parts of the United States, but not where I got them. Incredibly powerful. Incredibly addictive. Makes Oxycontin look like breath mints in comparison."

Kim shook the bottle, listened to the rattle of the thirty or so pills remaining. "Incredibly addictive. So are you addicted?"

Walker held out a hand for the bottle. "Oh, absolutely. So I'll need those back."

Blinking in surprise at his frankness, she gave him the pills. Then it was her turn to surprise him.

"Do you take them for pain stemming from the injuries you sustained in Guatemala, or do you take them to stop thinking about your wife?"

Even the wind went silent. Walker drew in a deep breath and smelled the age of the timbers. The suffocation he'd felt earlier wrapped more tightly around him.

He'd met Amanda Nemeth at a National Science Foundation conference, where she'd been presenting a paper on unknown species discovered in cave ecosystems. He'd approached her after the lecture, discovered she was a professor at Columbia, and surprised himself by asking her out for coffee. Such an ordinary thing, so casual, but not typical behavior for Walker. Since college, he'd been strictly the set-up-by-well-meaning-matchmaking-friends type. But Amanda had both a dry wit and a passion for her work. He'd thought they truly understood each other, but three years after they were married, she'd forced him to sit and listen and focus on her words, and she'd told him that she had been serious all of the times she had said she couldn't have a husband who refused to make their relationship a priority. Who couldn't even tell her the truth about what he did for work, where his journeys took him, what kind of danger he was putting himself in.

Where he'd gotten his scars. The injuries that had almost killed him.

She didn't want her son growing up in the shadows cast by his father's secrets and his mother's fears.

In the midst of this, his phone had rung and he'd been instructed to head to northern Canada, where retreating Arctic ice had revealed a system of subterranean catacombs full of artifacts and human remains that did not belong there. They had danced around it for weeks, known things between them were coming unraveled, but the moment she realized that he intended to go and couldn't tell her where he was headed, Amanda had taken his hand, brought him into their living room, and sat him down.

"If you go," she'd said, leaning toward him for emphasis, studying his eyes, "I will know I've chosen the wrong partner."

He had come home from the Arctic to find her gone. She had left a note that was uncharacteristically succinct for a college professor: *For Charlie's sake, I wish someone else had been his father.*

Now she had George, her artist boyfriend. Walker would stay in his son's life, but if George could be the right kind of father—be there for Charlie—he wouldn't deny his son that bit of happiness.

The mountain began to breathe around them again. The wind slid inside the stall and made the tents shudder and flap. Walker stared at the pill bottle, then clutched it in his hand and looked at Kim again. The chill cut into his flesh as if his thick layers of clothing meant nothing.

"If you'd seen the things that came after us in Guatemala, you'd want as many drugs as your body could handle," he said quietly. He shook the pill bottle again and then stuffed it into his jacket pocket. "I've got a couple of fused vertebrae in my back. The scars on my abdomen where they tore me open still pull and tug when I move, and there's pain inside where the surgeons knitted things back together. And when it's cold like this, the pins in my right leg feel like they're stabbing me. I'm in a hell of a lot of pain on a good day. Up here, right now . . . well, we both know it's not a good day."

Kim had paled even further. He saw the judgment and aloofness melt from her gaze. "I'm sorry. I didn't realize how—"

"Really, though," he interrupted. "It hurts like hell, even with the drugs, but probably half of the addiction is about my ex-wife. Some days that's worse because my spine and my other injuries . . . monsters did that. How badly I messed up my marriage, that pain is self-inflicted."

This time when she smiled, he smiled in return. They weren't happy people, but they understood each other now. Or at least they'd begun to.

"What about you?" Walker asked. "You doing all right? Any signs of you going mental again?"

Now she laughed. "The anxiety's still there," she said, shifting her weight from foot to foot. "And I had some terrible nightmares about the cadaver—"

"The horns are pretty unsettling."

"—but I'm all right."

He heard the hesitation in her voice and felt himself soften. They were all haunted in this cave, both by whatever ghosts they'd brought with them and by the fear they'd found when they arrived. The talk of nightmares also disturbed him, for he'd been having some fairly dreadful dreams of his own.

"Our horned friend is dead," he said. "I'm standing firm on it being human. There was a time someone born with physical defects would have been considered tainted or unclean, an abomination."

Kim shuddered and hugged herself against the cold. "Do you really believe that's what we've found? Some human abomination?"

"It's what I want to believe," Walker said, and suddenly the space vanished between them, leaving a quiet intimacy that made him hold his breath a moment.

"But?" she asked.

"The way people have been behaving—both of us included—is abnormal, even in a heightened situation like this one. We're all supposed to be professionals. Even the students had to have at least a bit of experience to be chosen for this. And the workers are Kurds who've lived on this mountain their whole lives."

"Don't underestimate the religious factor," Kim said, glancing over her shoulder as if afraid to be overheard. "If everyone's on edge, is that so surprising?"

Walker studied her face, the curve of her cheek, the glint in her eyes, and realized that they had become allies. They were in this together.

"It feels like more than that," he said. "Sometimes you run across a person you just *know* doesn't wish you well. You can feel it. And sometimes you wake up in the middle of the night to use the bathroom or get some water, and it's dark in the house and you get that feeling, the sense of a quiet *presence* there with you. I've never seen a ghost, but I've had that feeling, alone in the middle of the night, of something filling up the darkness in a room like air inflating a balloon. You ask me about this tomorrow, where people can hear me, and I'll deny it, but I've been feeling that since the second we got here. Both things. The weird closeness in the air that maybe is just claustrophobia talking but maybe isn't, along with that other thing, that—"

"Malice," Kim said.

Walker nodded slowly, staring at her, appreciating the surprising knowledge that he was not alone here.

"Yes, exactly. *Malice*."

Adam rubbed grit from his eyes and realized he had watched the same two minutes of footage five times. He'd hit PLAY, let the argument at dinner start to run, and then his mind would drift. Swearing quietly, frustrated with himself, he hit PAUSE and stared at the frozen image on his laptop. Meryam, angry and snapping at Hakan. Adam knew her better than anyone, but to him, the woman in that frozen image didn't look like Meryam at all. She had a gift for sarcasm and her temper could flare from time to time, but this wasn't her. More than that—she looked unwell. Her features were drawn and there were hollows under her eyes. Her pallor, normally a soft coffee, seemed almost jaundiced.

Enough, he thought, shutting the laptop. He left the tent, immediately wishing he'd put on his gloves and hat. Instead of turning back, he flipped up his collar and zipped his coat, rubbing his hands together as he moved through the walls and tents and plastic sheeting that made up the camp on level two. A lot of the sleeping quarters were here, but the crew had developed the habit of not hanging around unless they were sleeping, so he knew Meryam had to be elsewhere. More often than not, she could be found in a stall on level one, not far from where Helen's team had done their very first work on the project. There had been latticed remnants of what Helen believed were birdcages in the stall, but nothing else. Those remnants had been packed away with other artifacts and already removed from the site and Meryam had turned the stall into a sort of home base. Her office. As project manager, she'd claimed the space for herself. Meryam had embraced the KHAP with such ferocity that it left him feeling like an observer . . . an outsider on his own project. In the process, she had been running herself ragged, and every time he had tried to talk to her about it, she would change the subject.

With every passing day he felt more and more frozen out, until he had begun to feel like it wasn't his project at all anymore. Officially it was the Karga-Holzer Ark Project, but when people said KHAP out loud, the H was silent. As if Holzer contributed nothing at all.

The cold cut through him as he climbed down the ladder. Just touching the frozen wood seared his skin.

When he reached the bottom, he blew into his hands and rubbed them together. Her tenure as project manager had been taking a bad turn. Someone had to tell her, and it would have to be him, but he knew Meryam. She would never accept that she had been screwing up. They both knew that she loved the work more than she would ever love him, and she would assume that his criticism was rooted in resentment.

The blissful days immediately after their engagement seemed so distant now, and a joyful wedding day seemed almost impossible.

Adam took one more step and came to a halt as that thought took hold. Almost impossible. Was that what he really thought?

A hundred feet to his left, the mouth of the cave opened into the darkness. Snow had drifted in, several inches deep. Voices came to him on the wind and he turned to see several figures out at the edge of the cave, too near the drop-off for his tastes. They were smoking, bright orange cigarette tips glinting in the dark, but given the snow he was not going to rat them out to Meryam. No fire was going to start in the middle of this. Beyond them, he could see only the dark, as if those three burning cigarette tips were the last signs of life in the world, and nothing remained of humanity beyond them. Up here, in the storm, they might as well have been on another planet.

Freezing, his fingers numb, he hunched over and hurried toward the passage that led along the left side wall of the ark. Already he could see a warm golden light back there, and he knew he'd chosen correctly, that Meryam was in her "office" after all. He dropped his head again, staring at the footsteps in the snow as he tried to protect himself from the cold. When he lifted his gaze, he could see the open face of the stall twenty feet ahead.

Adam came to a stop. Standing in the darkness, his footfalls silenced by the wind, he stared at the two people bathed in that warm light inside the office stall. Meryam and Feyiz. Nothing unusual in their being together. They stood a few feet apart, perhaps a bit close—a bit intimate—but it wasn't as if they were in some kind of lover's embrace. They were colleagues. Friends. Meryam trusted Feyiz, and Adam had never been jealous of that because he felt the same way.

Yet though he could hear only the urgent tones of their voices and not the words being spoken, he saw the open, plaintive look on Feyiz's face and Meryam's broken, vulnerable expression—a piece of herself, a revelation of the real Meryam after weeks behind a hard mask—and he could not help but wonder. Breathless, face chafed by the wind, he watched them and asked himself if Feyiz might be the reason for the distance that had been growing between them.

Fists clenched, he turned and moved silently back through the passage, reversing his steps in the snow. He worked his way to the front of the cave and started for the ladder, barely noticing the figure that appeared beside him, as if from nowhere. A silhouette, one layer of darkness against another.

It loomed toward him and he jerked away, heart thumping.

"Jesus," he hissed. "Don't do that!"

In the soft glow of the work light that shone down from the top of the ladder, he saw Calliope smile.

"Sorry. I didn't mean to spook you."

"Sneak up on a guy in the dark, that's gonna happen."

Calliope put a hand on the ladder. "Especially here. What are you doing awake, anyway? Everything all right?"

Adam thought about lying. She stood close and he could smell the cigarette smoke on her clothes and knew she'd been one of the three people out there on the ledge, breaking the rules. Right then he liked her all the more for that. Some rules needed to be broken.

"Nothing's even close to all right," he said. "It's all going to shit, isn't it?"

Her face creased with compassion and then just the flicker of a new smile. The face of a friend. She reached out and took his hand. His fingers were so numb he barely felt her touch.

"It doesn't have to," she said.

Adam almost believed her.

Helen woke with a start, inhaling sharply, as if in the midst of sleep she had forgotten to breathe. Her eyes went wide for a moment and then fluttered closed again. She blinked, drifting in that twilight space between dream and wakefulness, content to be cradled in the thickly lined warmth of her sleeping bag. Her breathing slowed and she felt her muscles easing, body melting. The whistle of the wind created a comforting white noise. Her head lolled to one side.

She surfaced again. Her brows knitted and she lay listening for whatever had disturbed her. Well over a dozen people slept in the makeshift camp around her. Some were inside tents, while others buried themselves in all-weather sleeping bags. A few small stoves gave off warmth, but not enough to make a real difference with people spread out in stalls and a large room whose purpose they still hadn't determined. Just some kind of cargo hold, Helen felt sure, but wouldn't state without reservation. Not yet.

With a long sigh, she nestled deeper into her sleeping bag and just listened. In the middle of the night she had sometimes heard people making love, or engaged in quiet conversation, taking comfort from whatever they had to offer one another. She never begrudged them that comfort, although she herself would have found any kind of sexual or romantic entanglement far too much of a distraction. Though the paleopathologist, Dev Patil, did make that part of her sit up and take notice, prick her ears, and purr.

A smile touched her lips as salacious thoughts filled her head. That familiar pressure—her sister, Kristen, always called it "the original itch"—made her squirm a bit and she grew dismayed. No point in letting herself get hot and bothered when her only op-tions would be breaking her personal rules about fraternization on the job or finding some dark corner to get herself off and hope nobody came along to spoil it.

Her heart skipped a bit quicker than normal. Lying there, she listened to people breathing and wondered if any of them were awake. Would they hear her if she just went for it, right here? *Wrong question, Helen*, she thought. *Question is, how quiet can you be?* The answer, she thought, was not quiet enough.

Sighing, amused, she turned onto her side, relished the origi-nal itch a moment, and then tried to drift off again. Helen had spent much of her adult life at one archaeological dig or another, some of them in remote environments where this kind of com-munal living was unavoidable. For the most part, she didn't mind it, even took a kind of comfort from it.

But she couldn't go back to sleep.

A flutter touched her heart. Not excitement and not that old itch. This was something unfamiliar and uneasy. She felt a kind of pres-sure against her back—not a physical weight, but the weight of regard, the sense that someone must be there, just behind her. Her heart quickened and she swallowed hard, flooded with the sudden certainty that someone was there, very close now. Looming.

There. Was that the rustle of clothing or just someone shifting in their sleep? And that breathing . . . had it moved closer? Had it deepened?

Long seconds passed as Helen lay there and listened. She felt too warm, suddenly, only her face exposed. The sense of not being alone did not abate at all, but as the moments ticked by she began to recognize the absurdity of her fear. There were people only six feet away, and others beyond them. If some creepy bugger wanted to watch her sleep, she had only to turn and confront him. It was almost guaranteed to be a him, after all. Some men seemed to have a certain setting, a switch on their dial, that women hardly ever managed.

All right. Enough of this.

With a quick snicker of disdain at her childish fear, she began to roll over.

The first blow struck her nose, shooting a wave of obliterating pain through her face, enough to make her gasp and then hold her breath as the figure looming above took a fistful of her hair, yanked tight, and struck again. The second blow made her whimper, and she sucked in air, disoriented but not enough to blot out her anger and fear. She opened her mouth to scream and the third blow hit her in the temple hard enough to make the edges of her vision go black. So did the fourth. And the fifth.

If a sixth blow fell, Helen didn't feel it.

Darkness. A pulsing, aching, throbbing darkness that resembled the cradle of sleep in the same way that screaming resembled laughter. Awareness crept back in fits and starts and then she realized she was being tugged along, dragged along the snowy timbers in her sleeping bag. The only noise her abduction had made was a quiet shushing sound, and for a dozen long seconds, Helen could do nothing but blink and listen to that soft, lovely noise. The whisper of brutality. Of capture.

She blinked, wondering where her attacker hoped to take her. There was nowhere to go.

Snow whipped at her face, icy pinpricks on her bleeding, swelling flesh. The pain exploded in a brilliant flare and she thought her cheek must be broken, maybe the orbit around her right eye. The wind buffeted the sleeping bag and her blurred thoughts began to clear and quicken. She tried to twist herself inside the sleeping bag, tried to wrest her arms free, and her attacker picked up the pace.

"Stop," she rasped, her voice weakened by the beating she'd taken and stolen by the wind. The pain in her broken face exploded again, bursts of brightly colored agony like fireworks in her brain. "Someone . . ."

From the corner of her eye, in the strange blue-white darkness of the storm, she saw a body on the ground. Darvill, one of her students. The long, thin limbs and shaggy beard were unmistakable, so she recognized him instantly. He'd been on sentry duty tonight.

If her brains hadn't been scrambled by those punishing blows, she'd have sorted it out more swiftly. But *now* she knew.

Momentum picked up, and then she was sliding sideways, shushing against the snow until the swing lifted her entirely off the ground. Helen felt a moment of weightlessness as she sucked in a lungful of air.

As she plummeted over the edge, she screamed at last.

Too late.

TWELVE

Walker stands on the shore of the lake with an AR-15 in his hands, scanning the misty surface of the water. It ripples with a light breeze and he holds his breath, watching each tiny wave. The water is always warm, though the air is chilly. They are atop a volcanic mountain in Guatemala, three thousand meters above sea level, and the lagoon is an idyllic paradise of water and jungle born inside a volcanic crater. The mist atop the water might very well be steam. Walker hasn't clarified that with his geologist yet. He's been more focused on talking to the biologist about the things that have been slithering out at night and dragging the locals into the lake.

Witnesses describe them as nightmares. Serpentine bodies, long arms, hooked talons, and the teeth. All who've seen them mention the teeth.

Those they've taken eventually wash up on the shore of the lake, pale and bloated and drained of blood. The word "vampire" has come up several times, but Walker has laid down the law. Anyone who uses the word again is off his team, permanently. So they don't speak the word anymore, but he can't banish it from their minds. Only capturing or killing one of these fucking things will do that. Capture will be better. A previously unknown species showing up in such a remote location is a fascinating anomaly, and there will be a long study to determine their origin. His best guess is from inside the volcano itself, that the water goes deeper than anyone knew, through some kind of crack in the lake bottom. But none of that matters right now. Not when they've already killed three members of his team.

It's nearly dawn. He whispers the names of members of his team who began this long night at his side but whom he has not seen for hours. As far as he knows, he is alone. So the chill of the night breeze and the mist off the lake makes him think of lonely nights afraid in his boyhood bed, when his father would insist that only babies needed their mommies in the middle of the night. Dreams were just dreams and he needed to grow up.

He's nearly been killed seven times in his career. Walker is not afraid. Despite the chill and the mist and the fact that his team has vanished and he is alone, he is not afraid. But little Ben—his mom had called him Benny—that boy is terrified. Every breath he takes seems to have its own claws, and they drag inside his chest and cut him up with fear.

"Anyone?" he offers up to the predawn mist, and he hates how pitiful he sounds.

A splash out on the lake makes him freeze. Squinting to see through the mist, he takes a step into the water. Only ankle-deep, it's too shallow for them to hide, but still his pulse quickens. The darkness has turned that shimmering blue that exists only in the hour before dawn.

The mist eddies and begins to thin, just enough for him to make out an object on the surface of the lake.

He narrows his eyes, shuddering as he makes out the shape of it.

Not an object at all, it's a head, just barely above the surface.

A face, eyes glistening in the mist.

Human.

The curtain of mist draws back and in that blue darkness, Walker can't take his eyes off of that face.

"No," he whispers, and he takes another step into the water, heedless now of the danger.

He's been holding off, not wanting to draw their attention, but now he clicks on the light attached to his weapon, and the tight, powerful beam finds that face. The eyes blink, but the fear in those eyes . . . etched in that face . . . the sight of that fear just about kills him.

"Daddy?" Llittle Charlie calls to him, his voice slithering across the water.

Little Charlie. Like Little Benny. Two little boys, filled with fear.

"It's got me, Daddy," Charlie says, his voice a hitching whimper. "I can feel it down there, holding on. My legs are cut. It's got . . . I think it's got its teeth in me."

Walker wants to scream his son's name but the sound won't come out. He feels as if he's turned to stone, but still he forces himself to move another step, the beam of light from his weapon trained on Charlie's face . . . his weapon beamed on Charlie's face.

The boy whimpers again and then he jerks in the water, causing a little splash, like something has tugged him from below. He calls out for his father again and now Walker can see the tears on his cheeks. Worse than the tears, worse than the fear, he watches the spark of hope extinguish in his son's eyes. This little boy, only nine, knows he is going to die now.

That he is dying at this very moment.

"I love you, Daddy," Charlie whispers, the words gliding along the water's surface.

But Walker doesn't hear "I love you." He hears "good-bye."

And it breaks him.

"Charlie, no!" he snaps, and he wades into the water.

Wades deep. Not caring what might happen to him or what's happened to his team or the villagers. This is his son. The good thing he's done, the gift he's given the world that is meant to survive long after he's gone.

He screams now.

A hand rises, dripping, from the water, and long fingers wrap around Charlie's face. Walker can only see one of his eyes now, as Charlie begins to scream. The hand drags him down so slowly that the boy has time to call for his daddy one last time before the water enters his wide-open mouth and he is choking on it, drowning, just the top of his head and that eye and that horrid hand on him.

The thing rises up from the lake even as it drowns the boy. Its eyes glitter like cold orange embers. This is not the same as the monsters in the water. This is something else. . . . something worse.

Through the mist, Walker can see its horns. . . .

He woke sweating, despite the cold. Woke with a shout that startled Father Cornelius, who lay on the other side of the tent. Woke swearing, and then rolled over onto his side, legs pulled up tight against his body.

Walker whispered his son's name once, twice, and again, grateful to whatever gods there were that the boy was safe at home and not here with him. Not in the ark with the horned thing that had invaded his dreams.

Somehow it had infiltrated Walker's mind, and he'd felt it there, even while he was sleeping. It knew him now and he knew at least a tiny sliver of it. He'd felt its evil, and no matter what happened, he could not let it get down off the mountain. The evil had been unearthed, but it could be contained.

He lay for a time in that post-nightmare panic, ruminating on these thoughts until they came to seem awkward, even ridiculous. When at last he drifted off again, in that last hour before sunrise, Walker had convinced himself not to let fear make a fool of him. Though his determination wavered, he could not erase the certainty that the demon was somehow awake and aware, that it knew they were there. That it wanted them there.

Morning crept into the cave with a gray sprawl of daylight. Sometime during the night, the snow had stopped falling . . . at least for a little while. Word of the vanished staff members had spread quickly. Helen Marshall's team gathered in a private mourning circle beside the section of level one where they'd spent the past several days taking samples and preserving remains. They talked among themselves, wary of being overheard, and when Meryam passed by, she noticed that they fell silent and some glanced guiltily away, and she knew then that they were considering abandoning KHAP altogether.

Now she stood all the way in the back of level two, near the ladder that went down to the corner where the horned cadaver lay inside its tent, dead thousands of years, but still affecting the nerves and thoughts and behavior of everyone around it.

"I'm tempted to just set the thing on fire and be done with it," she said.

Adam held up a hand. "Now hang on—"

"I said I was tempted, love. I'm not going to do it." She rolled her eyes, shook her head, stared at each of the men around her in turn. Adam, the man she loved. Ben Walker, whom she'd welcomed but now wished was anywhere but here. Hakan, who hated her.

"I just wish it wasn't part of the conversation," she said. "If you'd told me we'd find a dead bloke with horns I'd have thrown a party. When we first opened up the coffin I felt almost giddy. That footage is gold for the documentary, but now every single thing that goes wrong gets blamed on us having a bloody demon in our midst."

Adam leaned against the dry timber wall. "It's not a goddamn—"

"I know it's not a demon!" she snapped. "But try convincing all these superstitious twats . . ."

She froze. Beyond Hakan, just at the edge of the passage that had brought them to this corner, someone stood eavesdropping. She spotted his shadow on the far wall, thrown by the bright work light just above her head.

"Oh, you little bastard," she hissed, storming past Hakan.

The shadow moved, squeaked like a mouse, but it was too late for him to run so he stepped out into the open. Olivieri, cheeks flushed with the cold and with guilt.

"Fuck off," Meryam said, biting off the words.

"I—"

"I'm not joking, Armando," she said. "Fuck off out of here right now. You weren't invited to this meeting. You know we came back here to speak privately or you wouldn't be eavesdropping."

"I wasn't—"

Meryam put a hand on his chest and shoved gently but firmly, walking him backward several steps to get him going. He used the momentum to turn and head back down the passage.

"I ought to be included in this," Olivieri said. "All of the senior staff should be. I don't know why Dr. Walker is here and—"

"Dr. Walker has a history of dealing with ugly shit and I wanted him here," she said. "I *don't* want you here."

But she didn't need to say any more. Olivieri was leaving.

Meryam turned and walked quietly back to the ladder, gazing a moment at the shadowy opening that led down to level one. To the box and the horned thing.

"What about my history?" Walker asked.

She studied his face. A thin scar creased the left side of his forehead and he bore several smaller ones on the right side of his neck. His eyes, though, were the real evidence of just how much darkness and trouble he'd seen.

Meryam sniffed. "Adam's here because he's my partner. Hakan's here because he's foreman. If I'd wanted someone in this little conference because of politics, I'd have Kim and Mr. Avci. When they were clearing you to come here, I studied up on you a bit. You've been in some tight spots, and though I don't understand who you really are or what you really do for the National Science Foundation, what information I found suggests you're capable of handling yourself pretty well when things go tits up."

"So you're saying you want my perspective?" Walker asked.

Meryam felt her anger at Olivieri abating. The cold settled into her again. The bright work light did nothing to make her feel more alert, more like morning had come. It still felt like midnight to her, like she hadn't slept in months and the shadows were closing in.

"Yes, Dr. Walker. That's what I'm saying." Her skull ached.

Walker rubbed at the dark circles under his eyes. He clearly hadn't been sleeping, either.

"You had two men go missing night before last," he said, looking pointedly at Hakan. "One of them is a guide, skilled enough to get down the mountain even with snow falling. The blizzard that's been forecast isn't here yet, so I was willing to go along with that theory. It made sense, to a degree. You have a lot of frustrated people working for you right now. But now two more people? A middle-aged archaeologist and one of her students, neither with a lot of climbing experience?"

The ladder drew her gaze again and Meryam forced herself to look away.

She turned to Hakan. "Could they do it?"

Hakan fell back on old habits, averting his gaze. He focused on Adam almost as if he wanted to wait for permission to reply. And what the hell was that about?

"It's possible," Hakan said, nodding slowly. But then he ticked his gaze toward her, eyes narrowed, full of dark wisdom. "But you know they didn't."

Meryam flinched. "What are you saying?"

Hakan's nostrils flared. He studied her with that familiar distaste. "You are not a stupid woman, no matter how hard you seem to be working to prove otherwise. Professor Marshall showed no hostility toward your leadership and no fear of dead things."

"I agree," Adam said quietly. For the first time, Meryam noted the absence of his camera. "These people didn't leave. There aren't any demons here, but that doesn't mean we're not dealing with a monster. Maybe more than one."

Walker moved to the ladder, put a hand on it, and gazed down into the darkness. They all watched him. Meryam saw the tension coiled inside him and felt it in herself, the urge to run or scream or fight.

"Murder," she said. "That's what we're saying."

"Yes," Hakan replied. "It can be nothing else."

"Murder, yeah," Ben agreed, glancing around to be sure there were no more eavesdroppers. "And sabotage."

Meryam felt her hands trembling. Her face flushed with heat.

"Hakan, tell Patil to put together whatever tools he needs, then get a few of Helen's students—the ones who can function—and meet me back at the box."

"Hang on," Walker began.

She ignored him. "Adam, make sure Zeybekci and Avci know what we're up to. You might as well tell Olivieri, too. And you and Calliope bring your damn cameras. We've wasted enough time."

Walker held up a hand. "Meryam—"

"You have no standing here, Dr. Walker. If you and the priest want to be there when we do this, I'm okay with that as long as you stay out of the way. But if I don't get that fucking demon out of the cave and away from these people, this project is going to unravel entirely."

Hakan and Adam nodded.

"Got it," Adam said.

They began to move away.

"Gentlemen," Walker said, "just one thing? Watch your backs. From now on, nobody should be running around alone in here. Even after we get rid of the cadaver, we've still got a real monster to deal with."

Meryam stepped onto the ladder and started down.

"One monster at a time."

The plastic tenting around the coffin had been dismantled. Bright lights illuminated the horned thing, a buttery yellow glow that cast haunted gray shadows in strange patterns on its withered remains and on the wall and floor around its box. Walker stayed out of the way as best he could, knowing that if anyone stumbled over him, Meryam would be within her rights to order him away.

Adam and Calliope somehow managed to be unobtrusive, weaving among the workers with their cameras. The workers Hakan had brought into the project had been excluded from this operation. Instead, Wyn Douglas and the archaeology students would be handling the removal of the remains, overseen by Dev Patil and Zeybekci. Olivieri hovered, studying the corpse intently. Meryam had twice barked at him and once physically maneuvered him out of the paleopathologist's way when Patil grew visibly frustrated.

"Is this typical?" Olivieri asked, sidling up to Walker with an air of disapproval. "I've never observed this process before, but I can't imagine there isn't a more methodical way to extricate the cadaver, particularly in the interest of preservation."

Under Patil's direction, the students had unwrapped a fresh package of thick plastic sheeting. Nobody could have been under the illusion that the opaque tarp was sterile, but at least it was clean.

"No idea," Walker said quietly, glancing at Calliope and her camera, not wanting his words recorded. "I'm not sure Meryam much cares at this point."

The students slid the stiff plastic tarp under the cadaver's head. When the horned skull shifted, they could all hear a dry crackle, like the crunch of autumn leaves underfoot. No. There was no way this was standard procedure in the archaeology world. This was *fuck-it-get-it-done-fast* procedure.

Walker wondered if the body would stick to the wood—if over the millennia the desiccated flesh would have melded itself to the bottom of the coffin—but as the archaeology team gently guided the tarp under the corpse, they encountered little resistance. The body rocked slightly. Bits of the dried skin that remained on the bones had reminded Walker of cobwebs, but they turned to dust as the body shifted, and the air at the back of the ark filled with a stale odor. Dev Patil sneezed into the crook of his arm, backing away for a moment as the students finished drawing the tarp underneath the body.

"We set?" Meryam asked.

Patil pulled a surgical mask up over his face and bent over the cadaver. With gloved hands, he checked the side of the head. The crinkling at the corners of his eyes made his displeasure clear and he sighed.

"There's damage enough already," he said. "So I'm going to say it again. Holding each edge of the tarp, we will gently roll the cadaver toward the wall. The board will be slid beneath the remains and then we will—again, gently—roll the cadaver back down. This will likely result in significant damage, but our goal is to minimize that damage."

At this, Patil glanced sharply at Meryam. Walker could feel the sting of the paleopathologist's disapproval from his place behind one of the lighting arrays.

A susurrus of mutterings came from off to the right, toward the other end of the passage, and Walker looked up to see Father Cornelius quietly arguing with Mr. Zeybekci.

"You may not," Zeybekci said firmly.

"You have no authority over me," the priest said, his caterpillar eyebrows knitted together. "Now let me pass!"

Walker swore under his breath.

"Dr. Walker—" Meryam began.

He held up a hand, staving off her admonishment, and pushed past Olivieri and one of the archaeology students. Adam's camera tracked him as he approached Zeybekci and the priest.

"Father, you can't be here," Walker began.

"I don't recognize your authority, either," Father Cornelius said.

"If you mention God's authority, I'll pitch you off the mountain myself," Walker heard himself say. He felt the flinch from the gathered team members, then realized what he'd said. Most of these people were worried that the missing staffers had been victims of foul play. If so, that almost certainly involved going over the cliff.

Father Cornelius ignored him, turning to Meryam instead. "Nobody here is going to listen to anyone but you, Miss Karga, so it's to you I must appeal. I've been poring over my transcriptions and notes from my examination of the bitumen casing and the coffin lid and there is no doubt in my mind that the writing thereon is a warning, one that seems to be repeated several times, and emphatically so."

Olivieri huffed and rolled his eyes.

Calliope swiveled to focus her camera on Meryam's face.

"Father, honestly," Meryam said, "I respect your faith—"

"This isn't about my faith. These are writings that have no root in Christianity. Only history. It's got nothing to do with being Catholic or Jewish or Muslim or any other religion."

"It does, though," Meryam said. "You're suggesting there's some kind of spiritual evil at work. That this thing"—she pointed at the horned cadaver—"is actually a demon. I'm not arguing your translation—"

"I am," Olivieri muttered.

"—but I'm saying it doesn't matter if the people who wrote those warnings believed they were necessary. *We* don't believe them." Meryam waved her hand around the space, her hand throwing long shadows in the bright, industrial light. "None of us but you, and priest or not, I'm surprised a man with your academic background would embrace such ideas."

Father Cornelius walked to the edge of the coffin. One of the students moved to stop him, but Meryam waved the young woman away, allowing the priest to stand beside the box and stare down at the horned visage of the "demon." The way the shadows fell inside the coffin, Walker admitted to himself that the thing looked terrifying.

"Back in my office, surrounded by books, I might not believe it," Father Cornelius said. "But I've felt it. And I know you've all felt—"

"Oh, enough of this," Olivieri interrupted. "You've translated only fragments, and I question the methods by which you arrived at even those limited translations. With all due respect, you're a frightened, elderly man who has heard one too many tales of evil from his fellow priests."

"The translation doesn't matter now," Walker said, trying to soften the inherent unkindness of the words as he gazed at Father Cornelius. "Even if this ugly bastard was an actual demon, *look* at it. The thing's been dead since long before the time of Christ. It's long gone."

Zeybekci moved in front of the priest. "Please step back."

Father Cornelius retreated a few paces, his face pale and his body tense.

"Do it," Meryam said.

The students moved into place at the head and foot of the coffin, while Patil picked up the thin, hard plastic backboard and rested it on the edge. On the count of three, Patil nodded and the two students slowly shifted the plastic tarp, rocking the body to one side. Patil lowered the board into the coffin and worked it beneath the cadaver as if he were trying to shovel the dead thing up. As he bent over, sliding the board into place, a dry crackling came from the corpse, like tinder catching fire. A crack appeared in the horned thing's chest, a puff of dust rose, followed by a little cloud of piss-yellow gas, enclosing Patil's head in a momentary fog.

"Get back!" Walker called.

Adam darted forward, camera hanging by his side, forgotten, and used his free hand to haul Patil away. The paleopathologist turned and fell to his knees. For a moment Walker thought the whites of the man's eyes had gone a putrid shade of orange. Then Patil twisted away from them and began to retch. The first groan brought up nothing, but with the next he spewed a torrent of vomit that splashed into the slanted corner of the cave, slipping into the places where the ark's timbers had separated under the pressure of passing ages.

"Wrap it up and get it out of there!" Meryam told the archaeology team.

The two students at either end folded the plastic tarp around the cadaver as Wyn Douglas taped it down fast, and they lifted the hard board like EMTs at an accident scene. In what seemed only seconds, they carried the cadaver toward the base of the nearby ladder, where they began to wrap it more efficiently.

Kneeling by Patil's side, Meryam put a hand on his shoulder. "Dev, are you—"

He shook her hand off and bent over again, breathing deep and fast, trying to control the surging roil of his guts.

Walker pushed past a student. "Meryam, get away from him. All of you, back away."

Adam shook himself, the momentary shock passing. "He's right. Come on, love. Whatever it was could be contagious." He turned toward another student. "Get the doc down here, right now. The rest of you, keep back."

Nobody else needed to be told. Calliope kept filming as Adam helped Meryam to her feet and they withdrew from Patil. Not all of them, however. Father Cornelius pushed past Calliope and started toward Patil and the now-empty coffin.

"Father—" Walker warned.

But the priest's eyes were locked on the brightly lit interior of the box where the horned thing had lain, and now Walker saw the markings there. The cadaver's fluids had stained the wood in some ancient era, but these were not just the striations from those stains—there were words here as well, symbols like those on the lid and the bitumen casing, carved or burned into the wood thousands of years ago. More messages from the past for them to translate.

"Not now," Walker began. "Seriously, we can't risk—"

Zeybekci shouted at the priest in Turkish, something short and angry at first, and then a long stream of guttural words that contorted the monitor's face with fury.

"Hang on," Meryam said as she and Adam turned toward Zeybekci, but too late. The man had already started moving.

Zeybekci lunged at Father Cornelius, hands outstretched, and his fingers hooked into claws as he snagged the priest's clothes and hurled him to the floor. People started to shout. Calliope jockeyed for position for her camera, getting the whole thing as they grabbed hold of Zeybekci and tried to pull him off. Zeybekci's stream of guttural language continued as he began to pummel the old priest, fists smacking Father Cornelius's head and throat.

Then he pulled his gun.

Adam snagged his arm, twisted it back, disarming him quickly, but then Zeybekci lashed out and cracked a fist against his skull, knocking him backward.

"Come on, help us!" Meryam called to the students.

But Walker had gotten leverage by then. With Meryam helping, he ripped Zeybekci off the priest and wrestled him to the ground. Then the students were there, holding the man's hands down as Zeybekci shrieked and fought them, strong in his rage. So strong that Walker knelt on his chest, shouting for him to stop, to come to his senses.

Zeybekci glared up at him. The industrial lights made his eyes gleam, but there were shadows there as well, and for half a second Walker thought they had the same glittery orange hue he'd seen in Patil's eyes when that gas had engulfed the paleopathologist's head.

Abruptly, Zeybekci just stopped. His eyes closed and he sighed and tears began to well in his eyes.

"What has happened to me?" he asked calmly.

Walker didn't trust it. Not yet. He and the students took their time, made sure Zeybekci really had calmed himself down. When he could exhale and the muscles in his back relaxed, Walker glanced back toward the coffin to see Patil sitting up and leaning against it. Patil wiped his mouth with a look of disgust, pale but otherwise seemingly all right.

"What the hell?" Adam said, rubbing at his skull as Meryam stared around the passage at the simmering aftermath of the chaos.

Walker looked at the gun in his hand. Zeybekci did the same.

"I'll take that, now," Zeybekci said, reaching for the pistol.

"I don't think so," Walker said, stepping between them. "Not yet, anyway."

He held out his own hand for the weapon. Adam hesitated, glancing at Meryam, but Walker would not wait for approval. Not when there was a firearm in play. Carefully but firmly, he took the gun from Adam's hand.

"As long as Mr. Avci seems fine, I'll return this to *him*," Walker said. That seemed to satisfy them all, for the moment.

Father Cornelius cleared his throat. They all turned to see the man rising shakily to his feet. Blood streamed from the priest's nose. His mouth had already begun to swell, his upper lip split, and his left cheek had split against the bone and would certainly need stitches.

"If you're through with your objections," the priest said, "I'd like to try deciphering what's written inside the coffin now. Maybe that noxious little cloud was nothing more than body gas. But just in case your insistence that all of this is perfectly natural turns out to be wrong, I'd like to know what we're dealing with."

Little patters of blood fell from his wounded face and dotted the timber floor.

No one attempted to argue with him this time.

There had been a lull in the storm. In midafternoon the wind dropped off to nothing for an hour or so, the world around the mountain going entirely still. Work had ground to a halt inside the ark, despite the moment of calm in the weather. Like the stillness of the sky, the cessation of activity inside the cave seemed a temporary thing, with the promise that both would soon be replaced by renewed vigor. In the case of the storm, at least, the promise was fulfilled an hour before dark.

Adam planted his feet, fighting the gusts that crashed across the mouth of the cave. Night had not yet fallen, but the darkness had come early. The snows of the past couple of days had been little more than flurries in comparison to the raging, churning whiteness that was now arriving. His back to the wind, he held tightly to his camera and recorded footage of the screaming white maelstrom, hoping the visuals were as stunning as he thought they would be. People would be familiar with the sight of a blizzard, but not like this, with thousands of meters of nothing stretching out below them.

He thought of the missing four, wondered if they had gone over the edge of that abyss and if their bodies were down there now, buried in the deepening snow, lost to their loved ones until at least the first thaw of spring. More and more, Adam had been keeping his thoughts and fears to himself. Meryam did not seem to want to hear them, and though that broke his heart a little, he reminded himself of the pressure she was under.

Pressure she put herself under, he thought. He'd have been happy to share the burden, but Meryam didn't want to share. *Doesn't want to share her troubles, and maybe doesn't want to share her happiness either. Is that really the woman you want to marry?*

Guilt washed through him. He loved her, and didn't regret that love. But sometimes Meryam didn't make it easy. Adam had viewed her as the perfect partner, someone with whom he could chase his dreams, side by side with her as she chased her own, each lending strength to the other.

Everyone with any sense was in the middle of taking whatever refuge they could find, firing up the heaters, and huddling down together, but he needed time to himself. A chance to clear his head. There were meetings going on, he knew that. A lot of decisions to be made. Dr. Dwyer had patched up Father Cornelius, and Hakan was observing while the priest tried to decipher the writing inside the coffin, with Walker and Kim assisting, and Calliope getting the process on film. Dev Patil and Zeybekci were still under Dr. Dwyer's care, though both were protesting that they were fine.

Adam tucked his camera into the deep pocket inside his jacket and zipped it back up, thinking he ought to head back inside. When he glanced he saw a figure moving out of the ark at a staggering hurtle. Head bowed, hands at its side, the figure trudged through the blizzard, straight for the edge and the long fall that waited there.

"Who the hell—" Adam began, starting to run before the words were even out of his mouth.

His feet skidded in the snow and he put his arms out like a child playing airplane, heart galloping with the fear that one wrong step would send him sliding right over the edge. In the ethereal blue light that breathed inside the blizzard, the silhouette picked up speed, but so did Adam. His feet had found their rhythm on the snow and he knew he was going to make it, to save this one life.

Then his left foot hit a patch of ice under the snow and went out from beneath him. He spun as he fell, crashing down on his right side with a grunt of breath and a shock of pain in his ribs. Momentum carried him a foot or two and he felt the nearness of the edge and the certainty that even to flinch might mean going over.

No, he thought, craning his neck, knowing he'd never make it now. He rolled onto his chest and started to rise, body tensed with failure.

A second figure came after the first. It emerged from the storm like an apparition, arriving between gusts of wind, a curtain of snow whipping back in revelation. Panic seized Adam as he imagined these only the first two of a sudden mass exodus, a flight of suicides as members of the team hurled themselves off the mountain.

Then he saw that the second figure was Hakan, and held his breath. Hakan shouted as he lunged after the first man, grabbed him by the back of the jacket and yanked him down into the snow. They tumbled over each other and Adam whispered a prayer when they came to rest on the ledge. Hakan's leg jutted over the side as the first man continued to struggle. Eyes wide with primal fear, desperate for his own life, Hakan struck the other man twice in the face.

Adam reached them then. He offered Hakan his hand, gave him leverage to move away from the edge. Together, they dragged the first man toward the cave. Hakan punched him again and then tore the scarf away from his face.

"You could have killed us both!" Hakan shouted, spittle flying from his lips.

Armando Olivieri stared back up at them without fear or shame, face filled instead with disappointment. Anger boiled up in Adam's chest. He grabbed Olivieri by the coat and dragged him onto safer ground. The professor cried out, slapped at Adam's arms, demanding to be released.

Adam slammed him onto the snow. "Are you kidding me? You pull this shit and bitch about me putting hands on you? I just saved your damn life!"

Olivieri went rigid and tears began to well in his eyes. Snow whipped at them, the icy temperatures slowing the professor's tears. Adam wondered if they would freeze on his face.

"You don't understand," Olivieri said, the wind so strong Adam doubted Hakan could hear it. "I felt it in me, like poison in my veins, and I knew God couldn't stop it. Do you see? God isn't here anymore. He can't help us."

The words were ugly coming from a man who had spent his entire adult life studying the Bible, but the tone of Olivieri's voice made Adam shiver in a way the blizzard never would. And his eyes . . . Adam had never seen hopelessness like that before. Haunted, he shuffled backward on his knees and looked up at Hakan.

"Take him to Dr. Dwyer. Tie him down if you have to," Adam said. "This is out of control. I've got to see Meryam."

Hakan took the man by the shoulders, making certain he would not run for the edge again.

"You may wish to wait to see her," he said with such disdain he might as well have spit the words. "Or you may not like what you find."

As they walked away, Adam stared at Hakan's back. A tight knot of silence in his chest blossomed into something larger, a strangely calming dread that accompanied his first step and his second as he began to follow.

His guard duties forgotten, even Olivieri's attempt at suicide only a vague motivation, he made his way out of the worst of the wind and along the level-one passage where most of the staff made their quarters. Some had moved up a level for a bit more protection from the elements while others had simply shored up their meager shelter. Adam and Meryam had their own quarters up on level two, but the stall she called her office was here, and he knew she would still be working.

Warm orange light glowed inside the stall, a combination of a generator-powered lantern and a small space heater.

Adam's footfalls were almost silent in the thin layer of snow that had drifted this far inside. He could not feel his own heart beating or the rise and fall of his chest as he came within view of the stall's interior.

Meryam stood inside, just as he had predicted. What he had not foreseen was that she might not be alone. In that warm glow, she had her arms around Feyiz, her face buried in his chest. From his vantage point, Adam could not see her face, but Feyiz had his eyes closed in an expression of heartbreaking contentment.

Adam began to shake his head as he backed away. Confusion and denial gave way to a bitter rush of bile and resentment as he started back along the passage. Then came the fury, at her for this betrayal and at himself for being so stupid. A phrase floated into his mind, something from a hundred books and comics he'd read over the years. *Lovestruck fool. That's you. Fucking idiot.*

Moments later he found himself back where he'd begun, out on the ledge with the blizzard screaming around him, snow whipping at his face, cold searing what little skin he'd left exposed. He stared at the place where Olivieri had tried to commit suicide, at the way the wind and snow seemed to create little swirling ghosts that swept off the cave's edge, mimicking the act Olivieri had intended to perform.

Adam took another step.

A hand touched his back. Anger seized him, a visceral inferno that radiated from within as he turned around, expecting Meryam. She must have heard him, must have followed.

Only it wasn't Meryam at all.

Calliope flinched at the severity of his expression, and Adam softened.

"Hey . . . what is it?" she asked.

Pain and humiliation stoked his anger but he forced it down, shook his head. "Nothing important. What do you need?"

Calliope refused to believe him. She searched his eyes and reached out to take his hand, shining with compassion.

"Adam," she said. "Please. What is it?"

There in the midst of the blizzard, lost in the darkness and the white scream of the storm, so close to the edge of the abyss, he kissed her. Calliope's lips were warm and soft and her breath against him had the faint scent of wintergreen.

She pushed him away. "Stop."

Adam breathed deeply and stepped back. Then he saw the worry on her face and he understood.

"Not here," she said.

So they went somewhere else.

THIRTEEN

The snow did not reach down into the farthest corners of the ark. At the back, where the coffin still rested on the slanted floor and space heaters provided at least a little warmth, Walker had no idea just how bad the blizzard might have gotten. What he did know was that nobody would be sneaking out tonight. If anyone went missing in this weather, there would be zero room for doubt as to what had become of them.

Murder.

The only question would be who had done it.

For now, the work in that back corner of the ark continued. Everyone else had gone to hunker down until morning, bury themselves in as many layers as possible, but there were pressing questions now. Questions that wouldn't wait for the sun to rise or the storm to pass.

Father Cornelius worked over the now-empty coffin, bright lights still shining into its interior. Kim stood next to him, taking notes longhand in a journal the priest had provided. Her position as UN observer didn't include assisting Father Cornelius in this way, but a trust gap had existed between Walker's team and the

KHAP staff from the moment of their arrival and it had grown into a vast gulf.

Polly Bennett and a couple of other members of the archaeology team stood watching. The distrust in the faces of the young archaeologists spoke volumes, but Walker knew it had been earned. Kim and the priest had both exhibited strange behaviors around the coffin and its occupant. Walker had contributed nothing in the past few hours, but he had stuck around for the same reason these archaeology students had—to make sure nobody went off the rails and decided to damage the coffin or, worse, themselves or someone else.

A short distance away, at the bottom of the ladder that went to level two, the cadaver had been treated and tightly wrapped, then placed inside a body bag and further sealed inside some kind of zippered canvas enclosure that would be simpler to transport. Ready to go, the moment the storm abated.

Walker tore his gaze away from the zippered canvas, forced himself to stop thinking about the ugly, twisted corpse inside and the wicked-looking horns on its skull.

"Well, that's not very nice," Kim said, frowning as she took a step back from Father Cornelius.

Walker felt a tremor inside him. *No, no*, he thought. *No more of this bullshit.*

But then Kim glanced over to let him in on the joke.

"He just said he wished Professor Olivieri was here," she said, nudging the priest playfully. "Honestly, I am offended."

The priest fumbled sheepishly for words. "It's only that, well, Olivieri would be able to understand the difficulties in translating—"

"He's disagreed with every word you've spoken since you arrived," Walker said. "He's unstable and, sorry Father, he was a prick even before he showed us he was unstable."

"No argument," the priest replied. "But he's a knowledgeable prick."

The archaeology students stared at him. Kim raised an eyebrow and pretended she hadn't heard, but Walker only laughed. It wasn't the first time he'd been in Father Cornelius's presence when the older man had said something off-color. If anything, it told him the priest was feeling more himself, more in control.

Polly Bennett joined Kim and the priest beside the coffin. In Helen Marshall's absence, Polly had become the senior member of the archaeological crew, their de facto boss.

"How different is this from what was on the lid?" Polly asked the priest.

Father Cornelius glanced back at Walker, so Polly turned as well, watching the silent exchange. The message was clear. This might be the Karga-Holzer Ark Project, but when it came to what Father Cornelius found here, the priest answered to someone else.

Walker nodded his authorization. All three of the grad students stared at him a moment—they didn't like the idea that they might be on the outside of new information.

"Same methods," Father Cornelius said, pointing into the coffin. "Whatever methodology was used by whoever wrote on the lid and engraved the symbols in the bitumen casing, the same mix of languages was employed here. I've found some things that are echoed. The Sumerian element is key. I feel as if I'm just not looking at it correctly, that if I can just make sense of why certain languages were used for certain phrases, I'll get it."

Polly glanced back at Walker again, although she did not work for him. "Languages are my specialty. I could help."

Walker expected the priest to scoff. There were times when he certainly would have. Instead, Father Cornelius cocked his head and studied the young woman with her half-shaved, green hair.

"I welcome it," he replied, but there was something in the way he said it—a kind of tremor in his voice, a darting of the eyes—that made Walker wonder if it was help he wanted, or just the solidity of Polly's nearness. The company of someone who seemed steady and strong when so many among them were frayed at the edges.

Kim shuffled to the side a bit to make room for Polly. Walker thought she might make a joke out of it, something about knowing when she was wanted, but instead she scribbled something in the journal and then stared at nothing for a few seconds. She seemed to waver on her feet. Concerned, Walker started toward her.

"Wait a second," Polly said, staring into the coffin. "The markings there—"

"The stains," Father Cornelius replied. "Yes?"

"You thought they were from bodily fluids."

"I still do."

The other students moved nearer. Shaken from her reverie, Kim craned her neck for a better look into the coffin. Walker stepped up behind Polly and the priest, peering between them at the etched symbols and the dark, striated stains where the body had lain. The pattern reminded him of the chalk outlines police made around dead people at crime scenes.

"I'd have to take samples to confirm," Polly said. "But to me, the outline is too clean to have been made only by stains."

Kim had her pen at the ready like some eager cub reporter. "What are you suggesting?"

Walker felt all of his doubts begin to unravel. All along he had come up with other explanations, not only for the behavior of the staff but for the one, huge, looming bit of impossibility that hung over it all—the location of the ark. There were ways to explain it, but they all stretched credulity. There had been several times in his career when believing in the supernatural would have made his work and life simpler, but he did not, and in each of those cases, he had found a tangible, biological explanation. Extraordinary, sometimes horrible, but not supernatural. He sought something more—that had become clear to him, hard as it was to admit to himself. But the occult, true evil, had no more bearing on his life than a bunch of fairy tales.

Now he stared into the coffin and he saw what Polly had seen. The darker part of the bottom of the coffin, where much of the writing had been hidden beneath the cadaver . . . the outline of that corpse hadn't only been darkened from being soaked in the fluids that escaped the body during putrefaction.

"The wood is burned," he said.

Polly had begun to explain, but now she looked at him and nodded. "I think so, yes."

"How is that possible?" one of the other students asked.

"There are ways to explain it," Polly replied.

And there were. Whoever had put the cadaver into the box might have burned the pattern into the wood beforehand, as part of the message. But Father Cornelius crossed himself, pulled the crucifix from inside his collar and kissed it before slipping it back within the cloth.

"I don't . . ." Kim began, lowering her head as she took a couple of deep breaths.

Walker moved over to her. "Kim?"

She straightened, closing the pen inside the journal. "I'm very tired. Would it be all right if I went to lie down? I think I'd like to sleep."

"Of course," Walker said. He glanced at Father Cornelius. "Unless you need her?"

"We'll muddle along," the priest said, studying Kim with only fleeting concern before he turned his attention back to Polly. "It may help me put all of this together if I talk through the various language elements I've already found."

As the priest started running through his observations anew, Walker took Kim by the elbow and escorted her away. They passed the wrapped cadaver of the horned thing. Walker barely looked at the zipped canvas transport bag, but he could feel its presence behind him as he waited for Kim to climb the ladder to level two, then made the ascension himself. Like the gaze of a spurned lover burning into the space between his shoulder blades, it seared him, until at last he was off the ladder. His thoughts were a jumble of questions, most of which had no satisfying answers.

"Walker," Kim said quietly, as they walked together. "Do you feel all right?"

"No," he said immediately, and then laughed at his dire tone. "But how should I feel?"

Kim bumped against him, keeping stride but somehow huddling into him with every step. "Cold, I suppose. But you know that's not what I mean."

Did he?

"Watched," he said, hating to admit to such a nebulous fear. "I feel watched."

Kim nodded, glancing around as if whoever might be observing them lurked in the shadows they passed, the dark places between the lights that were strung every ten feet or so along the passage. The stairs to level three were ahead, but Kim stopped and faced him. They were in the gloom between bulbs, but still he could see her breath plume in front of her. Winter had not just intruded, it had invaded.

"I feel that, too," she said. "But even more, I feel marked."

"As a target?"

Kim shook her head. "Not like that. I mean the way a dog marks its territory, puts its stink everywhere so the other dogs will know to stay away. I feel . . . claimed. And I know it's foolish, but I want to leave. I know I agreed to be a part of this mission. But now I . . . I've got to get out of here."

"The blizzard—"

"I know," she said, striking him on the arm, her brows furrowed. "I can't go anywhere until the weather clears. And I am ashamed of myself for how anxious that makes me."

Kim left her hand on his arm, stared at the timbers underfoot as she took a deep breath, unwilling to explain more. Or perhaps unable.

The day they'd arrived he would have admitted to at least a general dislike for her, but that had been a different woman. Beautiful, yes, but not his ally. Not his friend. Now, both of them stripped of their professional identities, he looked at Kim and saw someone smart and raw and full of curiosity, so much like himself.

"You're not the only one who's afraid," he said quietly. "I promise you, Seong, you're not alone."

His hand rose, almost of its own volition, and he cupped the side of her face. She leaned into his palm, and then forward into his embrace. And here it was, another thing he would have thought impossible.

They held each other, taking warmth and strength.

And for a time, neither of them was alone.

The cave ledge was like the mouth of a badly carved jack-o'-lantern. On its western half, much more of the ark's wall had given way in the landslide, leaving more of the interior open to the elements. The Ark Project had started work on this more exposed side in order to complete examination and collection of artifacts and samples as quickly as possible, so that their later work could be done behind whatever shelter they could take when they moved into the eastern side of the ark.

They were running behind. This storm had come too soon.

On the western side of that pumpkin/cave ledge, Adam huddled behind an outcropping of rock that blocked much of the wind. Still, the temperature had dropped precipitously low and he knew it had been foolish to come out here, especially in the dark. But it was the farthest he could get from the rest of the staff—

and from Meryam—without trying to scale down the mountain in the storm.

"Idiot," he whispered to himself, with lips that were chapped and dry behind the cloth of the balaclava he wore. His goggles pressed at the flesh around his eyes as the wind shifted direction for a moment, then eased again.

He told himself he was out here on the ledge because he had agreed to take the first shift on sentry duty tonight, but he couldn't make himself believe the lie. Not for a second. His hands still ached with the warmth and the softness of Calliope's curves, the memory of the hard, unyielding muscles in her arms and back as she moved against him, and he against her. She wore some kind of body spray with traces of vanilla and cinnamon, and the aromas floated in his head, the taste of her still on his lips.

Guilt burned in him, but guilt was not enough. When he closed his eyes, pressed them shut against reality, images flashed through his mind of Meryam holding Feyiz, of their intimacy and the contentment in his expression. But they were shuffled together like cards from different decks, mixed with images of the brief time he'd spent with Calliope only an hour ago, the way her mouth had formed a little *O* when she had rolled on top of him, both of them trying so hard to be quiet.

He hated himself a little. Maybe more than a little. But if he was being honest, he hated himself for betraying what he believed in more than he did for betraying Meryam. Right now she didn't deserve his guilt and self-recrimination.

"Fuck!" he rasped, out there alone in the storm.

He had to get off this mountain.

The emotions warring inside him were burning everything in their wake, scorched earth, and Adam had never been good at hiding his feelings. How the hell was he supposed to keep going even another hour past the moment he came face-to-face with Meryam again? His partner. His bride-to-be. Bad enough she was cheating on him with Feyiz. If it had been only that, he could have taken the high road. Stood tall. Broken-hearted, but at least able to tell himself that he'd been wronged. Now he didn't even have that.

All for what? Calliope didn't love him. They were friends and coworkers and they'd flirted occasionally but never with any real intent. In that moment when she had taken his hand and he'd seen the tenderness in her eyes, it had been as if someone else had taken over, as if his body had moved of its own volition. He could never say that aloud. All his life he'd hated people who fell back on the idea that they'd somehow lost control. So although her scent remained in his head and the feel of her body on the tips of his fingers, Adam would take the consequences.

Resigned, he pushed away from the wall and started back along the ledge. The snow coated his clothing and he had to wipe off his goggles as he marched toward the cave entrance, tempted to go back to the shelter he shared with Meryam and try to fall asleep before she came to bed, put the confrontation off until morning. He told himself it wouldn't be cowardice but practicality. They needed sleep.

But, no. The stew of guilt and anger boiled inside him and he knew he had to face her. His thoughts flickered back through the past few months and he wondered why he had never seen it. She had been in constant touch with Feyiz since their first trip here. Even as they planned their marriage, Meryam must have been carrying on with him at a distance. No wonder she had been so withdrawn, so disinterested in helping him make wedding plans. The day she had been so late to view a wedding venue and she had shown up with word from Feyiz of the landslide, of the cave, of the ark . . . no wonder she had been so determined to get back here as fast as they could travel, to push off plans for the wedding.

It had never been about the ark at all.

Snow crunched underfoot. The wind pushed at his back as if the storm itself wanted him to hurry toward the ugliness that awaited. He felt worst of all for Calliope. Their friendship shouldn't have to suffer from this but it would, and so would their professional relationship. He supposed there was a chance that somewhere down the line they would dig their friendship out of the wreckage that was about to occur, but Adam wouldn't have bet on it.

A gust of wind knocked him two steps to the left—toward the edge—and he bent forward, fighting the storm. Wiping the snow from his goggles again, he was surprised to see a figure emerging from the cave, backlit by the dull glow from within. The figure paused and glanced around, scanning for someone—*looking for me?* Adam wondered if it might be Meryam, or even Calliope. But as the figure spotted him and started toward him and their steps brought them closer together, he realized it was Feyiz.

His fists clenched. He could barely feel his fingers inside his gloves, but the bones ached when the anger tightened them together. His guilt muddied his feelings toward Meryam tonight, but what he felt for Feyiz . . . that was crystal clear.

"Thank goodness," Feyiz said, shivering and stamping his feet as he paused in front of Adam. "I couldn't find you and then Calliope told me you were on sentry duty and I thought 'tonight?' But then when I came out and didn't see you I thought . . . well, never mind. It doesn't matter. I need to talk to you."

"You shouldn't," Adam said quietly.

Feyiz barely seemed to hear. Adam wanted to smash him into the ground, to hammer at his face and make him bleed into the snow, to pitch him right over the edge.

"It's about Meryam," Feyiz said.

The words knocked the breath out of Adam. This son of a bitch dared to face him here, in the middle of this project, on the side of a fucking mountain, in a goddamn blizzard? He wanted to talk about the woman Adam had planned to marry? Just the look on Feyiz's face, that sanctimoniously earnest expression that suggested he knew Meryam better than Adam did was enough to earn him broken bones.

"Go on," Adam heard himself say, teeth gritted. Wanting to hear him say it, now. Wanting Feyiz to confess his sins before receiving the beating that was coming his way.

"I almost didn't seek you out," Feyiz admitted. "I promised her I wouldn't say anything, but I can't keep it to myself. I don't think it's right that I should know the secrets a woman keeps from the man she intends to marry."

Intends to marry, Adam thought. *Meryam still thinks we're getting married?*

Adam hadn't been in a fistfight since the eighth grade. As a boy, he'd struggled with a difficult temper and been in trouble more than once, gone home with scrapes and bruises and swollen knuckles. He had taught himself to be more civilized, to find another path in his life. But tonight he did not want to be civilized. He didn't want another path. His guilt over having sex with Calliope fell away as if it had been the one thing chaining down his rage.

"You've got balls, I'll give you that," he muttered.

The wind swept the words away. Feyiz frowned and studied him. He'd heard Adam speak but hadn't made out what he'd said.

"She's going to be furious," Feyiz went on. "But you deserve to know, Adam. She thinks she's protecting you or something, but I can see the way it's pushing the two of you apart." He threw his hands up. "Listen to me, talking in circles. I'm sorry. I hate breaking her trust, but you have to know she's sick. You must have noticed, right? Maybe you just don't see *how* sick."

It took several seconds for the words to sink in, to sift down through the fugue of his anger. When they did, the heat of his rage faded and the icy teeth of the wind bit deep. Frozen, freezing, Adam stared numbly at Feyiz.

"What did you just say?"

"She's sick, Adam. Meryam's been hiding it from you because she's afraid of how it will change things. She confided in me because I lost my father and my sister the same way and I've let her lean on me, but now—with all that's going on, all that she's been carrying on her shoulders—it just isn't fair for her to—"

"Sick how?"

"—keep it from you. I tried to get her to tell you, but she—"

Adam's hands moved on their own. Shot out and grabbed Feyiz by the front of his coat, dragged him forward so they were eye to eye, close enough to establish their own new and terrible intimacy.

"What is wrong with her?" he demanded.

Feyiz didn't try to push him away, didn't even fight the grip on his coat. It was that more than anything that told Adam just how bad the news would be. Full of sorrow, Feyiz only exhaled.

"She has cancer, Adam. Meryam is dying."

Trudging into the cave—into the ark—Adam felt like a sort of ghost himself, like a revenant in an old film, appearing from the maelstrom accompanied by an ominous clamor of chords. Somehow outside his own body, he watched powerless as the Adam Holzer he'd always seen in the mirror made his way past the staff encampment, where the warmth inside of plastic shelters caused the snow blown against the tarps to melt and run in small icy trickles.

He watched himself and saw only a kind of marionette. The human body was a puppet, wasn't it, with the mind—perhaps even the soul—pulling the strings? Adam didn't know who was pulling his strings now. His feet moved but he barely felt them. When he reached up and tugged off his goggles, drew down the scarf to bare his face to the cold emanating from the rock and timber and snow, he hardly recognized the motions as his own.

Numb, he came to stand outside the stall Meryam called her office. The heater rattled inside and the bright light created two Meryams, one who sat at the plastic table and a shadow Meryam, a dark twin whose silhouette seemed strangely misshapen. Inhuman. It occurred to him that neither of them was the woman he'd thought he knew.

His boots shuffled in snow, scuffed the timber beneath it.

Meryam looked up from her work with an air of impatience, almost consternation. Then she saw who it was, must have read the expression on his face, and she knew. Her lower lip trembled and for a moment she looked angry, as if she might have been nurturing some private reserve of rage that she would now unleash on him, or on Feyiz for telling her secret. Then the moment passed and she shuddered as she lowered her head.

"Damn it," she rasped.

The wind gusted in the passage behind Adam, almost shoving him into the stall with her. Snow cascaded from his clothes as he stumbled.

"It's true?" Two words. They were all he could manage.

Meryam met his gaze, spine stiffening with bravado, and she nodded. It was that moment of mustering her courage that broke him. Adam took three steps toward her and went to his knees. Meryam reached for him and he dragged her from her chair into an embrace that had them both on their knees. Body wracked with ragged breaths, sobs that could not seem to drag tears from his eyes, he cried out.

"I'm sorry," she said.

Adam inhaled sharply, the smell of Calliope still in his nose. Horror spread through him. He was still angry with himself and with Meryam, but the most terrible poison infecting him now was the truth he'd discovered. All his life, he had held himself up as one of the good guys. In old Western movies, he'd have worn a white hat. Now he was just as broken as everyone else, just as tainted. Not a bad guy, maybe, but not a good guy in the end.

What have I done?

"Tell me," he said.

She met his gaze firmly, chin high. Confronted, she would not shrink from it now. "It's a special brand. Acute myelogenous leukemia. They tried a couple of things, but even from the start I never saw a glimmer of hope in their eyes. I've been told to get my affairs in order."

Adam lifted a trembling hand to cover his mouth, grief hollowing him out.

"I'm so sorry," Meryam said again, amid her own shuddering tears. "I'm sorry I can't give you the life you wanted."

Adam held her at arm's length, studying her, as if he could see the cancer inside of her. "That's why you're sorry? Not because you didn't tell me? Not because you let me think you didn't care anymore, that you didn't want to get married? You're not sorry for that?"

Meryam waved her head back and forth, her whole body rocking. "I'm sorry for it all. But it wouldn't have been fair, love. Tying you to a dying woman. I prayed the diagnosis was wrong, and when the doctors confirmed it, I just prayed for another adventure, and then another. Adam and Eve conquer the world. I didn't know how many more adventures we'd have."

Adam stared at the dark, heavy circles beneath her eyes. He saw, at last, how prominent the bones in her cheeks had become, how thin even her neck seemed now. *It's not altitude sickness*, she had told him when she'd become ill that first morning, just before discovering the ark. He'd sensed something then but there had already been tension in their relationship and he hadn't wanted to press. Memories cascaded through his mind, moments when she'd stumbled or gotten sick or seemed so exhausted, and he had chalked it up to the stress of the project.

How could I not have seen it? How could I not have pressed for the truth?

"We're partners," he said, taking her face in his gloved hands, forcing her to meet his gaze. "This should've been us together."

Meryam scowled. "How does that work, Adam? How do we have cancer together? You're not the one who's going to die."

"Fuck's sake! I know I can't share your goddamn cancer! But you don't have to deal with this alone. That's always been the problem, hasn't it? You never really understood what it meant to be in love, to share your life—"

She ripped his hands away from her face and shoved him backward with such force that he fell on his ass. Shaking, she rose to her feet and retreated a step, glaring down at him.

"If you mean I never understood why people vanish into their relationships, you're right about that much. You knew that about me long before we were engaged. I wanted a partner, an ally, not the kind of romantic, fanciful bullshit spun by schoolgirls and women raised to cook your bloody dinner. I'm not looking for my other half, someone to complete my fucking puzzle. I'm whole unto myself, Adam. I wanted someone who was just as whole."

Adam heaved a shuddering sigh, anger seeping back into him. He pushed off the ground and rose to his feet.

"You want me to apologize for needing you? For loving you? For wanting to help you deal with this diagnosis?"

"And what would you have done?" Meryam demanded, shouting now.

She marched toward him and he stepped back out of the stall. The wind crashed along the passage, blasting snow around him. Heads poked out of the camp shelters and he saw the faces of some of the archaeology grad students, and then Mr. Avci. Silhouetted in the dark passage, he saw Feyiz standing and watching like some

silent monitor, a dark angel sent by God to record but not intervene.

Record, he thought. His camera was in his jacket pocket.
Calliope was nowhere to be seen. There would be no film of this
moment and for once Adam was grateful for the lack of footage.

"What the hell would you have done?" Meryam shouted, following him into the passage. "You'd have treated me like fine
China, locked me up in a cabinet somewhere to protect me, and
that would've killed me much faster than this damned mountain."

Adam couldn't argue against the truth. "I'd never have agreed
to this project, that's for sure."

Wiping at her tears, almost sneering, Meryam nodded. "My
point." She glanced at those who were watching them, then spotted the silhouette further up the passage. "Damn you, Feyiz. You
see what you've done?"

The whole of the ark seemed to shimmer with bitterness and
sorrow, to vibrate with hostility.

"Stop," Adam said.

Meryam wiped at her tears again, face red with anger. "It wasn't
his secret to tell! It's my life. Not his, and not yours!"

Adam had been feeling for a while that they had all been slowly
infected with a poison of the soul, and that it had been spreading.
But now it seemed so much worse, as if every time he exhaled, a
little more of him was leaving, and every breath he took was re-
placing him with something else. Some other, angrier, uglier
Adam.

Even as the thought struck him, he felt a tug inside him. The
strings of the marionette he'd imagined himself to be.

"It *is* my life," he said, but it wasn't him. His voice and his lips,
but not *him*. "How could you be so selfish?"

One of the staffers swore, shocked by the exchange. From
somewhere outside of himself, a sickness and horror spreading in
his mind, Adam could only watch and listen.

Meryam laughed. "Me? I'm the selfish one?"

Feyiz called his name. Adam heard the caution there, but could not respond.

His legs moved. His body turned. His arm cocked back.

He slapped Meryam so hard that she spun halfway round, the echo of the blow ricocheting off the walls up and down the passage. Moments of silence followed, filled only by the howl of the storm.

The ark itself seemed to hold its breath.

Something inside Adam began to laugh.

FOURTEEN

Walker woke to his name. Hands shook him roughly. His foot went astray, out from under the thick covering of the sleeping bag, the zipper scraping his shin. The cold air slithered inside and gooseflesh rippled across his naked flesh.

"Jesus, *what*?" he groaned, opening his eyes.

Father Cornelius knelt beside him, angry and urgent as he gave Walker one last shake. Polly stood behind him, just outside the tent. But her presence wasn't the problem. Walker glanced around, the past few hours coming back to him all at once. The tent did not belong to him and the heavy-duty sleeping bag was warm and soft but also not his own. Kim lay against him, her bare leg draped across him, and only now did her eyes begin to open.

The moment she saw the priest, she closed her eyes again and muttered something in Korean that Walker assumed was either a curse or a prayer. Then she slid down inside the sleeping bag, pulling it up over her head.

"Stop," Father Cornelius said, grabbing the corner of the sleeping bag and yanking it down to expose Kim's face and the upper part of her chest.

She cried out in alarm.

"Father, what the hell?" Walker snapped. "I know how this looks—"

"We don't care how it looks," Polly said, tugging the tent flap open further, staring in at the three of them.

"She's right." Father Cornelius patted his shoulder. "You two screwing is the least of my concerns. Get some clothes on and do it fast."

The priest reached up a hand and Polly helped him to his feet, rubbing one arthritic knee as he stood. When he'd left the tent and Polly had cinched the flaps closed behind him, Walker dragged his scattered clothes over to the sleeping bag and hurriedly dressed. Kim gazed at him in abject horror and then hid herself again.

"Come on," he said.

"I'm Catholic," her muffled voice explained from beneath the heavy sleeping bag.

"Didn't you see the look on his face? That wasn't about us."

Walker tossed Kim her clothes. She nodded and slipped into her bra, quickening her pace until—moments later—she pulled him toward her and kissed him so deeply that Walker had to break away to catch his breath.

"What—"

Kim smiled. "It's going to take a dark turn, now. Yes, I saw that look in the Father's eyes. So I wanted to let you know, right now, that this part, at least—this was good."

He took her hand, kissed her fingers, and she smiled again as she drew them back so she could finish dressing. Once they'd pulled their boots on, they left the tent and found Father Cornelius and Polly waiting in the stall, in front of the tent Ben had been sharing with the priest. Polly glanced out into the passage, glanced in either direction, and then nodded.

"I'm guessing whatever you translated from the bottom of the coffin, it doesn't bode well," Walker said.

Father Cornelius looked as if he might be sick. He ran a hand over the gray stubble that had appeared on his chin in the past two days.

"Some of it is a warning, like the writings on the lid and the encasement," the priest said. His pallor had turned gray and suddenly he looked very old to Walker. "And I won't claim I've cracked it completely."

"You've cracked it enough," Polly put in. "Just tell them."

The priest cleared his throat with a dry rattle. "Most of what's there—what was beneath the cadaver—is a history. An Apocrypha. In the era before Noah built the ark—"

"His name was really Noah?" Walker asked.

Father Cornelius fixed him with a searing glare. "Of course not. But I can't pronounce it and don't have time for guessing. It's Noah, all right? Or it's where the story began. Many ancient scholars believed that demons roamed the Earth in its infancy. In the fourth century Genesis Rabbah, Hebrews examining the early versions of the Bible interpreted certain passages to say that Noah took demons on board the ark. It's just one of the many examples of ancient texts that establish—"

"I'll take your word for it," Walker said, heart pounding. He didn't believe in any of this. So why did he feel a prickling at the back of his neck? Why did he wish he was anywhere but here?

"The same text, the Genesis Rabbah, discusses the idea that man existed in God's image until the days of Enos, and then we changed. I've never been persuaded by any of the translations I've seen. There's no clarity, but the suggestion is there that demons changed humanity in some fundamental way. This runs parallel to the myth of the Nephilim, who were supposed to have been born of a union between angels and human beings, or fallen angels and humans."

"Fallen angels?" Kim echoed. "You mean demons."

Father Cornelius grimaced. "Scholars can never agree. Tonight it doesn't matter. The only thing that does is that the history written inside the coffin tells the story of a world in which demons began to infect people with their own evil. Some kind of seer predicted the flood—a priest or magician or even something Noah saw in a dream. It's unclear, but Noah was persuaded. He built the ark for himself and his extended family. They brought plants and seeds and all the animals they thought they would need to settle wherever they landed, and they were ready when the flood came. But a demon called Shamdon found its way aboard. The demon murdered two of Noah's sons and a granddaughter before they were able to capture and kill it."

Walker waited, thinking there must be more to the story. Then he understood that he already knew how the tale ended. Kim and Polly were staring at the priest, but now both women turned their focus on him.

"The writing in the coffin—it identifies the demon by name?"

Father Cornelius nodded. "Shamdon."

Walker ran his hands through his hair, hanging his head. He could feel his pulse throbbing in his temples. "You know I don't believe any of this."

Kim moved nearer, drawing his eyes to hers. "I think you do."

"Is the body still back there?" he asked, looking to Polly.

"Still wrapped. It's just a husk. No way has that thing been walking around, hurting anyone."

"I agree," Father Cornelius said. "The cadaver is a shell. But the demon . . . I believe it's still here. Inside the ark . . . and inside one of us."

"We're talking about possession now?" Walker said.

The priest's gaze hardened. "We are."

Kim found her gloves and began to pull them on. "Come on, Walker. Meryam and Adam need to know. Whether they believe it or not, we've got to tell them."

His face flushed. Did he have to believe it completely himself in order to pass along what Father Cornelius had found? Maybe not. When Polly and the priest led the way out into the passage and Kim followed, he realized that his own feelings were of no consequence. Father Cornelius and Polly would pass along their findings. His only decision was whether or not to back them up.

He hurried to get his own gloves, then hauled on his thick, woolen hat. By the time he caught up with them, they were already to the reinforced stairs that led down to level two. Snow swirled up the steps, driven on gusts of wind, and Walker realized the noise he heard was the storm. They moved past the overhanging portion of the outer wall of the cave and into the open as they descended to the first level. Teeth chattering, he regretted not having taken the time to dress more thoroughly, but when Father Cornelius had woken him, he had not imagined he'd be leaving his quarters.

At first the shouts from below sounded as if they came from far away, carried on the wind or echoing off the mountainside. Kim had led them down the steps and now she started to hurry. Polly tried to take Father Cornelius by the arm but he barked at her to go and find out what the fuss was about.

Below, voices shouted Adam's name, ordered him to back off. Someone called out in urgent Turkish, but by then Walker was hurrying as well. One hand on the wall, he took the steps two at a time, the whole structure shuddering under his boots. Father Cornelius took his time, but old as he might be, he didn't need anyone's help. He'd used the word "fuss", but whatever had happened on level one, it was a hell of a lot more than that.

Another voice shouted. Meryam's. "Get your fucking hands off me!"

Walker hit the bottom of the steps at a run. Polly and Kim were ahead of him but he'd almost caught up by the time they'd reached the place where most of the staff were clustered. Kim shoved her way through, snapping at them, and Polly helped her clear a hole.

Through the gap, Walker spotted Meryam as she reeled backward. She staggered into shadow and then strode back into the light, blood pouring from her nose and a split in her lower lip.

"Keep back from him," she told the staffers gathered around. "He's lost his fucking marbles."

Polly pushed through them, ready for a fight. Feyiz stepped in front of Adam, blocking his access to Meryam. A cut by his eye had started to swell, and he put his hands up warily.

"Stop, Adam," Feyiz said. "This isn't what you want. Not if you love her."

Walker pushed through the staffers and came up beside Kim. His fists opened and closed, but there were others ready to step in as well.

Adam moved too quickly for all of them. Face carved with fury, he lunged at Feyiz, hammered at his face with such ferocity that Feyiz dropped to the snow. Adam straddled him, fists smashing down with a sickening, meaty sound. Blood smeared Adam's fist as four people got hold of him, one student yanking his head back by the hair. Savage, snarling, eyes wide, he surged upward and grabbed Polly by the throat. She whipped an arm up and broke his grip, struck him two solid blows to the chest with a speed that indicated martial arts training. Taking his wrist, she twisted and kicked him in the softness of his armpit, then kicked again, knocking him to the ground.

They were on him, then. Walker rushed in, put a knee on his left arm as Polly took the other, and two grad students held his legs. Kim stood above him, shouting at him to calm down, even as Meryam appeared beside her, wiping blood from her face.

Adam roared, trying to fight them off. Struck dumb, they all stared at him. In the midst of a lull in the whipping wind, Walker heard an all-too-familiar click and turned to see Hakan aiming a pistol at Adam.

Walker could have drawn his own weapon, but to do that, he'd have to let go.

"No!" Meryam barked, throwing herself in front of the gun.

"You don't see," Hakan told her. "Look at him again. This isn't your man."

Someone had helped Feyiz to his feet. He leaned on a student's shoulder, trying not to fall down again. "Don't do this, Uncle."

Hakan laughed softly. "I'm not going to kill the man. Not as long as he keeps his hands to himself from now on. Bind him hand and foot, and bind him well, so I don't have to shoot him."

Others moved in to take over. From somewhere they'd produced the sort of plastic zip ties that police officers sometimes used in place of handcuffs. Walker surrendered his position, but he watched carefully to make sure Adam wouldn't fight them. Polly had to twist one of his arms around, but beyond that, Adam only smiled, eyes cold, a thin stream of bloody drool sliding down his chin as if he'd bitten his tongue.

"There's an open stall a short way along," Hakan said, gesturing with the gun. "Take him down there and we'll figure out how to hold him. Someone bring a light."

As his Kurdish workers moved to help, Polly began to dismantle some of the lighting in the camp, repositioning it as Hakan had asked.

Walker stood, glaring at Hakan. "Is that Zeybekci's gun?"

"Better in my hands tonight than in his," Hakan replied.

Walker didn't argue, though he didn't trust anyone with a firearm right now. Even the weight of his own gun against the small of his back felt too dangerous, too easily turned against them all. Adam wasn't himself—Walker didn't want to think about what might happen if he himself lost control.

Kim stood with Meryam, speaking quietly to her, checking over her injuries. Approaching them, Walker saw that Meryam had begun to cry. The sight of tears on the face of someone so formidable cut him deeply. The whole scene had unfolded with a surreal quality, a nightmarish aura that made it all seem a terrible dream. But now he saw how tired Meryam looked, drawn and sorrowful and confused as the blood continued to trickle across her mouth and chin, and the realness of it all made him tremble.

"Hakan's right," Meryam said. "Adam wouldn't ever raise a hand to me. Especially now."

Walker saw Father Cornelius pushing through the gathered staff.

"Tell her," the priest said, the deep lines crinkling at the corners of his eyes. "It's all happening too fast."

Meryam wiped at the blood on her chin but did not try to erase her tears. "Tell me what?"

"What you already know," Walker replied. "What you and Hakan have both just said. That wasn't Adam at all. It was something else . . . and we think we know its name."

Meryam winced as Dr. Dwyer pushed the needle through her cheek, tugging the thread out the other side. She hissed air in through her teeth.

"Sorry," the doctor said. "I thought the topical I put on would dull the pain."

"I'm sure it did," Meryam said. "Still not a pleasant feeling, having someone stabbing holes in your face. How badly will it scar?"

Dr. Dwyer tugged on the thread and tied it off. "Four stitches. Not a huge scar, really, and it'll add character. But if it bothers you, a good plastic surgeon could make it barely noticeable."

The doctor stepped back, examined his handiwork. "You want to talk about this?"

His eyes were kind, but Meryam had no room for kindness now.

All it would do was soften her, and she needed to be nothing but hard edges and blunt force at the moment.

"I wouldn't know how to start."

Dr. Dwyer nodded. "Try to get some rest. The painkillers I gave you should make you sleepy and I'm sure your body's already exhausted. Decisions can wait for morning."

Meryam managed a half smile. "Get some rest yourself."

The doctor had dark circles beneath his eyes and as far as Meryam knew, *he* didn't have cancer. She figured that under the circumstances, she had been acquitting herself pretty well. Yes, she'd been burning the candle at both ends, but her light was going to burn out soon enough—no point in conserving that flame.

She lay down on her side on a thick bedroll, dragging a blanket over her. The heaters in the infirmary were doing their job, but with the frigid air blasting through the passages of the ark, there was a limit to what they could accomplish.

The doctor had allowed Patil and Zeybekci to go down to the mess to get something to eat. He'd sent one of the students with them, a young woman named Belinda, and she'd been instructed to bring them back to the infirmary as soon as they'd finished eating. But their temporary absence didn't mean Meryam was alone. Just a few feet away from her, Armando Olivieri lay with his head on a small pillow. Dr. Dwyer had sedated him, but even unconscious, the old professor's brow was furrowed, his sleep troubled.

Drowsy, she let her eyes close . . . and an image of Adam filled her mind, savage and cruel, his eyes bright with malice. She felt the sting of that first blow, the first time he had ever laid hands on her. Had she seen a flicker of strange fire in his eyes, a flash of color that didn't belong there? She imagined him smiling, saw a riot of sharp black teeth inside his mouth, jerked back and caught a glimpse of the horns jutting from his skull, pushing through his hair. . . .

Grunting, Meryam jerked awake. Her heart drummed in her

chest, filling up her throat so that she could barely breathe. She stared at the unmoving form of Professor Olivieri beside her. He'd turned on his bedroll, his back to her now. As she caught her breath she took in her surroundings, recognized that the lights in the infirmary had been turned down. *A dream*, she thought, but it had felt more like a haunting.

Catching her breath, she listened to Olivieri and watched his back expand and contract with his own deep breathing. Somehow she felt his breaths were too even, that he seemed not to be sleeping at all, but to be waiting. Listening.

Hugging herself beneath the blanket, she scooted a bit further from him, listening to the dark. Meryam forced herself not to dwell on the conclusions Father Cornelius and Ben had made. All she wanted now was for Adam to be all right, to be released by whatever had seized his mind.

Meaning you believe, she thought. *You believe in the demon*. Its body might be dead, but its essence remained. Ben had talked about ancient disease, some kind of contagion that nobody had been exposed to in thousands of years, and now Meryam realized it was precisely that . . . just not in any way either of them had been willing to imagine.

Her face hurt and a dagger of pain stabbed into her skull, just above her left eye. Fighting drowsiness, Meryam peeled back her blanket and climbed stiffly to her feet. Her boots and jacket were nearby and she winced several times as she carefully dragged them on. Dr. Dwyer was nowhere to be seen. Olivieri still had his back to her, but he seemed too still, so that she half expected him to speak to her, there in the gloom of the half light. She waited a moment, sure he would talk. It would have been good to have help and she knew Olivieri would understand. Others might try to stop her. Before she had seen the blunt malice in Adam's eyes, the glint of something she knew was not him staring out at her from his eyes, she'd have tried to stop herself.

Not anymore.

Quietly, she padded from the infirmary. Voices whispered along the passage off to the right, quiet footfalls headed her way, so she darted to the left and soon lost herself in the silent shadows of the ark. In the middle of the night, nobody would be back there, except perhaps a guard or two. Nobody would want to be there now, especially.

It was there. The demon. Shamdon.

Meryam hurried.

Walker's cheeks stung with the cold. Exhausted as he was, it seemed to affect him more now. His old injuries ached and he felt ancient as he trudged along beside Kim. Dr. Dwyer scurried ahead of them, frantic in his disapproval. Bringing up the rear was Father Cornelius, his age manifesting itself at last.

"Just let her sleep until morning," said the doctor, flustered by the way they ignored him, and growing more so with every step.

When Dr. Dwyer tried to stand his ground, blocking their way, Kim put a hand on his shoulder and gently brushed him aside.

"This is Meryam's project," she said. "If her partner were in any condition to make decisions, I'd defer to your medical advice. But unless you think it would be popular among the staff for Dr. Walker and myself to seize control of the ark ourselves, any decisions need to be approved by Meryam."

"In the morning," the doctor said, his voice a harsh whisper as they approached the infirmary. He didn't want to disturb his patients.

Walker liked that about him. "Look, Doc . . ." He paused, gave Dr. Dwyer a moment to gather his wits and calm his frantic heart. "What happened with Adam downstairs scared the shit out of everyone. That's bad because there's a lot of crying and praying going on down there right now, a lot of folks wishing they'd never climbed up here in the first place. But all of a sudden, nobody's fighting. Hakan's workers are helping keep watch over Adam. The grad students aren't arguing over whether or not this is really Noah's ark or whether they believe in angels and demons or whether there's an actual fucking demon in this cave with us. Pretty soon they're going to start wondering if Adam killed the four people who've gone missing in the last two nights, and if not, who did, because you damn well better believe they think those people are dead. But suddenly, for the first time and maybe not for very long, everyone is on the same page. We work together, gather as much of the research that's already been done, and the second the blizzard dies out, we get off this mountain."

Dr. Dwyer nodded vigorously, glancing from Walker to Kim. "Okay, that's good news, right? No more fighting. We evacuate as soon as possible."

Walker felt a thin thread of terror weaving through him. "That's the plan."

"But why disturb Meryam? Just let her sleep awhile," Dr. Dwyer pleaded.

Kim threw up her hands. "The arguing will begin again soon enough. The poison of this demon is in us now."

"I don't believe—" Dr. Dwyer began.

"Once people start fighting again, the argument's going to be obvious. What to do about Adam."

Father Cornelius cleared his throat. "And if Adam isn't possessed, then who is it? Everyone will hazard a guess, pointing the finger at someone they already don't like. The paranoia is going to turn ugly very fast."

Walker studied Dr. Dwyer. "We need to be ready for that, need to keep everyone on the same page and working together. If we can do that, maybe nobody else has to get hurt."

"Please just—" the doctor said, hurrying after him as Walker reached the entrance of the infirmary.

"Be quiet," Kim finished for him. "We know."

Walker stood just inside the infirmary. He'd mustered up some momentum from deep within, just enough to keep going. Now he felt it bleeding out of him. In the low light, he saw only Professor Olivieri on a cot. The others were all empty.

"Shit," Dr. Dwyer muttered.

"Where's she gone?" Kim asked sharply. "Doctor, we can't let anyone out of sight now, especially not anyone who's been exposed to the presence of . . ."

"Of the demon," Father Cornelius finished.

A rustling of cloth drew their attention, and then a rasping voice spoke.

"Father, you need to consider the bitumen."

Another rustle of cloth and Olivieri rolled over and looked at them in the half light. He had no idea what the man had done to end up in the infirmary, but his head lolled and it was clear Olivieri had been sedated. A thin line of drool gleamed on his cheek.

"Armando, now is not the time," Father Cornelius said.

Olivieri's face contorted into a snarl. "Now is the only time. Your arrogance will cost lives, perhaps your own among them. You are not the only scholar here, Father."

Walker flicked his gaze toward the priest, letting his confusion and curiosity show.

Kim looked back out into the passageway, searching for Meryam.

"Father?" Walker prodded.

The priest loosened his scarf. "All right, Armando. What about the bitumen?"

Olivieri coughed, a dry rattle that gave him a momentary paroxysm. He settled down and then stared blearily at the priest. "Helen Marshall's team studied the remains of many of the ark's passengers. Many of them wore charms around their necks on leather cords—shards of the same black bitumen that they used to encase the demon's coffin."

"Your point?" Walker asked.

"Have you read the historian Berossus?"

"We don't have time for this," Walker said, looking anxiously at Kim, who shook her head out in the passage. No sign of Meryam.

"Third century, b.c.?" Father Cornelius said. "I've read of him, seen some summaries, but have never had the opportunity to read the original text."

"Small wonder. A minor historian, at best, and he reported many stories passed down to him as if he'd heard them firsthand. It's only my research into the ark that led me to him. Even then there were scholars who argued the existence of Noah and of the ark, and tried to find evidence but instead found only more stories. Berossus reported that in his youth he had met a man who claimed to have found the ruin of the ark on one of the mountains of this range. The people who lived in the shadow of the mountain, Berossus reported, wore shards of hardened bitumen on cords around their necks as wards against evil."

"Like the ark's passengers," Father Cornelius observed.

Kim brushed her hair from her eyes. "Was the bitumen supposed to have magical properties? Or did they perform some kind of ritual to imbue it with those protections?"

"I thought of it when Helen showed me the charms, but that was before all of this and I'd forgotten until now," Olivieri said gruffly. "I don't recall it verbatim. Berossus may have said, or he may not, but if the family who built this ark took the time to cover the coffin with bitumen—"

"They coated the coffin with at least six inches of that shit," Walker said. "Why bother if they didn't feel it gave them some kind of protection?"

"They must have known something of the demon still lived," Father Cornelius said thoughtfully. "That its essence continued to be a threat."

"Forever," Kim added grimly. "Like nuclear waste, put in barrels and then buried inside cement and steel bunkers."

The infirmary went quiet. Walker glanced around at the people gathered there—the priest and the doctor, Kim and Olivieri—and knew it might mean nothing. But it might mean *something*. It might mean life or death.

"Father, can you work with Professor Olivieri? Find any of the charms that Professor Marshall recovered. Then dig out some of the bitumen from the encasement and separate out other shards. We need enough for everyone."

Dr. Dwyer huffed. "You believe this? It's a two-thousand-year-old folk tale."

Walker stared at him and couldn't stop the dry chuckle that escaped his lips. "Yeah? What the hell do you think we're standing in?"

The doctor started to argue, but Kim hissed for him to be silent, holding up a hand. She stood in the doorway, listening to the sounds of the cave.

"Someone's shouting."

An awful melancholy fell over Walker, and he saw in her eyes that Kim shared it, as if a moment before they had been attempting to stoke an ember of hope, and now it had been extinguished.

"Father, you and the professor get to work," he said, moving toward Kim. "Let's go."

They followed the shouting. With the stalls and passages and openings between levels, the ark could play tricks with sound, throwing whispers into dark corners. But as they reached the back wall, the shouts grew louder and more numerous. Walker hit the ladder first, his thoughts toward what it would take for his team to get down the mountain on their own. How long before they could be ready? Could Father Cornelius make the climb in the storm? Would one of the Kurds guide them? Maybe Hakan himself, who seemed so determined to halt the project.

He dropped to the floor, turned, and raced to the ladder that led down to level one. Through the opening, he saw the glow of flames. Meryam stood there, pools of orange light flickering on her face, shadows moving like some undersea hell.

"Kim," he said. "Fire."

She responded with a string of colorful English profanity. By the time she finished he was already rushing down that ladder, Kim following.

"Get back!" Meryam snapped.

Walker leaped the last three rungs and spun to face her, but Meryam hadn't been talking to him. Polly had arrived from one of the passageways, a fire extinguisher in her hands, and Meryam had rushed to block her way.

"Are you out of your fucking mind?" Polly screamed. "There's nothing but dry wood in here and you started a goddamn fire!"

Meryam jabbed a finger in the air, as if that alone would keep Polly from moving. "Then your job is to keep it from spreading, but you let it burn! You hear me? You let the fucking thing burn!"

Kim came up beside Walker. There were a handful of others there—Feyiz, Mr. Avci, and a grad student named Chloe—and Calliope stood in the corner, getting it all on film. Walker could see the reflection of the flames off the lens of her camera.

"Meryam," Feyiz said, starting toward her, his hands out in supplication.

"No," Meryam said, swallowing hard as she fought back tears. "Not you. You're the last person who should be talking to me right now."

So nobody did.

She had unwrapped the corpse of the demon, maybe doused it with some kind of accelerant, and set it on fire. The dry bones popped and the wisps of ancient papyrus-like skin crisped and curled, and ashes floated up into the rising smoke. Flames danced inside the skull, making a hideous jack-o'-lantern out of the wicked curve of the open jaws. The horns blackened further, somehow untouched by light or flame, as if determined to declare themselves infernal.

Walker saw the fire beginning to eat through the timbers under the cadaver, spreading to the wall. Polly and Chloe and Feyiz all shuffled forward, as if they might all rush in at once.

"Wait," Walker said, sliding past Meryam.

She started to protest as he reached for the fire extinguisher in Polly's hands. Polly resisted, confused, but then relinquished the metal canister. Walker took it, and turned to face the popping, crackling, blackening bones of the demon.

"Meryam's right," he said. "We're gonna let it burn."

FIFTEEN

Meryam's skin prickled with the memory of heat. The cadaver lay on the canted floor at the rear of the ark's lowest level, nothing but charred bones, ashes, and glowing embers. They flared orange, popped and hissed, and then went dark one by one. The demon's horns still jutted from its skull, but most of its skeleton had been burned down to withered framework, and some of the bones had crumbled.

Half an hour, maybe less, and the demon's remains were reduced to this.

The demon, she thought, staring at those glowing embers. In some strange way, she felt she ought to be celebrating. She believed in this thing, in its evil, and if evil truly existed, that opened up so many other questions she had thought she had answered for herself years before. Adam had lived with terror as a boy, real fear inspired by his grandmother's belief in an evil spirit hiding inside her clock. He'd always lied to himself and to her about how much of that he'd believed. He had fought against believing because of what it would mean about those days, those long nights.

Now the evil had slipped inside of him, almost as if the dybbuk had cracked open the door into his soul all those years ago, and this thing, Shamdon, had found its way in.

When she reached her soot-blackened hand to wipe at her tears, her whole body began to shake.

One of the dark figures at the back of the ark moved toward the crumbling, smoking remains of the demon. Walker, she saw. He wore a grim expression as he approached the thing, raised a heavy boot, and smashed his heel into the face of the demon. The skull gave way, crushed to black powder. A puff of sparks rose.

A line of fire had spread to the wall behind the remains, but Walker lifted the extinguisher and blasted it. He had kept the blaze under control the whole time. The cadaver had burned remarkably fast, nothing but dry skin and bones, but there had been a great deal of smoke. Meryam felt it in her hair and clothing and at the back of her throat. The stink would remain with her for days. Perhaps forever.

She winced and glanced around at the shadowed figures. For the first time, it occurred to her that forever might end for her right here in the ark. Meryam wasn't going to let that happen.

"How much of it do you think we can lay off on the demon?" she asked, scanning the faces of those around her. Wyn Douglas and Polly Bennett. Kim and Walker. Mr. Avci and Father Cornelius. Calliope, with her fucking camera.

No, don't hate her for that. Hate her if you want, but not for that. Adam would want this all on film.

"I don't know what you mean," said the old priest.

"Yes you do. Our behavior, mine included. I've got some ugly shit happening in my life even outside of this nightmare, but still I wonder if it's been influencing me. Influencing all of us."

Walker wiped his boot heel on the timber floor. "It has or it hasn't. Doesn't matter. From this point forward, we watch each other and we look inside ourselves. What's happened to Adam isn't just influence, it's full on . . ."

She could see he didn't want to say the word, so she said it for him. "Possession."

"Father," Kim said, "was it moving it from the box that did it? Allowed it to . . . move more freely?"

"That may be," Father Cornelius replied. "It does seem bolder now. But we have to assume those who've vanished have been killed, and that it used one of the people inside the ark to kill them, which suggests that either Adam or someone else had been possessed before we moved the cadaver."

"We can't trust anyone," Walker said. "I could be looking at you, talking to you, and you might be the demon. No way to know."

Meryam inhaled the smoky air. A cold wind slithered down the passage. For a moment they all stared at one another, wondering.

"No," Wyn Douglas said. "Right now, we *do* know. It's taken control of Adam. So whatever we're going to do, whatever decisions we're going to make, let's make them."

Mr. Avci agreed. Polly and Kim both nodded.

Father Cornelius coughed. Smoke inhalation had gotten to them all. "I disagree. The demon is going to continue to plague us. And we have no way of knowing what more it might be capable of."

"Meryam destroyed the remains," Wyn said. "There's nothing left of it."

"And yet I've just come from seeing Adam," Father Cornelius said. "He's awake. His eyes are open and he's grinning. When I asked who it was, lying there in the infirmary, he spit on me."

Walker whispered a curse that might have been a prayer.

"So what do you suggest?" Polly asked, shuddering. "And please suggest something, because just doing nothing—"

"I intend to do something," Father Cornelius interrupted. "It's all I can think to do. But I need you all to agree that it must be done, that there is no other recourse, and that you will exert your influence to calm the rest of the staff if it ruffles feathers. We can't be fighting about faith right now. This demon predates my own religion. If it is truly what I believe it to be, then it predates them all. But if there is any way to help Adam and to protect the rest of us, the only thing I can think of is an exorcism."

Mr. Avci began to shake his head immediately. "I think this is a very bad idea. Very bad. Several of the Turkish students are troubled enough already. And the guides, Hakan's workers—"

"Don't speak for them," Polly interrupted. "They've all just seen what's happened with Adam. If you have your own troubles with it, say so, but we've all been working together for weeks. The Muslims and Jews on staff don't need to believe in Christianity to want us to try everything to protect them."

Mr. Avci huffed and fell silent. Meryam nodded her thanks to Polly.

"Do you know the rite?" Walker asked, staring at the priest. "I've always thought it was pure bullshit, but I know that priests who are approved to perform an exorcism go through rigorous training."

"I haven't had that training," Father Cornelius said. "But I've observed the rite being performed. I understand its components. I'm sure the pontiff would not approve, but I'm not sure what other choice we have. The danger posed by the presence of the demon outweighs whatever danger the rite might pose to me, personally."

Walker reached up and massaged the back of his own neck as though he was fighting an oncoming migraine. Meryam understood, but she had come to a place in her mind where she recognized that certain things simply must be done. Setting fire to the cadaver had been a necessary step, and so was this.

"Our options are to sit and wait for the demon to kill someone else, or to at least try to do something about it," she said.

"Or climb down the mountain in the middle of a blizzard," Wyn Douglas added.

Meryam turned to Polly. "Go to the infirmary. Ask Hakan and Feyiz to bring Adam here. Make sure he's cuffed."

Mr. Avci began to speak her name and Meryam shot him a withering glance.

"Your objections are noted, Avci. Report them to your government if you get off this bloody mountain alive."

The air in the passage had grown close and stale, and strangely warm. Meryam told herself it had to be body heat, now that Feyiz and Hakan had joined them. She told herself that, and she tried to force herself to believe it. According to Polly, the storm still raged outside. She had gone to check on the rest of the staff and found most of them huddled together on level two, not far from the infirmary, and a handful of others in the camp on level one. Morning must only be a few hours away, but the temperature had continued to drop, and ice had formed on the outside of some of the plastic sheeting.

Not here, where the embers still glowed among the demon's scorched remains. Kim stood beside Father Cornelius. The old priest knelt on a pillow that had been brought to him. On the timber floor in front of them, Adam lay on his back, hands now bound in front of him. Another zip tie had been cinched around his ankles. He wore the same stupid, silent grin he'd had when they had marched him back here. Beads of sweat glistened on his forehead. His skin had an oily sheen and the yellowed hue of old parchment.

Something rose up the back of Meryam's throat when she looked at him. She didn't know if it would be a scream or a stream of vomit, but she fought it back down.

"He's Jewish," Feyiz said softly, standing beside her.

"And I'm Muslim," she replied.

But she felt the lie when she spoke the words. Adam might be more Jewish than she was Muslim, but neither of them had ever been very religious. They were both seekers, just looking for the truth. She'd always hoped the truth would reveal some hidden mysteries in the world, and Adam had hoped for the opposite. Now here she was, getting exactly what she'd wanted, in the worst way imaginable.

And it's warm back here, she thought. The wind did not seem to want to come back here now, the cold staying away. *Body heat*. But she knew that wasn't it.

Father Cornelius had been at it for the better part of an hour already. Prayer after prayer. For some of them, he had enlisted Kim Seong's assistance, as the only faithful, avowed Catholic among them. Hakan and Walker stood at the ready, looming over Adam, ready to step in if the demon lashed out. Polly and Wyn were guarding the passages that led toward the front of the cave, making certain they wouldn't be interrupted. Mr. Avci and Feyiz observed with Meryam. A strange crew to perform an exorcism. The word itself felt absurd when she rolled it around in her brain, so why not a group that felt equally ridiculous?

So warm, she thought. She glanced at the little dots of flame that still flickered in the demon's ashes. The smoke had been cleared by the wind blowing through the cave, before the wind had begun to refuse to sweep the passage clean. Even the smell of smoke had abated, partly replaced by something else. Something she could at first not identify. Then it struck her. The odor reminded her of the strong scent of rich, black tea, of loose leaves when she'd first open a container. Dry and old and earthen.

"It smells strange back here," Calliope said from behind the camera, as if reading her mind.

A frown creased Meryam's forehead. Was Calliope crying? She

glanced from the camerawoman to Adam and back again, noting the way Calliope looked at him. Really noticing for the first time.

Oh, you bitch, she thought, and then she forced her thoughts away, put her focus back on Adam. Jealousy would wait. For years she had envisioned herself as the one in the spotlight, the one who got the attention, and Adam had supported that vision. He was her partner and coauthor, but he was the man behind the camera. Had wanting the spotlight blinded her from seeing things she ought to have noticed?

Stop, she told herself. *There's nothing to be gained from this. Worry about your relationship when Adam's free.*

"Are you sure this is what you want?" Feyiz asked quietly as the prayers continued.

Meryam refused to meet his eyes. "None of this is what I want. Now hush."

Father Cornelius put his fingers in a mug full of water he'd already blessed and spattered a bit of it onto Adam's face. Adam inhaled sharply, grin widening, and snapped his head around to stare at Meryam.

"I should really tell you," he said.

The voice that came from his lips was not his. It was *like* his . . . enough like his that most of them probably would not have known the difference. But it had a ragged edge, a taunting quality that did not belong to him.

". . . hasten to our call for help," Father Cornelius prayed, raising his voice as if in response. "Snatch from ruination and from the clutches of the noonday devil this human being made in your image and likeness. Strike terror, Lord, into the beast now laying waste your vineyard. Fill your servants with courage to fight manfully against that reprobate dragon—"

He continued, splashing holy water onto Adam's face and body again. For the first time, that painful, rictus grin faltered. Adam's nostrils flared and he sneered at the priest. When Kim murmured an "amen," some punctuation for the priest's prayers, he gave a soft laugh.

It isn't real, Meryam told herself. *This is some kind of game, something Adam devised for the camera.*

Meryam's chest ached. Her right hand fluttered up to cover her mouth and she felt as if a barbed hook had been set deep in her gut and begun to tug hard, down inside her. In that moment she would have prayed to any god, given anything to be able to believe that it was all some prank, some hoax that Adam had not even shared with her.

Her eyes burned with tears she seemed unable to shed. Calliope had no problem weeping, but Meryam could not.

"Let your mighty hand cast him out of your servant, Adam," Father Cornelius went on.

Meryam forced herself to breathe, inhaling deeply the unnatural warmth of the passage, the scent of tea and smoke haunting her. Beyond the priest, the demon's charred horns still gleamed with reflected light.

On the floor, Adam began to shake. His grin twitched and his skull juddered against the ancient timber. A single fly buzzed past Meryam's head and at first it meant nothing to her, just an insect, until it landed on Adam's cheek and she heard Feyiz swear in Kurmanji beside her.

"Someone want to tell me where the fuck the fly came from?" Walker asked quietly.

For the first time, she heard fear in the voice of that stubborn, stalwart, brilliant man. Real fear, not simple trepidation. And it terrified her. Where had the fly come from, indeed, up on the side of this mountain in the middle of a blizzard?

The fly crawled across the bridge of Adam's nose, wings twitching. Calliope whimpered and began to lower her camera.

"Keep shooting," Meryam snapped at her, and she brought the camera back up.

Adam laughed as Father Cornelius continued his prayers. Adam's head turned again and he stared at Meryam with boiling contempt.

"I should tell you," the demon said. "I'm going to tell you, now, so I can watch your face when you hear it from this mouth."

Meryam stepped forward. The heat and the thickness of the air seemed to try to hold her back but she waded through it. Hakan stepped in her way, almost as if he did not hate her, almost as if he wished to protect her, but she thrust him aside and dropped to her knees and stared into the eyes of the thing behind her lover's eyes.

"He fucked her. Is that your big surprise? I don't need you to tell me."

The grin pulled so wide that she saw Adam's lower lip split, and then her tears came at last.

"So you know?" the demon whispered. "No. You suspected but you didn't know. Not until now. The pain in your eyes is glorious."

"You pulled the strings," Meryam whispered. "You made it happen."

The demon smirked. "Of course I did. But I promise you, he made it easy."

Meryam froze. She felt hands on her and shrugged them off, thinking they belonged to Hakan. Instead she heard Feyiz's soft voice in her ear, and when he touched her again she allowed him to pull her away, out of the priest's way. She glanced up and saw Walker's sympathy, saw Kim's fear, but she would not look at the camera again. Would not look at Calliope.

"Keep shooting," she said, just in case the woman lost her nerve again. Calliope might want to look away, but Meryam would not allow it. For Adam's sake, it would all be on film. After she was dead, he would be famous. He would be wealthy. He would always remember that she loved him.

Of course, she'd be famous, too. But she'd be dead.

The priest's voice lulled her. She could only stand and stare. The lights flickered and the wind gusted for the first time in long minutes, forever hours, but the wind itself felt warm. The fly buzzed around Adam's face and alighted on his lower lip. It crawled onto the teeth that were revealed by that terrible grin.

"I adjure you, ancient serpent, by the judge of the living and the dead, by your Creator, by Him who has the power to consign you to Hell, to depart now in fear. Yield not to my own person but to the minister of Christ. For it is the power of Christ that compels you, who brought you low by His cross . . ."

Adam continued to shake, slammed his head against the timbers again and again. The fly took wing again as he laughed, and then the insect landed upon the gleaming curve of his widened eye. He did not even blink.

Mr. Avci began to pray in his own language, to his own god. From far off to the right, in the shadows of the mouth of the passage there, Wyn Douglas sobbed loudly and began to shout denials, insisting that none of this could be happening.

Meryam's skin stayed warm. Ice formed at the base of her brain. Her vision began to darken. How long since she'd eaten or slept? She wondered as she lost feeling in her hands and feet.

How long till morning?

Detached from herself, she spoke his name. Then she screamed it, as if she were watching his grip loosen from the edge of a cliff, as if she were watching him fall into an abyss. And wasn't she, really? Meryam knew the answer, and screamed his name again.

Laughing, his whole body shaking, Adam began to utter the filthiest profanity. He lolled his head again, stared at her as he raised it and smashed it down on the timber floor, as if he wanted to watch her eyes while he split open his own skull. Meryam thought she might still be screaming, but she couldn't be sure.

Walker and Hakan dropped to their knees. Father Cornelius

might have shouted for them to do so. They grabbed Adam's shoulders and pinned him down, and Walker held his head in place so he could not smash it against the wood again. Blood seeped through Adam's hair and down the back of his neck, under the collar of his shirt.

When Meryam exhaled again, her breath turned to mist. She felt the warmth still, but the air had gone frigid. Something shifted beyond the priest and his helpers and she looked and saw that the horned, crushed skull of the demon had tilted to one side, as if the caved-in face, the charred and shattered eye sockets, had turned to gaze at her as well.

"Depart, then, transgressor. Depart, seducer, full of lies and cunning, foe of virtue, persecutor of the innocent. Give place, abominable creature, give way to—"

The lights went out. Someone shrieked. Seconds passed that Meryam could only count in the gallop of her heart, and then the lights flickered on again.

Adam's eyes were closed. His chest rose and fell in a sigh. His color had improved, although the beads of sweat remained. He hitched another breath and his eyes fluttered open for a moment, then closed again. Meryam was sure he had looked at her. That *Adam* had seen her, not the other thing.

Behind the camera, Calliope whispered a "thank you" to whatever power she'd prayed to.

"Did it work?" Kim said. "Is that . . . Father, did it work? Is it gone?"

Father Cornelius dipped his fingers into the cup of holy water and drew the sign of the Christian cross on Adam's forehead. Meryam felt a ripple of distaste, but beneath that ripple ran a river of hope.

Adam only sighed again at the priest's touch.

"Cornelius," Walker said grimly. "Damn it, *is it gone?*"

"I believe so."

Hakan muttered his disapproval but Feyiz hissed him into silence and turned to the priest. "You did it."

Father Cornelius did not look at him. Instead, he turned toward Meryam and for a moment she could only see the way Adam's head had lolled to one side, and the crumbling, burned skull of the demon that had done the same. Then she saw the gentle sadness in the priest's eyes.

"I did nothing," he said. "I hadn't even finished. I don't know if my prayers did anything at all. I may not be strong enough."

Kim backed away from them. "But you said it was gone."

"I think it is," the priest replied, the pain of apology in his eyes. "But I didn't drive it . . . and I don't know where it went."

Dr. Dwyer gasped as his eyes fluttered open, less startled to be woken in the night than by the fact that he'd managed to nod off in the first place. The last time he'd glanced at the clock in the infirmary it had been nearly two a.m. and his skin had been crawling with anxiety. Father Cornelius had admitted that they intended to attempt an exorcism and it had felt both unreal and terrifying. He had lain on a cot, warmer and safer than the rest of the staff, he felt sure, but he hadn't felt warm or safe. Somehow he'd fallen asleep.

Now he groaned and tried to curl into a slightly more fetal position to take the pressure off of those knotted muscles, hoping to find his way back to sleep.

Something scuffed the floor behind him.

He froze, his face to the wall and his back to the rest of the infirmary. The pain in his back crept into his neck and he knew he needed to exhale and stretch, but instead he could only listen. Outside the infirmary, the wind made the plastic sheeting flap. Not for the first time, he imagined the whole cave inhaling and exhaling, the ark breathing.

The doctor squeezed his eyes shut. Distant voices reached him as whispers, members of the staff camping just along the passage, where many had relocated tonight so they could be closer together, farther from the open cave mouth and the merciless storm.

From behind him there came the rustle of clothing. He wanted to ask who it was, but a smell filled the infirmary, a rich, earthen scent with a hint of rot beneath it. Suddenly he was eight years old again, trying to be brave now that he and his brother finally had separate rooms, but scared . . . so scared of the skeletal hand of the ash tree whose fingerlike branches scratched at the window with every gust of wind.

Dr. Dwyer blew out a breath and forced the memory away. For a second it had been so vivid, the fear in his heart so familiar from his childhood, that it felt as if he'd been back there, home in his bed. Some nights he'd get so frightened that he would go into his brother Teddy's room and shake him awake. Teddy, two years his elder, would punch him in the arm and tell him not to be a pussy.

Don't be a pussy, he thought.

Teddy would have been on target tonight. Dr. Dwyer exhaled again. In a sleep-fog, he'd forgotten he had patients in here tonight. They had taken Adam away, and Professor Olivieri had gone off as well, but Zeybekci and Dev Patil were still here.

Idiot. Laughing at himself, trying to shake off the fear that still clung to him, Dr. Dwyer rolled over on the cot and saw Zeybecki rising from his own cot, on the other side of the infirmary. With only one light on, a soft glow in the corner, the young Turkish monitor almost seemed as if he might be sleepwalking. Zeybecki hung his head, sniffed once, then wiped his hands on his sweater.

"You feeling all right?" Dr. Dwyer asked quietly, not wanting to wake Patil, whom he'd given antibiotics and a heavy dose of anti-anxiety meds that would also help him sleep. Whatever he'd inhaled when moving the cadaver had sickened Patil, but although more tests would be necessary, Dr. Dwyer didn't think the paleo-pathologist had suffered any lasting damage. He'd managed to go down to the mess with Zeybekci and eat a little something. Now the man needed rest and further observation.

Zeybekci, though, could leave anytime he felt up to it.

"It's still night," Dr. Dwyer said, trying to get a look at his face, wondering if the man might be sleepwalking after all. "Dawn's hours away. Maybe you should try to get some more sleep, stay in here till morning."

"His were the hands I used at first," Zeybekci said, holding up his own hands as if seeing them for the first time. "I whispered into his head so softly, he never even knew I was here. Never knew what he'd done. But I don't need to whisper anymore."

Zeybekci took two steps, then stood staring down at Patil.

"Mr. Zeybekci?" Dr. Dwyer ventured, thinking, *maybe he has to piss.* That must be it. But if so, why was he just—

Zeybekci reached down—it must have been quickly, but it seemed to happen slowly, so slowly, as if the infirmary were a fishbowl and they were moving under water. He put one hand over Patil's face, clamped him down against the cot. With the other hand, Zeybekci thrust his fingers into Patil's mouth, grabbed hold of his lower jaw, and ripped it off. Bones cracked and flesh tore and blood sprayed onto the cot and the floor.

"Jesus Christ!" the doctor screamed, staggering backward.

The words made Zeybekci flinch. He sneered, glared up at Dr. Dwyer with a sour scowl on his blood-spattered face, and then began to stab and claw at Patil's face with the broken edge of bone jutting out from the bloody piece of his own jaw. Patil's hands came up, trying to protect himself, and that was the worst of it. Worse even than the savagery of the attack. For a time, Patil was awake and aware, and screaming in a wordless moan that was all a man with no lower jaw could manage.

Then his hands fell away and his body went limp. Blood pulsed and sluiced to the floor, soaking through his clothes and sheets. Moments from death.

Zeybekci looked up at the doctor again, shuddered with obvious pleasure, and took a step toward him.

The hot stink of urine filled the doctor's nostrils. Only when he felt its heat drooling along his legs, soaking his pants from within, did he know it was his own piss.

It broke the little boy in him. There was no big brother Teddy to protect him now.

Screaming, he ran from the infirmary, skidding in the puddle of his piss. Zeybekci lunged for him, and missed. The doctor slammed into the doorframe, then stumbled into the passage and into the embrace of the icy wind gusting through the ark.

"Jesus . . . holy shit," he rasped.

Off to the right, he heard the voices of some of the staffers. Shaking, numb with the horror of what he'd seen, he stumbled in that direction, picking up speed as he went. Zeybekci lunged into the passage and crashed through some of the plastic sheeting, and the doctor began to scream for help.

A thick sheet of slashed plastic blocked the passage ahead. When he pushed through that hanging plastic, the voices seemed farther away. A bright bulb on the wall to his left made him cringe and blink, and then someone grabbed his arm and he lashed out, shoving the man away.

"Doc! Hey, calm down!"

Hands grabbed him again, by both wrists, a strong grip that made him snap his head up and meet the other man's gaze. One of the American grad students, young and good-looking, something Italian for a name. Bellucci. No, Belbusti. Steve.

"It's in Zeybekci," Dr. Dwyer said. "Let's move. We need weapons. Something to protect ourselves."

Others poked their heads out of stalls farther along the passage, men and women who were tired and afraid but who felt safe together. There were tents and clusters and right there in the passage, four people knelt on the floor with a space heater and had been caught in the middle of a card game—anything to while away the storm.

"Get up!" Dr. Dwyer shouted at them. A voice down inside him reminded him they couldn't understand, but didn't they see his fear? Did they think him just another member of the expedition whose sanity had become momentarily unmoored?

"Damn it, listen! He's coming! We've got to—"

"Doc, hey!" Belbusti said, gesturing to the others. "We're not stupid. Demon or no demon, we've got weapons."

Belbusti unclipped an ice ax he'd had hanging at his hip and brandished it for Dr. Dwyer to see. The silver metal shaft glinted in the harsh light, and the darker steel head had wicked teeth . . . terrible teeth. Dwyer nodded, taking some comfort in that awful instrument, and together they both turned toward the strips of heavy plastic that blocked the passage here. The doctor frowned. Where was Zeybekci?

"He was right behind me," Dr. Dwyer said. "He's the one who killed Helen and the others. He just murdered—"

"Maybe he went toward the cave mouth," Belbusti said. "We should warn the others on level one."

Climbing ax raised, brow knitted in fearless determination, Belbusti shoved the plastic slats aside and started forward. He'd taken half a step when Zeybekci came through as if he'd simply manifested out of the shadows on the other side. Zeybekci had one hand on Belbusti's throat when the American swung the climbing ax, grunting but still grim with purpose, still fearless. The kind of brave that Dr. Dwyer had never witnessed in his life.

Zeybekci ripped the climbing ax from his hand as if he were snatching a switch from a bullying child. The one burning light flickered and went dark for just a moment, but in that moment

Dr. Dwyer saw that Zeybekci's eyes burned with a sickly orange glint, the rotting light from inside the guts of a jack-o'-lantern.

"Please, God," Dr. Dwyer whimpered. "Please."

Zeybekci hacked the point of the climbing ax at Belbusti's face, puncturing his left eye and squelching six inches deep into the American's brain. Belbusti collapsed, the point of the climbing ax making a slick sucking noise as it slid from the dead man's eye.

Dr. Dwyer was already moving. Running. He saw the faces up ahead, all turned toward him, their eyes wide with terror. People were reaching for weapons. Others were screaming. One had already begun to run deeper into the ark, away from the horror and the cluster of people whose company she'd assumed would keep her safe.

The doctor could have told her there was nowhere inside the ark that would be safe now. But then he felt a solid blow at the back of his skull, heard the bone give way.

He died, then, amid a chorus of screams.

SIXTEEN

Olivieri stood inside the stall he'd been using as his own sleeping quarters. His bedroll had been bundled into a corner and three plastic chairs and a table now stood in the middle of the stall. Chunks of broken bitumen from the coffin casing lay in a pile on the floor. A dozen smaller pieces sat on the table, glassy smooth but with sharp edges. Some of them were those discovered with the cadavers Professor Marshall's team had studied, but the rest they would have to prepare for themselves.

Chloe sat in one of the chairs, using a cordless drill to make holes in the new bitumen shards while Errick threaded thick, rough twine through the holes. Olivieri had chosen the new pieces of bitumen for size, preferring bits that had lines engraved in them from that ancient, inscrutable language that Father Cornelius thought he could translate. Olivieri had tried not to think too much about the priest's ability to make sense of those engravings. He didn't have time for envy.

"This one," he said, selecting another piece from the floor. His back and knees ached from crouching to examine the bitumen.

Over the whine of the drill, Chloe hadn't heard him.

Olivieri tapped her shoulder and she took her finger off the drill's trigger.

In the resulting quiet, they heard screaming. Olivieri snapped up his head, muttered "no." Errick stood so fast that his chair crashed over backward. His hands opened and closed and he swore, realizing he was weaponless.

"Chloe," he said, reaching for the drill.

She frowned and turned her back on him. Olivieri understood. No way would she give up her only weapon so that he could have one. Chloe faced the stall opening, finger on the trigger of the drill. Olivieri took a step backward, though he knew that it meant his back would be against the wall. More screams came from the passage. He heard a thump that could only be a body hitting the floor, and then people were rushing past the stall opening, fleeing, and Olivieri knew they had to go.

"Run!" he snapped. "Both of you, go!"

Errick glanced at the pile of bitumen, snatched up the biggest, sharpest chunk from the pile, and stepped into the passage. A scream swept in on the wind and Olivieri saw one of the staff crash into Errick, who tried to sidestep, to free himself from entanglement. Olivieri watched Errick look up, ready for a fight, and then a climbing ax flashed through dim light as it whickered down and stabbed into Errick's flesh. He jerked aside at the last moment and the point pierced his shoulder instead of his chest. He went down, and his attacker rode him down, raising the ax for another swing.

Olivieri shouted, as if he might stop murder with only his voice.

Chloe hurled herself out of the stall and used the drill like a club, batting at the skull of Errick's attacker. The man swayed backward and Olivieri saw it was Zeybekci. Or the demon, inside Zeybekci.

Crying out, Chloe jammed the drill into his cheek and pulled the trigger, the bit whining as it dug into flesh and bone. Zeybekci only smiled wider as he reached up and grabbed Chloe by the hair. The drill bit plunged deeper into his face, blood spraying Chloe as he curled his fingers into claws, dug in his nails, and ripped out her throat. Inhumanly strong, the demon in Zeybekci stood as Chloe crumpled to the floor, blood gouting from her throat. The drill thumped to the floor next to Chloe's twitching, dying flesh, and Zeybekci turned to stare at Errick.

Olivieri could not move. He refused to breathe, for if he did, the demon might hear him. Might see him. Might come for him.

As if it heard his thoughts, the demon turned and looked into the stall. Zeybekci's mouth grinned.

Then someone else was there, moving fast. A fist crashed into that mouth, and Olivieri heard the demon snarl in surprise and fury. It didn't like that anyone might dare to fight back.

Walker heard people shouting his name. Kim and Hakan were right behind him, running along the level-two passage, but there would be no hesitation now. Mr. Avci would wonder, later, if he had done all he could to save Zeybekci. The Turkish government would launch a formal inquiry. As the UN observer, Kim Seong would have to do her best to explain what happened next. But for any of that to happen, there needed to *be* a next.

He threw the punch on instinct, but Walker's instincts had been honed through years of practice and deadly experience. When he hit Zeybekci, he did it from the waist, snapping his fist forward with the strength of his whole body. That blow would have dropped an ordinary man. Lights out. Zeybekci staggered back, twisted around and hissed at him, the hiss rising into a bestial snarl.

Walker had pissed off the demon. He wanted to be proud of that, but then its grin returned and he saw the corners of Zeybekci's mouth rip, blood running from the edges, the smile too wide for a human face.

He'd have given anything for a gun just then. He had one, but not in his hands. Not now. Hakan probably still had Zeybekci's, but he couldn't bank on probably.

The demon lunged at him. Walker sidestepped, dropped his elbow on top of Zeybekci's skull. Its hooked fingers clawed at his leg, tore his pants, and dug furrows into the flesh of his thigh as it went down. Walker pivoted, gave himself room, and snapped a hard kick at its head, pistoned his leg, and did it twice more.

With a scream, the demon wearing Zeybekci's flesh surged up at him, grabbed hold and lifted him off the ground. The stink of blood and death filled the passage. Red life steamed off the timber floors. The demon held Walker off the ground and rose up, its face only inches from his. Its breath made him retch, and its touch made his skin crawl. Fear moved like infection through his blood. He fought it, but its stink, the filthy grime that seemed to coat his own flesh just because it stared at him . . .

Unclean, he thought. *This is what evil feels like.*

"You wanted something to believe in," it rasped in Zeybekci's voice. "Believe in me and the things I will do to your little boy when I finally touch his flesh. The ways I will pull him apart. The door is open now, Benjamin. I am here. And now others will wake and feel my presence and they will remember the world of men and the pleasures of human flesh, and they will join—"

Walker heard a crack as Zeybekci went rigid. The demon's grip relaxed and Walker flailed as he dropped to the floor. Rage flooded him as he started to reach for Zeybekci, but the Turk was already collapsing on top of him. His eyes had gone blank, and Walker caught him by the arm and throat. As he twisted the body and dropped Zeybekci on his side, the body slumping, he knew the man was dead.

"Oh, no," Kim said, coming up behind him.

Meryam stood in the passage, the bloody climbing ax in her hand. Pale and shaking, bent over and dragging in big gulps of breath, she stared at the man she had just killed. The man she had murdered to save Walker's life. Behind her, like some kind of carrion creature, Calliope stood, filming it all.

"Where the hell did you two come from?" he asked, one hand on the wall as he pushed to his feet.

"Heard screaming . . ." Meryam said, sucking in breaths between words. "We went through level one, came up the steps. Thought it might be . . . better than following . . . in your footsteps."

Calliope kept shooting, and he wondered how much her footage would show.

Walker stared at Meryam, curious as to just what was wrong with her. The circles beneath her eyes were dark and sagging and her skin had a sallow quality that made her look pale despite her natural hue. Not possessed—not like Adam—but something had taken hold of her just as powerfully as any demon. They'd all gleaned enough from her fight with Adam to know Meryam was ill, but Walker wanted to know just how ill. He thought he ought to know whether the woman would be able to continue taking care of herself.

Considering she had possibly just saved his life, he thought maybe Meryam would take care of herself just fine.

Walker glanced at Hakan, saw the gun in his hand, dangling uselessly at his side, and silently damned him for not getting there sooner, for not pulling the trigger and taking Zeybekci's death on himself so that Meryam would not have the man's blood on her hands. That might not have been fair to Hakan, but he couldn't help thinking it. Besides, a bullet would have been cleaner.

"You killed it," Olivieri said, emerging from the stall just beside them, staring down at the corpse of the possessed man.

Meryam glanced around the passage. Walker did the same. Errick held one hand over a bloody wound on his shoulder.

Chloe lay dead, and there were several other corpses scattered on the ancient timber floors.

"No," she said, hollow-voiced. "I only killed Zeybekci."

The monitor lay facedown with blood pooling up through the hair at the back of his skull like groundwater from a fresh hole. Little rivers spilled down through the man's matted hair. It was no way to die. Walker glanced at the faces now beginning to gather and saw that they felt the same. Meryam had done it to save his life—maybe all of their lives—but still it seemed unfathomably cruel. Had been cruel, but the cruelty had not been Meryam's.

You wanted something to believe in. Believe in me, the demon had whispered.

He glanced up at Calliope, right into the eye of the camera, and pointed at her. Not at the camera, at her. "You're going to delete the vid you just shot of this. All of this."

Calliope ignored him, so Walker turned to Meryam. The footage would show her murdering Zeybekci. Nobody watching it would believe there had been something else driving him, something possessing him. Nobody who hadn't been inside the ark would know the way it felt to be tainted by that evil, to feel it on your skin and taste it on your tongue, to breathe it in the air.

"It's a conversation for later," Meryam said. "When we know who we're really talking to."

Walker looked around and studied their faces, watched their eyes as they processed her statement. Realization came to them slowly, but it did come to them. It began with Kim, then Hakan. One by one he saw brows furrow and eyes narrow and then they tore their gazes from the corpses and began to glance at the others in the passage around them, wondering—just as Walker worried— where the demon had gone. As Meryam had said, Zeybekci was dead. But the thing that had possessed him, and Adam before him, was still among them.

None of the faces around him betrayed the demon's presence. The wildly cruel grin and those ancient, knowing eyes were nowhere to be seen, but if Walker had learned anything thus far about his adversary, it was that the demon knew how to hide.

He nodded at Meryam, a silent acknowledgment that he shared her distress.

Meryam straightened up, hand still gripping the bloodstained climbing ax. "I want to cry. I want to scream. But I'm going to put all of that off until the time comes when I can do it knowing this thing is not going to be able to kill anyone else."

"So you're . . . you're sure?" someone asked.

Olivieri uttered a broken, humorless laugh. "You must be joking. Are we sure? You've just seen it with your own eyes!"

"So what now?" Errick asked, wincing as he kept one hand clamped over his shoulder wound. "If this . . . if it can just jump from one person to another, it's going to keep picking us off until we're all dead."

"You know we're working on that," Olivieri said, unclenching his fist to reveal a piece of carved bitumen with a strand of twine threaded through a hole in its center.

Errick shook his head. "This is insane. It can't be real."

"No?" Hakan said, stepping forward. "Ask *him*."

The guide nudged Zeybekci's corpse with one foot, as if to make sure he was dead. Unnerved, the others stared at him. Slightly hunched, Hakan's eyes were hidden, and Walker had a breathless moment when he wondered if the demon had not gone very far at all. Then Hakan looked around the circle. Gun still in his hand, as if he feared he might need to use it at any moment, he used his free hand to point at one of his workers and an archaeology student.

"You two. Go down to level one and bring everyone back here. Everyone, without exception. If anyone argues, tell them I will be unhappy if I must come and fetch them myself," Hakan said.

"I will go and gather Father Cornelius, Feyiz, and the others, and we will bring Adam here as well."

The worker started to turn immediately, but the student—Walker didn't know her name—hesitated and looked at Meryam. It was her project, after all. She was the boss, and Walker felt certain the entire staff was aware of the animosity between her and Hakan.

Meryam gave a single nod. "Go. Quickly."

The two rushed off even as Hakan continued, this time speaking to Meryam directly.

"We must remove them," he said, gesturing at the bodies of Zeybekci, Dr. Dwyer, and the others. "Anyone who has yet to see this horror should be saved from it."

"I'll handle it," Walker offered.

Kim volunteered to help, and immediately began poking into some of the stalls for blankets and things with which they might wrap the remains of their dead.

Meryam rapped on the wall between two stalls to get everyone's attention.

"I'm guessing there're a few hours left till morning," she said. "We're going to pull the heaters together. Bedrolls and tents and blankets. We're going to get a hot meal in us and then we're packing our gear, so we can be ready. At first light, we're evacuating the ark. We'll take it as slowly as we must, but we've got to get out of this cave and down the mountain."

"If the blizzard's still raging, we could die out there," Errick argued.

Meryam stared at him, and Walker knew what she had to be thinking. With that wound in his shoulder, Errick was in no shape to make a descent. But whatever disease had been eating at her, neither was Meryam. The difference between them was that one had already realized that they had no other choice.

"You could die out there," she said. "Chances are that some

of us will. The difference is in the guarantee. You could die if we go. But you'll most certainly die if we stay."

Meryam stands in the front room of the third-story flat in Mayfair where she and Adam have made their little nest. The view from the window is quintessential London, off-white row houses lining a road so narrow it can barely accommodate a taxi and a bicycle at the same time. Gray morning light creates a peculiar aura, a surreal quality that makes it seem like Faerie might be only steps away. In small flower boxes, vivid colors blossom amid the gray. This is spring in London.

The window is open just a few inches, the morning still a bit chilly, and she can hear the distant laughter of children. She imagines them playing some sort of game and steps to the window, craning her neck for a better view. A laughing boy careens into view, kicking a football into the road, careless of whatever traffic might wend its way along the narrow road. Morning dew glistens on the curb and the street, and shines on the windows of the flats opposite Meryam's.

A young woman rides by on a bicycle. Her hair is a vibrant, cobalt blue. Years ago, Meryam spent the better part of a year with her hair that color, and she wonders why she ever changed it. Then she spots the little girl in pursuit of the boy with the football. She runs with ferocity, arms pumping at her sides, face scrunched intensely, and it's clear to Meryam that the football belongs to her. The little boy has stolen it, perhaps for amusement, but stolen it nevertheless. The young woman on the bike calls out a warning and swerves, barely able to avoid the little girl.

Meryam wants to shout, her heart pounding. They don't need her warning, this young woman and little girl who each look something like Meryam herself. Other Meryams, from other times. Her face flushes even as she shivers with the chilly spring air snaking in through the gap in the window. The accident's been avoided, but her gaze tracks the running girl.

"*Mother,*" *a voice says, just over her shoulder.*

Icy fingers touch her arm and Meryam flinches. Where is Adam? Not here. Not where he ought to be. And where is her cancer? Not here. Not where it ought to be.

"*Mother.*"

Her eyes track the running girl as she catches up to the little thief, the boy who took her football. She is fierce.

Those fingers clutch at her forearm, cold enough to sear her. Again, that young voice whispers her name. Meryam forces herself to tear her gaze from the window, and she turns.

What is it, Jo? she asks.

Jo smiles back. JoJo, her little Josephine. "*Don't be sad, Mother,*" *her little girl says.* "*You were never meant to have me. They only let me live so they could take me away. If you're sad, you're only giving them what they want.*"

Confused—but you're not confused, are you—*Meryam crouches in front of her girl. Jo has the loveliest eyes, a bright copper that gleams and offsets the soft brown of her skin. Her hair falls in natural ringlets, such a beautiful little girl. One day she will make people catch their breath from the mere sight of her. One day.*

But why is Jo up here in the flat? How can she be here and down there on the street, chasing the boy who stole her football, all at the same time?

Have you caught the boy? Meryam asks her.

Jo takes her hand and clutches it tightly, staring into her eyes. "*Don't look out the window again, Mother.*"

Meryam hears the laughter of the little boy, the little thief, carried on the breeze and it seems to grow louder. The room around her is cast in the same gray, fairy light as the view out the window, but in here with her, among the meticulously arranged furnishings and the mementos from the adventures she and Adam had before Jo came along . . . in here the only color is the gleaming copper of her daughter's eyes.

"*Don't turn around,*" *Jo warns, but now her bright, new-penny eyes are more vivid than ever and the rest of her is fading. Those ringlet curls are little more than smoke.*

No, she says, and reaches out for her little girl. Her JoJo. But Jo vanishes as her hands pass through the place where she'd been only a moment before, as if it's the very act of trying to touch her, trying to hold on to the love that fills Meryam's heart, that makes her daughter turn to smoke and fade away. Those copper eyes are the last to fade, followed by the echo of her voice.

Don't look. Mother, don't look. Mother, don't . . .

Meryam turns to look out the window. It's as if not a moment has passed since she felt Jo's fingers on her arm. The touch of the little girl she and Adam brought into the world, the daughter she was never supposed to have.

Out on the street, fierce, determined Josephine catches up to the little thief and grabs him by the arm. The moment her fingers touch the boy's flesh, all of the flowers on their narrow little street in Mayfair wither and die.

The little boy leaves the football in the street. He turns to face Jo.

Meryam hadn't noticed the horns before.

Meryam is screaming.

And she wakes.

Meryam woke crying. She rolled onto her side, curled into a fetal ball before she could be completely sure that she had truly escaped the dream. Her body rigid, breath hitching as she shuddered and gasped, she held her eyes tightly shut, afraid of what she might see when she opened them. Her chest ached, heart drumming hard. Her whole body felt cold, icy breeze caressing the exposed skin of her hands and face and throat, and she wanted to scream.

To scream and scream and scream.

The echoes of her ragged-voice shrieking still lingered in her ears, but all she could feel was loss. Loss unlike she had ever imagined might be possible. Every dream she'd ever held in her secret heart, every hope of love and contentment, had been buried down deep the moment she'd learned she had cancer. Now they had been dug up and exposed, the flesh of her dreams flayed down to nothing but raw nerves.

"Meryam."

It sounded a little bit like *Mother*.

Cold fingers touched her hand and she leaped up, dragging the blankets with her as she threw herself off the cot and huddled against the hard plastic wall. Blinking, she realized she'd opened her eyes. The lights were dim but still seemed harsh and as the figure above her reached out for her again she batted his hands away.

"You're okay," he said. "Meryam, you were dreaming. It was a nightmare."

Lowering her hands, she stared at him. *Walker*, she thought. Pulse still pounding, she tried to steady her breath. Awareness finally bled back into her thoughts and she took in the room around them. They were in the infirmary. She'd been asleep on one of the cots, trapped in what felt not like a nightmare but like hell itself. The terror and screaming sorrow still raced around inside of her, searching for some way out, some way to expend itself before it destroyed her.

Walker had his hands out. "You're okay," he said again. "Why don't you get back onto the cot. Take a little time, let the dream fade. It will fade, no matter what it was . . . no matter how the nightmare's wormed its way inside you. Just breathe and let yourself wake up from it."

Exhaling, forcing herself to catch her breath, Meryam crawled back to the cot. The weariness of her disease had grown worse. The extreme nature of this project had taken its toll on her. Walker offered his hand but she ignored him, pulling herself up to the cot. She dragged the blankets over her shoulders and sat on the edge, looking around, feeling as if she were returning to the fabric of the real world for the first time.

Only slightly less hellish than my dreams.

She wiped at her tears. The pace had slowed, but they kept coming. The name Josephine kept circling around inside her head, like a snatch of song that could not be driven out. Josephine. Jo.

A baby she would never have.

The kind of daughter she would have been proud to raise. A girl who would never be born.

On the next cot over, a figure stirred beneath blankets. Meryam saw the mop of his thick, black hair and heard a groan as familiar to her as her own voice. Adam turned over and opened his eyes, squinting against the light. Scruffy and unwashed, angry and unfaithful, hurt and confused, he remained the man she loved. Josephine would never be, but this was the father she would have deserved. Human, and full of love.

"Meryam?" Adam said.

Walker stood back as Meryam climbed off her cot and lay down with Adam. She slid beneath the blankets with him, draped herself over him so that they could fit on the narrow cot. Memories of the night began to float up inside her head and though they were terrible, ugly things—full of horror and blood—still she preferred them to the endless despair of her dream, and so she embraced them.

"You want me to give you some time?" Walker asked, sitting on the edge of the cot Meryam had just abandoned.

Adam studied Meryam's face. She knew he was searching for an explanation, an answer to the question of how the tension between them had evaporated so instantly, but now was not the time for that conversation. She loved him. For now, that would have to be answer enough. Cancer had stolen her dreams long before this demon had insinuated itself into their hearts. But Adam could still dream. He might have a little Josephine someday, with someone else—someone who might be kinder to him. Death awaited Meryam just around the corner, at some time it had already chosen, or so she believed. But until the moment of that assignation, she would fight for Adam to live and dream, no matter his sins. She was certainly not without her own.

"You've been looking after us," she said, studying Walker from the cot.

"If we're going to make the climb down, you both needed time to recover," Walker said. He frowned as he studied them. "Truthfully, I'm not sure any of us will make it. The blizzard's still blowing like hell out there, and neither of you is strong enough for this. But the sun's rising in about twenty minutes."

"Not as if we'll see much sun," Adam said.

"It'll be light enough to see," Meryam said. "If not for the snow."

Walker rubbed at his eyes, dark circles beneath them. "It's the best we're gonna get, unless you want to wait this out."

Meryam dragged the blankets off of herself and Adam. His clothes were musky and stale, but the scent belonged to him. It meant he was alive.

SEVENTEEN

Adam allowed Meryam to sit him up on the edge of the cot. He forced a smile as she drew the blankets up over his shoulders and kissed his hand and held it tightly. Her gentle kindness—a side of her that he'd scarcely seen these past few weeks—helped him, but only a little. A spark in the darkness. No amount of loving attention could have burned off the taint he felt inside. If they'd had access to a hot shower, he might have scrubbed the ammonia-stinking film of sweat from his skin, but it would take time for the infection to leave his body. The demon might be gone, but his system still needed to purge the poison it had left behind.

"Hey," Meryam said, nudging him. "You with us?"

Again, he managed a smile. Weak as he knew it was, Meryam and Walker both seemed relieved.

"I'm here," Adam said. "Just . . . you know how it feels when you've had a bad flu, or you've had some kind of stomach bug. You feel shaky and . . . tentative . . . like it's still lingering—"

Walker stiffened. "You think the demon's still in you?"

Adam saw the way the other man's right fist clenched and wondered what Walker might do if he said yes.

"No. I think it's been pulling our strings for a while, but when it really moves in and takes over, that's something you know. It *wants* you to know."

Meryam's eyes filled with reflected pain and sympathy and he hated it. They had to act now, not let anguish and regret get in the way. There would be time for recriminations and doubts later.

If Meryam has any time at all.

Adam knew one thing—if her days on this earth would be as short as her doctor had predicted, he didn't want to spend those days negotiating truth and love. He just wanted to live it.

"I need to talk to you," he said. *About Calliope. About what I thought must be going on, and the role I think the demon might have played.*

He didn't say the rest of it, not with Walker standing right there, but Meryam seemed to understand. She ran the back of her hand across the scruff on his cheek.

"Later," she said.

Adam wanted to protest. To insist. A gulf had opened up between them and he wanted to know if that dead space could be bridged, if they could really find their way back to each other. They sat side by side, hand in hand, but that was only flesh and bone. The space between them couldn't be measured in physical inches.

"We have a lot to do," Walker said, leaning forward on the creaking cot. "I need to know if you can hold your own, or if you're going to need someone looking after you."

His hands were on his knees like some grandpa in a rocking chair, and it occurred to Adam that with so many dead and the rest of their lives in danger, Walker was in charge. The Karga-Holzer Ark Project was over. It was just about survival now.

"If I need help, I'll send up a flare."

"See you do," Meryam whispered to him.

Adam opened up the blankets she'd draped him with and put his arm around her, drawing her inside the warmth with him. The set of her jaw and the cast of her eyes revealed that there were words unspoken, but that was hardly a secret. The taint of the demon remained in more ways than one.

A shadow passed across the floor and Adam looked up to see Feyiz standing in the doorway, backlit by the garish glow of the industrial light out in the passage.

"I'm pleased to see you both sitting upright," Feyiz said.

Under the blanket, Adam felt Meryam stiffen. For a moment it was as if Walker had vanished from the infirmary and it was just the three of them and the tension of the past twenty-four hours churning in the space between them.

"Listen," Adam began. "You know it wasn't me."

Feyiz cocked his head. "Which part do you mean? The raving lunatic who attacked me? The jealous man who thought I was having an affair with his fiancée?"

Walker stood up, moving between the cots and the door. "Do we really need to do this right now?"

Feyiz stepped around him. "I think we do." He crouched in front of Adam and Meryam, glancing from one to the other. "I am and shall continue to be your friend. Of course I wonder, Adam, where your own emotions and behavior ended and the demon took over."

Meryam exhaled sharply. "We'll never know the answer to that question."

"That's right," Feyiz said, studying her face. "We never will. And so we go on, all three of us. We get off this mountain alive, and when we've accomplished that, we'll worry about what it means for old friendships."

He held out a hand. Adam took his arm from around Meryam and shook it. For the moment, at least, they could be strong together.

"That's lovely," Walker said. "Now do you want to give them an update on where we stand, or should I?"

Feyiz stood. "You're a man with sharp edges, Dr. Walker. Sharp edges and many secrets. I'm glad you're here with us. I'm also glad we're leaving."

"Get on with it," Walker said.

"Seven killed last night, in total." Feyiz shook his head, his hard shell cracking as he shared the news. "There are sixteen of us left, including the four people in this room. The bodies have been wrapped up tightly and stowed in a stall on level one for retrieval in the spring—"

"We're taking them with us," Meryam said. "I'm not . . . we can't leave them here."

"Meryam," Walker began.

Adam jumped in. "Feyiz just said there are sixteen people left alive. It's going to be hard enough getting down the mountain in this storm, not even taking into account whatever the demon might do to try to thwart that attempt. If it gets inside someone else"—*or back inside me*, he thought—"look, we just can't. You know this. Someone else will come back for them. I feel a responsibility toward them, too—I don't want to just abandon them, but our first priority has to be the people who are still breathing. The people we can save."

"Okay," Meryam said quietly. "I get it."

"We can't endanger them any further by asking them to carry the bodies of the dead down off the mountain," Adam went on.

"I said I get it!"

Her voice echoed in the little plastic box of a room.

Adam caught movement in his peripheral vision and looked up to see Calliope out in the corridor, filming the whole exchange. Heat flushed his cheeks, anger and shame in equal portion.

"Not now, Callie," he said. "Get the fuck out of here with that thing."

She flinched. Blond hair tied back in a bun, pale and drawn and exhausted, she looked as broken and vulnerable as the rest of them.

She'd been a friend and a comfort and when they'd made love it had felt like true shelter from the emotional wreckage in his heart. In that moment, it had felt right. Punishing her for it was a shitty thing to do, but he told himself this was not punishment. Just privacy.

"Seriously?" Calliope said. "One of us is doing her fucking job, and just in case the 'her' didn't give it away, it isn't you. I'm scared out of my mind right now, but I figured . . ."

She shook her head. "You know what? Never mind."

Calliope turned, lowering her camera.

Meryam called her back. "Hold on!"

The two women faced each other—Calliope in the doorway and Meryam on the cot—and Adam had to look away.

"Keep doing your job," Meryam said. "When this is over, we're going to want a record. Whatever happens, people need to know."

Calliope seemed about to reply, but was distracted by the arrival of Professor Olivieri. She backed up to let him into the infirmary, and Adam sent thoughts of silent gratitude toward him for the interruption.

"All right," Olivieri began, placing a cloth bag on the counter by the door. He glanced at Feyiz and Walker. "You two are squared away, yes?"

Walker nodded grimly. Feyiz reached inside his shirt and pulled out a black, gleaming charm—a bit of bitumen that hung from twine that he'd tied around his neck.

Reaching into the bag, Olivieri withdrew two just like it and handed one to Meryam and the other to Adam.

"I'm already wearing mine," the professor said. "Put mine on first, to be honest."

The bags beneath his eyes were dark and deep. His nose shone red but his dark complexion had gone pale. Adam thought he looked like hell, but he figured they all did. It helped him to not focus on Meryam's illness. They all looked dreadfully ill.

"Thank you, professor," he said.

Meryam slipped her bitumen charm on immediately, but Adam hesitated. Father Cornelius had blessed these things, but it wasn't the faith of the holy man that tripped him up. Rabbi, priest, imam—he figured a blessing was a blessing. But if he was looking for something to believe in, it wouldn't be a chunk of shiny, hardened, volcanic rock.

"Hey," Meryam said, nudging him. "It can't hurt."

Adam managed a weak smile and slipped the charm around his neck.

"Of course," Olivieri said, "with Dr. Walker's other skills, he may not need outside protection."

Adam tucked his bitumen charm inside his shirt. "I *am* curious, Walker. I've never seen a Ph.D. fight like that before."

Walker shrugged. "We're allowed to have more than one set of skills. Being able to handle myself in a fight has come in handy more often than I'd have wished."

Meryam toyed with the twine around her neck. "Can we focus, please? Has anyone else shown signs of being . . ."

"Possessed," Adam finished for her. "You can say the word, Meryam."

"All right," she said, glancing at Walker and Feyiz. "Any sign of anyone else being possessed?"

"Nothing overt," Walker said. "It could be hiding inside someone, pulling strings the way it apparently did with Zeybekci. Maybe he made it easy for the demon, I don't know. Right now, the only thing I'm noticing is a lot of tension, but that's natural."

"There is actually much less tension, now," Feyiz added. "The things that had splintered us apart before are no longer relevant."

"Terror is a great unifier," Olivieri muttered. "They've seen murder now. They believe in evil in one form or another. Everyone left alive up here just wants to survive."

"On that note," Calliope said from the passage outside the door, "can we cut the chitchat and get the hell out of here?"

Adam glanced at her, but saw only the eye of the camera. Calliope hid behind it, just as he so often did. With a nod, he placed a hand on Meryam's back, a moment of connection before he rose from the cot. He felt unsteady, but it passed quickly and he took a deep breath.

"Sounds good to me," he said. "Bundle up, folks. It's *cold* outside."

Olivieri stood with the others out on the ledge, and for the first time the impossibility of the task ahead sank in. Snow stuck to his goggles and he used his left glove to wipe it away. With the blizzard raging around them, it felt as if they were the last people on Earth. Like most of them he wore a balaclava that covered everything but his eyes and mouth. He told himself this was the reason he could not seem to catch his breath. It was the fabric and the storm, not his fear.

I'm going to die on this mountain, he thought. It was a cold sort of knowledge, like an awareness of his age or height or weight. He would die long before they reached the foot of Ararat. Perhaps that would be best.

Around him, people shouted to one another, trying to get in some semblance of order. Hakan had been project foreman, but now he and Feyiz had returned to their roles as guides. The two of them were working with a third guide, a cousin or something, to get the rest started down the mountain. Some carried heavy packs while others helped the weak or wounded, but the people around him had lost their identity beneath hats and parka hoods and behind goggles and balaclavas. They'd become strangers to one another. He wondered if the demon hid inside one of them, its eyes peering out.

Olivieri wore his crampons. He had a climbing ax dangling at his hip and poles that Hakan had given him. There were ropes and pitons, but only for emergencies. Once they moved away from the cave, sidling westward, back toward the normal path that would lead them down to Camp Two, the mountain wasn't steep enough to require them all to be tethered together. But he thought there might be another reason why Hakan didn't want them all tethered.

Nobody wanted to be tied to a climber who might attempt to murder them at any moment.

A man grabbed his arm. On instinct, Olivieri yanked it away.

"You're next, professor," the man said, his voice thickly accented. It might have been Feyiz or his cousin, face hidden like that. Or it might have been something else.

Olivieri wanted to weep. "I don't think I can."

"You have to," the voice said, muffled by a gray balaclava. "We're going, and we're all in it together. You've climbed a dozen mountains, you told me. This one's easy."

Olivieri laughed. It was Feyiz, after all. The guide had such kindness in him, not like his uncle. "Easy in the summer."

But he started moving. The wind gusted and he stumbled, but Feyiz took his arm and helped him over to the western corner of the ledge. The cold had numbed him already and they had thousands of meters of climbing to do. In good weather they could have made the full descent in a handful of hours. This would be different.

All morning he had felt a sickness twisting inside him. Screams that wanted to erupt from his throat. Frantic tears he had to fight to keep inside. Adam had been possessed, but he wasn't the only one. Zeybekci had committed murder when the demon had taken the reins of his flesh, and Adam had attempted to do the same.

But not Olivieri. The demon had used him as a different sort of puppet. It had gotten down deep in his bones, insinuated itself there and gnawed at all of his doubts, every instant of self-loathing he'd ever felt. It had feasted on the sorrows and regrets that Olivieri believed everyone must have within them. The demon had torn open the wounds on his soul and made him try to take his own life.

It was the demon, he told himself now. *Laughing at you. Pulling the strings.* He told himself that. But the true hell of the thing was that he couldn't be sure it had been the demon at all, because the urge remained. As Feyiz led him to the rope line that they had set up to guide them away from the snow-covered rockfall and onto more reliable terrain, he had to fight the temptation to hurl himself off the ledge.

"Come on, professor," Feyiz said, making sure he was holding onto the guide rope. "It's time."

His boots crunched down on the snow and he slipped a few inches. His hands surprised him by holding tight to the rope. He froze a moment, and then started moving west, bent toward the mountain, digging the crampons on his boots into the snow and the mountain beneath.

Death beckoned to him. But the professor held on.

Time, Walker thought. *That's the key.*

He held onto the rope line that Feyiz's cousin had set up, leaning into the mountain. His knees crunched in the snow and his climbing ax tapped his thigh as he shuffled sideways. They were leaving the ark in groups of three or four, moving along the guide rope to a section of the mountain face that Hakan assured them was safe. Already, several groups were gathered in clumps thirty meters to the west, and Hakan had begun to coach them on how to maneuver the descent. With crampons, they could dig at the snow with the toes of their boots and get a good foothold. Facing the mountain, they could descend carefully for the first thousand meters or so, after which they might be able to simply hike down. The frigid air and the blasting winds were a challenge, but now that he'd been out in the blizzard for a short while, Walker felt confident they were not the real danger.

Time, he thought again. They needed to get as far down the mountain face as possible before nightfall. In the midst of the blizzard it was dark enough, but when evening arrived, the temperature would plummet further and even with flashlights, the footing would become more treacherous. He had left all of his samples, all of his notes, back in the cave and he didn't care. He could write DARPA all the reports they wanted, but only if he got off Ararat alive.

"Let's go, Father!" he urged. "We've got to keep pace."

Walker kept one hand on the guideline and put the other at the small of Father Cornelius's back. The priest had been using the same kneeling shuffle as Walker but he'd already become winded. Beyond him, Kim Seong stood at an angle to the mountain, holding onto the rope and watching them patiently. The grooves left behind by the knees and footsteps of the dozen or so who had gone before them had created a path in the snow and she seemed more confident in her balance than Walker felt in his own.

"Father," he said again, his voice muffled by his balaclava and the whirling snow. Even through the cloth, his face stung.

"I'm doing my best!" Father Cornelius huffed. "I'm an old man, Walker!"

"If you want to get any older, you're gonna have to put a little more effort into it."

The priest grumbled, but started to shuffle his knees faster. After a moment, he gave a muttered curse, dug his boots into the snow, and stood up.

"Father, I don't think that's a—"

"My knees are killing me," Father Cornelius said. "If we keep on like that, I'm not going to get anywhere fast."

Walker didn't bother to explain how much work lay ahead for the old man's knees. The priest would either make it or he wouldn't. If they had to wrap him up in some kind of makeshift travois and slide him down the mountain, that was exactly what they would do. But Father Cornelius had his pride, and Walker did not want to undermine it so soon into the climb.

Grunting and chuffing, Father Cornelius kept one hand against the mountain and the other one wrapped around the guide rope. It wasn't safe—none of what they were doing was safe—but there were other dangers here, and speed was of the essence.

Time.

"Look at that," Kim said, nodding westward, into the storm.

Walker turned to see a red glow flickering in the blizzard's heart, rising at first and then beginning to fall.

"Well, that's a good sign," Father Cornelius said.

Walker agreed. Feyiz's cousin had been instructed to climb down two hundred meters and send up a flare to let them know the descent could be made without difficulty, at least to that point. They all watched as the flare flickered momentarily, its light refracted a million times inside the white, rushing silence of the storm, and then it vanished, hidden in the driving snow.

"Your superiors will be disappointed," Father Cornelius said, his voice a muffled rasp. "With you coming back empty-handed."

Walker saw him slip, the snow buckling under his left foot, and reached out to steady him. The priest went down on one knee but was back up in a moment. Kim had a hand on his back as well, and she met Walker's gaze and gave a small nod, letting him know that they were in this together. Whatever might come, they were getting Father Cornelius off the mountain.

"Under the circumstances, I don't think they can really hold me responsible, do you?" Walker asked. His fingers were already stiff and cold inside his gloves. He looked forward to no longer need-ing the guide rope.

"Actually, I'd think they would be even more disappointed," Father Cornelius said. "You found a demon, Dr. Walker. A super-natural force with real, malignant power. Whoever you really work for, I get the impression they would dearly love to dissect that power and see if they can figure out how to wield it."

Walker stiffened. They were only a dozen feet from the end of the rope line now. Wyn Douglas and Polly Bennett stood at the end—their group had gone right before Walker's, and they were waiting, apparently to lend a hand. With the storm blowing and the way they were all swaddled against the cold, they were still too far away to hear the conversation. Walker wanted to keep it that way.

"You know who I work for," he said, glancing from the priest to Kim.

"We know who you say you work for," Father Cornelius replied.

"The rest is an educated guess," Kim added, leaning slightly toward them, making sure he could hear her over the wind and through the cloth covering her mouth. "We've decided it's DARPA. Some of the hints you've given of things you've seen are beyond the life of an ordinary researcher, and your background is a bit too colorful for something as ordinary as the National Science Foundation."

Walker kept shuffling to his left, digging his boots into the snow. They were smart, both of them. The UN had chosen Kim for a reason, and Walker himself had picked Father Cornelius for his brilliance and comparative open-mindedness. He con-templated telling them the truth, but he couldn't really do that. On the other hand, he refused to lie to them. After what they'd endured together already, and the peril they found themselves in now, he owed them that much.

"Does it matter, now?" he called, stumbling a bit, slamming

a knee into the snow. "We all had certain responsibilities on this trip, and we all tried our best. Part of my job was exactly what I said it was. My credentials in biology and anthropology are genuine."

"Oh, I know they are," Kim said. He wanted to think she was smiling, but so much of her face was covered. All he could see was the barest hint of her eyes behind her goggles, and the snow and the gray light nearly took that glimpse away as well. "You don't think the United Nations vetted you before sending me along?"

Father Cornelius paused to rest a moment, both knees back in the snow. He was closer to Walker, his eyes clearly visible behind his goggles.

"That's *why* they sent her," the priest said. "To make sure that she learned whatever *you* learned."

Walker couldn't help laughing. "I guess we're both out of luck."

Father Cornelius wasn't wrong. If he got off the mountain alive, General Wagner and the others he answered to back at DARPA would be supremely unhappy that he had nothing to show for the journey. He had responsibilities, they would remind him. Obligations to his country. But fuck that, he was no expert on demons. Meryam had burned the thing's remains, but clearly its real power no longer resided in its bones. It might be possible to trap the thing inside a person the next time it possessed someone, but he had zero idea how to even begin figuring that out, and it was clear Father Cornelius didn't know any more than he did. If DARPA wanted to play around with demons, they could send a team back up to the ark after he filed his report. The only thing Walker knew for certain was that he wouldn't be on that mission.

If there was a way to harness evil, to use a demon for their own ends, DARPA would do it, and worry about the moral implications later, the way they always did. But Walker would be damned if he was going to try to grab the tiger by the tail himself.

Damned, he thought, and he laughed again.

"What's so amusing?" Father Cornelius asked, huffing with exertion as he clung to the guide rope.

"Nothing," Walker said, smile fading. "Nothing at all."

Unsettled but determined, he shuffled westward. A moment later he glanced up to see Polly reaching out a hand to him. He stood back, steadying Father Cornelius and Kim as they joined Polly and Wyn, and then he let go of the rope at last.

One of the guides was there, shouting instructions and advice. Walker smashed his gloved hands together to get the blood flowing again, and then snatched his climbing ax from where it hung at his hip. The incline wasn't terrible, but the snow would make every step uncertain. He planted his ax into the mountain face, back to the storm, and began to descend, leading the way for the others.

He exhaled, feeling ice crystals form on the inside of his balaclava. Every step away from the cave eased a little more of the tension from his shoulders.

No question lingered in his mind. He was never coming back to Ararat.

Adam watched as Meryam and Feyiz started across the guide rope. Once upon a time he would never have been able to resist the urge to catch this with his camera, but despite what Meryam had said to Calliope, he had no desire to film their exodus. It ought to be captured—he knew that. With so many dead or presumed dead, every bit of video they could present to show how things unfolded in the ark would go toward defending the choices they'd all made. But he still felt sick, his head muzzy and his guts queasy, and a layer of invisible filth seemed to cover his flesh. He was too focused on how ill he felt, and battling that, to give a damn what did or did not end up on film. So it was good that Calliope was there.

He glanced over his shoulder and saw that she'd followed him. The eye of her camera looked dark. Snow whipped around her, so strong she visibly leaned into it. She was formidable. Beautiful. The memory of her kiss, the touch of her skin, rushed back into his head and he squeezed his eyes closed, forcing it out. Maybe she didn't mind at all, maybe to Calliope there had been nothing romantic in what they'd done. Just sex. She'd practically said as much. But still he felt as if she was the one who'd suffered the greatest injustice here.

You're such a shit for even thinking that.

Digging the toes of his boots, the claws of the crampons, into the snowy mountain face, Adam readied to step off the ledge.

"Hey," Calliope said, putting her hand over his on the rope.

Startled, Adam jerked to his left and nearly slid right off the edge.

"Sorry," she said. "Shit, I'm sorry, I just . . ."

She had lowered the camera for a moment, but now she lifted it again, shooting footage of Meryam and Feyiz, tracking their progress with the camera.

"Calliope, we've got to get out of here," he told her.

She nodded, but he saw her hit the button on the camera that stopped the recording. This was between them.

"I know," she said. "You're right. I just figured once we were climbing down, there wouldn't be a lot of opportunity to talk. And I just wanted to say I was sorry."

Adam stared at her. He tugged down the front of his balaclava to make sure she could hear him clearly. "I got you into this situation."

Calliope smirked. "Men and their arrogance. Don't be stupid, Adam. You're engaged to be married. I knew that. I saw the stress fractures in your relationship. I didn't know if Meryam had really been screwing Feyiz on the side or not, but when you thought that, you were broken up inside. You're guilty. I'm not saying you're not. But I took advantage, and that makes me guilty, too."

Adam glanced past her. Hakan had come out of the shelter of the cave, a huge pack on his back. Behind him, inside the darkness of the cave, orange light flickered and grew and a plume of black smoke began to spill out, eddying away on the gusts of wind.

"Holy shit," Adam said.

Calliope turned, took it all in, and clicked the camera back on. Hakan had lit the timber skeleton of the ark on fire, and the flames were spreading fast. Burning light flickered in the dark mouth of the cave, and Calliope got it all on film as Hakan marched toward them, a grim phantom in the maelstrom of white.

"Best to move now," the guide said. "There will be a great deal of smoke."

Adam turned to Calliope, speaking more quietly and hoping she could hear him, not caring if the camera picked up his voice.

"I get what you're saying," he told her, "but I'm still sorry. I never thought I was the kind of person who would do something like that."

"Maybe you're not," she said, her back to him, filming the flames licking out of the cave mouth. "Maybe it wasn't you at all."

"Do you really believe that?" he asked.

Calliope glanced back at him. "Get out of here, Adam. And good luck to both of you."

He nodded. Pulling up his balaclava, he started out along the guide rope at the quickest pace he could manage. The path had been worn down enough that it wasn't too difficult now, and he made good time.

He thought of the dybbuk in his grandmother's clock, and wondered what would happen to his own spirit if he died on Ararat. Would he haunt the mountain, lingering here forever, or would he be trapped inside an object himself, like that old dybbuk? Locked inside his camera, perhaps, viewing the same fragments of footage, little bits of digital memory that would be all that remained of his life?

He decided that he did not want to die here. He refused.

Head down, he held the rope so tightly that his knuckles hurt. His sins followed him every step of the way.

EIGHTEEN

Meryam wished she could go numb. Even with thick layers, wrapped in insulated tights and shirt, and a sweater with the right wicking, she felt the cold digging down into her bones. The cancer had not just weakened her, it had lessened her, eroded her flesh and muscle and the warmth her body normally could have regenerated on its own. Her limbs felt like hollow pipes, nothing but frozen glass, so easily shattered if she were to fall.

Teeth clenched, she kept descending. Tugged the climbing ax from its hold, planted it a couple of feet lower, dug the claws of her crampons into the snowy mountain face, then did it again.

As they climbed, she heard the occasional muttered or shouted profanity and glanced down to see people skidding downward thanks to a misplaced foot or an unreliable toehold. The angle allowed for mistakes, permitted anyone sliding downward to cling to the snow and rock face, dig in their boots and hands and climbing axes, and correct their mistakes. The wrong fall could break bones, or much worse, no question.

Her teeth chattered behind her balaclava. Bones aching, breath rattling in her chest, she kept moving, all of her focus on her grip and the placement of her feet.

The blizzard swept across the mountain face, turning the world into white silence. The storm breathed, the wind pushing and then holding its breath a moment before blowing again. When the gusts came hard enough, she had to pause and wait for it to stop clawing at her, and what little strength she had continued to be leeched away.

She could make out the two figures above them on the mountain. Hakan and Calliope were making steady progress. They were like ghosts, clothes coated in so much snow that they were white against white, only their constant movement separating them from the maelstrom.

"Hey," Adam said, pressing a hand against her back as if he was worried she might just tumble.

Confused, Meryam glanced at him, saw the knitted brow just above his goggles, and realized that they had both stopped climbing down. The ice in her bones, the pain—*oh, God, the pain*—that she hadn't allowed herself to feel, had made her stop without even realizing it.

"We've got a long way to go," Adam said.

Meryam exhaled, a breath of mist sieving through her balaclava.

"I'm good," she said, nodding.

She bit down hard on her lip, sharp pain waking her up. This was different pain, hot and stabbing, and as she tasted the copper of her own blood, it got her moving again. Toehold, handhold, toehold, tear the climbing ax out, smash it into the snow and rock a couple of feet lower, then start over again. And again. And again.

The numbness reached her thoughts, but she kept moving. Adam moved beneath her, and Meryam thought she would be all right. A thousand meters or so and the slant would change, allowing them to hike down instead of climbing. In her mind, she could already imagine pausing briefly at Camp Two to have something hot to drink, maybe even make a small fire. She'd burn someone's gear if she had to do that to get some heat into her bones.

Something shifted to her right.

She glanced that way and blinked in surprise. Feyiz clung to the snow there, his head against the mountain. He had been below last she'd looked, but at some point, he'd stopped moving just as she had a moment before.

Even through his goggles she could see there were tears in his eyes.

"Feyiz?"

His eyes widened. He looked at her with such imploring sadness that she first thought he'd lost hope or become ill.

"I feel it," he said, the words almost lost in a gust of wind. Snow built up on his hat and goggles and the collar of his jacket.

"What's wrong?" Adam called loudly, starting to climb up toward them again.

I don't know, Meryam wanted to say.

But that would have been a lie. She did know. She saw it in Feyiz's eyes. There ought to have been terror there, but he did not look frightened. Only sad and resigned.

"I feel it inside me," Feyiz said. "I can hear it laughing."

His gaze hardened. A deadness entered his eyes and he stared at her, but she knew that it was not Feyiz.

He gasped as the demon released its hold. She saw it happen, the moment when he had control of his body back. And she saw the sorrow and hopelessness fill his eyes.

"No," he said. "Oh, Meryam, the things it *shows* you . . ."

Feyiz tugged his climbing ax out of the snow. He cocked back his arm. She screamed his name, reached out and grabbed hold of his jacket, tried to scramble close enough to take his wrist, but she was too far away, too late, too weak. With a ferocious strength,

Feyiz struck himself in the head with the ax, the point punching through flesh and bone and brain.

Meryam screamed her throat ragged. She kept her grip on Feyiz's jacket as he slumped downward, head lolling back, his full weight dragging on her. Adam called her name and then she felt his arm around her waist, holding on, shaking her hard to make her let go.

Her fingers were so cold, so numb, that she simply couldn't feel it when Feyiz slipped away. All she felt was the absence of his weight. She screamed curses at a God in whom she'd never believed.

Feyiz's body spilled down the mountain. Meryam kept screaming. The air was too thin for hysteria and she couldn't catch her breath between screams. Blackness swarmed in at the edges of her vision and she felt herself sag against Adam, suffocating in the darkness. Then the world was gone.

Blinking, she dragged in a breath and her heart began thudding in panic again. Adam was there, soothing her, talking to her in that comforting voice, as if he hadn't stopped at all. Which meant she hadn't blacked out very long, and that was good.

Long enough, though, that Hakan and Calliope had caught up to them.

Calliope had her camera out, filming it all.

"Fuck you," Meryam slurred. She gritted her teeth, then bit her lip again, sending bright pain surging through her, waking her up fully. "Fuck you and that camera."

"You told me to—" Calliope began to argue.

Meryam snarled at her. No words were necessary. But Calliope did not put the camera away, and Meryam knew that was right. God damn this woman for doing her bloody job.

Then she saw the way Hakan was looking at her and she remembered Feyiz.

"Hakan," Meryam said, drowning in grief. "I'm so—"

"Can you continue?" Hakan asked, voice colder and more dangerous than the storm.

Heart breaking, Meryam took stock of herself—of her pain and what little strength she thought she could muster.

"I think so."

"Then keep moving," Hakan said, studying both her and Adam with revulsion. "And go quickly, before I kill you both."

Walker had Father Cornelius pressed against the mountain. The priest had been moving slowly but surely, conserving both strength and breath. He might have been old, but he had a vitality and persistence that many people at his age could not manage. His skin had gone nearly as white as the blizzard, so pale he looked more like a cadaver than a living man, but those bushy eyebrows knitted together in determination above his goggles and he kept moving.

Until Feyiz's body had tumbled past them. The guide's skull had struck a rocky outcropping perhaps a dozen feet away and the loud, echoing crack had erased any doubt as to his fate. Blood smeared the snow below. Arms and legs twisted at wrong angles as he kept falling. Further below, someone screamed, days of pent-up fear and horror escaping in one, mournful wail.

Walker and his group had paused, paralyzed for a moment. He pressed Father Cornelius against the mountain, while a few feet away, Kim and Polly tried to persuade Wyn Douglas to keep going.

"Come on, love," Polly urged. "Keep moving."

"But what . . . how could it happen? Did he just fall?" Wyn asked, and then questions kept coming.

"It doesn't matter how," Polly replied. "We've got to—"

"Doesn't matter? He's dead! He was so kind, and now he's—"

"Wyn, you've got to keep moving!" Polly snapped.

"I can't!" Wyn shouted, as if her voice was an assault against the storm.

Kim shot a hard look at Walker, not a demand for him to intervene but a silent question: What would they do if Wyn would not move?

"We've got to go," he said firmly.

His little boy waited for him back home. Yes, there was work for him to do. He had responsibilities. But he wasn't going to die here, so far from home, with Charlie waiting for him there.

"Kim—" he began.

She didn't need his prodding. Nudging Polly aside, she grabbed a fistful of Wyn's jacket and tugged, forcing the archaeologist to hold on even tighter.

"What the hell are you doing?" Wyn shouted, staring at her, perhaps thinking the demon had entered her.

"Moving on without you!" Kim called over the storm's howl. "You can keep moving, or you can stay right here. If you stay here, eventually you'll freeze to death or you'll fall. But there is no scenario in which you stay here and live."

Kim started climbing down. Walker tapped Father Cornelius and they both began moving as well, one foothold, one handhold, at a time. Polly stayed with Wyn, arguing quietly for several seconds before they, too, began to move. As they passed the rocky outcropping where the snow had been stained with Feyiz's blood— black-red in the gray gloom of the storm—nobody but Walker turned to look.

Kim made her way over to him, so that they were climbing almost side by side, close enough to hear each other's grunting exertions.

"This shouldn't be happening," Kim said. "The charms are supposed to keep the demon out."

"We don't know," Walker said. "Feyiz might not have worn it—"

"Or it's just another myth! We've gambled our lives on a myth!"

Father Cornelius paused a moment, wheezing behind his balaclava. He craned his neck to look down at them as they continued.

"You don't know that," the priest rasped loudly.

"And we don't have any other answers!" Walker snapped. "We're committed now."

Memories flashed through his head. Images of Charlie. He thought of Christmas mornings when Charlie was still small and theirs had still been a happy home. He wondered now why he had never caught any of them on film. *Did people ever appreciate the moments they were in while they lived them?* he wondered, and the wondering tore him apart.

Walker glanced up to make sure Wyn and Polly were keeping pace and saw fear in Wyn's eyes . . . and Polly's left hand clutching Wyn's throat, squeezing.

He shouted, adrenaline searing through him. Crablike, he scrambled sideways and upward, grabbed hold of Polly's leg. She whipped her head around and through the swirl of whiteness he saw the glint of orange in her eyes. Polly snatched up the climbing ax that hung at her hip, turned and hacked it down at him. Walker tried to defend himself with one hand but she had such grotesque strength that he had to take his other hand away from the mountain. Polly gave a high, giddy squeal and kicked at his side. Her boot thumped his ribs and then Walker was falling.

He twisted as he fell, hurling himself sideways instead of down so that he could land flat on his chest. If he'd fallen outward, begun to tumble, broken bones would be the least of it. Instead he thudded against the snow and rock, dug his fingers in, and then jabbed the toes of his boots in deep. The edges of the crampons caught. Momentum almost tipped him backward, but he pulled his feet away from the mountain again, let his hands drag, let his knees create furrows in the snow, and then he dug his feet in once more.

Walker heard his heart thumping in his ears and he gave a shout of triumph and fury. Kim and Father Cornelius were shouting at Polly from below. Shouting at Walker to make sure he was all right. Every part of him told him to keep climbing, to get away from the demon, but when he looked back up he saw Wyn trying to scrabble away, clawing at the snow, clinging to the mountain.

Polly dragged her back. Steam came from her mouth and began to mist up from her eyes, as if the demon brought its own inferno and that hell burned now inside of her.

Below, Father Cornelius had begun to pray loudly. Walker could barely see him through the blowing snow, but the old man's rasp turned into a bellow now that he was praying, and Polly winced as if the words hurt her.

"Leave her!" Walker shouted, climbing toward them again. "In the name of God—"

The thing inside Polly did not wince this time. It laughed. "When have you ever believed in God?"

Wyn screamed, her face briefly visible as Polly wrapped an arm around her neck. The demon glanced back toward Walker, the gleaming embers of its eyes pinpricks of color in the white, churning sea of the storm.

"You have no faith, Benjamin," it said with Polly's lips, from behind that balaclava.

Then she wrenched Wyn's head to one side and the whimpering ceased. The struggling halted.

"No!" Walker cried.

Polly shook her head as if in disappointment, a parent schooling a recalcitrant child. "You don't believe in anything."

She kicked away from the mountain face, arms wrapped tightly around Wyn's lifeless body. Inhuman strength carried them out fifteen feet or more, and then they began to arc downward, plummeting through the storm. The other climbers screamed, watching it happen. Like a spider enshrouding its prey, Polly wrapped herself around Wyn for a moment . . . then sprang away from her, limbs pinwheeling as she reached for a handhold.

Polly struck, slid, rolled, and slammed into the jagged ridge of a crevice.

Wyn's body dropped out of sight, lost in the whistling swirl of white. Walker listened, but the storm had taken them so completely that he did not even hear the impact. Nearby, someone was choking back sobs. For a moment he thought it might be Kim, but then he saw her put a hand on Father Cornelius's back and he knew it was the priest who had begun to cry.

From above, he heard Meryam and Adam shouting at them to keep going, and he knew they had no choice.

"Keep moving," he said icily, making sure Kim and the priest heard him. "Go."

They started to climb, silent and resigned.

And then they heard the screaming from below.

Walker dug his ax into the mountain and leaned out as far as he dared, peering through the white. It took him a moment before he saw movement where no movement should have been.

Polly's body had struck that jutting stone ridge. Bones would have shattered. Blood would be everywhere. But still she was moving, crawling back up the mountain with one hand, humping up a few feet at a time, unnatural and inexorable.

"Kill her!" Walker roared down at those below. "You've gotta kill her!"

Something broke inside him as he said the words. He felt smaller, diminished, and farther away from his little boy than he had been before, even up inside the ark.

Olivieri clung to the mountainside, lost in despair that swallowed him more completely than the storm. The climb had gotten easier in the past few minutes, the angle lessening as they moved toward the cleft below. The first group—one guide and two archaeology students—had already passed the cleft and continued onward.

Then the bodies had begun to fall.

"Who was that?" he asked. "Did anyone see?"

He craned out farther to try to get a look, but it was no use. The blizzard swept around them in a blur of white that seemed to turn them all into ghosts, as if each climber were a spirit, already dead, wandering the slopes of Ararat forever.

"No idea who fell first," Errick said, "but I think there were two just now, both women. I saw green hair. Had to be—"

"Polly," Olivieri said numbly, dry lips cracking. He let go of his grip on his climbing ax, almost unconscious of the urge to give in completely, to just fall with the others. The strap on his climbing ax tugged against his wrist but he did not grip it again.

Mr. Avci shifted downward, boots digging into the snow. The wind gusted so hard that his jacket rippled with it and his body rocked slightly leftward.

"We must continue," Avci said. "We'll stop at the crevasse below. Just a few minutes of rest before we—"

Errick swore loudly.

Olivieri looked down and could barely take in the hideous white nightmare unfolding there. Through the veil of snow he saw Polly Bennett's green hair, a splash of color against the ghostly white world. Her left arm hung loose at her side, useless, and she dragged one leg behind her as she used her right arm and left leg to climb, leaving a smear of bright blood on the snow. Polly grinned so wide that her mouth had torn at the edges and blood flowed from her cheeks. Her eyes glinted like tiny flames as she scrambled upward, inhumanly fast.

Mr. Avci screamed. Errick let himself slide down toward Polly, by accident or in their defense, Olivieri didn't know, but suddenly he felt himself doing the same. He tugged his ax from the ice, moving, desperate to do something to fight back against the terror inside him, against the evil that he felt stained his heart and soul. Polly clawed at Errick's leg. He cocked back a boot and kicked her in the face, the claws of the crampon tearing her cheek even further open.

Errick lost his balance and his grip. Skidding farther down, he found himself first parallel to Polly and then slightly below.

Olivieri forgot his age. He forgot the extra inches around his middle and the years since he had last done any regular exercise. He pulled his hands and feet away from the snow and began to slide. Snow went up inside his coat and sweater and inside the cuffs of his pants and for a flicker of a moment he wondered if he would be able to stop.

He slid right into Polly. Snow flew up into her bloody, pale features, but those orange eyes blazed through the mask of white. Her green hair blew wild. A flap of skin from her torn cheek quivered in the roaring wind. Something gray jutted out through a tear in the sleeve of her coat, a jagged edge of broken bone that had burst violently from inside her arm as she fell.

Her one good hand closed on his jacket. Together, they began to slide again. Olivieri dug into the mountain with his boots and one hand as she thrust her face toward him. Her breath had the reek of rancid meat and though her lips did not move, he was certain he heard a chorus of voices whispering and laughing from the darkness at the back of her throat.

For a moment he had thought he could fight this, thought he could face evil and stand fast. Instead he began to weep and to bat at her with his free hand, wishing he had never come here, that he had never been so foolish as to think he could protect anyone. She grabbed his head and smashed his face against the mountain. The snow saved him, soft and yielding.

Other voices shouted. One belonged to Errick. He felt Polly tug away from him and forced himself to look, saw her fighting with Errick . . . saw her plunge her fingers into his left eye socket and pluck out something wet and squirming. Saw her dig in deeper, and when she pulled her hands away again, Errick began to skid away and then to roll, now that the slope was not so drastic. He tumbled into the cleft and came to rest against a ridge of rock, snow dancing around him.

Polly came for Olivieri again.

The others nearby were climbing away, desperate to escape, no delusions of heroism for them.

Only Mr. Avci remained.

Olivieri blinked in mute surprise. Avci had moved nearer, had climbed up to within five feet of them. He held a black pistol in his left hand, took aim, and shot Polly through the skull. A swatch of blood and green hair blew out the back of her head and hit the snow, skittering downward in its own grotesque little snowball.

"Oh, my God," Olivieri gasped, turning to thank Mr. Avci.

Avci aimed the gun at Olivieri's face. "You bastard. You said the charms would work. I should kill you next."

Then others were shouting and they both looked up to see Walker, Kim, and Father Cornelius scrambling down to them, and the moment passed. The fury—the hatred and fear—in Mr. Avci's eyes had been purely human.

Or, at least, he thought it had.

NINETEEN

Meryam and Adam sat together in the cleft. She lay against him, allowing him to hold her, and to hold her up. There had been a time when she would have contemplated the way this might look to the others, the way it might undermine the leadership she had established. They were beyond that point. Even without the storm and the horror, there was the cancer. It had worn away at her long before the cold had dug in its talons. Her weariness pulled at her like a siren's song, luring her into the darkness of unconsciousness. But unconsciousness meant surrender, and surrender would mean death.

They couldn't sit here long. She knew that. As long as they kept moving and kept well covered, they wouldn't suffer too badly from exposure. There was bound to be some frostbite, but if they could set a decent pace and make it off the mountain within a few hours after nightfall, at the latest, they would be all right. She reckoned less than an hour to reach Camp Two, maybe twice that to Camp One—less if the blizzard weakened at lower altitude, as she expected it would.

You can make it, she thought. But she rested against Adam and thought maybe, just maybe, she was telling herself a lie.

The survivors were clustered around her. She thought of them that way now. *The survivors*. Olivieri, Mr. Avci, Belinda and another student Meryam didn't know well. Hakan—*fucking Hakan*—and the other guide, his cousin or nephew or whatever. And Walker's little team. Somehow they were still intact, that trio of Walker, Kim Seong, and Father Cornelius. She didn't wish them dead, but she couldn't fight the jealousy it inspired to see them together, now that Feyiz was dead.

Then there was Calliope, with her camera. Meryam didn't know whether to murder her or admire her. *Maybe both. She fucked my fiancé.* But damn, the work ethic on this woman. She knew it might not be work ethic at all, that maybe it was more about the idea that viewing this horror through the lens seemed to keep it at arm's length. Calliope might feel safer with the distance the camera seemed to provide. Meryam knew it was a false distance, a false protection, but as much as she hated Calliope right now, she wasn't going to take that away from her. Not when she would have given anything for a little distance, a little sense of security.

"Hakan," she said, clearing her throat, mustering some residue of energy. "How much further before we can start hiking instead of climbing?"

Smashing his hands together to get the blood flowing, Hakan stood and looked over the ridge to get his bearings. His grief and fury were well hidden.

"Ten minutes if we move quickly," Hakan said. "Fifteen at most. It's really not far. After that we must still be very careful. Help one another. Use climbing poles if you have them."

"We're *all* going to stay together," Meryam told them, surveying the faces around her, gauging their terror and shock.

"Like hell we are," Belinda said, hidden behind goggles and

balaclava. "Every single one of us should be climbing alone, and should retreat if anyone comes near. That's what I'm gonna do. I'll keep in visual range, but I'm not going near any of you until we're down."

No one spoke. Instead, each of the survivors began to study the others around them, almost vibrating with fear and paranoia. Meryam felt it as well. She wasn't immune. From one face to the next, she searched for hints of the lunatic grin on their lips or the glint of orange in their eyes. They were all doing the same thing.

Was it here among them, even now? Was the demon inside one of them, relishing every moment?

"If we all stay together," Walker said, "then if the demon attacks, there will be enough people around to prevent more fatalities."

"Or try to, anyway," Calliope said.

"Try to," Father Cornelius agreed. "We will stay together. Those who wish to be on their own, we do understand. But if the evil enters you, takes you over, it may just make you hurl yourself down the mountain, or worse. We should be watching over one another."

"I still don't understand why this is happening," Mr. Avci snapped. "Professor Olivieri said the bitumen charms—"

"It was a theory!" Olivieri shrieked, so fragile Meryam thought she could see little bits of his psyche breaking off with every word. "I had reason to believe . . . the Apocrypha spoke of it . . . and Noah's family was wearing the damn things!"

The survivors had begun to pick themselves up again, shouldering their packs and making sure their faces were fully covered before they slipped over the ridge and began the careful descent.

Meryam took a deep breath to steady herself, then pushed off Adam's shoulder and rose to her feet. Her thoughts blurred and for a moment she thought she might fall over. Adam reached out to steady her but she waved him away.

"No. If I can't do this myself, you'll have to carry me down, and it's too dangerous."

Taking long, even breaths, she managed to clear her head. She'd had a protein bar while they rested and she could feel the little bit of energy it gave her starting to take hold. Somewhere in Adam's pack there were caffeine pills and she knew she might need those before long, too. For now, though, fear was all the motivation she required.

"Okay," she said. "Let's go."

The others had all gone over the edge of the ridge by the time she started to clamber backward over the rocks.

"Meryam," Adam said.

She glanced up to see him digging down inside his turtleneck, pushing his gloved fingers between the sweater and balaclava.

"What are you doing?"

Adam found the bitumen charm, snaked a finger around the twine from which it hung, and yanked it off. Before she could object, he tossed it into the snow behind him.

"I know what you're going to say," he told her. "But we both know they're not working. Maybe the demon's already in us, maybe the evil's taken root. Doesn't matter. I think our only hope is getting beyond its reach."

"Its reach?" she echoed, fresh fear buzzing inside her.

"Like a ghost can't leave the place it haunts," Adam said, his eyes hurt but hopeful. "I'm hoping that's what it is . . . that once we really get away from the cave, it can't hurt us anymore. If I'm wrong . . . well, if I'm wrong, we'd all have been better off going off the ledge that first night, dying right then."

"Don't say things like that."

Adam glanced away. "Let's just go."

He stayed by her side as they caught up to the others, descending more quickly now that the slope was less treacherous. His words echoed in her mind and that look in his eyes lingered, breaking her heart by degrees with every moment of reflection. She knew about the dybbuk, about the fear that had been his constant companion as a child, and she had always hated his grand-mother for having instilled that dark faith in him. He had never been able to escape it. Now he wouldn't put his faith in anything, including the charm Olivieri believed might save his life.

But Meryam had to keep the charm around her own neck. She had never believed, and now this horror had instilled her with the faith she had always lacked. There was no way she was going to take off that charm.

Which meant she would have to watch Adam very carefully from now on.

For a handful of minutes, they scrabbled down the mountain face in silence replete with wary glances. Walker stayed with Kim and Father Cornelius at the center of the line of climbers, the comfort-ing weight of the gun against the small of his back. Cold and numb as he'd become, he wondered if his fingers would cramp up if the time came for him to hold that weapon, to pull the trigger again.

When screams broke the silence, rising on the wind, he steeled himself and looked down with grim resignation. How could he be surprised, now? The demon had become their curse.

Kim swore and started to quicken her descent, but Walker barked her name and reached out to stop her.

"What are you doing?" she demanded. "We have to . . ."

Her words faltered as she gazed into his eyes. She looked at Father Cornelius for support and found none.

"We have to what?" he asked.

Only twenty feet below them, Hakan's cousin had turned on a student, a scruffy guy named Markus. He had a knife, and in-fernal strength, and with those tools murder took only seconds.

Blood flew in the falling snow, whipped away on the wind. Belinda tried to stop it, but that knife and that strength did their gruesome work on both of them, and soon the blood had splashed in hideous patterns across a stretch of snow, right where the slope became more accessible . . . right where things should have become easier for them.

The demon brandished its knife, and that soulless grin, and it started to climb back up toward them in the body of that guide—the last of Hakan's family on the mountain.

Walker pulled his gun. He held onto the mountain with one hand and aimed downward.

Shouting, Hakan skidded down from above, wanting him to stop, to let him try talking to the young man, give him a chance to drive the demon out. But the guide had that bloody knife and he was clambering spiderlike toward Walker and Kim and the priest, and Walker had been trained to eliminate the immediate threat.

He shot the guide twice in the chest. The bearded young man flopped backward, rolled down the hill, through the bloody snow, and tumbled to a halt where the ground became hikeable.

Hakan put a hand on Walker, who knocked it away with the barrel of the gun and then took aim at Hakan. For a full five-count they stared at each other, breathing deeply, until Walker decided Hakan had not been possessed—not yet—and Hakan apparently decided he did not want to be shot.

Scrambling down the snowy slope, sliding and then trudging, Hakan fell to his knees beside the corpse of his cousin. He closed his cousin's eyes, muttering prayers in their own language.

Walker held back with his team as Meryam, Adam, and Calliope passed them and went to stand by Hakan. Olivieri and Mr. Avci joined them.

"As soon as we get a little ways past the blood," Walker said quietly, turning to Kim, "I want you to go. Move as fast as you can.

I studied the hiking maps before we came. Camp Two isn't far. You can probably make out some of the path based on the way the snow has accumulated, but either way, you'll be safer on your own than you will be with any of us."

Kim stared at him, then glanced at Father Cornelius. "I won't leave the two of you behind."

"You're here to observe, not to die," Walker told her. "We'll be able to hike down from this point, but Cornelius can't go very quickly. Just the way it's got to be."

"Walker's right," the priest rasped, leaning against the mountain as if he hadn't any fear the demon would enter him next. "You should go."

"I'm safer with the two of you than on my own," Kim said. "But . . ."

Walker frowned. The weight in that one word, the thick lines in her forehead, showed just how much it disturbed her.

"What?" he urged.

Kim glanced at the others below, the handful of people gathered around Hakan while he mourned.

"What if we shouldn't even try?" she said. "What if the demon isn't poison, but more like a virus, and if we bring it down off the mountain we're just setting it loose in the world?"

Walker stared at her. He had no reply. What Kim had said terrified him more than any idea he'd ever heard.

Adam held Meryam's hand, but there was nothing romantic in the gesture. He had tried to get her to lean on him, to sling an arm around his shoulder so that he could help keep her on her feet, but she had refused. Only after she had stumbled several times and nearly sprawled face-first onto the snow-covered trail had she relented enough to hold on to his hand.

They trudged downward, some of them with hiking poles and others just aiding one another, lost in the shock of death and bloodshed. Nearly an hour had passed since the demon had made its last appearance, and Adam could feel the shock beginning to abate. He didn't dare hope that they had passed beyond its influence, but the spark of hope was hard to extinguish, particularly since he so wanted to believe it. Every minute that passed, he saw those around him beginning to relax the tiniest bit. And to feel. To grieve. Half an hour ago, Calliope had begun crying quietly and let her camera dangle in the grip of her right hand while she used the left to wipe her tears away.

Meryam stumbled. Adam gripped her hand tightly and pulled her to him, almost as if they were dancing. Face-to-face, he crushed her against him, watching her breath mist through the cloth of her balaclava.

"Camp Two is just ahead," Hakan called back to them.

He had taken the lead some time ago, with Calliope just behind, and Meryam and Adam trailing them. The rest were stretched out in an irregular line, but nobody more than fifty yards back.

Camp Two. The terrain would still be rough, particularly with a foot of snow on the ground and the wind still gusting, resisting their progress. But from Camp Two the trail would get easier, more pronounced, enough so that Adam thought he might be able to get down from there even without a guide. Camp Two was good news.

Don't be stupid, he told himself. *Don't hope. There's still a long way to go.* They had hours yet, and Meryam would only grow wearier. Adam didn't want to think about how complicated things would become if he had to carry her.

"Hakan!" he called, taking Meryam's hand again as they began again to follow the trail. "Wait for us!"

Up ahead, Hakan turned slowly toward them.

"Wait for you?" he said. "It takes all of my will not to leave you here."

"Now hang on," Adam replied.

Calliope shifted the weight of her camera from one hand to another but did not lift it to begin filming.

"What?" Hakan snarled, marching back toward Adam and Meryam, glaring his hatred at them, face nearly as full of malice as if the demon had taken him. "What do you want to say to me, you two disgusting beasts?"

"Fuck you, you obnoxious—" Adam began.

Meryam put the back of her hand over his mouth to stop the words, but she kept her gaze on Hakan.

"I'm sorry," she said, a hitch in her voice. "Feyiz was my friend, Hakan. I wish I could hear him laugh again and feel the openness and acceptance that he gave to everyone around him. But wishing won't fix anything. This group is all that's left. I don't know if this is just grief or if the demon's pulling your strings, bringing out the worst parts of you, but—"

"Slut," Hakan sneered.

Adam took a step forward, letting go of Meryam's hand. "That's enough!"

"Look at the two of you," Hakan said. "A Jew and a whore who has turned her back on God. I know the torment that awaits you both, but it is not enough. You parade yourself in front of my nephew until the stink of your sex fills his head so that he forgets himself, so that he can't do anything but what you desire," he said to Meryam, and then he turned to Adam. "And you . . . what do you do, *man* that you are? You seek out another whore to—"

"Hey, fuck you!" Calliope snapped.

Adam waded toward him, fists bunched, knowing that Hakan could thrash him within an inch of his life but not caring. The man needed to stop talking, he needed to be bruised and bleeding and unconscious. Even better if he were dead.

A gunshot cracked the sky, echoing off the mountain.

Hakan and Adam both spun to see Mr. Avci pointing his pistol at the clouds. The little man hunched over in exhaustion, glaring at them both. Walker and Kim came rushing down the trail, leaving Olivieri and the priest behind. Barking orders, trying to play alpha the same as he had since his arrival, Walker pulled out his own gun and leveled it at Avci.

"Get hold of yourselves," Avci said, ignoring Walker.

Adam's hatred seethed inside him. Hakan had been a bastard since the moment they'd met him, long before his grief and loss. But the things he'd said were unforgivable. Adam turned to Meryam.

"What do you say?"

Meryam stood up to her full height, pale but alive. When Adam reached for her hand, she batted it away, slogging through the snow so that she and Hakan were eye-to-eye. She spat in his face.

Hakan hauled back a fist as everyone began to shout. Adam rushed toward them, but he wouldn't make it in time.

Calliope did. She stepped between Hakan and Meryam and grabbed his arm before he could throw the punch. Whatever she might have said to him, Adam couldn't hear it. He wanted to thank her, but what could he say?

"You didn't have to—" Meryam began.

Calliope whirled on her. "Don't talk."

Meryam stuttered and took a step back.

"No, really," Calliope went on. "Don't say anything. Everything he said, about you . . . about Adam and about me . . . it's all true, and you know it. If there's a demon inside us, we invited it in. Don't you see that? The thing up in the cave might have been evil, but the awful parts of us are what fed it and made it grow."

The camera fell from her hand, thumping into the snow. Tears filled her eyes as she staggered backward, off the trail.

"Don't be stupid, girl," Hakan said.

Calliope only glanced at him, not bothering to wipe her eyes. She picked up her pace, cutting her own path away from the trail.

Hakan started after her, angrier than ever. Adam expected her to stop, to cry and catch her breath and then rejoin them, but it wasn't until Calliope started to run and fell, sliding down the mountain slope, bumping over rocks under the soft layer of white, that he realized she really meant to abandon them.

"Damn it, Calliope!" he shouted, striding off the trail.

Meryam grabbed his arm, her grip too weak to hold him but enough to get his attention. He turned to her, torn and panicked. Without a guide, off on her own, Calliope would die. Even if she made it to the base of the mountain, the odds of her being anywhere she could find refuge without freezing or starving to death were pitiful.

"I have to—" he began.

"No. You don't."

Heart pounding, he stared at Meryam, then turned to watch Hakan skidding and clambering after her. The wind kicked up again and for several seconds the storm swallowed Calliope entirely. They could still see Hakan, but she was gone.

"Calliope, come on!" Adam shouted. "You can't do this on your own!"

Hakan paused on the mountain, turned to point back up toward them.

"Stay on the trail. Camp Two is just below!" Hakan shouted. "Rest there no more than ten minutes, then carry on. I will bring her back."

"Let her go, Hakan!" Mr. Avci shouted. "We must have a guide!"

But Hakan had gone. Adam could see him slipping, knees bent, maneuvering down the slope. He watched until, like Calliope, Hakan had vanished in the swirl of white.

"I hate him," Meryam said, standing beside Adam.

"He hates you, too."

They stood another few seconds, staring into the frozen landscape, where the rush of wind and snow seemed to stretch out forever.

Then Meryam took his hand and they marched down into Camp Two.

Seven of them remained, and only Adam, Meryam, and Olivieri had any history climbing this mountain, all with more courage than skill.

TWENTY

They gathered behind a ridge of black rock that half encircled Camp Two, eating protein bars and drinking water. Walker wanted coffee, but none of them dared to take the time to make it, him least of all. They spoke little, still smothered in the paranoia that had been with them all day. They eyed one another, took a drink or a nibble, and then they packed up again. At first they had all been glancing the way Hakan and Calliope had gone, expecting them to return at any moment, but after the first ten minutes, there had been few glances in that direction. They had left enough people behind on the mountain that they were getting used to it.

Walker ejected the magazine from his weapon, checked it over, and then slammed it back into place. He wouldn't take any more chances.

"Let's move," he said, standing up.

Kim and Father Cornelius rose immediately. The others all glanced at Adam and Meryam, still thinking they were in charge. But Adam had to help Meryam to her feet, and the way he held onto her arm, assisting her, Walker wasn't confident she would make it to Camp One, never mind off the mountain. Part of him wanted to abandon them all, to just get himself home to Charlie. He would be a better father now, he promised any god who might be listening. He would be kinder to Amanda, a friend to her in the aftermath of his failures as a husband. If he left Meryam behind—and the priest, damn it, because Father Cornelius was so old and so fucking slow—he could be a better man.

But that made zero sense. How could he be a better man back in the world he'd known if he abandoned these people now? He couldn't be a father any son would look up to if he left them to die.

And you'd probably get lost and die without at least someone *who's climbed Ararat before.* Walker trudged down the snow-covered trail, claws of his crampons keeping his footing firm. He peered through the snow, watching Adam and Meryam moving slowly up ahead, and tried to tell himself that wasn't it—that he would have stuck with them even if he had climbed this mountain a thousand times.

It's not just that you need them, he thought.

And he tried to believe it.

He watched them carefully, now. For the first twenty minutes out of Camp Two, he kept his gun in his hand, but after awhile he had to holster it so that he could stretch his fingers and clap his hands together to get the blood flowing. The temperature ought to have risen at least a little as they dropped elevation, but if it had, Walker noticed no difference. If anything, the wind seemed to bring even colder air, frigid and biting, and there were spots on his mouth and around his eyes that had gone numb, places his balaclava didn't cover. He tried not to think about it.

Just as he tried not to think about the one thing on all of their minds with every step. Walker's back prickled with his certainty that he was observed, that evil descended the mountain with them, burrowed inside their hearts or minds. If he let himself think about it, he found he couldn't breathe. Fear trapped him between the desire to just stop and curl into a ball, huddling in fear, and the atavistic urge to simply run, screaming.

The demon was here among them, and Walker could practically feel it relishing their dread. Each of the survivors knew it was only a matter of time. He watched Adam and Meryam up ahead, wondering. On edge, afraid, but also ready.

"Slow down, Walker!"

Startled from his reverie, he realized he'd nearly caught up with Adam and Meryam. Snow had gathered on his goggles, as if for several minutes he had been sleepwalking. A hot jolt of dread ran through him. Sleepwalking, or not in control of himself?

He stopped and turned. Reached up and wiped the snow off his goggles, letting his hand come to rest on the lump beneath his thick layers of clothing, the hunk of bitumen rock on the twine around his neck. Anger flashed through him. They had relied on Olivieri. Even Father Cornelius had bought into the scholar's logic, but obviously it had been no better than a guess. *A guess we all wanted to believe.*

The curtain of snow parted and Kim emerged, Father Cornelius holding her arm to steady himself. A gust of wind embraced them, a squall of white that obscured them again, as if the storm were reluctant to reunite them. Then Kim was there, her eyes narrowed with frustration at being left alone with the priest.

"Sorry," he said. "Just got into the rhythm of it."

"Do not leave us behind," Kim replied with such emphasis it was nearly an accusation.

Walker stood aside and let them pass. "I won't. I swear."

Father Cornelius had been watching his own feet with determination, as if unsure of his steps. Perhaps he couldn't feel his feet touching the ground. Walker swore silently. That would be very bad.

"I need to talk to you about the charms," Father Cornelius said.

Walker thought he heard a cry behind him. His pulse quickened and he turned, holding up a hand to block the wind as he tried to peer through the storm. The other three members of the group had fallen back farther and were nothing but silhouettes in the storm. He cursed himself for not noticing, for getting so caught up in his own fear that he'd forgotten the people depending on him.

"Walker?" the priest called weakly.

But as Walker glanced back again he saw one of those silhouettes stumble, saw it fall, and then another began to hurtle through the veil of snow toward him. The third followed, running and sliding along the trail, moving with silent strength and confidence, and Walker knew. Just knew.

Irritated by his lack of response, Father Cornelius pulled away from Kim and turned around, starting to berate him for his rudeness. Then the priest saw the figure springing along the trail with agility none of them could have duplicated.

Kim shouted that *it* was back.

It emerged from the storm, figure solidifying enough that Walker could make out the familiar shape of Armando Olivieri. But Olivieri had never moved like this, never been graceful or powerful or fearless, and this thing was all of those and more.

Walker reached for his gun, drew it out with numb fingers, and those same numb fingers fumbled with it. The weapon bobbled, seemed almost to dance away from his grip. Reaching after it, he knocked it into the snow at the edge of the path, and then all of the calm he'd mustered fled him. Flushed with fear, heart seizing in panic, he dove after the gun and hit the ground, scrabbling in the snow. The gun had made an imprint but vanished into it. Father Cornelius and Kim shouted at him and at Olivieri even as Walker dug around for the gun, and he knew he was about to die.

The thing came at him and he heard it laugh as it grabbed his head, ripped away the hood and the fabric of the balaclava that covered him. With the other hand, it tangled its fingers in his hair, got a fistful, and yanked backward in the same moment that his own fingers found the gun.

As it hauled him back, he twisted in its grasp and spun, aiming the gun at Olivieri's face. The professor's eyes gleamed with that internal fire, the glint of tainted orange light, and the demon grinned. Olivieri released Walker and stepped back, raising his hands as if in surrender. With Olivieri's mouth, the demon laughed.

"Shoot him!" Adam called, rushing up now to shove between Kim and the priest. "You can't give it a second to—"

"Oh, yes," the demon said with Olivieri's lips. "Shoot me."

Walker stared at it. For a moment his vision had shimmered and in the billowing snow he had thought he'd seen another face, a misshapen thing with horns and a mouthful of black needle teeth. Then still a third face, his little boy's. Charlie's.

Shoot me, he heard inside his head.

"What's the point?" he snapped. "It's only going to jump again!"

The orange eyes flared brightly and Olivieri snarled. Then, abruptly, the professor's face changed. The light went out of his eyes and he stumbled forward a step. Walker nearly pulled the trigger, prompted by that step forward, but then he saw Olivieri's sorrow and confusion and he understood that the demon had left him.

He only had a moment to wonder *where*, and then he felt it slide into him. A shudder rocked him, a mixture of pleasure and regret and a sorrow so deep that he yearned for the release of death. The filth spread through him and he imagined it as a kind of poison or infection, a stain seeping deeper and deeper, so that the urge to peel away his skin gave way to the desire to dig deep into the flesh, to drain the marrow out of his own bones. Anything to be rid of the filth inside him.

In that moment, Walker understood insanity. He opened his

mouth to scream, but the screams were only silent things that echoed inside his mind, because his mouth was no longer his own.

Neither were his hands.

Walker could see out through his own eyes, but he felt the evil inside with him. He felt his arm move and tried to fight it, but the demon had control. The intruder violated his flesh and his heart, the core of his soul, and he could feel its glee. Its jubilation.

"No," Professor Olivieri said, arms out, moving through the blizzard toward him.

Walker's right hand lifted the gun. He felt the twitch of his finger as the demon pulled the trigger twice. The shots rang out, echoed by his own screams, lost inside his head . . . and then he fell forward, dropping to his knees.

The demon had left him.

"—it, Walker!" Kim was screaming. "Fight it!"

You can't fight, he thought, not sure if his voice would be his own.

Olivieri lay on his back on the snow, hands over his chest. Blood welled up through holes in his coat, steam rising as the bright red spilled down the fabric and began to melt snow, a vivid pool of color.

"I'm sorry," Walker said. "Oh, my God, I'm so sorry."

Olivieri coughed and blood sprayed from his lips, then began to drool from the corner of his mouth. Meryam and Adam went to him, kneeling on one side while Walker stared in mute horror on the other, his flesh afire with shame that he had been so easily used, his body perverted for such evil purpose.

Kim stood behind him with Father Cornelius, who had begun to say the prayers that accompanied the last breaths of the dying in his church.

Walker bent forward, eyes pressed shut, cradling his own gut as he fought to hold on to some sense of himself.

When he opened his eyes again, Olivieri had stopped coughing.

The dying man stared at him, but it wasn't Olivieri anymore. The demon grinned up at him, eyes gleaming, and it laughed softly, a wet chuffing almost lost in the whistle of the wind.

"Poor Ben," the demon rasped, blood bubbling out of its mouth. "You thought you could fight me, but how easy it was to cast your will aside. I can't wait to meet Amanda. I can't wait to get inside Charlie. The things I'll make him do."

Walker stiffened, all of the self-loathing and guilt burning right out of him.

"You're not getting anywhere near my boy," he said.

Again the demon laughed. He spoke again, more quietly this time, but Walker bent forward and he could make out the words, even in the storm.

"You'll never get away from me, you fool. You've taken me with you."

Sneering, Walker raised the gun again, this time in full control. But then the light went out of Olivieri's eyes—both natural and unnatural—and the professor's head slumped to one side. His body went still.

Walker got up, legs unsteady.

"It isn't right to just leave him," Father Cornelius said.

"What else can we do?" Meryam asked weakly.

Walker spun and took aim at her left eye. Meryam froze, but he swung the gun over to aim at Adam's chest, then at Father Cornelius.

"It's me, Walker," the priest said, his voice a tired rasp. "It's only me."

For a long, breathless moment, Walker stared at him, then glanced around at the others. They were all just themselves, it seemed. But only for now. It had gotten inside of him. Adam had been possessed as well. Father Cornelius and Kim had each been at least temporarily tainted by it. It could take any one of them, any time it wanted. Which meant that Walker had to start thinking differently. He was not going to let the demon off this mountain. It would never get the chance to threaten the people he loved. If that meant he had to kill them all, and then eat a bullet himself, then that was exactly what he would do.

A last resort, he thought.

But as a shaking Mr. Avci came stumbling along the trail, his own gun trembling in his hands, Walker wondered how long he could wait before the last resort became the only choice.

Somewhere out there in the storm, Hakan and Calliope might still be alive, but he wasn't counting on it. Without them, that left six survivors.

And a long way still to go.

"Adam, lead the way," Walker said.

Hesitating, Adam stared down at Olivieri's corpse. At last, he gave a nod, but his eyes were devoid of hope. He took Meryam's hand and they started down again. The others fell into step, all of them keeping close now.

Walker knew the demon moved with them. There was only one way to stop it.

Father Cornelius walked with Kim's assistance, with Mr. Avci taking up the rear. The officious little man had his gun out and his gaze shifted left and right, peering into the storm, as if what they had to fear was out there somewhere, instead of within.

"Walker, you must listen," Kim said. "Cornelius and I have been talking. There's no way to know what limitations this creature has—"

"It's a 'creature' now? I think we all know what it is," Walker replied.

Father Cornelius erupted in a rattling cough, then spit into the snow. After all they'd been through, he looked his age at last. More than his age. He looked a hundred years old, but Walker figured they all looked like walking cadavers by now.

"In all the priesthood taught me and in all I've learned in my secular research, there's never been any reliable account of anyone dealing with demons like this," Father Cornelius said. "Exorcisms, certainly, and loads of ancient writings about evil spirits, but always with the caveat that they could be driven out . . . and once they were driven out, they would either lose their power or one could guard against the return of that evil. I've never run across an account in which a demon could move from one person to another with such ease."

"In your vast experience," Walker said drily.

"Walker, you're being an asshole," Kim observed. "He's the only one here who's ever been to an exorcism, and I don't know about you, but he's certainly spent a lot more years researching all of this than I have."

Shuddering, Walker reached up to pull shut the collar of his coat. The more tired he became, the more the cold sapped his strength and will.

"I know," he said. "That's frustration talking."

"The charms are not working," Father Cornelius said. "That much is clear. But what if they're actually hurting instead?"

The question made Walker falter a step, so that Kim bumped into him. He kept moving, but shot the priest a hard look as he went.

"How do you figure?" he asked, but his own thoughts were already shifting.

"Maybe it's not a good idea for us to have taken anything from the ark that had any contact with the cadaver," Kim answered. "Maybe the demon's consciousness was still in its bones or still in the ark—we have no way of knowing—but if so, do we want to walk around with bits of its sarcophagus around our necks?"

Seemed like a good idea at the time, Walker thought. Olivieri had convinced them the bitumen shards could protect them, but Olivieri was dead now. The fingers on Walker's right hand twitched, muscle memory from the moment he had pulled the trigger and murdered the professor. Only he hadn't pulled the trigger at all, had he? The demon had done that.

But Walker's body remembered it.

"I've been thinking the same," Mr. Avci said, closer behind them than they'd realized.

Walker flinched and glanced back at him, watching the gun in Avci's grasp. The man seemed himself, but there was no way to be sure.

Mr. Avci reached his left hand up to his neck and dug through the layers of fabric, pushed his fingers in and then yanked hard, tugging out the gleaming black bitumen shard and the twine on which it had hung. Without hesitation he flung it away and Walker saw him visibly relax, as if the charm had been a terrible weight on his spirit.

Anger rippled through Walker and he felt his brow furrow. He faced forward again, picking up his pace to catch up with Meryam and Adam. Kim and Father Cornelius did their best to keep up.

"What do you think, Walker?" Kim demanded.

"I think you should do what you want."

"But—"

"Wait a second," he said, shaking his head as he slowed again. Meryam and Adam kept going. Mr. Avci caught up, but Walker paid him no attention. His thoughts had drifted back to the cave— to the first time he'd seen one of those charms. Nearly the whole descent he had been ruminating, flipping through images in his mind, trying to find any hint at the demon's nature. Something that would help them.

Father Cornelius put a hand on his shoulder. "What is it?"

Walker trudged on, staring at his feet without seeing them. His mind returned to the ark, to the moment he had first encountered Helen Marshall.

"The archaeology team found them on some of the cadavers

in the ark," he said, as much to himself as the others. "Why not all of them?"

"Maybe they had the same disagreement we're having now," Father Cornelius suggested.

"When we first got there," Walker continued, "I talked to Professor Marshall. She and her team were working on several sets of remains, but one of the passengers had died trying to claw her way out of the ark, through a door that had been jammed shut against the side of the mountain. She'd lost her mind, obviously, but she was trying anything she could to get out of the ship . . . to get away."

He glanced over at the priest. "There was no charm on that cadaver."

"I remember it," Mr. Avci said, behind them.

"Are you saying the demon drove her mad because she wasn't wearing one?" Kim asked.

"Maybe," Walker replied, boots crunching on snow. The cold slithered inside his clothes. He'd gone numb inside and out. "But what if it wasn't just madness? What if she was trying to escape the others on board the ark, the ones who were wearing the charms, because she'd figured out that they'd made the wrong decision? That instead they were making it easier for the demon to possess them?"

"But why would that be?" Kim asked. "It makes no sense."

Father Cornelius stumbled on the snow. Walker caught him, helped him right himself. He saw just how pale the priest had become, just how much the climb had taken out of him. Ahead, Adam and Meryam did not even seem to notice. They marched downward, slowly but relentlessly, never turning around to check on the welfare of their charges. Walker hated them a little bit for that.

"What if . . ." the priest said. "What if they trapped its spirit? Somehow they killed it and they boxed it up in that coffin and encased *that* in bitumen. They thought they'd imprisoned the demon's essence, but instead it . . ."

"It seeped," Kim said. "They'd have felt it, the evil getting under their skin, the same way we did. If it infused itself into the bitumen, then when they put those charms on, all they were doing was giving it more intimate access, keeping it with them. . . ."

Her words trailed off, and the four them stopped dead on the trail, turning to face one another, giving each other a bit of protection from the wind and the whipping snow. Mr. Avci still had his gun in his hand, but Walker noticed that he held it as if he'd almost forgotten it was there. He looked up at Kim.

"We're saying they knew the same legend Olivieri told us about?" he said. A gust of wind bumping him forward, so they were all even closer. He could see the exhaustion in their eyes, and the dreadful realization.

Father Cornelius swayed, squeezing his eyes closed as if he might collapse. He put a hand on Mr. Avci's shoulder to hold himself up.

"What if Olivieri isn't the one who told us about that legend?" the priest asked. His eyes opened and he gazed into the gray nothing in the space between them. "What if it was never his suggestion to begin with?"

"Shit," Kim whispered. "Shit, shit, shit." Her fingers were at work, digging into the folds of her clothing in search of her charm.

As Kim hurled the charm off into the driving snow, Walker turned to shout down the trail. "Adam! Meryam!" They'd only gotten another twenty yards or so along the path, but they were ghosts in the white veil now. "The charms . . . you've got to take them . . ."

He hissed icy air in through his teeth and stood up straight, spine rigid.

"Walker?" Father Cornelius asked, reaching for his arm.

The evil slid into him so easily, as if it had blazed a trail before and now possession had become effortless. Walker screamed, but only inside. On the outside, he felt the grin that tore the edges of his mouth and he heard the laugh that came from his own throat.

Mr. Avci pointed a gun at his temple, too close to miss, and Walker felt gratitude and transcendence. Inside, he waited for the bullet. Outside, he heard Kim shout and saw her lunge and knock Avci's gun hand aside. The gunshot echoed off the mountain, the sound bouncing around inside the maelstrom.

Walker could taste the blood seeping from the torn edges of his mouth, but he could not control his hands as he reached out and grabbed Father Cornelius's skull in his hands. The demon relished that moment, and Walker felt its pleasure.

"Good-bye, holy man," it said through him.

Father Cornelius clawed at him, trying to fight back.

The priest yanked back a fist and Walker caught a glimpse of frayed twine and of the black shard that dangled from it. He gasped as he felt the sudden release, and fell to his knees as the demon left him. Left him utterly. A giddy relief swept him and he threw his head back and gazed with love at Father Cornelius, not caring about the pain at the corners of his mouth or the taste of his own blood.

"Thank you," he said, staring at the priest but thinking of Charlie. Thinking of the life he'd given up hope of living. "Father, thank you so—"

The priest's eyes glittered with orange light.

Father Cornelius snarled as he turned on Kim. She swore and began to stagger backward, but he struck her with a blow that sent her sprawling off the trail. Mr. Avci raised his gun again, but the priest grabbed him by the wrist and twisted, snapping bone. Avci shrieked in pain and the gun fell into the snow.

Walker drew his own gun, aimed it at the old priest's face.

Father Cornelius laughed. The sound came from somewhere

far away, like the hideous whisper in a nightmare from which there could be no waking.

"Go on, then," the demon said. "Murder another one."

Walker gripped the gun. His chest ached as it rose and fell. The copper tang of blood in his mouth made him want to retch. He hesitated two seconds, perhaps three, but then the old priest turned and sprang away from them, darting into the snow with strength and speed no man could have.

He pulled the trigger. The priest had already become a ghost in the storm, but Walker saw him stagger as the bullet caught his right shoulder. The wound did not slow him. Walker fired twice more, but by the time the echo from those shots faded, the figure had vanished completely, lost in the swirl of frozen white.

Father Cornelius was gone.

TWENTY-ONE

An hour or so later—it was difficult for Meryam to keep track of time now—she fell to her knees in the snow. Adam tried to help her up. Failing that, he tried to comfort her, but she weakly pushed his hands away, sucking air in through her nose. She whispered tiny prayers, quiet pleas, not caring what facet of God might be listening but hoping some higher power would hear her, and take her pain away. Take her fear and regret.

Instead, her stomach convulsed and she retched, heaving a torrent of stinking vomit into the snow. She hadn't eaten much, but it was all there, along with plenty of stomach acid and a smattering of blood. It relieved her to know that Adam wouldn't see that blood—people had an instinctive urge to look away from vomit. There would be no questions about that blood. It occurred to her that he might not have asked even if he'd seen it. They both knew the cancer had invaded her, that it was eating her from within, slowly killing her. The demon from the ark had not been the first poison, the first evil, to infect her.

"Hey," he said in her ear. Gently. Kindly.

His hand had rested on her shoulder and she hadn't even

noticed. Now she leaned into him, shuddering as she choked back her tears. She took his hand and began to rise.

"Meryam, you can rest," Adam said, studying her face. "We have time."

She steadied herself on him and stood, holding on as a gust of wind tried to push her backward. "We *don't* have time."

Adam held her face in his gloved hands. Nose wrinkling at the taste of bile in her mouth, she tried to smile at him in spite of the balaclava covering most of her features. She had come to hate the storm and the heavy clothing that erased so much of their identity.

"We threw the charms away," he reminded her, and then he turned toward the others, who had stopped a respectful distance away while she puked up her guts. "All of us. It's been an hour or more and it hasn't come after us again. More than that . . . I can feel it and I know you can, too."

She was still turning it all over in her mind, trying to make rational sense of the theory Kim and Walker had presented. The way they'd worked it out, the demon's spirit had been trapped inside the coffin and its bitumen encasement. Its malevolence had settled into the bitumen, had driven the people on the ark insane and possessed them and forced them to murder and despair, just as it had done to the people Meryam and Adam had brought into the ark thousands of years later. Adam had suggested the possibility that it had been inert, somehow—almost hibernating—but that they had woken it by breaking the encasement around its coffin.

The rest—what Walker believed about the demon influencing Olivieri, convincing them to wear the charms—that much seemed irrefutable. Back inside the ark, the demon had grown strong enough to influence or possess whoever it wanted. Now, this far from the place where its remains had been turned to cinders, it could still exert its evil, but it could only possess someone who remained connected to it through contact with one of those bitumen shards.

Meryam glanced at Walker and Kim, and poor Mr. Avci cradling his broken hand against his body. Mr. Avci didn't need her sympathy. He was still alive. They all were—him and Walker and the brilliant, lovely Kim Seong, and even Adam—the four of them were going to make it. Meryam might still be walking, but she was just as dead as the people they'd left bleeding in the snow. The others were going to live. They were the survivors, not her. And she hated them for it.

"Maybe you're right," she said, noticing for the first time that the blizzard had calmed. The snow still fell and the wind still blew, but not with the same level of rage. "I'd like to think it can't get inside us now, but even if that's true, Father Cornelius is still out there. So are Hakan and Calliope, if they're alive. So we're not safe. Not yet."

Adam gave a curt nod. He didn't want to hear it—she knew that. Adam wanted her to let him pretend the danger had passed, but Meryam could not give him that. No matter how much she loved him.

"Let's go," Adam said.

He slid an arm around her and helped her along the trail. Meryam would have liked to do it on her own, but they both knew she could not. Her strength had ebbed so low that she barely knew where she was going at this point, and throwing up had weakened her further. So she leaned against him, and nothing mattered but the touch of his body against her and her living long enough to make sure he got out of this. That was the engine that drove her, the fire that burned inside—making sure Adam made it home alive.

"I love you," she rasped, but the wind kicked up and her voice betrayed her.

"Hmm?" he asked, frowning as he glanced at her. "What'd you say?"

Meryam coughed and wiped her glove across her mouth, shaking her head to indicate that she'd said nothing important. That they should just keep moving.

The snow kept on, the wind rising and falling but never returning to its former fury. Meryam trudged onward, her vision blurring and her head bobbing as if she were on the verge of nodding off while she walked. Black spots danced in front of her eyes and edged in at the corners of her eyes and she knew her body wanted to stop. To fall.

Walker and Avci had their guns out. Several times, Adam paused and forced them to rest a minute, and Meryam saw those guns and wondered what good these foolish men thought they would do. Bullets might rend flesh, but the demon had no flesh of its own. She supposed she did understand the logic. If they encountered Hakan or Calliope or the priest, possessed, the guns would stop them. Bullets wouldn't kill the demon but they would free those it possessed. And if those guns managed to kill everyone still wearing a bitumen charm, then perhaps these so-called survivors really would have escaped.

But Meryam felt haunted. The demon's touch had carved a place at the base of her skull and it huddled there, even now, like a runaway hiding in the shadows of an alley. In her secret heart, the place where she kept only the most precious and the most horrible bits of herself, she thought it might be a good thing she was dying. It might be for the best.

She lost track of time. It blurred like her vision, came and went like the wind, but after a while she blinked and realized they had stopped for another rest. Drawing a deep breath, she looked around and saw Walker holding Kim in a tender embrace.

"Adam?" she said, oddly numb. Most of her pain seemed to be gone.

His face appeared beside her and Meryam realized they were seated, side by side, on a large rock.

"I'm here," he said. "You still with me?"

Cheerful. But beneath the cheerfulness, she saw his grief. He knew she was dying. Of course he had known for a while, but now it was real. Even more real than the fear that had driven them down the mountain.

Meryam forced herself to perk up, reached down into a reserve of will that she had never known she had, until now—when she needed it.

"I'm still with you," she said. "And we're going to live. We're going to make it."

Adam smiled, and she saw that the snow had abated enough that it had become beautiful. The sky had turned gray instead of white and she knew they were well into the afternoon. Then she saw lumps beneath the snow on the ground, noticed the rock formations and recognized the shape of the clearing they were in, and she realized where they were.

"Camp One," she said. "Have we come so far?"

"We have," Adam said, squeezing her hand. "But we've got a long way still to go."

A thought occurred to her. She glanced at Walker and Kim again. "Where's—"

"Avci had to piss," Adam told her.

Meryam almost managed a smile.

Then they heard the gunshot, and Avci screamed, and they all looked over to the edge of Camp One and saw the body slump from behind a rock and sprawl on the ground, pushing snow ahead of it.

And Father Cornelius stepped out of the storm. For a moment Meryam wavered on her feet, vision blurring again, and a muffled bit of consciousness at the back of her mind wondered if any of this were really happening. She could barely feel the cold, and the world around her had the not-quite-there texture of a nightmare. Sounds were muffled.

The priest stepped over Avci's bloody corpse in a single, smooth stride, and she saw his grin. He'd torn off his balaclava and his jacket. Now he strode toward Walker and Kim with a smile so wide it had ripped his cheeks almost as far back as his ears. Blood painted his jaw and throat, streaks of vivid red that stood out against the white of the falling snow.

But his eyes were on Meryam. The grin seemed meant for her, and those eyes held a knowing gleam along with the glitter of orange fire, as if they shared a secret.

She wanted so badly to scream. Instead, she started toward the thing that had been Father Cornelius. Adam grabbed the sleeve of her coat and dragged her backward. Meryam tried to fight him and he shoved her to the ground.

"You can barely stand. He'll kill you."

"I'm—" she started to say. *Dying. I'm dying anyway.* But Adam had already rushed over to stand with Kim and Walker, leaving Meryam on her own, sprawled in the snow.

The demon in Father Cornelius crouched forward, lifted his hand, and gave her the same kind of little wave a circus clown might give a child in the audience, as if to tell her that this show was for her. Then it sprang on top of Walker, beating him with both fists as it rode him down into the snow.

Meryam could only watch the nightmare unfold.

Walker felt the blows in his skull like savage music thumping his brain. He'd seen the priest and he'd hesitated. So stupid. No hat, no coat, no balaclava, out there on the mountain more than an hour after they'd last seen him, an old man in priestly black and a white patch at his collar . . . zero chance he had gotten there without the demon driving him.

Its fists came down. Father Cornelius's fists. An old man's paper-thin skin and blue veins and age spots and chafed knuckles. Walker felt his nose break, tasted a rush of fresh blood, and he roared and whipped himself side to side, but the thing inside the priest had strength born of hell instead of muscle.

Hell, he thought, as a fist thumped his left temple and he felt the orbit around his left eye crack. He believed in Hell now. Which meant that somewhere up there, God existed, and Walker was beneath his notice. They were all, the people dying here on the side of Mount Ararat, not worthy of his attention.

Another punch. The right side, breaking off an upper incisor. God, he decided, was an asshole.

Grunting, he jerked his arm, turned the gun, and pulled the trigger. The shot went wide, but the grin left Father Cornelius's face. The orange glitter in his eyes flared brightly and he snarled as he wrapped both hands around Walker's throat, as if he'd had enough of playtime and decided the killing moment had arrived.

Seconds. All of those blows, all of those thoughts, had taken only seconds.

Walker's vision darkened. The lights were going out in his head.

Then he heard shouting—two voices, and one of them belonged to Kim Seong. The demon's grip loosened and Walker blinked, focusing enough to see Kim and Adam struggling with Father Cornelius. Adam had an arm around the priest's throat, wrestling him backward, trying to drag him off Walker. Kim had him by the left arm, clawing at his eyes with her free hand as she attempted to twist him away.

She stopped clawing at his face. Her hand dropped to her side and came back up with her climbing ax. The metal gleamed wetly as she swept it down and buried it into the priest's chest. Sputtering and wheezing, Father Cornelius reeled backward. Adam shoved him and the priest went rolling to the ground with the climbing ax still jutting from a place high on his left side.

Father Cornelius whipped his head up, staring murder at them all. The orange fire in his eyes blazed so bright it might have been actual flame.

Walker lifted his gun and shot the priest once, the bullet taking him in the right shoulder and knocking him backward. It wasn't too late, he told himself.

"Adam, get the charm off him!"

The demon twisted, hissing as Adam lunged. Kim wrapped herself around its left arm and tried to drag it back, but as Adam snatched at the priest's collar, he came away only with the white tab that marked his office.

Father Cornelius grabbed Adam by the neck and dug in his fingers, then ripped out his throat in a spray of bright blood.

The snow fell.

Walker screamed as if he could deny what he'd just seen. He hurled himself at the demon, momentum crashing them both to the ground. Shouting for Kim, he jammed the gun snugly beneath the priest's chin.

Kim's hand flashed in front of him, dug inside the now open collar, and tore the bitumen charm from around Father Cornelius's neck. Her fist pulled back, trailing loose twine, and she cocked her arm and threw the gleaming black shard out into the storm, as far from Camp One as she could manage.

Walker saw the priest's eyes go clear as the demon departed. He saw the knowledge of what he'd done flood Father Cornelius's eyes, and then the old man began to weep, lying on the ground as snowflakes danced gently down upon his face.

From behind them, Walker heard Meryam begin to scream, her voice weak, ragged, and full of an anguish he had never heard from another human.

Adam lay on the ground with his throat flayed open and pumping blood, as if wolves had been at him but had run off without their prize.

"Oh, God," Kim said, the gentle snow eddying on a light breeze that caressed them all, living and dead alike.

She stumbled past Adam's corpse and made her way toward

Meryam. Walker listened to her attempts to comfort the other woman, but Meryam would not listen. She could only cry out to her dead fiancé, telling him to get up, that he was the one who was meant to live, that none of it meant anything without him.

"Father," Walker said, looking down at the priest where he lay in the snow.

The climbing ax still jutted from Father Cornelius's chest, and blood oozed from the bullet wound on the other side. But Walker doubted these injuries were the worst of what had been done to the old man. His face had been torn so badly and he had lost so much blood that it seemed impossible he had even made it to Camp One. The elements should have killed him if the blood loss had not, but the demon had been the furnace inside him, the engine that drove him.

Now that fire had gone out.

"Father," Walker said again.

The old man's lips were moving, despite the horrible injuries to his mouth and face. He managed only a bubbling whisper, a rasp made almost unintelligible by those mutilations, but Walker understood. Father Cornelius had begun to pray. They were words Walker had heard before, at the bedside of his mother, when the hospital had summoned a priest for last rites. The words were a prayer for the dying, but Father Cornelius spoke them on his own behalf.

Walker remained silent, held the old man's hand, and prayed with him as he died.

Just in case God was listening.

The three of them made their way down from Camp One together. Meryam staggered along between Kim and Walker, doing her best to stay upright. Sometimes she managed to walk freely, though never without a steadying hand, and other times she grew lightheaded, and darkness swept in around her, and they had to sling her arms around her shoulders and practically carry her down.

Human wreckage, they kept going, and by the time night began to fall they had made it nearly back to the place where there would be trucks and people and food. *Oh, my God, food*, Meryam thought, in a moment of ravenous lucidity.

The snow kept falling, though only very lightly now, almost as if the heavens offered beauty in apology for the cruelty of the blizzard that had lashed the mountain.

Meryam staggered to a stop, nearly falling as she tried to get away from the others, to go back up the trail.

"Stop," Kim said. "What are you—"

"There!" Meryam said, pointing a shaking finger. "Don't you . . . do you see him?"

They hadn't.

In the shadows of a copse of leafless trees, Hakan sat alone with his shoulders hunched. An orange light gleamed in the near darkness and Meryam almost screamed, but then she saw the light flare and diminish, and she realized it was the tip of a cigarette. Hakan sat awaiting them, smoking, exhaling plumes of gray cancer into the air.

Walker broke away from them, leaving Meryam to lean on Kim. He drew his gun, approaching Hakan warily.

"How the hell did you get down here?" Walker barked.

Hakan cocked his head. "I should be asking you that question."

"Show me your throat! Open your shirt and show me you're not wearing one of those fucking charms!"

Hakan let his cigarette dangle from his lips as he complied. Its orange tip flared brightly again, and flashes of memory flickered through Meryam's mind. The gleam of orange in the eyes of the possessed would stay with her for as many hours, days, or weeks as she had remaining to her.

"Turn out your pockets!" Walker demanded.

Hakan took a long drag of his cigarette and stood to comply. "You're wasting your time. I never had one. Feyiz gave me one of the charms but I left it back up in the ark. It felt wrong to me. If the demon wanted me, I didn't see how a little piece of rock . . ."

He let the words hang in the air. Meryam wanted to ask why he had not made the argument up on the mountain, before they evacuated the cave, but she knew the answer. They never would have listened to him.

Walker lowered his gun but did not put it away.

"What happened to Calliope?" Kim asked.

Hakan nodded slowly. He reached carefully inside his jacket, watching Walker to make sure not to alarm him, and he withdrew Calliope's camera. Meryam couldn't be sure in the faded light, but she thought it might be smeared with blood.

"I thought you might want this," Hakan said, showing the camera to Meryam.

Trembling, she thanked him. "Please . . . you hold onto it for now."

His eyes, so often full of anger and disdain, softened as he studied her. "Adam?" he asked.

"Back up there," she said quietly, gesturing toward the peak of Ararat. "With the rest."

Hakan nodded slowly. She saw a flicker of something in his expression, some decision, and then he moved Kim aside and lifted Meryam into his arms. She stiffened, remembering all of the hatred he had inflicted upon her, but then she let it go. Let herself relax into him. The man saw a dying woman and had decided to show her a last kindness. She would not take that away from him.

Walker began to argue, but Kim silenced him, and these few

last survivors began the final stage of their descent. Meryam thought about the burned remains in the cave, and the slabs and chunks of broken bitumen up there. She thought about the dead they had left behind, and the shards of bitumen around some of their necks, as well as the other charms that had been cast aside, somewhere on the face of Ararat. Where was the demon now? Still inside the ark? Suffused into the bitumen? Haunting the shards they'd left behind?

Or was he still with them, these few survivors, quietly waiting to meet the modern world?

Meryam wept quietly in Hakan's arms. As he walked, her body rocked against him, and soon she lost consciousness.

Her dreams were filled with screaming.

TWENTY-TWO

On the second Tuesday in April, Kim Seong sat at a small, round table in Pizzeria Paradiso and waited for her lunch appointment to arrive. She'd taken a table right by the windows that looked out on the sidewalk so she could watch pedestrian traffic passing by on M Street, but also because it was an unseasonably warm early spring day in Washington, D.C., and she wanted to feel the sun on her. Ever since Ararat, she could not get enough of the sun.

"Can I get you a drink while you wait?"

Kim blinked and glanced up at the waiter, a thin young man with perfectly groomed hair and artful stubble on his chin.

"Just water for now," she said.

The waiter vanished as if she'd summoned him out of her imagination in the first place. She sat and waited in the sunshine, relishing its heat and light. For a moment she closed her eyes, just basking in it, but she opened them quickly again. Whenever her eyes were closed, she saw things she hoped never to see again.

A bell rang over the door and she looked up. The way the little table was situated, a corner and a column and a tall plant obstructed her view of the entrance, but she heard the muffled voice of someone speaking to the hostess and she knew it was Walker even before he came into view. He smiled when he saw her and raised a hand in greeting, and Kim did the same. For the first second or two, they studied each other's faces, searching for signs— for a grin that seemed too wide or a glint of orange light in the eyes that defied both sunshine and shadows.

It had become her habit when she encountered anyone, studying them a little closer, wondering when she might encounter someone who was not who they pretended to be. Kim's pulse quickened in relief when it seemed to her that Walker was only Walker. With the way the corners of his mouth had been torn and then sewn up, he seemed reluctant to smile too widely, and that was for the best. He had healed quite a bit, but the scars would be with him forever.

Walker stepped aside, beckoned back toward the entrance, and a little dark-haired boy joined him. He put a hand on the boy's back and the two of them approached the table.

"You made it," she said pleasantly.

"Made it?" Walker replied. "We live here. You're the one who came from so far away. I appreciate you making the time."

Kim gave a nod. She didn't want to correct him just yet.

"This must be Charlie," she said, lowering into a crouch.

The boy smiled shyly. He took after his father, but he had a softness to his features, an open kindness, that undermined the resemblance.

"Charlie, this is my friend Seong. Can you say hello?"

The boy held out his hand to shake. "It's nice to meet you, Seong."

"And you, sir," Kim replied, sharing the boy's formality. "Your father tells me this is your favorite place to eat."

He brightened and launched into a litany of pizza toppings that were acceptable to him, all shyness gone. The three of them sat around the table in the sunlight and with the boy entertaining them, Kim and Walker managed to avoid discussing the horrors they had in common. By the time the waiter had returned, Charlie had already helped each of them perfect their pizza orders and seemed proud of his expertise.

"The fresh mozzarella—the drops—not the shredded stuff," the boy told the waiter.

"Absolutely, sir," the waiter said as if the kid were a Congressman instead of a fourth-grader, and then went off to put in their orders.

"All right, buddy, what now?" Walker asked.

"Hands," Charlie replied good-naturedly, sliding his chair back. He stood and looked at his father expectantly.

"You first," Walker told his son. "I'll go right after."

The openness faded from Charlie's face. His nine-year-old innocence receded, to be replaced by keen perception as he glanced from his father to Kim and back again.

He nodded. "Got it. But no kissing in public. It's embarrassing."

As Charlie marched off to wash his hands, Kim felt herself flush. Walker watched him a moment before turning toward her.

"Sorry about that."

She cocked her head. "Is there a reason he expects us to kiss the moment he leaves the table?"

Walker offered a small shrug, with no trace of a smile. "He interrogated me on the way over. One of his questions was whether or not we'd ever kissed."

"And you said we had."

"There are a lot of things I can't tell him," Walker replied. "I've made myself a promise that I'm going to be honest with him about everything else."

Kim scraped her fingernails over the textured cotton tablecloth. She wetted her lips with her tongue.

"How much do you know?" she asked.

Walker glanced around to make sure they weren't overheard. He leaned slightly forward. "I know they've pulled most of the bodies off the mountain. My employers have been paying very close attention to their progress, but so far we haven't had any reports of violence or . . . anything like what we experienced up there."

Kim nodded. "So far. But they haven't let anyone go into the cave. The Turks are adamant that the ark is off-limits and the UN is inclined to agree with them."

They locked eyes and Kim saw her own fears reflected back to her. Walker glanced out the window, watching two women stroll hand-in-hand, one holding the leash of an energetic black terrier. *Ordinary people living ordinary lives,* Kim thought. *If they only knew.*

"Have they released Adam Holzer's body?" Walker asked.

"Just a few days ago. I thought about trying to attend, but I feared it might be an intrusion," Kim replied. "Besides, Meryam doesn't want to see us. She wants to put the mountain behind her for whatever time she has left."

Walker glanced deeper into the restaurant. Kim followed his gaze and saw that Charlie had emerged from the bathroom in the back corridor and was wiping the excess water from his hands onto his jeans. It made her smile.

"I'm sort of amazed she's lived this long," Walker said. "She can't have much time left."

Kim hesitated, then plunged ahead. "You never know how much time you'll have," she said. "Which is why I wanted to see you."

Walker must have heard something in her tone, because he studied her more closely, searching her face for whatever he'd missed. "What is it?"

"I just thought you should know that I've taken a job at the embassy. A two-year posting as special advisor to the ambassador.

So, I'll be here in D.C. for a while. I thought we might get together now and then."

His expression was hard to read.

"I'd like that very much," he said, but there was a stiffness in him that made her wonder if he might be just being polite.

"I'm not expecting anything," Kim told him. "It's just that I have nightmares. All the time, I have nightmares. And there isn't anyone else who could understand."

Charlie arrived back at the table and hiked himself up onto his seat just as the waiter arrived with waters for all three of them. The little boy thanked the waiter politely.

Walker reached across the table and took her hand, holding it there.

"I have those dreams, too. You're not alone."

Anyone overhearing him might have thought the words implied romance instead of dread. Charlie wrinkled his nose and rolled his eyes. The role of little gentleman that he played so well apparently did not extend to public displays of affection.

"We're not kissing," Kim told him, forcing herself to smile, her heart lightened by the presence of the boy. "Or is holding hands also on the list of forbidden activities?"

Charlie pursed his lips in contemplation and then sighed as he relented.

"I guess holding hands is okay."

Walker laughed softly and held Kim's hand a little tighter. She was grateful. The contact helped, the knowledge that he understood her nightmares. The job offer, to come to D.C. and work for the ambassador, had nothing to do with Walker or her experience on Mount Ararat, but she could not honestly say his presence here hadn't played a role in her accepting it. Not because she loved him—she didn't know him nearly well enough to even consider the idea of love. But ever since Ararat she had gone through periods of terror and paranoia during which she wondered if she might be insane . . . and then periods in which she feared that, in fact, she was entirely, terrifyingly sane.

"Thank you," she said to father and son alike.

But when the waiter came to deliver their pizzas, she cast another glance at Walker's eyes, searching for that telltale orange glimmer. Just in case.

Kim knew she would always be watching for it.

Always.

A light spring rain darkened the sky over East Meadow, Long Island. Meryam had met Adam's father only once, at the launch party for their first book, when it seemed like investing their own money in a trip to New York just to celebrate the publication of the book made sense. In his late fifties, Mr. Holzer had been widowed for more than fifteen years, but had never remarried, despite a long love affair with a stock market analyst named Sylvia. Meryam had wondered if Adam's father had never married Sylvia just so his son wouldn't have to come to terms with having a stepmother.

She hoped Mr. Holzer would marry Sylvia now, after an appropriate period of mourning. Adam's feelings weren't an issue anymore.

Meryam stood just outside the black, wrought iron gates of the United Synagogue Cemetery. Rain pattered onto her umbrella, dripping down from its edges, and she tried to make herself small beneath it to avoid getting wet. She wore a long, black, fleece-lined coat and a thick gray scarf. That morning before leaving her hotel she had tied her hair back with a band, but it had broken and now her wild mane fell thick and unruly around her face.

Her heart ached as she peered through the gate at the cars that lined the narrow roads around the mausoleum, in the western corner of the cemetery. Meryam had worked with the Turkish authorities, connected them to Adam's father so that Mr. Holzer could arrange for his remains to be returned home. If the aging Holzer had known of his son's engagement, he never mentioned it.

Mr. Holzer had invited her to be here, but she had told him that she was not well enough to travel. A lie, on so many levels. Instead of joining the small gathering during the funeral service, and now inside the mausoleum, where they would be inserting Adam's cremated remains into a wall niche, she had flown to New York in secret and rented a car for the drive to Long Island.

If she had accepted the invitation, she would have felt like an intruder. Or an impostor.

Cars growled past on the street behind her, splashing through puddles, but there were no other pedestrians. Only Meryam with her umbrella, watching through the gate as the mourners emerged and began to make their way back to their cars. From this distance she could not tell which of those dark figures might be Mr. Holzer and Sylvia.

She wished that she could cry.

In a moment, she would walk away. She didn't want them to see her, to know that she had come all this way but had been unwilling to join them inside.

Not unwilling, she told herself. *Unable.*

Even if she'd wanted to, she wouldn't have been able to walk through those gates. Not any more than she'd been able to enter the synagogue where the funeral had taken place. If she wanted to mourn Adam, she had no choice but to stand in the rain, though she didn't worry about pneumonia. Meryam didn't worry about illness at all now.

The first cars began to move slowly along the road toward the gates and she forced herself to turn and walk back along the sidewalk toward her car. As she did, she slipped her hand into her pocket—just the way she had that night when Hakan had carried her down off the mountain—and just as she had that night, she felt the sharp edges and smooth surface of a bitumen shard.

Meryam had no idea who had slipped it into her pocket. The demon could have compelled any of them to do it, possessing someone for a moment and sliding the charm inside her jacket with her none the wiser. A safeguard, to give it one last opportunity to find its way off the mountain . . . find its way into the new world. It had chosen her because it had something to offer her.

Life.

For as long as she complied with its wishes, it would make her well again. Make her whole. It had eradicated the cancer that had been killing her, and taken its place. A different sort of cancer.

A painful grin split her features but she fought against it, forced it away. The demon might not let her cry, but she refused to allow it to make her smile. Not today.

Had it been just for herself, Meryam would never have taken the demon's bargain. Death would have been so much better than this.

But she hadn't done it for herself.

Numb, she put a hand over her belly and felt the roundness there, four months along and a little bigger every day. If her baby was a boy, she would name him Adam, and pray that he took after his father.

Sometimes, though . . .

Sometimes she let herself consider the possibility that the thing growing inside her might not be a baby at all. And then she would scream, just for a moment or two until it became irritated and seized control from within, silencing her. It didn't like her to scream like that.

Bad for the baby, the demon would whisper inside her mind. *And the baby needs to be strong.*

Meryam wondered how much it would hurt to give birth to something with horns.